A COUNTRY GIRL'S HEART

By the Author

Where the Light Glows

Unchained Memories

A Country Girl's Heart

Visit us at www.boldstrokesbooks.com

A Country Girl's Heart

by

Dena Blake

2018

ISBN 13: 978-1-63555-134-1

This Trade Paperback Original Is Published By
Bold Strokes Books, Inc.
P.O. Box 249
Valley Falls, NY 12185

First Edition: March 2018

Credits
Editor: Shelley Thrasher
Production Design: Stacia Seaman
Cover Design by Jeanine Henning

Acknowledgments

Thank you to Len Barot and Sandy Lowe for yet again giving me the opportunity to share my characters with the world. It's still surreal to see them in print. This book is near and dear to my heart, and without my editor extraordinaire, Shelley Thrasher, it wouldn't be the best that it can be. Shelley makes me a better writer. I'm also genuinely grateful for the BSB family; they have welcomed me completely, and the friendships I've made are truly wonderful.

Thanks to my big brother, Paul, for teaching me everything I needed to know about horses and rodeo. Thanks to Robyn for reading everything I write and giving me good, tangible feedback. To Kate for your direct, honest opinions and unwavering support, particularly when I'm deep into a book and don't come up for air. To my kids for supporting me in life as well as in my writing. And always to my family for being the most awesome support system a girl could ever want.

To all you readers out there, thank you for reading. I hope you enjoy this book as much as I enjoyed writing it.

For my cousin Dave, who had the most generous heart I've ever known. I miss you every day.

CHAPTER ONE

I told you before, Ms. Whatever-your-name-is. I don't want anything to do with her." Kat slammed the phone into the cradle and whirled around to the kitchen counter. She snatched her leather work gloves from the table, threw open the screen door, and stepped out onto the porch.

Kat had tried to ignore it, but she couldn't miss the headline plastered across every newspaper in town: MONTCO OIL CEO DIES IN FATAL CAR CRASH. Just two months before, the horrific collision between her parents' Mercedes and a semi truck had taken her father's life and left her mother critically injured with a broken pelvis.

Squaring his jaw, Virgil scratched at the day-old, gray-spotted beard emerging from his chin. "She's your mother, Kat. Why don't cha just see what she wants?" he said calmly from the rocking chair positioned in the corner of the old, rickety wrap-around porch.

"I know what she wants." Kat held her tongue. Her father-in-law obviously meant well, but he had no idea what a huge concession communicating with her mother would be. It would split open a wound she thought she'd forgotten long ago. From the twisting in her gut, she now realized it hadn't quite healed. "She wants me in Austin to take care of her." Kat blew the fundamental statement out with a slow, heavy breath. What came without a doubt for most children would not come so easily for Kathryn Jackson. She remembered clearly how that was her mother's own doing.

She grabbed hold of the porch railing, tightening her fingers around it as she stared out onto the dream ranch she'd put so many years into creating. Sucking in a deep breath, she inhaled the marvelously pungent scent of horses and freshly cut hay.

Virgil's foot teetered back and forth on the edge of the floor railing, prompting the chair to rock slowly. "Your mother needs you, Kat."

"She needs me?" She squealed, vulnerability slipping out involuntarily. "Where was the mighty Elizabeth Belmont when I needed her?" Roughly smoothing her hair, she fastened it with a plain black hair band. "If she thinks I'm giving up everything I've worked so hard for to take care of her, she has another think comin'."

Kat yanked her gloves on and headed down the steps and across the grounds to the horse stable. She didn't want anything to do with her mother now. The only thing she'd ever wanted from her was love, and Elizabeth had never been able to give that freely.

"Will I see ya for lunch?" Virgil shouted, still settled comfortably in the rocker.

"Not till about one. I'm gonna take Minow out and check the trails for divots." She glanced over her shoulder at him. "I don't want any injured horses this week." Besides that, she needed some space this morning. The constant battle between her conscience and her free will was about to do her in. After all, Elizabeth was her mother, but after what had happened between them, Kat couldn't bring herself to see her, no matter what the circumstances. She needed to settle the problem in her mind, and the best place to be when she needed to think was out on the range.

She went inside the stable, took a bridle out of the cabinet, and continued into the first stall. "Hey, baby." She stroked the horse gently. "You want to take me for a ride today?"

The beautiful black Arabian clicked her hooves slightly in response to Kat's voice, and she slid the bit into the horse's mouth.

"Okay, come on." She led Minow out of the stall and across the breezeway to the tack room, where her custom-made saddle hung on a separate wall from the rest. Kat lifted the fifty-pound seat of leather from its peg, slung it across the horse, and cinched it tight. Minow held perfectly still while Kat mounted her and then trotted out by the corral when she nudged her sides with her heels.

Giving Virgil a quick wave, Kat took the first trail leading up the hill into the towering cottonwood trees. She weaved the horse through the massive shadowy patch of trees and emerged on the other side into the wildflower field, dotted with bluebonnets and paintbrush. She looked up into the sky and let the sun warm her face. Closing her eyes, she sucked in a much-needed breath of fresh country air. This was definitely the best way to clear her head. Riding had always been Kat's release. Even when she was away at college and it seemed like she couldn't manage the never-ending studying and constant pressure, all she had to do was close her eyes and she was out on the range again. The smell of wildflowers, the touch of early morning moisture in the air, and the endless sight of the vast, rolling countryside had always made her happy.

She stopped at a small stream about two miles out on the lower valley trail, slid off Minow, and propped herself up against a large walnut tree. Sleep hadn't come easy these past few weeks, but here in her sanctuary, she could relax. She stared into the distance until her vision clouded and her lids dropped over her eyes.

Then she was there, Arizona Jackson, the only thing Kat loved more than God's green earth. The woman who'd swept her off her feet almost ten years ago. The very same woman that her parents had forbidden her to marry.

"Arizona," she mumbled, letting out a ragged breath. "What should I do now?" Her voice deflated, confusion filling her head. "I know I shouldn't be bitter, but I just can't help it."

Without saying a word, Arizona put her mouth on Kat's and their tongues mingled softly. Kat shuddered as Arizona unbuttoned her blouse and let her fingers tickle across her chest. After pushing the shirt from Kat's shoulders, Arizona quickly replaced her hands with her lips, slowly roaming across the hollow of Kat's neck to the soft skin of her breast. She let out a soft shudder, captivated by the touch of the woman she loved so much. Arizona's mouth lingered, touching, teasing her wildly. Sensations rocketed through Kat, commanding her to react and quiver uncontrollably as she always had with Arizona.

The tremors subsided, and Kat heard the rapid rhythm of Arizona's heartbeat pounding in her head. She opened her eyes as it faded with the dream. Arizona was gone again.

The sound of a galloping horse in the distance had replaced the comforting sound. Kat dropped her head forward, and tears streamed down her cheeks. Swiping the sleeve of her denim shirt across her face, she shrugged off the remnants of the dream and hauled herself to her feet. She stood waiting for her neighbor with her arms crossed across her chest as the pounding hooves of the horse came closer.

Victoria Maxwell was the kind of neighbor you wouldn't wish on your worst enemy. A far cry from the kind of ranch owners Kat had encountered over the years, she didn't seem like the kind of woman who would be interested in owning a ranch, much less smart enough to run one. For almost seven years, the woman had given Kat nothing but grief.

"I thought I told you to stay off my land, Victoria," Kat shouted to the tall, surly woman on the approaching horse.

"Oh, come on, Kat." She slung her leg easily around the rear of the horse and dismounted. "I thought we were friends." Her voice took on its usual irritating drawl.

"With friends like you, a woman doesn't need many enemies," Kat said, firming her stance as Victoria strode toward her.

"You know I could be a lot nicer if you'd just let me." Victoria backed her up against the tree.

"Not in this lifetime," she said, tilting her head upward as Victoria's six-foot frame towered over her. The blackness filling her eyes dampened the clean, engaging features of her long, narrow face as she moved closer and forced her mouth onto Kat's.

"Get away from me." Kat's voice was muffled as Victoria's hard mouth covered hers. She struggled against the powerful arms keeping her pinned to the tree and then decided to take another route to force her away.

A groan of pain gurgled from Victoria's throat, and she flew back, wiping the blood from her lip. "You bit me." She raised a hand to slap her, and Kat stood perfectly still, narrowing her eyes and silently daring her.

Victoria clenched her fingers into a tight fist and lowered her hand. "No." Her thin lips flattened into a smile. "You're not going to force me to damage that pretty face." She ran her finger the length of Kat's jawline. "You'll come 'round eventually." She let out a laugh and climbed on her horse. "And then you'll be beggin' for a lot more than a kiss." She twisted her lips into a smile and rode off slowly.

"Stay off my land." Kat didn't move until Victoria was out of sight. Then she dropped to her knees and spewed what little she'd eaten for breakfast into the weeds. Just the smell of the woman turned her stomach. The thought of Victoria touching her again made her skin crawl. Things had just started to improve financially at the Jumpin' J when Arizona died four years ago. Although Kat hadn't asked her, Victoria had stepped in to help with the day-to-day operation of the ranch whenever needed, making herself available to Kat under the guise of friendship. Easing herself into Kat's life through her grief, the woman also offered some much-needed comfort in her time of loss. Kat didn't know exactly how it happened, but out of gratitude more than anything else, she made the mistake of allowing Victoria into her bed. That was a lesson in trust Kat would never forget.

She leaned against the tree and remembered how Victoria had inserted herself into the business at the ranch and tried to take control—a testimonial to Victoria's loathsome character. She'd taken advantage of Kat at her lowest point. Thankfully, she hadn't given her any financial control, or Kat would've found herself out on the street. She didn't know how she could've been so blind to Victoria's motives. It was clear now that all she wanted was her land.

Kat hauled herself to her feet and shouted into the sky, "Why can't they all just leave me alone?" Her voice echoed through the valley as she climbed onto her horse.

Kat looked up. If only Arizona were here now. She would know exactly what to do. She'd always been able to see through the anger and lead Kat in the right direction. She mounted Minow, kicked her heels into her sides, and the horse trotted up the hill.

After she inspected the trails without finding any major divots or obstructions, Kat made it back to the house just before two o'clock. She headed up the steps and saw the salad and large glass of iced tea Virgil had left waiting for her on the table. Entering the kitchen, she smelled the sweet aroma of freshly baked biscuits.

She slid into the old padded metal chair and scooted closer to the matching Formica table she'd bought many years ago at the antique mall in town. It didn't look like an antique, but it certainly was aged enough. After she and Arizona had bought the ranch, Kat had furnished the house piece by piece as they could afford it. Like the rest of the furniture she'd picked out, the dining set had its own unique style.

Virgil appeared from the doorway to the living room. "Get your head cleared?"

"For today." She glanced up and noticed his chin was clean shaven now, and he'd combed and waxed the ends of his handlebar mustache in his usual fashion.

He ducked through the doorway, crossed the small kitchen, and tugged open the oven door. Reaching in bare-handed, he cursed as he plucked the biscuits from the baking sheet and tossed them into a basket one by one. Then he slammed the oven door closed before dropping the basket onto the table.

Kat's mood perked up a bit at his twisted expression. "I have hot pads in the drawer, you know."

"Yeah, I know," he mumbled, rubbing the callused tips of his fingers together.

Kat smiled. The man had his own way of doing things and was too old and set in his ways to change now.

"How 'bout I make you a little chicken fry to go with that rabbit food?" He jerked open the refrigerator door and took out a package of cubed steak.

"This is fine, thanks." She doused the salad with vinaigrette dressing before taking a biscuit from the basket and setting it on the edge of her plate.

He tossed the package of meat on the shelf inside the refrigerator and let the door close. "You need to put a little meat on those bones if you're gonna keep working so hard," he said as he flopped into the chair across from her.

"There's plenty of meat on me to survive, Virgil." She stuffed a fork full of lettuce into her mouth.

"A hundred and twenty pounds of pure strength, right?" Virgil chuckled, raking his fingers through his thick silver hair. "Arizona always said you could take her down in a minute."

"I think she liked it that way." She smiled lightly before pressing the napkin to her lips.

"I bet she did." The edges of Virgil's mouth tipped up slyly, forcing his hazel eyes to squint in the midst of his tan, weathered face.

Kat moved a wedge of tomato to the side of her plate, and her smile faded as her morning visitor entered her mind. "I ran into Victoria by the river."

"Pushing the boundaries again, huh?" Virgil asked, his furrowed brow reflecting his concern.

"She tried." Kat didn't go into the particulars, knowing Virgil might set out to take care of her himself. Acting as both her protector and mentor after Arizona died, her father-in-law had been her savior at the ranch. The squirrelly old varmint had warded off many a hostile cowpoke. Without him, Kat wasn't sure she would've been able to keep the ranch running this long.

He hopped up from his chair, sending it clanging against the counter. "Why don't you let me have some of the guys rough her up?"

"Because she's a woman, Virgil. We don't rough up women. Besides, you know that won't solve anything. She'll just come back at us with her guys." Kat set her fork on her plate and reached for her glass. "I really need to find out how she came by that land in the first place."

"We've been through this before, Kat. The records in town say it's been in her family since before you were born."

"Something's just not right about those records, Virgil." She took a sip of sweet tea. "My grandfather owned all this land. Including the portion Victoria claims is hers."

Virgil turned the knob on the window air conditioner and then slapped it when it didn't fire. "Damn things never work when you need 'em." He untied the bright-red bandanna from his neck, wet it in the sink, and replaced it before picking the chair up and sliding into it. "You could always ask your mother."

Kat flashed him a firm look of warning. "Not gonna happen, Virgil."

Virgil's forehead creased. "Well, where else can you look?"

"I'm not sure, but I'm going to have to find out." She finished the last of her salad, washed her plate, and set it in the drain board to dry.

"You sure you don't want somethin' else to eat?" he asked.

"No. I'm good. But if you have a little extra time on your hands, maybe you could fix that air conditioner." She winked at him as she opened the screen door. "I'll be in the barn if you need me."

CHAPTER TWO

D amn that woman." DJ slid the receiver from her ear and slammed it into its cradle. "She won't even let me talk." She slapped the open file folder on the desk closed. "Hell. I've called her about twenty times, and she acts like she doesn't even know my name." She was exaggerating the numbers, but it irked the hell out of her that the woman could be so rude.

Danica Jane Callahan wasn't used to having someone dismiss her with such venom. She sank into her high-backed leather chair and mulled over the conversation. Twisting the chair around, she looked up at the cream-colored certificates strategically placed on the wood-paneled wall behind her. This was only one of the many aspects of being Elizabeth Belmont's personal attorney she didn't enjoy. She didn't care for her methods, specifically the way she'd forced DJ into completing this particular task. If she was really looking for a response, she should still be calling her daughter herself.

She knew what came next and wasn't looking forward to it. She was going to have to see face-to-face just what kind of heartless woman wouldn't take the time to find out how her mother was recuperating after an automobile accident.

"Marcia," she called, shooting up out of her chair. Swiping the file off her desk, she slid it into her leather briefcase and snapped it closed.

A small, red-haired woman poked her head through the doorway. "Yes, Ms. Callahan?"

"Unless I missed something, I'm not due in court for anything this week, right?"

"No. Not this week."

"Good. I need you to make a reservation for me at this place." DJ tossed a small pamphlet across the desk. "And cancel all my appointments for the next few days."

Marcia's lip slid into a sideways smirk as she picked up the brochure. "You're going to a dude ranch?"

"It's business." The type of business DJ didn't like to conduct.

"It must be, to make you take a trip to the country," Marcia said with a chuckle. "Can I go?" Her eyebrows rose. "I'd love to see you on a horse."

"Just make the reservation, Marcia." DJ picked up a few more files and brushed past her to the doorway.

Marcia followed her out. "When would you like to arrive?"

"Tomorrow." DJ dropped the files on her desk. "I need to go by and see Mrs. Belmont this morning." Her stomach churned. DJ knew she wouldn't be happy with her daughter's adamant response. DJ had been a little surprised herself. "Then I'll be heading to the courthouse to do some research. Call my cell if you have any problems." She walked to the elevator.

"How many days?" Marcia said.

"Two or three." Without turning, DJ held up her hand and wiggled her fingers indecisively.

"So, I can take the next couple of days off?" Marcia shouted after her.

"Nope." DJ shook her head. "You still have some work to do on those files I just put on your desk." She smiled as she rounded the corner to the elevator, catching what she knew was just the beginning of Marcia's stinging protest.

DJ took the short drive west on Sixth Street to Winsted Lane and then drove through Old Enfield to the upscale neighborhood of Tarrytown. Elizabeth Belmont's historic New Orleans–style estate was one of the oldest in the neighborhood. DJ often wondered what it would be like to own a house in this area, but property in this part of town was priced way out of her league. This neighborhood was filled with old money and dot-com millionaires who had housekeepers to answer doors and gardeners to keep the grounds groomed. Even if she could afford it, this lifestyle wasn't for DJ.

She rang the bell and admired the architecture as she waited. She loved these old mansions. Clandestinely embedded deep in the heart of Austin, they were extraordinary treasures. After a few minutes' wait, the head cook, housekeeper, and self-proclaimed protector of the Belmont household met her at the door.

"Mornin', Maggie," she said with a nod as she entered.

"She's upstairs," Maggie said without hesitation. "And she's a little on the crotchety side today, so mind your manners, young lady."

"Thanks for the warning. I'll try to improve her mood for you." DJ gave her a wink and headed up the winding staircase.

"I know you will, darlin'. You're the only one who's managed to keep her sane for the past five years."

Elizabeth Belmont sat propped up in bed eating her usual breakfast of oatmeal, fresh fruit, and coffee.

"Good morning, Elizabeth," DJ said, in the usual polite manner she took on with all her clients, wealthy or not.

"What a nice surprise, Danica." Elizabeth gave her a creeping smile. "Come sit. Have some coffee with me."

DJ crossed the room, the heels of her shoes clicking against the hardwood floor. Picking up the small china coffeepot from the night table, she poured herself a splash before adding a touch to Elizabeth's half-empty cup.

"I haven't received a favorable response from Kathryn over the phone. So I'll be heading to Kerrville in the morning." DJ sat between the wooden arms of the small antique chair next to Elizabeth's bed. She did so as ladylike as possible in the short chair, swinging her long legs to the side as she kept them pinned together at the knees.

"Will you be gone long?"

"That depends on how receptive she is." DJ pinched the bridge of her nose. "Hopefully I'll wrap it up right away. I have a lot of work waiting for me at the office."

Elizabeth gave her a troubled look. "You remember our deal, correct?"

DJ squeezed her eyes closed as the gnawing in her stomach reappeared. "Yes. I remember."

"You must bring her home to Austin." Elizabeth spoke so nonchalantly, no one would ever know she was holding DJ's feet to the fire. "You seem tired, Danica. You should really take a little more time to enjoy life."

DJ didn't acknowledge Elizabeth's observation, but she was right.

Looking in the mirror this morning, she'd seen the dull redness and dark circles surrounding her sunken eyes. The vibrant green color she remembered seemed to have faded to a pale sage. There wasn't enough makeup in the world to hide the stress or her loneliness.

"Then I'd be really behind." She tensed, thinking of the many cases she'd had to shuffle in order to make the trip to the ranch.

"Are you going to tell Kathryn who you are right away?"

"Telling her I'm your attorney might not be the best way to introduce myself." DJ took in a mouthful of coffee and rolled her eyes slightly. "I've already experienced your daughter's quick-tempered reaction a number of times on the phone." *Like mother, like daughter.*

"It might be wise to become acquainted with her first. She might be more apt to listen." Elizabeth reached into the drawer of her night table and took out an old porcelain-backed hand mirror.

DJ watched as she held the mirror up in front of her and narrowed her eyes at her reflection. "I'm not sure it will make much difference. As you know, I've made many calls that have gone unanswered. I don't think she'll be very agreeable."

"I'm sure you'll find a way to bring her around. For the sake of your family." Elizabeth poked at the beehive surrounding her head, then swept a few stray strands of platinum hair into place.

"And if not?" DJ's pulse raced as she shifted to look past the pattern of petite pink roses covering the back of the mirror hovering between them.

"Then, if nothing else, you'll have a few nice relaxing days in the country." Once she was satisfied every hair was in its appropriate place, Elizabeth cupped her hand behind her head and smiled before sliding the mirror into the drawer.

DJ clenched her jaw behind the cup she held to her lips. "I'll get her here somehow." Elizabeth Belmont had enjoyed the life of Texas high society since she was a small child and wasn't accustomed to being disappointed. She wouldn't be happy if she returned without her daughter, and the livelihood of DJ's family depended on it.

"I know you will, dear." She reached for the small china pot on the night table. "More coffee?"

"No, thank you." The cup rattled against the saucer as DJ slid it onto the table. Carefully extracting herself from the clutches of the vintage chair, she let out a weary groan and stood up. "I'd better be

going. I have a few more things to do before I head out in the morning."
This trip was going to be far from relaxing. She wanted to find out a
little more about Kathryn Jackson before she landed on her turf. "Can I
do anything for you before I go?"

"No, thank you, darling. Other than Kathryn, I have everything I
need right now." Elizabeth's ruby-red lips curved into a satisfied smile.

DJ pasted on a smile and moved quickly to the door. "I'll be in
touch."

As the elevator doors retracted, DJ could see Rosa dancing around
the table to the tune playing on her iPod. The feathers swept across the
table, sending dust into the air and onto the apron tied snugly around
her waist. DJ set her briefcase and the bag of Chinese takeout on the
decorative bench near the door and crept up behind her.

"Hello, Rosa," she shouted, making her jump a foot.

Rosa took off her headphones. "I told you not to do that anymore!
One of these days you're going to give me a heart attack."

DJ laughed as the woman who often boasted of being her second
mother swung around and slapped an open palm to her shoulder. "That
iPod is hands down the best present I've ever given you."

"You're home early today." Rosa shrugged, impatiently turning to
the foyer table to arrange the vase of fresh flowers.

"I thought I'd work a little from home this afternoon." DJ retrieved
her briefcase and food from the bench before heading into the kitchen.

"I haven't started your dinner yet. Would you like me to make you
a snack?" Rosa asked, trailing behind her.

"No, thanks. I picked up Chinese food on the way home." She set
the bag of food on the counter. "Want to join me?" She cocked her head
and let the girlish grin she knew Rosa had grown to love creep across
her face.

"Thank you, no. Chinese has much too much salt. Makes my
ankles puff up like balloons." She pursed her lips and blew her cheeks
out.

DJ chuckled at her animated expression. Visiting with Rosa was
always a treat, one of the few forms of entertainment DJ allowed

herself. On the occasion Rosa did join her for a meal, DJ always came away from their conversations knowing more about life than she had before. Along with being a skilled life advisor, Rosa was an excellent cook. DJ knew she had a family of her own and didn't like keeping her later than necessary.

"You can go on home now if you want," DJ said.

"Great!" She gathered her purse. "My sister's coming to visit tomorrow, and this will give me a little extra time to prepare."

"Rosa," DJ called as she walked to the elevator door. "I'll be gone for a few days. Why don't you stay home and spend some time with your sister?"

Her eyes widened and a smile spread across her face. "Oh, that would be wonderful."

DJ couldn't help but enjoy her delight. "I'll let you know when I'm back in town."

"You'd better not be eating any of that fast food while I'm gone." Rosa turned, her eyes darkening as she assessed her. "If you're not careful, you'll soon be very large, like my Antonio."

"I won't, I promise," she said, following her to the elevator. "Don't worry about me. You just have a nice visit with your sister." DJ pressed the button, prompting the doors to open, and waited as Rosa entered and the doors closed again.

DJ walked into the kitchen, grabbed a beer from the refrigerator, and twisted off the cap. After taking a fork from the drawer, she slid the food across the counter before planting herself in the plush leather bar stool and crossing her legs. As she ate, she opened her file on the Jumpin' J Ranch and thumbed through it. She'd spent most of the day gathering as much information as she could on Kathryn and Arizona Jackson. Elizabeth had filled her in on some of the specifics, but DJ knew Elizabeth well enough to suspect she'd probably left a few things out. DJ had hoped she'd be able to take care of this matter over the phone, but as Elizabeth had told DJ many times, her daughter was just as stubborn and hardheaded as her mother, and since she wasn't receptive to one of their calls, the trip was unavoidable.

From the financial figures she'd obtained, DJ saw that the ranch had been running in the black for the past three years. Before that it had jumped back and forth a bit, slipping into the red during the winter months, which would be considered off-season for the ranch. Overall, it looked as though the Jumpin' J Ranch was a profitable venture for the Jacksons.

After finishing her dinner, DJ tossed the empty food cartons into the trash before going into the bedroom to pack. She rolled a small designer carry-on bag out of the closet. Rethinking her choice, she pushed it into the corner and took a navy-blue duffel from the top shelf. DJ didn't want to be too obvious about who she was. She didn't know exactly how Kathryn would react to her mother's lawyer in the flesh.

She dropped the bag onto the bed and threw in some shorts and a few golf shirts, along with a flannel shirt and some colored T-shirts and jeans. When she had everything packed, she reached up to the top shelf of the closet, fetched a large box, and opened it. She hesitated before lifting the vanilla felt cowboy hat out.

She slid it on her head and turned to the mirror. The size was still right, but the hat really didn't fit her anymore. Wearing it used to be part of her daily life, but it hadn't been out of the box for the better part of fifteen years. Now, staring at herself in the mirror, she felt strange and out of place with it on her head.

After DJ became a lawyer, she'd never put it on again. College and law school were her father's choice, not hers. The anger and emptiness she'd felt when she'd left the farm had faded over the years, but her love for that way of life still burned deep inside. It took her a while, but DJ finally realized her father only wanted more for her than he'd ever had himself. She definitely had that now, and it was her turn to help out the family if she possibly could.

DJ took the hat off her head, set it on top of her bag, and then raked her hand through the short hair she waxed to stand at attention every morning. That style would have to go. She'd wash it and leave the curls free tomorrow. She stripped off her slacks and blouse and hung them in the closet. She wouldn't need any clothes like that on this trip either. She needed to be natural, or she'd never make it past the front gate.

She crawled into the massive feather bed centering the room, and all but a few of the many pillows slid off onto the floor. Ignoring the irony of her current situation, DJ propped herself up against the headboard, opened the folder she'd filled with information about Kathryn Jackson, and studied it again.

Chapter Three

D J was just leaving the Austin city limits when she picked up her cell phone, punched in her assistant's number, and waited for her to answer.

"Danica Callahan's office. May I help you?" Marcia's unusually sweet voice resonated in her ear. She must have been enjoying her time alone in the office.

"Good morning, Marcia. Did you make my reservation?"

"Barely," she said, her voice slipping into its familiar cantankerous tone. "You're lucky they had a last-minute cancellation. It appears the Jumpin' J Ranch is a very popular vacation spot."

"Really?" *The ranch must be doing better than the figures indicated.*

"I practically had to beg, borrow, and steal to get the woman to give you a room." Marcia's voice rumbled with irritation. "Then I had to listen to her speech about May being the cusp of prime season. According to her, if I'd waited another hour, there wouldn't have been anything available until the fall."

"I'm sorry you had to go through all that, Marcia." DJ smiled as she smothered a chuckle at Marcia's exaggerated distress. Marcia wasn't the sweetest assistant in the building, but she always got the job done and usually managed to take good care of DJ along the way. "Do you have the brochure handy? I didn't have a chance to look at it yesterday."

"I have it right here. What do you need to know?"

"Tell me about the place." DJ changed lanes and sped around a car.

"It says here, the ranch is made up of roughly a thousand acres of pasture and small mountain terrain located in the Texas Hill Country on the outskirts of Kerrville, Texas, about one hundred miles southwest of Austin. Close enough to drive to for the weekend, yet far enough away to escape the big city."

"Marcia," she said flatly. "I know where it is. Just give me some basic information about the ranch."

"Why didn't you just say that?" Marcia's voice rose in irritation. "The grounds consist of a working horse stable and corral, a regulation-size rodeo arena, and various riding trails throughout the hilly terrain. There's also a seven-acre pond stocked yearly for fishing and a river snaking through the property used primarily for swimming and kayaking." She sucked in a breath. "Is that enough basic information for you?"

"That's perfect, Marcia. I *do* appreciate your patience."

"Oh, and they're LGBTQ friendly. Maybe you should stay a few weeks and find yourself a wife."

"I'm happy just the way things are, Marcia."

"Right." Marcia let out a breath. "Anything else?"

"Not at the moment, thanks. I'll let you know if I need something." DJ caught sight of a mileage sign ahead. *Seventy-five miles to paradise.*

"It says here to stop at the gate and push the button on the intercom for directions to the office." Marcia's tone sweetened. "Now, you just relax and have a good time. I'm sure you can use the break."

"Thanks." DJ hit the end-call button on the screen and tossed her phone onto the passenger seat.

By the time DJ drove up to the huge wrought-iron gates of the Jumpin' J Ranch, it was almost eight o'clock and the gates were wide open. They were probably left that way during the day. They looked to be electronic and were most likely controlled by the key-card slot on the intercom. Rolling the car up next to it, she pushed the button and waited for a response.

"Jumpin' J Ranch. May I help you?" a woman's voice chanted.

"DJ Callahan. I have a reservation."

"Yes, Ms. Callahan. We're expecting you. After you come through the gates, take an immediate right, and that road will lead you directly to the registration office."

"Thank you." DJ threw her BMW 440i convertible into gear and sped through the gates. She drove the short distance and cursed as gravel from the road clanked noisily against the wheel wells of the car. She parked, and after superficially inspecting the black clear-coat paint, she proceeded up the steps to the registration building.

"Don't they believe in asphalt out here?" she said to the wisp of a girl behind the counter, who was probably barely into her twenties.

"I'm afraid you're in the country now, Ms. Callahan. Things are a little different out here." The young woman behind the counter smiled politely. "I'll need a credit card and a driver's license, please."

DJ raised an eyebrow. "Then I would think, being in the country and all, you people would be a little more trusting."

"Things aren't *that* different." She gave her a subtle wink.

She managed a smile as she fished her wallet from her bag, then tossed the items onto the counter. "What kind of room do I have?"

"You're staying in what we call a guest lodge, complete with a minibar and Jacuzzi."

"King-size bed?"

"Extra-long, eighty-five inches."

"My assistant booked it," she mumbled in explanation. In truth, after one too many nights of sleeping in beds not quite long enough to accommodate her six-foot frame, DJ made a habit of asking before paying.

"I just need you to sign here, and you're all set." The girl marked the spot and handed her a pen. DJ signed and pushed the paper across the counter.

"Here's your key card, Ms. Callahan. You'll need it for both your room and the main gate if you come or go after hours. If you happen to lose it, just let us know, and we'll get you another one."

"Thanks," she said, slipping it into her back pocket. "Where do I go to find my room?"

She slid a small map of the grounds across the counter. "Here's where you are now." She tapped her pen over a small structure on the paper. "And here's your lodge." She trailed the pen an inch or so and circled a larger building. "Go back out to the road you came in on and then take a right. After about a half mile, you'll see the barn on your left. Take the next right. Yours is the first one on the left."

"What are these other buildings?" She traced her finger across the map.

"Those are bunkhouses."

She drew her brows together. "Bunkhouses?"

"They're used for deluxe cowpoke packages. With that package, you room in a bunkhouse with up to ten other guests of the same gender."

Her eyes widened as they flew up to meet the young lady's. "I do have a private room, don't I?" She'd had her fill of roommates in college and wasn't about to put up with a bunch of cowhands snoring through the night. She was too old and set in her ways to make those kinds of sacrifices.

The young lady's smile broadened. She was apparently amused at her frenetic reaction.

"Sort of. Your sleeping space has a sliding door, but you do have to use the community bathroom in the building."

"That's all you have available?"

"I did have a private room when your assistant booked, but she thought you'd like this better."

"Seriously?" *I'm gonna kill her.*

The girl nodded. "I can probably have you moved to one in a day or two, but right now they're all full."

"It'll have to do." She hoped she could finish her business with Kathryn Jackson right away and wouldn't have to stay more than a day or two.

"The rooms really aren't bad for the amount of time you spend in them." She moved her pen across the paper, continuing with her detail of the grounds. "This is what we call the chow shack, but it's really just a cafeteria. The bar and the general store are located in the same building."

"You have a bar?"

"Yep. It's a friendly little place. Stays busy most nights with guests and townfolk."

"What's this little house here?" DJ pointed to an unlabeled square on the page.

"That's Mrs. Jackson's house. It's off-limits to the guests," the girl said.

"Jackson as in Jumpin' J?" DJ kept her eyes glued to the map.

"Yep. They should probably take it off the map, but it's a good landmark."

DJ looked up at the girl. "She doesn't like to mingle with her guests?" DJ's mind was working. The house was off-limits, but the map didn't show any kind of barrier between it and the rest of the grounds.

The girl's lips spread into a soft smile. "Don't worry. You'll see plenty of her during your stay."

"Thank you for your time, miss." She tipped her hat and headed out the door.

A gravel road, framed in white iron-rod fencing, actually did lead DJ directly to paradise. Horses grazed in the fields, and abundant trails meandered up into flourishing, tree-covered hills. The ranch was beautiful. Almost too beautiful. As she inched the car forward, the usually dormant feelings beginning to twist in her gut overwhelmed her. Who would've thought the scent of horse manure would bring them out in such force?

DJ threw the shift knob into neutral and let the car glide to a stop on the side of the road. She had to get a grip on her emotions. She couldn't very well show up on Kathryn Jackson's doorstep with tears streaming down her cheeks. While she'd been living full-time in the city, she hadn't had to deal with the persistent feelings that still dwelled in her heart. She wiped the moisture from her cheeks, sucked in a ragged breath, and flipped the visor mirror open to check her reflection. She removed the small amount of black from under her eyes before she popped the gearshift into place and continued farther.

Definitely a cowgirl's paradise, she thought, gliding into the space in front of the guest lodge. The building looked like an old horse stall. Noting the old-fashioned carpentry, she laughed. That's exactly what it was, an old horse stall. Only now, it had been framed out into separate rooms. She roamed the hallway and found her space, as the young lady called it, to be the third stall on the left. The room consisted of a bed, not very wide, but extra-long, a dresser with a mirror, and a small refrigerator. The space wasn't great but not as bad as she'd imagined. After tossing her duffel and hat onto the bed, she walked to the end of the hall, found the bathroom, and surveyed the multiple sinks, toilets, and shower stalls. This part of the ranch wasn't DJ's idea of paradise, but at least the place was clean.

After unpacking, DJ went outside and took the short walk over to the little white house with blue trim. She wanted to get a look at how the ill-mannered eldest daughter of Elizabeth Belmont lived. She stopped at the corral just across from the house, slung her arms across the top railing, and nodded at the young, dark-haired man leading a horse carrying a little girl around the circle. She looked enough like him to be his sister, but at second glance, seeing the gentle way he tended to her, DJ figured he was more likely her father. DJ's father had started her and her brother and sister riding the same way.

Chapter Four

Virgil picked up the phone on the second ring and pressed it to his ear.

"Oh yeah?" His lips curved into a wide smile.

He chuckled. "We'll take good care of her."

"You got another live one coming." Virgil winced as he took a sip of hot, black coffee. "City girl, straight from Austin. DJ somethin' or other."

Kat kept her eyes fixed on the work schedule for the day. "Good. I can use an extra set of hands today. Is she ready to work?" The Jumpin' J Ranch was definitely not the place to go if you were looking for a relaxing vacation. All the guests here were required to participate in the many tasks that kept it running, from cleaning out horse stalls to herding cattle. When you stayed at the Jumpin' J, you received the full experience, which also meant pulling your own weight.

"Dunno, but I get the feelin' she didn't book the stay herself," he said as he peeled away a stray fleck of peach-colored paint from the window pane.

Kat eyed her father-in-law. His voice was too cheerful. Something was up. "What makes you say that?"

"Take a look." Without turning, he raised his hand and gave her a two-fingered motion.

Kat pushed away from the kitchen table, and the metal chair legs vibrated against the old linoleum floor. She wandered over to the screen door and peered out through the mesh. There, by the corral, stood a tall woman with a head full of short, unruly curls the color of a pearl palomino. Dressed in khaki shorts, a white polo shirt, and loafers, she leaned easily with her arms draped across the top rail of the corral, stroking Minow's cheek.

"Not another one." Kat let out a groan of aggravation. Plucking her baseball cap from the door peg, she slipped it on and tugged her ponytail through the hole.

Virgil grinned in amusement. "I'm sure you'll have her whipped into shape in no time."

"Thanks. I appreciate the confidence." She went out the screen door, letting it slam behind her. Virgil enjoyed watching Kat break in the city folks. It drove her crazy when someone showed up expecting to be catered to as if they were staying at a luxury resort.

"Welcome to the Jumpin' J, Ms..."

"Calla...Callen." DJ cleared her throat. "DJ Callen."

"Ms. Callen." Kat gave her a slight nod of acknowledgment. "I'm Kathryn Jackson. Most people call me Kat."

DJ casually glanced over her shoulder, and Kat got the feeling she was being checked out. The woman was attractive enough, but that kind of attention was something to which Kat had never grown accustomed.

"Do you know how to work a horse, Ms. Callen?" Kat asked in a pleasantly sweet Texas drawl.

"I'm not here to work. I'm here to relax," DJ said as she turned to face her.

"Well, I'm afraid you're out of luck. This is a working ranch, Ms. Callen. Everybody pitches in. Including the guests," Kat said, her voice turning firm yet still holding its soft, feminine edge.

Not making eye contact with DJ, she led Minow out of the corral. Kat was careful not to give the solo guests any sort of encouragement. She preferred families, but unfortunately, part of her clientele consisted of single women and men looking to work more than just the ranch.

"Good morning to you, too." DJ's pointed tone prompted Kat to stop and square her shoulders.

Kat bit her tongue, swallowing the caustic retort waiting to roll off the tip of it. After all, the woman was a guest. Maybe she was just at the wrong place. "If you're not up for it, perhaps you'd like to move to the lodge down the road. They have a nice pool to float around in there. I'm sure you could handle that."

The woman's bland expression didn't change until one side of her lip tugged up into a cockeyed smile. "I think I'd rather stay here."

The way DJ looked at her prompted a fleeting shiver to run the gamut through Kat. She suddenly felt like DJ was a hawk and she was her prey.

"All right then. All you have to do is walk the horse around the corral a few times." Kat led Minow to DJ, reached up, and took the bridle off. "It goes on like this." She slid the bit into the horse's mouth and the leather strap over her head. "There's another bridle on the fence." She flipped her head toward it. "Now, if you would, Ms. Callen, please get that filly over on the other side of the corral and give her a little workout." Kat hiked her leg up, slid her foot into the stirrup that hung just about at her waist, and then swung onto the horse. "Oh, and when you're finished with that one, you'll find five more in the stable," Kat added before riding off to the barn.

What was that about? Her first instinct had been to welcome DJ, as she usually did with new guests. But when she'd caught a glimpse of DJ's sea-green eyes, Kat's survival instincts had kicked in at full force. She'd totally surprised herself with the attitude-filled banter she'd spluttered.

Kat climbed the steps, leaned against the loft opening, and watched DJ slip the bit into the filly's mouth. After sliding the leather strap over the horse's head, she stroked her gently before guiding her around the corral. A welcome breeze swept through the loft, and Kat smiled. She wasn't impressed, just a little surprised to see that the city girl seemed to have a way with horses.

Kat was busy tossing hay from the loft when DJ came into the barn with the freshly exercised filly.

"Any particular horse you want me to take out next?" DJ shouted up to Kat, sputtering when a pile of hay flew down on top of her.

"Sorry," Kat said, doing her best to contain a chuckle. "Stall number five, the brown one with the white spot on her nose." She continued tossing hay on top of her. "But be careful. Sometimes she can be a little temperamental."

Kat peeked over the edge and saw the horse tied to the barn door latch but no sign of DJ. She jumped at her voice behind her.

"Didn't you see me standing there?"

"Geez," she said, spinning around and losing her balance.

DJ grabbed at her arm in what Kat took to be an attempt to lessen her fall, but she was too far gone, and DJ fell along with her into the hay. Sprawled out flat on top of her, DJ chuckled as Kat struggled beneath her.

"This isn't funny, Ms. Callen. Please move." The weight of DJ's shoulder smashed against Kat's face, along with the potent smell of her cologne, was smothering. She struggled and twisted, fighting to catch just the smallest amount of fresh air.

DJ eased up onto her elbows, and her smile widened when Kat put both hands on her shoulders and shoved DJ off to one side.

"Ouch." DJ's smile faded quickly.

Kat shrugged, scrambling to her feet. "Really? Like little old me could actually hurt you."

"I'm not kidding," DJ said gruffly, her voice showing definite signs of anguish.

Kat brushed the hay aside and saw that three out of four pitchfork tips had punctured the fabric of DJ's shorts.

"Oh my God!" She dropped to her knees and quickly removed the implement.

"Hey, take it easy there." Her voice rose momentarily.

Kat pushed DJ's shorts up slightly to examine the small scratches. She swept her fingers across the bare skin below them, and DJ tensed momentarily, magnifying the muscle in her thigh.

"They're just flesh wounds." Kat lifted the fabric to check for further damage and hesitated when a rush of warmth cursed her body. "You'll be all right." She took a bandana from her pocket, soaked it with bottled water, and cleaned the wounds.

"You sure?"

"Uh-huh." DJ would be fine, but Kat didn't know what the hell was going on with her. She dropped the cotton fabric quickly and offered DJ her hand, hoping she didn't notice the heat simmering in her cheeks. "If you go over to the house, Virgil will tend to it for you."

"Thanks." DJ rubbed her thigh gently as she stood up. "I'll take care of it myself."

"Suit yourself," Kat said and returned to moving the hay.

DJ descended the steps and stood just beneath the loft.

"If you're sure you're okay, those horses still need to be worked." She tossed another pile of hay on top of her. "Oh, and you might want to cut back on the cologne a bit. The horses don't care for it much."

"Do you see me standing here?" DJ shouted, brushing the hay from her shoulders.

"Yep." Kat tossed another pile over the edge and smiled. "If I were you, I'd have moved by now."

"People actually pay for this?" DJ left the barn, plucking hay from her hair.

❖

Kat pushed the hay to the side and stood at the edge of the loft opening. Plenty of guests were in the corral today, but without the faintest idea why, Kat kept her eyes glued on one in particular, DJ Callen. She just couldn't seem to take her eyes off the city girl with the muscular thighs.

She watched her lead another horse out of the stable and gently stroke the powerful animal before sliding the saddle onto its back. After cinching it tight, she tried to put her foot in the stirrup, and the horse jerked away quickly.

Kat could see DJ talking as she circled around to face the horse. She stroked the horse's neck and seemed to be soothing it with her voice until the animal rested its head on her shoulder. Then she moved slowly next to the horse and slid her foot into the stirrup again. The horse stood perfectly still for DJ this time, and she mounted her easily. Riding slowly at first, she had the horse worked into a gallop before they went up the trail and into the trees.

Kat skipped down the steps and smiled to herself about the unwavering stranger. *Not as much of a city girl as she makes herself out to be after all.* She filled the water barrel in the corral before walking across the yard to the house. Virgil met her at the door with a large, cold glass of water.

"Hot out there today, huh?"

"Muggy is what it is." Kat drank half the glass and let out a sigh of satisfaction. "And it's not even summer yet."

"What were you and the new gal doin' in the barn for so long?" He folded his arms across his chest and leaned against the counter. "She had quite a grin on her face when she came out."

Kat finished her water and wiped the small trickle running down her chin. "She's a little clumsy. She tripped and fell on me in the loft." Virgil didn't need to know the woman had scared the bejesus out of her.

"Oh, yeah?" He smiled curiously. "That all?"

Kat turned to the sink to refill her glass. "I forked her," she mumbled, bringing the glass to her lips again.

"You had sex with her?" His voice cracked in surprise.

Kat's eye widened and she choked, sucking enough water in her lungs to strangle herself. "Certainly not, Virgil." she sputtered, dragging her sleeve across her face. "She fell on me, and when I pushed her off, she rolled onto the pitchfork. It scratched up her leg."

Virgil chuckled and smiled sheepishly. "I'm sorry. It just sounded like you said…"

"Like I ever talk like that. You need to have your ears checked, Virgil." She raised an eyebrow and brought the glass to her lips again. "Or your mind scrubbed." The picture of the city girl's cream-skinned thigh popped into her mind, and Kat shuddered. "Maybe we both do," she mumbled, yanking the screen door open and going outside. Virgil had beaten her to the thought. Her imagination hadn't made it quite as far as his yet, but after seeing that bare skin, that's where it was heading.

❖

Kat slipped out of Minow's stall and waited until she saw her newest guest go into the general store. She'd had enough interaction with the city girl today. Spending her time running around in circles, accomplishing absolutely nothing, didn't make for a productive day on the ranch. She hurried across the yard, up the steps, and jerked the screen door open.

"Hold on a minute there, missy."

She whipped her head around and looked over her shoulder. She saw Virgil through the mesh screen, sitting at the end of the porch in his usual rocker. "Oh, hi, Virgil. I didn't see you."

"Who ya hidin' from there, Kat?" He bounced his brows at her. "The new gal?"

Even though Virgil had made it clear he'd be okay if she found someone new, she'd told him repeatedly she wasn't looking for any female company. Looking or not, Kat couldn't deny the fact that the wrong kind of women always seemed to flock after her.

She narrowed her eyes and let the door slap against the jamb. "Virgil, don't even go there." She dragged another rocker over next to his and sank into it.

"You want a beer?"

"No thanks." Virgil knew she didn't like beer, but he still managed to offer her one every night.

"The more you run, the more they chase." He took a swig of his beer and rested his head against the chair. "Everyone loves a good chase."

"Is that coming from experience?" She crossed her arms and waited for what she knew would be an interesting tale.

He nodded. "You betcha."

"How many did you catch?" She shifted sideways in the rocker, giving him her full attention. She'd spent many an evening out here on the porch listening to Virgil's adventures, but he'd never revealed much about the women in his life.

"A few, but only one mattered."

"Arizona's mother?"

His eyes rolled, squinting as they focused upward. "Her too." He tipped up his beer and finished what was left in the bottle.

Kat shook her head and blew out a short breath. "Virgil." Her voice took on a low, demanding tone. "How many of those have you had?"

"One or two." He gave her a half smile and winked. "Just like the women." Looking past her, he flipped up a finger and pointed across the yard. "There's the new gal now."

She spun around in her chair to catch the city girl standing on the porch of the store, watching them. Reluctantly she threw up her hand and waved. DJ dipped her chin in acknowledgment before heading across to the guesthouse.

"Well, I think you can probably go ahead and add that one to *your* list."

"Not if I can help it." Kat pushed out of her chair and went inside.

CHAPTER FIVE

It was nearly five o'clock by the time DJ finished with the rest of the horses. She led the last of the lot into the stable and scanned the grounds, looking for the commanding little spitfire who'd been ordering her around all day. Kathryn Jackson was nowhere to be seen. She'd been captivated by Kat's honey-sweetened voice and had stood speechless when Kat fired out orders to her earlier. DJ had felt as though an angel had slapped her. She'd barely been able to catch a glimpse of Kat's face under the brim of her baseball cap. Icy blue eyes, full lips, and long dark hair. *Absolutely gorgeous.* She'd turned and taken a good, hard look, catching only Kat's backside as the horse trotted off. Long, slender legs that led to a shapely body. Tight-fittin' Wranglers never looked so good. DJ shook the thought from her mind. Kat was nothing at all like she'd expected the hardhearted woman she'd been dealing with over the phone to be. Well, except she *was*—everything like her.

DJ had to admit Kat had spunk. She probably weighed a good twenty pounds less than DJ, but she certainly had a lot of fire in her for such a scant piece of woman. She'd watched her ride across the yard, ponytail as black as the horse she was riding bobbing up and down with every stride. She had definite form. Maybe coming out here wasn't such a bad idea after all. DJ had taken note of the once-over Kat had given her and had cursed herself for not putting on her jeans before coming out to the corral. Lesson one, learned.

After taking the saddle off the horse, DJ stroked the horse softly, shoveled a small pile of hay into the stall, and closed the gate. She carried the saddle into the tack room and hung it on one of the empty posts sticking out from the far wall. As she turned to leave, two custom-made saddles hanging alone on the opposing wall caught her eye. She let her hand slide across the cool, slick seat of the first, then lifted the stirrup and saw the emblem: MYERS, YUKON, OKLAHOMA. The saddle was tooled in a basket-weave pattern.

DJ had to admire Kat's taste. She'd never owned one herself, but DJ had seen a few Myers saddles in her youth when she ran with the rodeo circuit. Each one was custom-made by hand to suit. She let the stirrup drop and swiped a finger through the dust on the seat of the other saddle. No one had used this one in a while. She found an old horse blanket and wiped it clean before heading out the door and across the grounds to the general store, where she picked up a bottle of hydrogen peroxide before going to her room for a long, hot shower.

DJ opened the shampoo bottle and inhaled its honey-laced scent. Unbidden thoughts of the soft, sweet-smelling woman she'd had trapped beneath her earlier tumbled through her mind. The heat of her breath against her shoulder. The fleeting touch of her fingers across her thigh. She tossed the small bottle onto the basin, took the shampoo from her travel bag, and went into one of the showers.

When Kat had lifted DJ's shorts in the loft earlier to look at her wound, she'd heard a waver in her voice, and it wasn't because of the blood. The tyrannical little ranch owner had been a little flustered at the sight of her bare thigh. If she played her cards right, DJ could use this attraction to her advantage and be out of here within a day or two. She hadn't expected to become quite so close so quickly. She smiled, thinking about Kat's blushing cheeks. This was going better than DJ expected. She always found women were much more apt to listen once they knew her intimately.

DJ dialed the control back and let the icy water cool her before she flipped it off. While she was still dripping, she wrapped a towel around her and stepped out into the common bath area. She looked in her bag, saw the small bottle of unisex cologne, and remembered what Kat had said about the horses. DJ closed her eyes and shook her head. She should've remembered that. She picked up her stick deodorant and swiped it under her arms before she gathered her things and went to her room.

She threw her duffel onto the bed and dug to the bottom, searching for a cotton T-shirt. After tugging it over her head, she sat on the edge of the bed, took the top off the bottle of peroxide, and poured it over the three scratches on her thigh. Without replacing the cap, she set it on the nightstand before lying on the bed and drifting off to sleep.

When DJ woke, her room was completely dark except for the bright-red light of the alarm clock. She wasn't quite sure where she was until she roused herself out of the sleepy haze brought on by the workout she'd received earlier. She looked at the clock. Almost seven p.m. She rolled off the bed, flipped on the light, and put on her jeans. On her way out, she took her cowboy hat from the wall hook and headed across the yard to the chow shack.

The cafeteria was empty and most of the food already gone. DJ picked up a tray and began to scrape the small amount of cold chopped brisket left from the metal pan.

"Missed supper, huh?" a voice said from behind her.

"I fell asleep." She slapped a spoonful of cold, lumpy mashed potatoes onto her tray.

"She did work you pretty hard for your first day." The man pushed the door open into the kitchen and shouted, "Hey, Jake. Any brisket left?"

"Just the usual hold-back," the cook shouted.

"Got enough for two plates?" He continued through the swinging doors into the kitchen and soon came out with two heaping plates of brisket, mashed potatoes, and green beans. "Grab a couple of forks over there." He pointed to the utensils at the end of the counter.

DJ left the tray of food scrapings on the counter, took two forks from the utensil tray, and followed the man to one of the large picnic-style tables.

"Thanks." She slid onto the bench across from him and dug her fork into the brisket. "I didn't realize the kitchen closed so early."

The man nodded. "Everything runs on a schedule around here. The sooner you get used to it, the better off you'll be."

"How about the bar? What time does it close?" DJ asked between bites of green beans.

"It stays open till one, but I wouldn't advise staying that late if you have a shift in the morning."

"Duly noted." DJ stuffed a fork full of mashed potatoes into her mouth. She could see the man was giving her the once-over.

"Heard you had a little accident today." The man's lips spread into a smile before he looked back to his plate.

DJ shifted in her chair, trying to relieve the dull ache in her thigh. "Just a little flesh wound. Nothing to worry about."

"Did you clean it out good? Those pitchforks are mighty dirty."

"I picked up some things from the store and took care of it." DJ surveyed the man as he ate. She'd seen him watching through the window of the house earlier. He looked a little old for Kat, but it seemed age had no boundaries these days. "You live in the house with the boss lady?" DJ felt him out, trying to find out the nature of their relationship.

"No. I live in the little shack next to the stable." His stare held no expression. "But I do spend a lot of time in that house, and I know everything that goes on there."

DJ's mind-wheels spun, and it clicked. The man sitting before her was the famed Virgil Jackson, Kat's father-in-law. Elizabeth had told her on many occasions what a wonderful horse trainer he was.

"Again, duly noted." DJ returned her attention to her plate. Only the sound of clicking forks filled the room for the remainder of the meal, until she sat back in her chair, her stomach fully satisfied. "By the way, my name's DJ. Can I buy you a beer?"

"Mine's Virgil." He stood and placed the huge, black Stetson on his head. "Maybe another time. I have someplace to be tonight." He motioned across the room. "Take the door on the left. It goes past the general store right into the bar."

DJ nodded and carried the trays up to the dish return before heading through the door into the dimly lit room. She took a seat at the corner of the bar and admired the huge mahogany piece of wood covering it. The lack of people made the small dance floor in the middle of the room look much larger than it was. The array of tables scattered throughout the place gave the bar a rustic mountain atmosphere that made DJ feel strangely comfortable.

"What can I bring you, miss?" the bartender asked.

"Let me have a beer, and the name's DJ."

"Okay, DJ. Mine's George." George had shoulder-length sandy hair that fell across his eyes as he reached into the cooler and took out a bottle of beer.

"Where is everyone tonight, George?" DJ asked, taking note of the silence.

"It's rodeo night. Everyone's over at the arena."

DJ raised an eyebrow in interest. "Exhibition or competition?"

"Around here, it's always competition." He raked the hair out of his face.

"Open registration?" DJ's pulse quickened. It had been a long time since she'd been to a rodeo arena.

"Yep." George looked at his watch. "But you'd better hurry. Cut-off is in about fifteen minutes."

"Put a hold on that beer." She reached into her pocket and threw a few dollars onto the bar.

DJ could see the lights of the arena lighting up the sky just beyond the barn. After walking the short distance across the grounds to the entrance, she climbed the steps to the announcer's booth and read the list of events scheduled for the night. She poked her head into the booth where Virgil and a few other men were laughing as they made moneyless bets on the entrants.

"Can anyone sign up?"

The conversation stopped abruptly when DJ spoke.

Vigil's brow hitched. "You like rodeo, DJ?"

"I can take it or leave it." She leaned across the railing into the booth. "Does the boss lady participate in any of the events?"

"Only by special request," Virgil said.

"Which ones?"

"She can *do* everything on the board, but she's partial to team ropin'."

"Team roping's good. Sign me up with her."

Virgil's lips came together, pursing slightly at DJ's request. "Okay, but I have to warn you, she's not always in the mood."

DJ gave Virgil a confident grin. "Just put us in. I'll take care of her mood." DJ had no idea why she was trying to impress Kat. She was here for one reason, to reunite her with her mother.

The men gathered again, chuckling and mumbling to each other as DJ walked away. They seemed to be looking forward to the show as much as she was.

❖

Kat approached the arena and squinted, trying to read the event board. As she came closer, she made out her name listed for team roping. There must be a mistake, she thought as she climbed the steps to the announcer's booth. Virgil knew better than to enter her in any event without asking first.

"What's going on, Virgil?" She pushed her way into the small booth crowded with men. "Why's my name on the board tonight?"

"We had a special request." He pointed to DJ, standing at the railing above the competition box.

Shit. Kat's stomach fluttered as she turned, pressed back out between the men, and stood just outside the booth. Maybe she should just go to the house and forget about this. She turned to leave but then swung around. That wouldn't be right. She was a guest, and Kat should treat her with the same courtesy she would anyone else. Kat had a reputation to maintain. Sometimes she just needed to suck it up and do what was necessary. She found DJ standing just where Virgil had pointed her out—at the railing, looking over the box, where the first team was preparing to compete.

"I'm sorry, Ms. Callen. You'll have to find another partner. I'm not participating tonight." DJ turned to face her and stared into her eyes. DJ was looking at her with such intensity Kat had to fight the heat simmering within her.

"You want me to pair you with someone else?" Virgil shouted, with no response. "DJ, do you want to team with someone else?"

"No." DJ shook her head. "Just take me off," she said, not breaking eye contact with Kat. "I understand if you're not up for the challenge." She raised an eyebrow and cocked her head. "I hear there's a carousel at the lodge down the road."

Kat knew from the immediate silence in the booth that all eyes were on her. Glancing over her shoulder, she saw Virgil and the other men awaiting her reaction. If she didn't accept the challenge, they'd never let her hear the end of it. The channel gate clanged open, and DJ returned her attention to the arena.

Following the line of her lean, muscular shoulder, Kat could see blond, curly strands of hair protruding from just under DJ's hat. The arena lights, bright and glaring, made the curls flicker with her every move. Her full cheeks led to a rigidly clenched jaw as she watched the competition.

Any other night, Kat would've just walked away, but for some reason she felt compelled to prove a point to this woman, even if she was just a city girl. In addition, she felt the need to show DJ her skills. What was that about?

"Okay, Ms. Callen. If that's what you want, I'll team with you. But you'd better know what you're doing," she said firmly, before turning to Virgil. "Did you bring Minow up tonight?"

"Bring her up every night," Virgil confirmed with a whimsical smirk.

"Put us up next." Kat reached into the booth, took a rope off the wall, and tossed it to DJ. "And wipe that stupid grin off your face," she added as Virgil chuckled. "Come on. Let's find you a horse." She headed down the stairs and into the corral.

As DJ followed, she stopped to stroke the side of a young palomino. "How about this one?"

Kat continued across the corral. "Buck should do the trick for you." She handed her the reins to an old paint horse. "He's fast out of the gate and knows the routine." She put her foot in the stirrup and threw her leg across Minow. "You take the rear. I'll give you a few seconds to catch up, before I throw the front." As she approached the gates, she slowed and looked at DJ. "As soon as my rope is on the steer, throw yours and hold it tight."

"Whatever you say." DJ's tone was slow and even.

As Kat waited in the box for the gate to open, she kept her expression blank. She watched DJ slide her hands up her arms one at a time, bunching her light-gray T-shirt up around her biceps. She couldn't help but notice the definition of muscle flexing rigidly as she kept tension on the reins to settle the horse. Was that a tattoo peeking out from under her sleeve? Kat squinted to get a better look. No. It wasn't a tattoo. It was some sort of scar. DJ's gaze flashed back to meet Kat's, and the gate opened.

The horses bolted out of the chute. Kat threw her rope perfectly around the steer's horns, then dallied her rope around the horn of the saddle and led it around the arena. DJ followed, clumsily throwing her rope just out of sync with the steer's stride. It slapped across the animal's legs and then dropped to the ground. The crowd clamored, hooting boos and hisses. Kat worked her rope loose from the steer's horns, tempted to match the crowd's belligerence, but she held her tongue, trapping the string of obscenities threatening to escape.

"If you didn't know what you were doing, why did you ask me to team with you?"

"I wanted to see you in action."

Kat widened her eyes as her irritation flared. "Unbelievable!" she muttered, sliding off her horse. "Well, I hope you got a good look."

"There's nothin' better than seeing a woman hold her own in the arena." She chuckled. "Listen to them." She motioned to the crowd chanting Kat's name louder and louder in the stands. "They want to see what you can do too."

"I don't think so." She coiled the rope up and hung it over the saddle horn. "I'm not very fond of being made to look like an idiot."

"I won't do it again, I promise." She smiled, seeming to fully enjoy her irritation.

"I said no, Ms. Callen." She turned to lead Minow into the corral.

"You don't want to disappoint your guests, do you?"

"They'll survive." God, she was irritating, smiling at her with those damn rosy-red cheeks.

"Okay. If that's the way you want it." DJ rolled her eyes and feigned a heavy sigh. "I'll just have to go out alone."

She swung around quickly to face her. "You can't do that."

"Why not?"

"It's *team* roping."

"I'm not going to disappoint that crowd." She reached down, took the rope from Kat's saddle horn, and headed to the gate.

Anxious to see what an ass DJ was going to make of herself, Kat tied Minow to the fence and hurried up the stairs to the announcer's booth.

"Virgil, go ahead and give her a three-second delay."

"Made you mad, did she?" Virgil said with a chuckle.

"Now we'll just let everyone see *her* in action," Kat muttered, planting herself on the edge of the railing.

DJ was set to go in the channel and waited for the gates to open. When the buzzer sounded, the steer gate clanged open, and the longhorn raced out into the arena. The box gate remained closed, and DJ glanced up at Kat. Her brow rose, and she caught the glint in Kat's eye as her lips twisted into a sly smile.

She looked to the arena and waited patiently until the gate opened. When it did, she dug her heels hard into the horse, and it sprang out of the box quickly. After positioning herself next to the steer, DJ threw the header and dallied the rope tight around the horn of her saddle. Then she jumped off the horse, threw the loop around the steer's hind legs, wrapped the rope around her arm, and dug her heels in deep. The steer jerked and went down quickly, launching DJ forward on her belly, hard into the dirt. The crowd cheered wildly as DJ stood and dusted herself off. She looked up at Kat, smiled, and tipped her hat.

"Touché, Ms. Callen. Touché." Kat caught her bottom lip between her teeth to hold back a grin. She was still irritated with her previous performance but seriously impressed to see that, even with the delay, DJ had taken her fastest steer down within ten seconds.

"City girl's quite a crowd-pleaser." Virgil grinned.

"She's something all right," Kat mumbled as she went down the steps. "I should've forked her in the ass."

"Where you goin'?" Virgil shouted after her.

"To the bar. I have to make a few changes to tomorrow's work schedule." She threw up her hand and gave him a wave without looking back.

Chapter Six

After a full day out on the range, herding cattle in eighty-degree weather, DJ was completely beat. She rotated the aching muscle in her shoulder and winced as the sharp pain shot through her. After the stunt she'd performed in the arena last night, she was sure the jerk of the steer had dislocated her shoulder and the fall had popped it back into place. She'd been out of practice, and it was a stupid thing to do but a small price to pay for Kat's attention. Kat might not like her very much, but DJ had piqued her interest.

After hanging her hat on the fence post, she put her hands under the spigot and splashed water onto her face and neck before dipping her head under the running water and holding it under the slow, steady stream. The navy cotton T-shirt was soaked as she shook the water from her hair. She pulled her shirt hem from her jeans, tied it into a knot, and splashed water on her stomach before she took the short walk to her room.

Virgil wandered out of the barn chuckling. "I wouldn't push her buttons again if I were you."

"Got to her, did I?" DJ said with a grin.

Virgil's smile widened, deepening the rugged creases in his cheeks. "By the work detail she gave you today, I'd say you irritated her a bit."

"Humph." DJ let out a short breath. "If today was her response to a little irritation," she curved her lip slightly, "I'd hate to see what she'd do if I really made her mad."

❖

Kat picked up a bag of feed and slung it across the barn. This was the third delivery in a row where they'd stacked it wrong. She heard the faint sound of Virgil in conversation with someone just outside the barn.

"Damn it, Virgil. They stacked the feed on the wrong side again," Kat shouted from just inside the barn.

"Settle down. I'll round up some of the hands in the morning and move it," he said calmly.

"It has to be moved tonight." Kat stepped out of the barn and let out a sigh of exhaustion. "We have—" *Skin, belly button, abs.* She fixed her gaze on DJ and stood there open-mouthed, searching for something coherent to say. The babbling voice in her head rambled on like an oversexed teenager, and the only thing she could think of was…*Wow!*

"What?" Virgil's question along with his puzzled look interrupted her brain freeze.

With an irrepressible heat rushing to her cheeks, Kat jerked her hand up to cover her mouth. *Oh my God. Did I say that out loud?*

"Why does it have to be moved tonight?" he asked.

"Huh?" Kat said, relieved her reaction had remained in her head. She still stood motionless, keeping her gaze fixed on DJ, watching the beads of water trickle slowly across the well-defined muscles of her stomach.

Virgil traced her stare to DJ and then back again. His lips pressed together, skewing into a grin. "*Why* do we have to move it tonight?"

She snapped her eyes to Virgil. "We have more hay coming first thing in the morning," Kat said, her voice regaining its strength.

DJ hung her hat on the fence post. "Well, then we'd better get moving." She groaned and headed into the barn.

Kat stood staring suspiciously for a few minutes, wondering why DJ was being so helpful. After all, she'd sent her out on the nastiest detail on the ranch today just for spite. She thought she'd be packing her bag to leave by now for sure.

"Not the kind of help you're used to havin' around lately, huh?" Virgil took Kat by the arm and drew her along. "Now come on. We don't want to be out here all night."

Kat climbed into the cab of the bucket loader, drove it over to the feed, and jumped out to help DJ and Virgil throw the bags into it. Stacking twice as many bags as Kat and Virgil, DJ made lifting the fifty-pound bags look easy. Even after the third load, she was still tossing them effortlessly into the bucket. Kat moved out of the way so DJ could hoist the last few bags, and she couldn't help but sneak a look at her again. As Kat watched the muscles flex in DJ's arms, she tingled from head to toe, a reaction she hadn't felt in a very long time. After throwing the last bag into the bucket, DJ turned suddenly, and Kat knew she'd caught her assessment.

Kat hopped into the bucket loader, shot across the barn, and dumped the last batch onto the stack. Trying to keep some distance between them, she grabbed the broom and began to sweep the loose feed from the newly bare corner of the barn.

"Is that all?" DJ asked.

"I think so," Virgil said, scanning the barn. "We sure do appreciate your help." He offered DJ his hand, and she shook it.

"I'm sure you could've done it without me."

"Yes, we could have," Kat said, straightening her stance. "But we did it a lot faster with your help. Thank you," she added humbly. It would be too dangerous to look up again. Thoughts of skin and sweat would pummel her and... *Snap out of it!*

"She's not so bad once you get to know her," Virgil said as he walked with DJ to the barn entrance.

DJ smiled and shook her head. "She certainly doesn't make it easy." She took her hat from the fence post.

Virgil's eye squinted into a wink, prompting his weathered face to wrinkle. "Try the bar after supper. Corner table. She's usually there."

Kat waited a few minutes before heading to the entrance and sliding one side of the barn closed. "You know I heard everything you said."

He nodded. "Yep."

She closed the other door. "I might just decide to stay in tonight."

"No, you won't," Virgil said as he flipped the latch shut, turned, and headed to his room.

And he was right. DJ Callen was making it hard for her to stay away.

❖

Today was a tough but good day. DJ had forgotten how much she liked to be out on the range, so close to nature. She opted for the community Jacuzzi to soothe her muscles before her shower tonight. She considered herself in good shape for a woman her age. She ran five miles every morning and lifted weights three times a week, but this kind of workout was a lot tougher than her usual routine. DJ listened to a few other guests talking about their cowhand adventures, but unless directly asked for her opinion about something, she tried to keep mainly to herself.

After soaking until her energy was zapped, she heaved herself out and cooled down in the shower. Clean but not quite revived, she tugged a fresh shirt over her head and collapsed onto the bed, contemplating whether to hit the sack or eat first. Her stomach won out with a loud growl. She rolled off the bed and headed to the chow shack.

After a dinner of chicken-fried steak and mashed potatoes, DJ picked up a roll of antacids at the general store and popped a few into her mouth before she wandered into the bar.

"What can I bring you tonight, DJ?" George asked.

"Let me try that beer again." She swung her leg around and slid gingerly onto the bar stool.

"Long day?" George set a frothy mug of draft beer in front of her.

"It's been a while since I've been on a horse for an extended amount of time," she said as she picked up the mug and took a sip.

"You'll get used to it after a few days."

"I don't know about that. It hurts in places you don't even want to imagine." She rubbed the back of her neck. "I thought this was going to be a vacation."

George let out a hearty laugh. "You didn't read the brochure, did you?"

"Read it." Her voice rose. "I never even saw it." She'd have to remember to thank Marcia properly when she returned to the office.

George smiled. "Mrs. Jackson does expect the guests to do their share." He motioned toward the corner of the bar, where Kat was sitting at a table, sorting through a pile of papers. "She's tough, but she's a good lady."

She looked different tonight, DJ thought as she turned to watch her. She hadn't noticed her appearance before, perhaps because she'd never seen her without a hat on. Kathryn Jackson had beautiful, long, dark tresses, which tonight were flowing like silk across her shoulders. DJ sat at the bar, watching her absently run her fingers through her hair and smile patiently as several guests approached, one by one, making conversation or possibly asking her to dance. She gave them all a few minutes of her time but eventually sent each one on their way without so much as a stroll around the dance floor. She hadn't experienced Kat's good nature personally, but she was impressed by her constant smile and seemingly favorable responses. Most of the women she knew would've been out of the bar by the third person.

She turned to the bartender. "She married?" DJ already knew the answer. She just wanted to see what the staff knew.

"Nope."

"Boyfriend?"

"Nope."

DJ peeked over her shoulder and observed the sparkle emanating from the thin golden band as her hand moved through her hair. "She has a ring on her finger."

"Widowed, about four years ago."

"Does she wear it to fend off all the sharks in this place, or is she still hung up on a memory?"

"A little of both, I think." George filled two glasses with scotch and slid them in front of the couple sitting at the corner of the bar. "She goes out every once in a while, but she's pretty selective nowadays. She doesn't seem to have much free time."

"Did you give it a shot?"

"Thought about it more than once." His lips curled into a sly smile. "But she's partial to women suitors. Besides, it wouldn't be the best idea to mix it up with the boss."

It was obvious Kat wasn't interested in anything besides the books tonight, but DJ decided to press her luck anyway. Maybe she could gain a little insight as to why she seemed to hate her mother so much. After downing the last of her beer, DJ wandered over to Kat's table. It looked like she was busy going over the next day's schedule and didn't even acknowledge DJ when she planted herself in the chair next to her.

"Can I buy you a drink?"

"No thanks. I'm not drinking tonight," Kat said without looking up.

"In general or just alcohol?"

Kat peeked up at DJ through her thick, darkened lashes, and her lips curved into a slight smile. "Alcohol."

When Kat's electric-blue eyes met hers, DJ was stunned. She hadn't really noticed the resemblance to Rebecca before, but now, with her dark hair flowing, framing her face, it was uncanny. The shape, the lines, even the expression were almost a carbon copy.

"Have a little too much last night?"

"*No.*" Kat's voice hung on the O as her tone dropped. "I still have a lot of work to do tonight."

DJ stared, still trying to get over the resemblance between Kat and her sister. Her naturally arched brows were dark in color against her tanned forehead. They hung perfectly over her wary blue eyes and rose slightly as she stared back at her. Except for the tiny lines around her eyes, DJ would have never guessed her to be almost eight years Rebecca's senior.

"What?" Her full sensuous lips, void of any artificial color, pursed into a grimace before she swiped her hand across her face. "Do I have something on my face?"

"Sorry," she said with a smile, amused by Kat's discomfort. "You just look really familiar." She rocked her head to one side and drew her brows together curiously. "Have we met before?"

"That's an old one." Kat let out a short laugh, tucked a swag of her dark, silken hair behind her ear, and focused on her paperwork again.

"I'm serious. I think we've met before." DJ swept Kat's hand up in hers and held it firmly.

A startling sensation shot through Kat, and she popped her head up quickly. Her eyes went straight to DJ's, and the warmth she'd been cursed with earlier returned in a frenetic fury.

"Ms. Callen," she managed to rasp out. "I can honestly say, the first time I ever laid eyes on you was yesterday." She would've remembered a woman like DJ Callen, so commanding, so sure of herself in every way. A woman who made Kat yearn for every pleasure in life she'd forbidden herself in the past year. Kat slowly slipped her hand away and sank into her chair, hoping the sensation would subside as quickly as it had emerged. It wouldn't. The feeling would linger, chiseling away at her resolve, just as it had before. The best she could hope for now was that DJ would find her company lacking and leave her to find better conversation.

"All right, if you say so." DJ conceded. "I'm gonna get myself a drink." She gave her a polite smile and stood up to go to the bar. "You sure you don't want anything?"

"No thanks. And you can save yourself the trouble of coming back."

DJ's smile only seemed to broaden at Kat's words of rejection. "Oh, it's no trouble, ma'am," she said smoothly, tipping her hat as she walked away.

Kat watched out of the corner of her eye as DJ made her way across the room to the bar. She wore fancy-pocket jeans and walked with the sort of confidence that screamed attraction. As DJ leaned against the bar, she rested a foot on the rail, leaving one long denim-clad leg glued to the floor. Following the line of her leg from boot to butt, then belt to hat, Kat noticed how she certainly had the look of a cowgirl now, which threw her into a full-blown frenzy of desire. Roping that one in was bound to bring her a whole lot of heartache.

DJ turned abruptly and glanced over her shoulder at Kat. The attraction hit her right between the ears again, tossing her mind into a spinning haze and her eyes back to her paperwork. That was definitely not the city girl she'd met yesterday.

After a short time, Kat relaxed into her chair, relieved that the woman who made her stomach tighten and her palms sweat seemed to have found someone else to occupy her time. She was deep in thought when DJ appeared in front of her holding two shot glasses filled with an amber-colored liquid.

"Try this." DJ set one of the glasses on the table and pushed it to Kat.

Kat shook her head. "I don't think so."

"Afraid I'm going to poison you for sending me out with the cattle today?" DJ's voice was low and deceptively tame.

Kat reluctantly picked up the glass and held it to her lips. She inhaled the intense aroma of the caramel-scented liqueur before letting a small amount float across her tongue. Pleasantly surprised at the taste, she held it up in front of her and stared through the liquid at DJ before filling her mouth with another sip and setting it on the table.

"Like it?"

"It's not bad." Kat did her best to conceal her enjoyment as the unique taste lingered on her tongue. "What is it?"

"Tuaca. It's an Italian liqueur." DJ lifted her glass. "I was a little surprised to find it here. Most places don't stock it." She skimmed the bar. "Apparently your bartender's been around."

"Really?" Kat's voice rose. "I could've sworn he told me he was from some little town in Oklahoma." She took another sip and stared over at the young, scraggly-looking bartender curiously. "I must have misunderstood." She didn't think she had. She'd have to ask him about it sometime.

DJ moved closer, her eyes widened, and she flashed Kat a mischievous grin. "There's only one problem with Tuaca."

Kat backed away cautiously, noting the flush, rosy color that had settled into DJ's smooth, rounded cheeks. "What's that?"

"It tastes really good and goes down smooth. But if you're not careful, it can knock you on your ass."

Kat drank the rest of it. "You just worry about yourself, Ms. Callen."

"Whatever you say," DJ said in a slow, even tone, then drank hers in one swallow. "I'll be right back."

"Bring me another," Kat said. DJ turned at the demanding tone. Kat was caught by dark-green eyes, and her insides did an unexpected flip-flop. "Please," Kat added, filling her voice with reluctant, sweet allure as she stared down at her papers. If Kat looked into those steamy green eyes again, she literally might do something she'd regret.

"Why certainly, ma'am." DJ brushed against her as she left the table, and liquid gushed between Kat's legs. DJ somehow had encompassed all of her senses. She hadn't been so aroused in years. This was something Kat hadn't seen coming and couldn't seem to prevent.

As Kat watched DJ walk across the dance floor, her desire increased with her every step. *Zing!* There it was again, that feeling. Somehow, curly, unkempt hair, Miss Me jeans, and a flannel shirt made her even more attractive than before. It was clear there wouldn't be any more work done if she stayed here tonight. She shuffled through the papers and snagged one out as DJ strolled to the table.

"Here you go." DJ set one shot in front of Kat and took a sip out of the other as she slid down into the chair.

"And this is for you." Kat handed DJ a single sheet of paper.

"What's this?"

"Your work detail." Kat gathered her papers and stood up. "I usually give first-time guests an every-other-day schedule, but since you seem to like working so much, I went ahead and put you on again tomorrow."

DJ squinted at the schedule. "Lucky me."

Kat picked up the shot of Tuaca and gulped it before leaning over to whisper in DJ's ear. "Thanks for the drinks," she said, knowing she was playing with fire. She caught a glimpse of DJ's breasts. Only a few small pearl snaps were holding them captive, and she could easily pop them open in one swift tug. Kat closed her eyes as need shuddered through her. She turned and shot across the room, not stopping until she was safely through the hallway and inside the office. After closing and locking the door, she fell against it, clutching her papers to her chest and totally baffled by her own behavior. She should be staying as far away from DJ Callen as she possibly could, but instead she'd scheduled DJ to work right alongside her all day tomorrow. She tossed her papers onto the desk and dropped into the chair. Who was she trying to kid? Kat knew why she'd done it. She hadn't felt a rush like that from any woman's touch since she'd lost Arizona. It felt good to have these feelings and desires stirring inside her again. Kat wasn't sure what, if anything, was going on between her and DJ Callen, but tomorrow it would be just the two of them, and she would have ample opportunity to find out.

DJ was still at the table when Kat came out of the office an hour later. Kat moved from table to table on her way out, stopping to chat momentarily at each one. She took an occasional peek over at DJ. When DJ's gaze met hers, she smiled and took a quick left, circling around the bar away from her. The wetness in her jeans had just begun to dry, and now, with just a glimpse of her, Kat was completely soaked again. She hoped tomorrow didn't turn out to be a huge mistake.

CHAPTER SEVEN

The vision of Kat leaning down to whisper in her ear last night played through DJ's mind. The scent of her honey-sweetened tresses draped across her face still filled her senses. When Kat had asked her to bring her another drink, DJ hadn't expected to react so strongly. She'd been mesmerized by how quickly Kat's steel-blue eyes had softened and her lips had curved into the sweetest of smiles. At that point, bringing Kat a drink was the very least she wanted to do for her. She'd walk through fire for another look like that.

Yesterday, DJ had seen Kathryn Jackson as a demanding ranch owner with an unbending schedule, but last night a very different woman sat in the bar. A kind, beautiful woman who seemed to genuinely care about the people who took time out of their busy schedules to visit her ranch. DJ had watched her mingle, totally at ease in her own element, and wondered how a woman from such a prominent family had wound up in the middle of nowhere running a dude ranch all by herself.

The pounding on the door shook DJ out of her drowsy state. "Rise and shine, Ms. Callen." Virgil's voice came through loud and clear. "You decent?"

"Of course." She didn't sleep naked in strange places. She heard the lock click, the door flew open, and the light blinded her.

DJ smashed the pillow over her head. "I thought I locked that last night?"

"You did, but I have the passkey." Virgil's voice rang with an odd tinge of humor, as though he enjoyed rousing all the guests out of the sack at the crack of dawn.

DJ moaned and rolled over to peek at the clock. "What time is it?" Still adjusting to the light, she squinted. "The sun's not even up yet." "Almost five thirty. Come on now. Breakfast's at six." Virgil went out the door, closing it behind him.

DJ swung her legs out onto the floor, reached to the bottom of the bed for her jeans, and tugged them on. She stepped into her boots, took her hat and flannel shirt from the bedpost, and headed to the bathroom.

The door clanged shut behind DJ as she wandered into the chow shack. She gave another foggy-eyed guest a nod before taking one of the thick diner-style mugs out of the rack. She slid the cup under the spout, flipped the lever, and let the coffee drain into it. She skimmed the area, caught sight of the short-order cook, and watched the man juggle five breakfast orders at once without missing a beat. After taking a sip of the piping-hot liquid, DJ winced as she strolled across the room and sat at the table across from Virgil.

"Is every day like this?" She rubbed her eyes and raked her hand down her face.

"Nope." Virgil chuckled. "You'll earn a day off if you make it through the first couple."

"I'm gonna kill Marcia." DJ brought the cup to her lips and slurped in a mouthful of the thick, black substance they had the nerve to call coffee.

"Who's Marcia?"

"My assistant."

Kat's voice came across the room, and DJ looked up to see her poking her head through the doorway.

"Virgil, you in here?" she shouted.

Virgil threw his arm up. "Over here."

Kat continued inside, picked up a coffee mug, filled it halfway with the hot brew, and doused it with cream before making her way to the table.

"Did the boys set all those posts yesterday?" Her face twisted in response to the bitter taste of the mocha-tinted sludge.

"Sure did. Every last one of them."

"Great." She veered her eyes to DJ as though measuring her carefully.

"Good morning." DJ looked warily over her cup at Kat, wondering what kind of torture she had in store for her today.

"Good morning, Ms. Callen." Kat took another sip of coffee before setting the mug on the table. "You'd better put some food into you. You're gonna need it today." She turned quickly and headed out the door.

"What the hell is she talking about?" DJ dropped against the hard, wooden chair and watched Kat cross the room.

"Didn't she tell you?"

DJ drew her brows together. "Tell me what?"

Virgil's lips spread into a wide smile. "You're working with her today."

"How'd that happen?" DJ shook her head. The woman was confusing her no end. "I thought she didn't like me." She jerked her lip up, thinking whatever torture Kat had in store for her today wouldn't be all bad if she could coax a smile or two out of her like she'd seen last night.

"Don't get too excited," Virgil said, apparently catching the glint in her eye. "Her work details are usually the hardest. She's gonna make you use those muscles of yours."

DJ didn't mind. She liked using her body to the fullest, in work and pleasure. The hardest part would be looking at Kat's curves all day without being able to touch them. After a sleepless night filled with erotic dreams, she wanted to do a whole lot more than that.

"That should be a treat." DJ gave him a wry smile, then eased up to fill a plate with eggs, bacon, and homemade biscuits.

After breakfast, DJ stroked her stomach on the way out the door. She shouldn't have eaten that last biscuit. It had been a long time since she'd allowed herself a country breakfast. Fifteen years, to be exact. She spotted Kat by the barn loading some tools into the bed of a beat-up old pickup.

"Why don't you use the big truck?" DJ looked over at the Ford dually parked next to the house.

"That's for towing the horse trailer." Kat picked up a roll of barbed wire and hoisted it into the truck. "Old Blue, here, does just fine out on the range."

As Kat reached for another roll, DJ stepped in front of her, creating a barrier between Kat and the truck, forcing her to stop and look at her. Kat's soft, blue eyes drifted up across her face, meeting DJ's in a stinging union. No one spoke, but DJ understood the woman standing in front of her this morning was offering a truce. Kat was taking the first step by putting herself out there. DJ wouldn't disappoint her by refusing the offer.

"I'll get that." She took the roll of wire from her, then retrieved the last few from the ground and tossed them into the truck bed. "So, what are we doing today, Boss?"

"We're gonna stretch some fence." Kat lifted her eyebrows. "Have you ever done that before?"

"Nope. Never have." DJ was lying. The first time she'd strung fence, she was only ten or twelve years old. You learned early on the farm, especially when you didn't have enough money to pay anyone else to do it. DJ and her brother, Junior, had done these kinds of chores. Her sister Marilyn, a delicate wisp of a girl, helped their mother in the kitchen instead.

"Don't worry. I'll show you how," Kat said with a smile as she walked around and slid into the driver's seat without giving DJ so much as a glance.

"Whatever you say." DJ spoke in her usual low, even tone. She gave the old rusted door a yank. It flew open and rattled loudly as it smacked against the hinge stop. She hopped into the cab and swung the door closed gently, afraid it might fall off any time.

"How's the leg?" Kat asked hesitantly, giving DJ the once-over.

"Doing good, thanks." She reached for the waistband of her jeans. "You wanna see?"

"No." Kat's eyes darted to DJ's. Her cheeks reddened as she turned the key and revved the engine. "I'm glad to see you're wearing the appropriate attire today." She let her lips break into a smile. "Barbed wire can be hell on your legs." She threw the truck into gear and hit the gas, throwing DJ against the seat, scrambling for the seat belt.

It didn't take long to drive to the area high above the rest of the ranch. DJ hopped out of the truck before Kat could put it into reverse and back up to the fence posts. She stood mesmerized by the blanket of vibrant wildflowers leading down to the string of trees framing the river. Her mother always said that nature was a beautiful canvas, and she was right.

"Wow. Is this your property too?" She looked out above the trees, finding something magical about being able to look out so far on the countryside.

"Just to the other side of those trees." Kat pointed into the distance. "How beautiful." She wasn't exaggerating. In her youth, DJ had worked country like this, but she'd long forgotten it. The sight made memories flood back, giving life a completely new perspective, one she hadn't thought about since she'd left the family farm years ago.

"That's why I'm here." Kat's voice filled with the velvety sound of contentment as she walked around to the rear of the truck and opened the toolbox. "I hope these fit." She tossed a pair of leather work gloves to her.

DJ gave her a playful grin as she slipped them on. "You take advantage of all your guests like this?"

"Just the ones who pay extra." Kat smiled casually as she lifted the toolbox out of the truck and carried it to the first fence post. "Will you grab a roll of wire and bring it over here, please?"

DJ veered her gaze from the view. "Whatever you say."

"We'll do the top and bottom strings first, then fill in the middle." She pointed to a completed section of fence they'd be continuing.

DJ nodded, still holding the roll of wire. "How long have you had this place?"

"Almost eight years."

"How come you've waited until now to put up a fence?"

"My neighbor and I don't see eye to eye on much." Kat took the roll from her, then wrapped the wire around the wooden post and tacked the end to it. "Recently she's been trying to take a few more liberties than I'd like."

"Are we talking about your property or you?" DJ followed her to the next post.

"Both." Kat handed the roll of wire to DJ. "Pull the wire as tight as you can." She reached into her shirt pocket, took out a heavy-duty staple, and set it before she pounded the hammer against it to fasten the wire securely to the post. "It's nothing I can't handle." She raised her eyes, giving DJ a subtle look of what seemed like warning before continuing past the metal supports and on to the next wooden post.

"Message received." She gave her a slight smile of admiration. She could see her putting anyone in their place if they got out of hand. What would Kat do if she took her into her arms right now and kissed her?

As the morning progressed, the two of them worked well together, like right and left hands, one not having to ask the other what to do. DJ actually found working alongside Kat enjoyable with or without occasional conversation. They'd talked about many topics, including horses, Texas, the ranch, and barbed wire. She'd even opened up and told Kat she had a brother and sister who lived close by. DJ had surprised herself with that disclosure, even though she'd let her assume they lived in Austin and that she had a good relationship with them. Something about Kat made her want to tell her everything. The only subject that created silence was Kat's family. Each time DJ brought it up, Kat diverted to something else.

"You're pretty good at this." Kat dropped her hammer into the grass and headed for the water cooler. "If I didn't know better, I'd think you were a farmer."

"What makes you think I'm not?" DJ followed her, took her gloves off, and slid onto the tailgate.

Kat took a paper cup from the dispenser, held it under the spigot, and let the water run into it. She handed it to DJ and filled one for herself. DJ felt the cool water all the way down. Kat finished hers, crushed her paper cup, and threw it into the truck before reaching up and tugging the collar away from DJ's neck. "Pale skin." Kat took DJ's hand, stroked her palm with her fingers, and a jolt shot through her. "Soft hands." Kat stared into DJ's eyes and hesitated. "And your clothes, of course. No farmer would wear a hundred-dollar pair of jeans to stretch fence. I may be a country girl, but I'm not stupid." She dropped DJ's hand and headed to the fence.

DJ moved her eyes quickly, looking down at her jeans, then darting back up. "Maybe I'm a rich farmer." She followed her to the fence, where Kat had started collecting the tools.

"Right, and your idea of a vacation is to be a ranch hand." Kat let out a short laugh. "I don't think so." She narrowed her eyes before she walked to the box and dropped the tools into it.

"You hungry?" They still had a lot of work ahead of them, but for the past hour, Kat's stomach had been rumbling. Running into DJ in the chow shack this morning had thrown off her routine. The sight of DJ looking so gorgeous first thing in the morning had made her too jumpy to eat. Food wouldn't settle well. If she didn't put something in her stomach soon, she'd be passed out in the brush before long.

"I could eat something." DJ loaded the toolbox into the rear of the truck, then took off her flannel shirt and tossed it into the cab. It was warming up to be another hot, humid day.

"Get in." Kat opened the door and slid into the driver's seat. She studied DJ for a moment and noticed that the red T-shirt seemed to accentuate her breasts more than the gray one had at the arena the other night. DJ gave her a subtle smile, and Kat warmed as she thought about letting DJ into her life a little more. Kat veered right and drove down the hill to the same shady area she'd ridden her horse to a few days before. After parking just behind the tree, Kat climbed up into the truck bed, slid a cooler to the edge of the tailgate, and then jumped down to lift it out.

"Let me take that," DJ insisted, picking it up easily.

Kat led her to a flat, grassy area under the tree, where she spread out an old hand-sewn quilt.

"Did you make this?" DJ ran her hand across the material.

"You must be kidding." Kat laughed. "If I didn't have Virgil, we wouldn't be eating right now."

"Not very domestic, are you?" DJ smiled as she lay back on the blanket and stared up into the sky. "This is a nice spot. Come here a lot?"

Kat nodded. "It's peaceful here." She opened the cooler and rummaged through it. Second thoughts about bringing DJ here flew through her. She took a deep breath and pushed them out of her mind. "Turkey or roast beef?" She held up two sandwiches.

"Roast beef." She propped herself up on one elbow.

Kat tossed DJ the sandwich, took out a couple of sodas, and sat down on the corner of the quilt across from her. Kat was so hungry, she inhaled the first half of her sandwich and slapped DJ's hand when she reached for the second. Stretching fence in eighty-degree weather was taxing, and from the weather report she'd seen this morning, it was guaranteed to be even hotter today.

"You have anything else in there?" DJ asked.

Kat raised the top of the cooler. "Apples, bananas, and grapes."

"Let me have an apple." She held her hand up.

Kat tossed it to her, then took out a small bag of grapes for herself. As DJ bit into the apple and sucked the juice into her mouth, she caught herself wondering what it would be like to kiss those lips and feel them on her body. The thoughts produced a reaction she'd thought no longer possible.

DJ tossed the apple core into the grass, then crawled over to the cooler, lifted the top, and looked inside.

Kat shook herself out of the erotic thought. "There's another sandwich in there."

"Not anymore." DJ peeked over the cooler at her. "And I have to say, your grapes are looking mighty good right now too." She raised her eyebrows and grinned.

"I wouldn't count on getting anywhere near my grapes." Kat squared her shoulders and playfully tossed one at her.

DJ let the lid drop, picked up the grape, and popped it into her mouth. "Um...Sweet. I gotta have some of those." She crawled across the quilt next to Kat and put her hands out. "Come on, just a couple," she said, begging comically.

"I don't think so. You've eaten just about everything else. Do you want me to starve?" Kat held the grapes above her head as DJ reached for them. She had Kat down and pinned in an instant.

Unprepared for the urgent passion rising within her, Kat suddenly wanted DJ to touch her. She felt DJ's lips slowly drag across her cheek and then the smoldering heat of her mouth. Kat trembled and the grapes fell from her hand. She tugged softly at DJ's lips with her teeth. What was this woman doing to her?

"I knew I could get them." DJ sat up and straddled her before she swiped the grapes from the quilt and popped them into her mouth one by one.

Still pinned beneath DJ, Kat propped herself up on her elbows—shaken, annoyed, and embarrassed that she'd let her body control her actions. Her cheeks burned with unwelcome heat. "You can move now."

"Oh, come on. I thought we were having fun here." DJ dipped her chin and covered Kat's mouth with hers.

Sweet-tasting nectar filled Kat's mouth, and her mind spun. Heat spiraled through her, igniting her senses one by one, but she felt guilty for enjoying it. Her mind was telling her no, but her body was all in. When DJ's tongue dipped into her mouth, Kat snaked her arms around her neck and held on for dear life. Their tongues danced, softly baiting each other until Kat heard a faint moan. When she realized it wasn't coming from either one of them, she popped her eyes open. It took a minute, but she recognized the sound in the distance.

"Did you hear that?" Kat turned her head to focus on the faint wail.

"What?" DJ's mouth trailed down the newly opened path of Kat's neck.

Kat's mind went hazy until she heard the moan again. It rapidly grew louder until it turned into a blood-curdling screech. "Damn!" Kat twisted to maneuver out from under DJ, jumped up, and raced to the truck. She took a rope from the cab, ran to the riverbank, and headed upstream. "Come help me," she shouted.

Kat saw the calf's head bobbing in and out of the water. She didn't have time to think. Her instincts kicked in, and she waded knee-deep into the water. DJ scrambled to her feet and ran to the edge of the river, waded in next to her, and started out farther.

"Wait," Kat ordered her, slapping her hand to DJ's arm. "It's stuck in the net. We have to get it loose or it'll drown." DJ's eyes fixed on the flailing calf before she brushed Kat's hand aside and continued into the rushing water.

Kat held on to DJ's arm, and she whipped her head around. "What?"

"The river's too rough. Anchor me. I'll go in." Her voice steady and firm, Kat handed one end of the rope to DJ, then tied the other around her waist. "Don't let go."

DJ held the rope tight as Kat waded deeper into the icy, rushing water and fought to free the flailing calf from the fishnet wrapped around it. She struggled uselessly to undo the tangled net before losing her footing on the slippery moss-covered rocks and sinking into the rushing water. Kat caught sight of the river bank and saw DJ wrestling with the line as she thrashed her arms and legs, fighting to keep her head above the surface. The rapid monster-current continued to force her downstream, threatening to consume her in one big gulp. DJ seemed to have dug her heels in as she struggled to hold the rope. Gradually gaining momentum over the water, she towed Kat in as she sputtered and gasped for air.

DJ's breaths were short and labored. "Are you all right?"

"I'm fine." Kat coughed and choked, then staggered to the river's edge, intending to go back in after the calf.

"No, you don't." DJ pushed her to the ground. "Stay here." She gave the orders this time, treading through the hip-deep water.

Kat watched as DJ held the top of the net and waded out to find a place to anchor her feet in the rocks just behind the calf. The force of the water held the animal hard against her. Kat noted the path of the river. They could both end up downstream, and eventually DJ would have to make it to shore, without the calf. Kat's stomach clenched. She hated to lose a baby, but she didn't want to consider losing DJ.

Kat could see her trying to work her hand into the pocket of her soaked denim jeans to find something. It was a knife. Relief washed through her. She could cut the net. Kat held one end as DJ hacked it and held the calf. She used the net as a tow rope, moving slowly to the riverbank one step at a time until she could dig her heels into the rocks for balance and guide the exhausted little one close enough to shore for Kat to help it out of the water. The tired animal quickly scrambled to its feet and ran up the riverbank to its mother.

"They have such strong family instincts," Kat said, watching the mother tend to her baby. "Sometimes they seem more human than us."

DJ collapsed onto the ground.

"Damn Victoria Maxwell," Kat muttered, pacing back and forth, clothes and hair dripping. "This is the second calf I've almost lost because of her." She wrapped her arms across her chest and shivered when the wind picked up.

DJ went to the truck, peeled off her T-shirt and jeans, and hung them over the side. Then she reached into the cab and took out her flannel shirt and a couple of old wool blankets from behind the seat.

"Take off your clothes," DJ said as she walked to the quilt where they'd picnicked.

"Excuse me?"

"You heard me. Come over here and take off your clothes."

"You have to be kidding." Kat let out a funny-sounding snort, planted her hands firmly on her hips, and let her eyes sweep DJ.

"If you don't, you're going to catch a chill." DJ held the blanket up in front of her. "Here." She handed Kat her flannel shirt. "Put this on."

Kat lifted an eyebrow. Even though she wanted to be naked with DJ, she felt oddly self-conscious all of a sudden.

"I'll close my eyes." DJ waited while Kat removed her wet clothes and dropped them to the ground. Kat glanced up and caught DJ as she opened her eyes and immediately snapped them shut again.

Kat put on DJ's flannel shirt, then said, "Okay," before she ripped the blanket from DJ's hands and quickly wrapped it around her waist.

DJ gathered Kat's clothes, took them to the truck, and hung them over the tailgate next to hers. She went to the quilt, spread it up onto her shoulders before she took Kat's hand, and led her over to a small patch of sunlight shining between the thick, leafy branches of the trees. The chill of the river ran through Kat again. At least she thought it was the river. The way DJ was smiling at her could've triggered it too.

"It'll be warmer over here in the sun." DJ spread the quilt, then motioned for Kat to sit. She dropped down next to her and wrapped herself and one of the other blankets snugly around Kat.

"Relax," DJ said. She must have felt Kat's back stiffen against her. She took Kat's ice-cold hands and warmed them with hers. Kat reluctantly molded into DJ. As she settled in, Kat's bare thigh brushed against DJ's, provoking unbidden thoughts and a simmering heat between her legs. Being this close to DJ felt good. No. It was more than that. It felt natural.

CHAPTER EIGHT

The sun had shifted to the west by the time Kat woke. As she lay with her face nestled against DJ's chest, her arm had somehow found its way across her stomach. Oddly, she didn't feel the slightest twinge of discomfort. Something about this woman made her feel very much at ease. Kat still didn't know why she was here. DJ had given Kat the impression that she didn't want to work, yet whenever she assigned her a task, DJ did it well and without complaint. She acted as if her stay at the ranch was more of an imposition than a chosen experience, yet she hadn't hesitated to go into the river after the calf. Kat thought about what she'd seen after DJ came out of the river. *Sports bra, nipples, boyshorts—dripping-wet, body-clinging boyshorts.* It was absolutely unreal. First the rodeo, then the kiss, and now this. Was there anything about DJ she wouldn't like? She was just *too* perfect. This had to be a test.

Before she'd fallen asleep, Kat had felt a sudden change in DJ's embrace. It was gentle yet rigid. From the moment DJ had arrived, she'd been so laid-back and relaxed, Kat had been unable to provoke the slightest rise out of her. She'd turned her head to see her eyes clamped shut. Was it her that was making DJ so very tense?

DJ shifted, and Kat gazed slowly across the compressed rounded breasts down to her stomach. The sight of her boyshorts still clinging to her catapulted her mind into a wild spin of forbidden imaginings. Acutely aroused, Kat was suddenly aware that her sexual desire hadn't died along with Arizona. Trying to ignore it, she snapped her eyes closed and took a deep breath, but the unbearably overpowering scent

DJ emitted made the attraction zing even stronger, and the perpetual wetness between her legs she'd experienced over the past few days began again. Kat resisted the temptation to trail her fingertips across DJ's stomach. She clenched her hand into a tight fist instead and withdrew her arm. Kat felt DJ stroke her arm lightly. The cool air fleeting across DJ's bare stomach must have sent her an immediate wake-up call.

"That calf really wore you out," DJ said.

"How long did I sleep?" Kat rolled and propped herself up on her elbow.

DJ squinted at her watch. "A little over two hours." She swept a single finger across Kat's forehead, moving a few strands of hair.

Kat rubbed her face to shake off the sleepy remnants still fogging her head. "I guess we're not going to string much more of the fence today."

"I think you've done enough for one day." DJ smiled as she slowly dragged the back of her fingers across Kat's cheek and down the side of her neck.

DJ caught her gaze with her drowsy green eyes, and without hesitation, Kat's mouth was on hers, their tongues entwined again. Heated hands moved under the flannel shirt, searing like a red-hot brand against Kat's cool skin. DJ's thumbs slid under the silken material of Kat's bra and captured the stiffening peaks, sending a shuddering jolt of pleasure through her. Kat crawled willingly onto DJ, the inferno raging inside her fueled even more when DJ's thigh pushed up against Kat's center. Whatever vows she'd made to protect her heart in the past year had now been shattered into a million tiny pieces. Kat would never be able to abide by them again. Not as long as DJ was around.

At the sound of galloping horses on the upper trail, Kat jerked away and slid to DJ's side. She sucked in a ragged breath and searched the hillside before she darted her gaze to DJ. "I'm sorry. I don't know what the hell I'm doing."

DJ stroked the pad of her thumb across Kat's lips. "Would it make it any easier if I told you I feel it too?"

"Nothing is easy for me." She sat up, clasped her legs to her chest, and let out a heavy sigh.

"Baby steps," DJ mumbled.

"What?" Kat asked softly.

"Oh, it's just somethin' my momma used to tell me." Her lips tugged up into a soft smile. "Whenever I had a problem, she'd say, if you can't do it all at once, darlin', take baby steps."

Kat's heart unlocked a little. She'd just caught a completely new insight into the city girl that she wasn't expecting. "Your momma sounds like a smart woman."

"That she is." DJ nodded, and a moment of silence drifted between them. "You wanna go back now?"

Kat gazed into DJ's eyes and could see she'd rather stay, but going back was the best thing for Kat right now. "I need to," she said and broke eye contact, afraid of being spellbound again by DJ's perilous green eyes. Kat really wanted to dive full-force into that wonderful pool of pleasure she'd just begun to experience, but she couldn't. Not now, not here in this place. That would be wrong.

"Okay. Let's go." DJ stood up and offered Kat her hand. "Only this time, if you don't mind, I'll drive."

"No. I don't mind." Kat smiled softly, letting DJ open the passenger door for her. "I don't mind at all." Her voice was a quiet whisper as she slid in onto the seat.

Kat watched DJ in the side-view mirror as she folded up the quilt before taking her still-damp jeans off the side of the truck and tugging them on a little at a time. She circled around, loaded the cooler, and picked up Kat's clothes before climbing into the truck.

"Your clothes are still pretty wet," DJ said, putting them on the seat between them. "I'll drop you at your back door."

"I'd appreciate that," Kat said with a slight smile.

DJ pulled up as close as she could to the steps of the house.

"Thanks for everything you did today," Kat said as she gathered her clothes from the seat.

"Aw, shucks. I really didn't do all that much," DJ said with a wink. Her charmingly boyish manner helped lighten the mood, and Kat gave her a smile, barely managing to keep a tickled grin at bay. If DJ thought that passively flip attitude of hers was the slightest bit attractive, she was absolutely right.

Kat opened the door before she reached over and touched DJ's hand. "I mean it. I wouldn't have been able to save that calf on my own today."

"You're welcome." DJ's smile seemed sincere and unassuming this time.

Trying to suppress the overwhelming urge to kiss her, Kat turned quickly, hopped out of the truck, and hurried up the steps. She only stopped to peek over her shoulder at DJ as she threw her wet clothes across the porch railing. After a simmering look from DJ that sent a jolt straight to her midsection, Kat raced through the screen door and stood just inside. Her head pressed against the doorjamb, Kat watched DJ drive off. She touched the collar of DJ's flannel shirt to her cheek as she stared into the dust trail left hovering just above the road. *I'm in big trouble.*

"What happened to you?" Virgil asked.

Startled out of her thought, Kat whirled around nervously. "Don't sneak up on me like that."

"I didn't sneak. I just walked in the room."

"I'm sorry, Virgil. I guess I'm just a little on edge. Another of the calves was caught in Victoria Maxwell's fishnet." She tightened the blanket around herself.

"You get it free?"

"I couldn't, but DJ did."

"DJ, huh." Virgil smiled as he observed the flannel shirt she was wearing. Kat knew he recognized it as the same one he'd seen on DJ that morning. "Yer on a first-name basis, now, are ya?" He looked out onto the back porch, and his smile broadened. "Those your clothes out there?"

"I was in the river, Virgil. They got wet." Kat didn't know why she felt the need to explain. She was free and unattached. She hadn't done anything wrong.

Virgil stood silently staring at her, his goofy grin growing bigger by the minute.

"Virgil, don't give me a hard time. I'm way too tired for that right now." She rushed down the hallway to her bedroom and slammed the door, making the old house rattle. She'd known DJ only a few days and was becoming much too familiar with her. How could she be so attracted to a woman she knew absolutely nothing about? *That's not entirely true.* She flopped down onto the bed. Physically, she knew a lot about her, from her misty green eyes to the musky smell of her skin. Kat was fully aware that DJ hadn't offered much about herself personally or professionally.

Kat floated into the shower, closed her eyes, and let the steaming hot water run down her face. She couldn't get DJ out of her head. All she could see were pink cheeks surrounding that cocky grin. Even peering out from beneath her cowboy hat, her smile was magnetic. She didn't know what it was about her, but for the past few days she'd had Kat dreaming of things she hadn't thought were possible.

Since Arizona died, Kat had been dealing only with the present, struggling through each day as it came. The idea of loving someone again or any speculation of what the future might hold had long since left her thoughts. Working with DJ today had been easy. Easier than it had been with anyone in quite some time. Being close to her hadn't felt strange like it had with other women. With DJ it felt natural, like coming home, but Kat knew deep down inside it wasn't realistic to hope for something with a woman playing ranch hand for only a few days.

CHAPTER NINE

DJ yanked at her jeans. They clung to her like a wet suit. The denim material raked at her legs, pinching every hair along the way as she peeled them off. She flipped on the shower and closed her eyes. DJ thought about what Kat had said earlier as they watched the mother tend to the calf they had rescued. How could cattle have such strong family instincts? Why had those instincts changed in Kat's family? Thoughts of her own home filled DJ's mind. Not her current home in Austin, but her childhood home near Johnson City. The sight of the wedding-ring patterned quilt had brought those to the forefront of her mind today. Her mother and sister used to make similar quilts and sell them in specialty shops to help earn a little extra money for groceries. DJ's heart raced and her muscles tensed. She should've turned around and left this place the first day. It was too much like home. Hell, it was only fifty miles from her family's farm.

The last time she'd seen her sister, Marilyn, she'd shown up in Austin at her office unexpected. She'd begged DJ to come back, said their mom missed her terribly. They'd had a long discussion about what went down when DJ left, and Marilyn had tried to convince her that it hadn't been her mom's decision. She could see her point. Her dad had pushed DJ out, but her mother had let it happen. She shook her head. She didn't want to revisit that wound. Instead, she focused on the beautiful woman she'd spent the day with, who was nothing but confusing.

Her mind fogged with the warmth of Kat's body, sucking her deeper into this cowgirl's paradise. Kat was much more vulnerable than she'd expected, and the lines were clearly becoming blurred. DJ still couldn't shake the physical resemblance between Kat and her sister, Rebecca, but now she was beginning to realize that they were two very different people. The past few days, Kat had acted as though it pained her just to acknowledge DJ, yet she'd purposely set DJ up to work alone with her on the fence today. Earlier, as she'd watched Kat pop grapes into her mouth one by one, Kat had given her a soft smile, and something in the pit of DJ's stomach had twisted. She was every cowgirl's dream. Smart, beautiful, and tough enough to handle any job on the ranch. DJ was afraid Kat was beginning to handle her as well. She needed to back up and remember why she came.

After having a bite to eat, DJ wandered into the bar. The usual slow, even pace of her heart raced at the thought of seeing Kat again. She'd been close enough today to notice the delicate woman buried deep inside the tough exterior she donned. She couldn't shake the feel of Kat's warm mouth and soft skin now embedded in her mind. There she sat at the same corner table as the night before, looking through another endless pile of papers. DJ stopped by the bar and ordered two shots of Tuaca before she headed over to see her.

"Hello there." DJ smiled and let her voice rumble with subtle seduction.

Kat popped forward in her chair and glanced up. "Good evening, Ms. Callen. I wasn't expecting to see you here tonight." Her voice was cool and detached.

DJ noted and ignored her distance. "Surprised I survived again?" she asked, smiling as she sat down and slid a shot across the table in front of Kat.

"No. I just thought after a day like today, a city girl would probably be in bed by now." Kat smiled at her, raised the glass to her lips, and took a sip.

DJ locked her gaze for a moment. Her eyes sparkled even more tonight, the deep red of her V-neck cotton shirt intensifying the electric blue in them.

DJ downed her shot. "I'm tougher than you think."

Kat raised an eyebrow. "Should I schedule you again tomorrow?"

DJ let out a low, grumbling sound. "If you need to."

Kat looked over the schedule for a minute. "Looks like I have some new guests coming in the morning, so you'll have to find something to do on your own instead."

Relieved, DJ shifted gingerly in her chair. "Whatever you say." She wasn't as young as she used to be, and her body was shouting that fact loud and clear. "How about another drink?"

"Sure. Why not?" Kat finished the last of her Tuaca and handed DJ the glass.

DJ went to the bar, then returned with two more shots. She slid into the seat next to Kat this time and draped her arm across the back of her chair. "So, tell me a little about this situation with your neighbor."

"You don't really want to hear about my problems."

"I wouldn't have asked if I didn't." DJ sipped her drink.

Kat let out a short breath and dragged her teeth across her lower lip. "She thought it would be the perfect plan if she and I got married."

DJ shifted, removing her arm from Kat's chair. "I take it you didn't agree."

Kat shook her head. "Nope." She sat back against the chair and crossed her arms. "She figured our properties would merge and we'd own this whole territory together. She said she'd take good care of me." She flattened her lips and rolled her eyes. "She wasn't too happy when I told her I wasn't interested." She locked her simmering blue eyes with DJ's. "If I want to be with someone, when and where will be my decision."

DJ grinned. She could see Kat didn't need anyone to take care of her. Wanting someone was a different story. "What's her name again?"

"Victoria Maxwell."

"How long has she been your neighbor?"

"She showed up about two years after Arizona and I started the ranch."

"Just like that, out of the blue?"

"Yeah. At the time I thought it was kind of strange." Kat frowned. "I was pretty sure my grandfather owned all the land in this area."

"What's your grandfather's name?"

"Francis Montgomery."

"Do you think your grandfather may have sold it to her?"

"That was my first thought." Kat reached across her chest and kneaded her shoulder with her fingertips. The river must have taken its toll on her as well today. "I checked the county records, and they show Maxwell's family has owned it for more than fifty years."

"What about before then?"

"The county records don't go that far. They had a fire a few years ago that destroyed all the archives."

"Have you checked the ones in Austin?"

Kat crinkled her nose and cocked her head curiously. "Which ones in Austin?"

"Whenever someone files papers with the county, a copy usually goes to the land office at the state capital as well."

Kat widened her eyes. "You know, you're right." She shook her head. "I don't know why I didn't think of that." She smiled broadly, picked up her glass, and clicked it against DJ's. "Thank you, Ms. Callen." She threw back the shot, then slapped the glass to the table.

DJ chuckled at her continued attempt at distance. "After this afternoon, I think we know each other well enough for you to call me DJ, don't you?"

"All right. DJ it is." Kat's voice was low and silky. "If you insist." Her lips curved into a reluctant smile.

The sound of her name rolling off Kat's tongue made the swirling in DJ's belly resurface like a raging twister.

"So tell me, DJ. What do you do when you're not out saving calves from the river?"

DJ settled into her chair and took a long, slow drink. "I'm sure we can find something more interesting than me to talk about."

Kat reached over and slowly traced the back of DJ's hand with her fingertip. "I'd really like to know."

The memory of Kat's skin and the taste of her lips flashed through her mind. Soft and yielding, her sweetness still lingered on her tongue. DJ's pulse quickened, and the storm inside her raged out of control again. DJ shifted in her chair and struggled with what to tell her as she tried to clear the images of Kat from her mind. Images that were producing physical reactions she'd rather Kat didn't discover at the moment.

"What do you think?" DJ didn't want to lie, but tonight would be the end of it if she told Kat the truth. At this point she couldn't risk that, not professionally or personally.

"To be honest, when I first laid eyes on you, I figured you were some kind of yuppie corporate raider." Kat laughed, sitting back and crossing her arms. "But now that I've seen you in action, I'm not quite sure."

"You're close." She chuckled. "I'm an attorney."

"Where did you learn so much about horses?"

"I grew up on a farm just outside of Johnson City," DJ said hesitantly. The last time she'd felt comfortable enough to tell a woman about her family, she'd run for the hills.

"Really?" Kat's voice rang with obvious surprise.

DJ nodded. "I started working the horses when I was ten. By the time I was eighteen, I thought I was going to be a rodeo star," she added uneasily.

"From what I saw the other night, you probably could've been." Kat's voice was soft and reassuring.

DJ smiled lightly. "Those were the dreams of a young girl who didn't have the slightest idea what the real world was like."

Kat relaxed in her chair and crossed her legs. "That sounds a tad cynical."

"Just being realistic."

"I don't know about that. I've always believed if you try hard enough, any dream can become a reality." She lifted her hands. "This ranch was my dream." She let her hands drop to her lap. "Mine and Arizona's."

Obviously the only thing missing from that dream now was Arizona, and those were big shoes to fill. "Maybe the rodeo just wasn't my reality."

"Don't you ever regret leaving it behind?" Kat seemed genuinely interested, which made DJ want to tell her everything.

"All the time," DJ said matter-of-factly. "I never wanted to leave in the first place."

Kat's brows drew together, creating a tiny crease in her forehead between her eyes. "Then why did you?"

"My father insisted."

"Oh?" Kat's voice faltered, and DJ wondered why. "Do you mind if I ask why?"

"Before I left, a fire burned through the wheat crop and part of the barn." DJ rubbed her neck. "It was my fault."

Kat propped her elbow up on the table, supporting her chin in the palm of her hand. "How so?"

"I was off messin' around at the arena when it happened, and the fire was in full force when I got there. If I'd been home, I could've helped. We could've put it out sooner." The guilt rushed DJ as if the fire had happened only yesterday.

"Well, I don't think you can take the blame for that. It's not like you started the fire."

"I might as well have. It was bad enough that the barn burned, but my pop was hurt too. The next week he sold my horse, said we needed the money to fix the barn. I didn't give him any trouble for doing it, but after that I was gone." She shook her head. "Didn't go back until I'd finished law school."

"I bet he was proud of you then."

"I guess so. I offered him some money, but he wouldn't take it. Stubborn as a mule." Her stomach rushed to her throat. If he had, the farm wouldn't be in the financial situation it was in now. "My father worked that farm from the day he was born until the day he died." She stared out onto the dance floor, trying to conceal her emotions, but they still came through loud and clear. "I got my education. That was my obligation to my father." DJ absently circled her finger around a knot in the table. "He made sure I had the opportunities in life that he didn't."

Kat shifted in her chair. "How come you never moved back?"

"After he died, my brother took over." DJ hesitated, embroiled in thought for a minute before sipping the last of her Tuaca. "I'm not really needed there anymore. He and his wife take good care of my mom."

Kat touched her hand lightly again. "What about you? What do you need?"

DJ directed her gaze at Kat. She sucked in a deep breath, then leaned forward and took Kat's hand. "All I need right now is a smile from you." She curved her lips into a grin. Kat's cheeks reddened, and DJ's heart quickened. "Tell me about you. Do your folks live around here?"

Kat slid her hand from DJ's and tucked it under her leg. "They live in Austin. I mean, my mother does. My father passed away recently."

DJ noticed a sadness in Kat's voice she hadn't heard before. "I'm sorry to hear that."

Kat smiled slightly and let out a short breath. "Thanks," she said as she fiddled with the empty shot glass in front of her.

"Were you and your father close?" DJ already knew some of Kat's family history from her conversations with Elizabeth, but she wanted to hear more from Kat.

"Not really. I haven't heard from my parents at all in the past ten years." Kat took in a deep breath. "I guess you could say we had a falling-out."

"It's hard sometimes when things are left unsaid." DJ understood her plight and tried to lighten her burden, but it didn't seem to help.

"Plenty was said between us before I left." Kat's voice trailed to a whisper as she stared into her glass.

"Ten years is a long time, Kat. People change." That hadn't been the case for DJ, but she'd always prided herself on being the exception, not the rule.

"You don't know my mother." Kat shook her head. "She's a very stubborn woman."

"She's probably a lot like you," DJ said, her voice guarded.

"Probably." Kat flattened her lips. "For better or worse, I've acquired many of my mother's traits."

"Has she tried to contact you since your father died?" DJ continued her charade, still not knowing how she was going to tell Kat the truth about why she was here.

"Yes, but I don't want to hear what she has to say. Apparently, she hasn't received the message. Her lawyer won't leave me alone." The shot glass flipped out of Kat's hand and across the table. DJ quickly scooped it up before it crashed to the floor.

"Sorry."

"No problem." DJ slid it across the table to her. "What does she want?"

"I'm sure it's something about settling my father's estate."

DJ looked around the room, noting the wear on the dance floor and the old wooden tables surrounding it. "You could probably use a little extra money around here."

Kat launched out of her chair. "I don't want their money. They couldn't let me live my life the way I wanted then, so I'll be damned if my mother is going to try to manipulate it now." Kat gathered her papers into a chaotic pile. "Nothing from my parents ever came without strings."

DJ knew that for a fact from her own situation with Elizabeth.

She followed Kat as she headed across the dance floor and down the hallway. In one swift move, Kat turned the knob, used her shoulder to push through the office door, and then tossed her papers across the desk.

DJ stepped into the office behind Kat and observed the wide variety of books, including horse care and finance, that filled the shelves behind the desk. Pictures covered the rich wood-paneled walls. Many of them included Kat, Virgil, and a tall brunette woman, whom DJ took to be Arizona. DJ fixed her eyes on Kat again, and she followed the long raven hair draped across her back. The straight-cut ends hung halfway down the snugly fit, red cotton shirt she had tucked neatly into her jeans. Her body tensed as she thought about what was underneath the well-fitting denim surrounding Kat's curvaceous hips. DJ sucked in a deep breath and calmed herself. This wasn't why she'd come. She should leave right now. Kat turned around and she couldn't.

Kat peeked over her shoulder and caught DJ's assessment of her backside. Her heart thudded wildly in her chest as she turned slowly and cleared her throat, demanding DJ's attention upward. When their eyes met, Kat saw the desire in DJ's eyes. DJ wanted Kat as much as Kat wanted her. She wished she could forget DJ was a guest, if only for one night. These feelings had to stop, or she would soon be left used and brokenhearted.

"I'm sorry," DJ said, looking up at Kat. "I didn't mean to hit a nerve."

"No, I'm sorry." Kat leaned against her desk and kneaded her forehead with her fingertips as a rush of confusing emotions hit her. "My parents just aren't a good subject to discuss."

DJ took Kat's hands in hers and coaxed her from the desk. "Dance with me. You'll feel better." She whirled her around the office to the country music emanating from the bar.

DJ was wrong about that. This wasn't making Kat feel any better. It was making her realize what she no longer had in her life. Someone to listen, to lean on, and to love her when things got rough.

Kat pushed out of her arms. "I'm not really in the mood right now."

"Well, then let's change that." DJ used Kat's resistance along with her own momentum to throw her out for a twirl and snap Kat hard against her.

Kat knew DJ was only trying to help, but the erratic thud in her chest told her she shouldn't be nearly this close. With her hand on the small of her back, DJ tucked Kat in tight. The warmth of her strong, firm body pressed hard against her, Kat could feel DJ's heart thundering against her chest. She was undeniably aroused, and Kat's newly rebellious body reacted in turn. She looked up into DJ's simmering green eyes and wished she hadn't let her touch her. Then she wouldn't be here, dangling helplessly, begging for her to do more.

"Let me help take your mind off things for a while." DJ charmed her with a wink. "You see? It's working already." The tempo slowed, and DJ wrapped her arm around Kat's waist, bringing her closer than she thought possible.

Kat let herself melt into DJ and floated with the music, ignoring her instincts to move away. It was working all right. Kat couldn't think of anything but DJ—her eyes, her lips, the warmth of her body. The spring that had been coiled so tightly inside Kat for the past year was quickly unwinding, and there would be miserable recoil. What was it about this woman she barely knew? In an instant DJ had made her forget all the problems plaguing her. The ever-present uncertainty in her life had suddenly vanished. Kat had hoped it was the circumstances drawing her in earlier—her special place by the river under the tree, along with the moment of comfort she'd felt in DJ's arms. Being this close again made it painfully clear it was DJ, not the situation, making her body react in ways she'd thought weren't possible anymore.

Kat took in a slow, deep breath to try to calm herself, but her mood heightened instead. No pungent odor of cologne surrounded DJ tonight, only the light, woodsy smell of scented soap. Kat had another problem now. She'd already gone further than she should with DJ Callen, and from the looks of it, DJ was still making headway.

"Walk me home?" Kat whispered as the music faded.

"Love to." DJ opened the door and motioned Kat in front of her.

The sky was clear, a crescent moon shining softly in the midst of a few scattered stars. As they walked to the house, they could hear the rustle of the trees in the wind, along with the bullfrogs croaking like a symphony in the distance.

"Today brought back some memories for me," DJ said easily.

Kat gave her a soft smile. "Good ones, I hope."

"Definitely," DJ said with a chuckle. "Even though I worked

my butt off, was kicked by a calf, and almost drowned." She stopped for a moment. Kat searched DJ's eyes and saw something she hadn't expected—a longing within them, possibly for something she'd lost. "I'm not quite sure why, but I thoroughly enjoyed it." DJ hesitated as though she were memorizing Kat's face. "It must have been the company."

She caressed Kat's face with her thumb, and DJ's warmth radiated through her. Her fingers roamed slowly down her neck and across the hollow of Kat's neck. She looked up into DJ's eyes, shimmering in the moonlight. *Beautiful.* Kat's heart pounded wildly, and suddenly she wanted to know everything about DJ. Her thoughts, her dreams, and her innermost desires. She wanted more, so much more. She fought the urge to dive into her, to feel the softness of her lips again. DJ's fingers, slowly and deliberately, traced just inside the collar of Kat's shirt. Alarmed by her guiltless feelings, Kat tensed, and DJ must have felt her reaction. Her fingers trailed back to Kat's neck, and she moved closer. The heat of DJ's breath warmed her cheek. Her eyelids lowered as Kat anxiously awaited the softness of her lips. She was disappointed when DJ's lips brushed her cheek before she turned abruptly and walked on. Kat was left feeling embarrassed and abandoned…again.

As they approached the house, Kat rubbed the inside of her wedding ring nervously with her thumb, wondering just how this evening was going to end. Should she invite DJ in or ask if she wanted to sit on the porch and look at the stars? Kat quickly headed up the steps, tripped on the top step, and fell forward.

DJ rushed to help her. "You okay?"

"I'm fine," Kat said with a laugh as she rolled onto her elbows.

DJ stared at the gorgeous woman in front of her, and the familiar expression made her shudder. She offered Kat a hand and laughed along with her at first, but then Kat's eyes became dark. A rush of heat filled her body, and it suddenly felt like it was ninety degrees outside. Kat's laughing gaze had changed into a steamy look of want, and DJ's willpower puddled. Kat took her hand, and DJ brought her up against her. Kat's mouth covered hers, and she kissed her with such intensity, DJ gasped for air. Her lips left Kat's soft, hungry mouth and dipped lower, roaming the soft white skin of her neck. DJ submerged herself in the pool of senses Kat was creating within her. Everything seemed to slow as the jolt fired all her senses. Liquid gushed between her legs.

Her body was immediately and completely ready for this woman to take every part of her. DJ drew back and sucked in a deep breath. This was too much. *She* was too much.

"I'll see you in the morning," DJ stuttered, stumbling down the porch steps, leaving Kat standing at the top looking embarrassed and confused. She turned, slapped a hand to the back of her neck to suppress the confusing tingle still lingering, and tottered across the grounds. Unsettled by her own actions, DJ headed to the stable, knowing full well she wouldn't sleep anytime soon.

DJ had seduced many women before for many different reasons, and she'd thoroughly enjoyed doing it. Becoming romantically involved with Kat was a stupid move. She should've told Kat who she was right away. She was beginning to care for her a little too much. Leaving this romance behind would not be easy.

"It's a little late to be tending the horses, isn't it, Ms. Callen?" Virgil asked from the darkness.

"Couldn't sleep. Thought I'd come out here and clear my head."

"From the looks of you, that may take some time." Virgil jabbed the pitchfork hard into a bale of hay and left it standing. "What's going on between you and Kat?"

"What do you mean?" DJ said, giving him an innocent look as her mind flashed to the face of the woman she couldn't seem to purge from her thoughts.

"I'm talking about this afternoon when you dropped her off at the back door." Virgil motioned to the house. "And just now up there on the porch."

DJ jerked her lip up into a half smile as she shook her head. "I'm not really sure." And she wasn't.

They both turned and looked at the house when they heard the screen door slap closed in the distance.

"You're either serious about her or you're not. Which is it?"

DJ moved closer to one of the horses and patted it on the neck. "That's what I've been asking myself all evening." She could see Virgil was dead serious. He'd probably seen Kat hurt more than once. "When I first arrived, I knew exactly why I was here. Now I have absolutely no idea what I'm doing." She wasn't lying this time. Kat had yanked her string and spun her around so hard, DJ still hadn't shaken the dizzy feeling.

"Well, you'd better make up your mind soon, young lady. I don't need you hangin' around messin' up her routine." Virgil closed and latched the door. "That is, unless you're willin' to stay for good."

DJ leaned against the stable wall and stared across at the house. Virgil was spot-on. She had some decisions to make. Otherwise, this whole thing was going to blow up in her face, and Kat was going to get hurt. She shouldn't care. Business was business, but this time it had become personal.

CHAPTER TEN

K at stormed into the bedroom and threw herself onto the bed. She stared at the old ceiling fan, watching the chain clink against the glass as it slowly rotated. *What did I miss?* DJ's eyes were dark, aware, and wanting as Kat had stared up at her. She knew that look. Just thinking about it made Kat shudder. Things between them had been so good all day. The thought never entered her mind that DJ might not be interested. She'd never had a problem seducing a woman before. Finding one she wanted to keep around afterward was the challenge.

Kat had gone full circle since Arizona died. At first she couldn't even think about touching another woman. Then after plying herself with enough alcohol, sex became something she did just to try to make herself feel again. Then she found she needed more, some sort of bond. She needed intimacy. Without it she was left feeling empty and unfulfilled. For the past year Kat had lived like a nun, purposely isolating herself from everyone. She didn't take sex lightly anymore. Somehow, DJ had made her feel beautiful and vibrant again. She had Kat questioning things in her life that she'd been certain of for quite some time.

Tonight, she'd taken a chance and put herself out there, and DJ had walked away. It had been a long time since Kat had kissed anyone like that, but she could still tell when a woman enjoyed it. At least she thought so. *Damn it!* She sprang up, hugging her pillow to her chest. She was sure of it. DJ had enjoyed it, whether she wanted to admit it or not.

Kat stared at the curtains, which had a strange glow about them tonight. She heard voices outside her window—loud, urgent voices.

She tossed the pillow to the chair, ran to the window, and nudged the fabric aside. The immediate grounds were lit up like a night baseball game. She pushed the curtain open farther. The tack room was on fire.

"Shit!" She raced through the house, grabbed the phone from the wall, and dialed 9-1-1. "There's a fire at the Jumpin' J." She let the phone drop, and it clanged against the floor as she flew out the door and started belting out orders. "Get the hoses and buckets." She watched the flames lick the roof. "And move the horses out of the stable."

DJ shot out of the stable with a few of the horses. "Is anyone inside?"

"I don't know." Kat searched the area. "Where's Virgil? Was he in there with you?"

DJ shook her head as she scanned the area. Virgil had left her just a little while ago, and she hadn't paid attention to where he'd gone. She looked over at Kat, saw the fear in her eyes, and started for the fire-engulfed tack room.

"Stay back," DJ shouted and took off to the blazing building, grabbing the doorknob. "Damn," she growled as the knob singed her hand. She jerked it back and looked at her blistered fingertips. She ripped off her pearl-snap shirt and used it as a buffer for the searing metal knob as she pushed the door open slowly. "Virgil, you in there?" No answer. The fire flared as part of the roof fell in, and the door flew in her face.

"Is he in there?" Kat shouted.

DJ heard the sirens in the distance, but she didn't look back. She couldn't. She had to go in now. Sweat poured off her forehead. She closed her eyes and prepared herself for what was to come. Scorching heat, burning flesh, and stinging lungs. She knew the scars of fire all too well. The burning barn at her family farm flashed through her mind, and she threw herself against the wall. She closed her eyes and willed herself to move. She pressed her shirt to her nose and mouth and pushed through the door.

"Virgil." She coughed, then dropped to the floor, trying to suck in clean air. Water spewed through the roof as the stench of burning leather filled her nose. The fire department was on it, but the fire was still spreading. She searched the room—no one. She turned to the door—blocked. She swung around. The only way out was through a wall.

The hair stood up on the back of her neck, and she hesitated. Agonizing memories clouded her thoughts, nearly paralyzing her. She could hear the screeching horses clearly in her head. She panicked and barreled through the raging fire into the wall—nothing.

She held her head. It spun with splitting pain, and her stomach lurched. She turned to the wall and snatched the saddle from its peg to use as a shield. She plowed into the wooden wall planks. One or two cracked, but not enough to break through. She slapped at the flames burning her shirt as she hopped through the fire. Then she reversed direction and ran full speed into the wall again. Fresh air filled her lungs, and her body cooled. She'd made it through. She dropped the saddle and stumbled—everything went black.

Kat darted into the corral, ran across it, and jumped the fence to reach the far side of the tack building. She grabbed a horse blanket from the railing and threw it across DJ's smoldering black T-shirt. She slapped at her face, trying to rouse her, but she was out cold.

"What the hell happened?" The sound of Virgil's voice sent an overwhelming sense of relief through Kat.

"Jesus, Virgil. We thought you were inside." She rolled DJ to her back and put her cheek to her mouth. DJ's breath brushed across it. *Thank God.*

A paramedic sprinted over with a tank of oxygen. It was Mike Carpenter, one of her frequent riders at the arena. "Is she breathing?"

"Yes."

Mike placed an oxygen mask on DJ's face, and she coughed. "Help me move her away from the building."

"Hang on. Let me get the guys." Virgil threw up a hand. "Jimmy, Brett, come give us a hand here."

One of the men picked DJ up and started to the guest quarters. Mike followed with the oxygen tank.

"Bring her to the house," Kat directed, and Virgil gave her a strange look. "I can't afford to be sued, Virgil." They both knew that wasn't what this was about. DJ had risked her life to save Virgil, and that act had skyrocketed her into the realm of possibility.

"The ambulance should be here soon," Mike said.

"Alrighty. Take her in and put her on the couch," Virgil said.

"No. Put her on my bed."

"Kat." Virgil's voice rose in objection, and Kat met him with a don't-cross-me look. Virgil swung his arm, motioning them on. "Do what she says, boys."

Mike carried the oxygen and his medical box into the house behind them. "Lay her on her side, if you can. I need to take a look at those burns."

Kat took a small plastic bowl from the kitchen cabinet and filled it with water before taking a couple of washcloths and some antiseptic from the bathroom cabinet. She rummaged through a basket under the sink, found some gauze and medical tape, and then went into the bedroom after them.

She watched Mike check DJ's forehead. *No cuts. Just a growing bump.*

Kat dipped a washcloth into the water and wiped the black soot from around DJ's mouth and nose. She dipped it again, wrung it out, and dabbed her face and neck before letting the cool cloth rest on her forehead. DJ was pale and clammy. She was in shock. Kat rounded the bed and removed DJ's boots before she took an old hand-sewn quilt from the rack in the corner and covered her legs with it.

"Hope this shirt didn't mean anything special to her." Mike clipped the edge of DJ's T-shirt with the scissors and ripped it up the back. "Not a vintage rock T-shirt, is it?" He looked up at Kat and she shook her head. "Plain black."

"Good. I'd hate to ruin one of those." Mike drew it away to reveal scattered pink burns across her shoulder and upper arm. "She's been burned before." He motioned to the rough, puckered skin on DJ's back and arm. "Do you know how old these are?"

Kat kneaded her forehead. "She said something about a fire before she went to college."

"What is she, in her mid-thirties?"

Kat lifted her hands. "I have no idea." It sounded about right.

Mike ran a gloved finger across the scar. "These are probably fifteen to twenty years old."

The new burns weren't as bad, probably second-degree, but Kat could tell from the look of the scars on DJ's shoulder, the previous burns had been much worse. DJ had told Kat about the fire at her family farm, but she hadn't mentioned that she'd been hurt.

Mike took a packet of gauze from his kit and ripped it open. He sprayed saline on the gauze and gently dabbed the burns. He took another small foil packet, tore off the top, and spread ointment onto the burns. Then he took a dry piece of gauze and taped it to DJ's shoulder.

Virgil touched Kat's shoulder. "Why don't you go meet the ambulance and bring the medics inside?"

"No. I'm not leaving her." She could hear the ambulance siren in the distance. "Is she going to be all right?" Kat looked at Mike, anxiety overtaking her.

"She hit her head. She has to go to the hospital," he said, and Kat could see the concern in his eyes.

Two other men came through the door, and Kat's world spun as she was forced to the corner of the room while they moved DJ to the rolling stretcher they'd brought with them. The woman with whom she'd found an incredible connection was going to be swept away to the hospital. Panic rushed her. *What if I never see her again?*

"I'm coming with you." Kat followed them through the hallway and outside to the ambulance.

"There's not enough room for everyone in the ambulance. Are you next of kin?"

Before Kat could answer, Mike spoke up. "Yes, she is. You guys don't need me. I'll stay behind."

"Thanks, Mike. I owe you one." Kat didn't know if Mike realized just how grateful she was. After all, DJ had gone into the fire because of her.

"I'll collect that some night in the arena." Mike smiled. "Keep an eye on her, and call me if you need me."

Kat nodded. "I will. Thanks."

They'd been in the hospital room a couple of hours before DJ coughed and bolted up. "Pop!" The oxygen mask muffled her voice. She ripped it off, and the desperate, terrified look in her eyes caught Kat off guard. "Shh. Just lay down. He's fine, the fire's out." Kat could see the panic fade. "You have quite a bump on your head, but you're gonna be fine." She didn't know if that was completely true. DJ had screamed for her father, not Virgil. Those old wounds seemed to have left more than just physical scars.

DJ swiped her palm across her forehead and dropped against the bed.

"You need any help?" Virgil asked, standing in the doorway.

"I think I have it." Kat slid the elastic around DJ's head and placed the oxygen mask back on her face.

"I'll come back in the mornin' to getcha." Virgil motioned with his head toward the hallway. "Gotta make sure the boys moved everything out of the tack room." He stopped and turned for a minute. "Call me if you need me."

"Thanks, Virgil. I will." Kat rewet the cloth on DJ's forehead and spread the blanket up over her chest.

For the next few hours, Kat sat on the edge of the hospital bed next to DJ, watching her breathe. She thought about the fire and shivered. When DJ had run into the burning building, Kat's heart had all but stopped. She was torn between being terrified that DJ wouldn't come out again and the thought that Virgil, the only person she considered family, was inside being engulfed by the fire. When DJ had thought Virgil was trapped inside, she'd gone straight in, without even a glimmer of doubt in her eyes. She was a hero.

Kat looked at the remnants of soot filling the creases in her forehead and let her fingers trail across her cheek—still clammy. She took the cloth from DJ's neck, rewet it, and blotted her face, then her lips. They were soft, pink, and relaxed now. Kat didn't know what she would've done if DJ hadn't made it out, if she didn't have any chance of feeling those lips pressed against hers again. She remembered the mischief in DJ's eyes the night she'd challenged her at the arena. She'd hated it. The silent laughter she saw in them had infuriated her, but that had changed now. The roguish sparkle in those emerald-green eyes earlier tonight had made her body heat with desire. She'd do anything to have DJ look at her like that again.

DJ bolted up. Kat sat up next to her and said, "You're all right." She touched her cheek, and DJ turned to her, staring blindly, almost as though she were looking right through her. Then DJ ripped off the oxygen mask, wrapped her arms around Kat's waist, and took her down on the hospital bed with her. She couldn't move; DJ had her trapped. She looked at DJ's tense face and sighed. This was what she'd wanted, just not quite the way she'd imagined it happening.

DJ mumbled something and smiled. It was a name she couldn't quite make out, but she knew it wasn't hers. *Jesus, Kat. What the hell are you doing? She probably has a girlfriend or possibly even a wife at home.* She shifted, slipped from DJ's grasp, and scooted to the side of the bed. After placing the plastic mask back on DJ's face, she eyed the clock. Five a.m. Time to go.

Kat took the flannel shirt she'd hung on the chair earlier and pressed it to her nose, inhaling DJ's scent. It was the shirt she'd given Kat to wear at the river. Thoughts of DJ's hands inching up her sides made her tingle in places she didn't want to right now. She dropped it on the bottom of the bed and headed to the nurses' station to call Virgil.

CHAPTER ELEVEN

The morning sunlight flickered at DJ's eyes. *Where the hell am I?* She drew back the blanket covering her. Noticing her hospital gown, she peered around the room, took in her sterile surroundings, and spotted a pair of jeans and a shirt on the chair along with a new pair of flip-flops on the seat.

"Kat," she called but heard no response.

Her shoulder stung as she propped herself up on her elbow. The fire hadn't been a dream. She swung her feet to the floor and held on to the bed to steady herself. Hopefully the dizziness would subside soon. Shuffling across the room, she inspected herself in the bathroom mirror. She hissed out a breath as she peeled back the bandage on her shoulder to look at the burn. *Not as bad as the last time.*

DJ went into the room and took off the hospital gown. She swiped the shirt from the chair, slid it gingerly over her shoulders, and then put on her jeans and the flip-flops. She picked up her cell phone and called Marcia. She had to find Kat.

❖

DJ had survived the ride from the hospital to the ranch with Marcia. Her well-meaning attempts to convince DJ to stay in Austin, as well as the snarky comments about her curly hair, had been needless and unwelcome. DJ's usual business look included perfectly spiked hair that gave her a masculine edginess she used to her advantage.

Apologizing to Marcia for her curt, unyielding stance, she'd sent her on her way before opening the screen and pushing through the unlocked door. The kitchen was empty. She went down the hall to the bedroom and knocked on the door.

"Kat, you here?" No answer. She opened the door and warmed when the scent of the woman she'd come to know in such a short span of time greeted her. She studied the room—no paintings or pictures on the walls and a mix-match of furniture, including a pinewood nightstand with a Tiffany lamp resting on it next to the bed, a quilt rack in the corner, and an old oak dresser lining the wall. She caught a glimpse of a photo of Kat and Arizona perched on a lace doily atop the dresser, and her heart clenched. She shouldn't be here in Kat's bedroom—not without her. She hadn't been invited.

DJ located her boots on the floor at the bottom of the bed and headed down the hallway. Just like the rest of the house, no one was in the small living room. She continued to the kitchen, slid a metal chair from the table, and pulled on her boots before glancing outside through the rickety wooden screen door. The fire had destroyed nearly all of the tack building. DJ raked a hand across her face, and it smelled of wet embers. The unbearable heat flew through her mind, and she remembered going in, then hitting the wall, but that was it. A flash of terror shot through her, and the back of her neck prickled as her adrenaline spiked. *Where's Kat?*

"Kat," she shouted, rattling the screen door as she pushed through it.

"She's not here." Virgil popped up out of his rocker as if out of nowhere. He hadn't been there when DJ arrived.

"Is she okay?"

"She's fine." Virgil brushed by her and went inside.

"Where is she?"

"Could be anywhere by now." Virgil squinted at his watch. "She's a busy woman, you know."

DJ followed him in and watched him pour himself a cup of coffee.

"Want a cup?" he offered.

"In a minute." DJ looked at the single mug left to dry in the drain board and then at the clock. Only seven thirty and Kat was long gone. What had she said last night? She couldn't remember anything past the warm body lying next to her in the darkness.

"Heard you had a rough night."

DJ looked toward the hallway. "She stayed there with me, didn't she?" DJ remembered hearing Kat's voice during the night. She must have let something slip.

"Yep." Virgil filled his cup before leaning against the counter. "You did a good thing last night, goin' in there after me."

"But you weren't there."

"No matter. It was still a good thing." He took a sip of his coffee.

"You sure Kat's all right?" If DJ had let anything slip about who she really was and why she was here, Kat had probably worked up enough steam by now to blast her pretty good when she got back.

"She's fine. Looks like you were the only one hurt."

"Well, I'm thankful for that."

"Yep. Lost a few saddles and equipment, but all that can be replaced." Virgil's voice trailed off for a second. "Tell me, Ms. Callen. What're you really here for?" His eyes swept DJ from head to toe, then back again. "You didn't come here to play ranch hand. You've got some skills most others don't. I can see you're a country girl at heart. You can't hide that. You're all cleaned up and citified now, and you can't hide that either."

DJ walked the short distance across the kitchen and plucked a cup out of the drain board. "It's a long story, Virgil, and I'm sure you're not going to like it."

He cocked his head to one side. "Why don't you let me be the judge of that?"

DJ filled her cup with the steaming hot brew before wandering across the kitchen and leaning against the opposite counter.

"I'm her mother's lawyer."

Virgil's brows flew up. "The one she's been hanging up on?"

"Yep." DJ took a long, slow drink of coffee and let it burn across her tongue.

"But I thought the lawyer's name was Callahan."

"Danica J." She took a thin leather wallet out of her pocket, plucked a business card from it, and handed it to Virgil. "I didn't think she'd talk to me if she knew who I was." And DJ needed Kat to talk to her for her own family's sake.

"You're right about that." Virgil looked at the neatly embossed rectangle and then dropped it onto the table. "Should've figured the Belmonts would find a way to get to her."

"What do you mean?"

"Sending out a woman like you to make sweet with her. To try to convince her to come back."

DJ shook her head. "I didn't come intending to seduce her."

Virgil raised an eyebrow. "Well, whether you intended to or not, that's what it looks like." Virgil refilled his coffee cup and settled against the counter. "You don't know the family very well, do you?"

DJ stopped mid-drink. She knew Elizabeth Belmont's tactics better than anyone, but telling Virgil about her own dilemma wouldn't make her circumstances any less complicated. "I know that Kat's father was killed in that car accident and she wasn't at the funeral. I told her on the phone myself that her mother was seriously injured, and Kat hasn't contacted her either." She rattled the details off without missing a beat.

Virgil looked over his cup at DJ. "You'd better settle down, young lady. Talking like that 'round here isn't gonna get you anywhere."

"I'll tell you something else, Virgil. I don't understand it," DJ said as she set her cup down. It rattled when it hit the counter. "Kat seems like a very sensitive woman. You'd think she'd at least take the time to see if her mother is all right."

"Well, like I said before, she's a busy woman." Virgil's voice deflated, and he turned to the door. "Is Elizabeth all right?"

"She's recuperating well."

"Glad to hear it." Virgil tipped his hat.

"It's nice to know someone around here is. What kind of a daughter ignores her ailing mother's calls?" DJ asked, the words coming out harsher than she'd expected. She knew in her heart that Kat must have reasons to ignore her mother.

Virgil swung around quickly. "Listen, miss. That woman is the best you'll ever lay eyes on. Been hurt more than once, and she's still got a bigger heart than I've ever seen." He poked a finger into her chest. "Besides that, her mother's not the one making the calls. You are."

DJ brushed Virgil's finger aside, wandered to the door, and slung it open. "What difference does it make who's doing the calling? If her mother needs her, she should go." Blowing out a short breath, she lifted her arms and let them drop to her sides. "Look at this place. You'd think she'd be a little grateful." DJ was pushing because she needed more information about the relationship between Kat and her mother.

Virgil closed the door and held it there. "How long have you been working for the Belmonts?"

"I've been Elizabeth's personal attorney for the past five years." *Long enough to know how manipulative she can be.*

Virgil pinched his lips together and shook his head. "You know, you really oughta get your facts straight before you go shootin' off your mouth."

DJ widened her eyes. "I think I'm pretty familiar with the facts."

"Not hardly." Virgil let out a short breath. "You think they gave her this ranch?"

"I think they gave her seed money to help her start it."

"Open your eyes, DJ." Virgil spread his arms and rotated slightly, motioning to the surrounding furniture. "Does this place look anything like the Belmont estate?" He snatched a chair out. "Do they have old metal chairs with worn vinyl padding in their dining room?"

DJ let her eyes roam the kitchen, then the living room, taking note of the mismatched decor and the aged condition of the furniture. Her opinion didn't falter.

Virgil's eyes narrowed. "Well, let me tell you, DJ, or whatever your name is. That little lady and Arizona built this ranch from scratch. Without any help from the Belmonts." He hesitated. "Charlie Belmont didn't like me or my daughter much. Said we were beneath 'em. Told Kat if she married Arizona, she'd be on her own." He slammed the chair under the table. "As you can see, she's on her own, and better off that way, if you ask me."

DJ raked her hand through her hair, regretting everything she'd just said. "I'm sorry. I just assumed." The anger in her voice dissipated. She should've known better. Just from the short time she'd known her, DJ could see Kat was too prideful to take anything from anyone. "What happened to Arizona?" DJ scratched her head. She knew Arizona had died a few years ago, but she didn't know how.

Virgil sucked in a deep, ragged breath. "It's been a little over four years now. Arizona was out checking the trails when a flash thunderstorm hit. The horse spooked and threw her into a tree by the stream. Broke her neck. My baby girl died instantly."

DJ could see the pain in Virgil's eyes as he spoke. "I'm sorry. I didn't know."

Virgil cleared his throat. "People tend to think it shouldn't hurt so much, her being my stepdaughter and all. She may not have been my flesh and blood, but she was *my* little girl since she was three years old." His voice cracked. "The only thing that hurt as much as losing Arizona was losing her mama." Virgil turned and rinsed his cup out in the sink, then set it in the drain board. "It's been hard on Kat—running this place without her, goin' to sleep in an empty bed every night. I've never seen a woman love another like she did Arizona." Virgil smiled. "And believe me, Arizona loved her just as much. She knew exactly what she had with Kat." His smile faded. "And then to have Arizona taken from her just like that." He raised a hand and snapped his fingers.

DJ wandered across the kitchen, opened the door, and stared at the remnants of the tack house, wondering how it could be rebuilt. "So, now she runs this whole ranch on her own?"

"And does a damn good job of it," Virgil said proudly. "She has a lot of people depending on her. She may have to turn away guests and cut staff for a while, but she won't let 'em down."

DJ rubbed her neck. "Elizabeth didn't tell me any of this."

"That doesn't surprise me," Virgil muttered. "You know they didn't even come to the funeral. Haven't heard word one from 'em till now."

She'd made a huge mistake, judging Kat without knowing near enough about her to do so. All she'd had to go on was what Elizabeth had told her. She should've known better than to believe her. Kat was special. She veered her gaze to the steps where Kat had put her head into a spin last night. It hadn't been easy for DJ to resist her last night. The feelings she'd developed for Kat had truly surprised her. DJ knew now it could never be just a casual affair. She had to take care of some things before she dug herself in any deeper.

"Now I suggest you pack your things, go back to Austin, and tell the Belmonts to leave her alone," Virgil said, his voice settling a little.

"Listen, Virgil." DJ turned to face him. "I'd like to help."

Virgil's brows flew up, causing his weathered forehead to crease. "Why would you do that if you work for the Belmonts?"

"Because Kat *is* a good lady."

Virgil let out a short chuckle and planted the heels of his palm on the counter behind him. "You came all the way down here to do the

Belmonts' dirty work, and now you can't do it." His lip curled slightly and he cocked his head. "You really are sweet on her, ain't cha?"

"Let's just say she's not quite what I expected," DJ admitted, returning Virgil's smile.

"What can you do to help her?" Virgil studied her as he twisted the waxed end of his mustache between his fingers.

"I'm curious about this neighbor of hers. Something just doesn't sound right."

"Maxwell?"

"Yeah. That's the one."

"Thinks she can do whatever she wants to her."

"Why would she think that?"

Virgil rubbed his hand across his face roughly. "I tried to warn her, but a while back, Kat made the mistake of gettin' personal with her."

"Oh." DJ had a sick feeling in her gut. Kat had mentioned her neighbor, but she'd failed to give her all the intimate details. It was stupid to think Kat was just waiting around for someone like DJ to show up and sweep her off her feet.

"Can't blame her, though. She went through a bad stretch after Arizona died. After she broke it off with her, the backwoods vermin did everything in her power to force Kat into selling the ranch to her. She had her men bully the guests and scatter the cattle across the countryside nightly."

"She wants the ranch that bad?" The wheels began to spin in DJ's head. Who was this woman, and why did she want the ranch?

"I don't think it's the ranch so much as the sting of rejection that fired her up." Virgil crossed his arms. "You might be feelin' that sting yourself soon."

DJ smiled and let out a short breath. "You're probably right." She said it but didn't believe it. Last night, Kat had shown no sign of rejecting her.

"Maxwell just didn't realize who she was dealing with." A wide smile crept across Virgil's face. "Runnin' a business like the Jumpin' J, Kat's made all kinds of friends. Includin' ones with money and power." He snorted out a laugh. "All she had to do was call a few of our regular guests, and in no time at all, they had Maxwell and her boys running home to lick their wounds."

"So, why is she bothering her again?"

"Don't know. It's been almost two years since she backed off, and now she seems to be creeping around just like poison ivy in the trees."

DJ's eyes narrowed. "Has she threatened her in any way?"

Virgil shook his head. "No, not really. She just keeps pushing the boundaries."

"Like the calf stuck in the fishnet." DJ was lost in thought for a minute about the day before. It had been an unwelcome but necessary interruption. DJ would've found herself in a whole different situation if they hadn't been disturbed. "Kat said she had some questions about property ownership."

"She seems to think that all this land belonged to her grandpa," Virgil said.

DJ rinsed her cup and set it in the drain board. "That's what she told me last night. Who checked the county records?"

"We both did. Checked and double-checked. They all say the land's Maxwell's."

"My number's on the card." DJ reached down and slid it across the table to Virgil. "Call me if she needs me."

"Where you goin'?" Virgil picked up the business card.

"To Austin, to do some research on Victoria Maxwell." DJ pushed the screen door open. "I'll be back tonight." She let the screen door slap against the jamb behind her and headed down the steps.

She heard the door whoosh open behind her and looked over her shoulder to see Virgil following her. "You gonna tell her?"

DJ didn't turn. "If she was with me all night, she probably already knows by now."

"Don't think so. If she'd found out something like that, I'd have gotten an earful this morning." Virgil looked at the card DJ had given him and then slid it into his shirt pocket.

"I sure hope not." DJ gave Virgil a sideways glance and continued to her cabin. She needed a chance to redeem herself.

Chapter Twelve

Rebecca Belmont parked her black Mercedes in her usual parking space in front of the Montgomery Building. After taking a moment to check her makeup in the visor mirror, she reached over to the passenger seat to retrieve her leather valise and Gucci purse before opening the door and sliding out. Rebecca adjusted her skirt, then headed to the front entrance of Montco Oil. She swung her hips lazily, knowing that the cut of her Armani suit perfectly accentuated her long, slender legs and shapely hips. This was one of her favorite ensembles. It made her shoulder-length, highlighted, dark hair shimmer in the sunlight against the contrasting midnight-blue color of the jacket.

"Good morning, Randy." She smiled at the young security officer, whose usually unruly hair was conspicuously absent this morning.

He held the door open for her to enter. "Morning, Miss Belmont," he blurted nervously in a deep voice.

She stopped and looked at him momentarily. Without the massive mat of amber locks strewn across his forehead, he looked as though he wasn't old enough to be out of high school yet. "You cut your hair, didn't you?"

"Yes, ma'am." His eyes held hers as his head lowered slightly. "My mom said it was too shaggy."

"Well, your mom was right," she said, smiling slightly before continuing through the doorway. "That face is adorable. You shouldn't keep it hidden under that mop."

As she entered the elevator, Rebecca turned to see the young man smiling broadly, still holding the door as though she hadn't come through it yet. She rode up to the twenty-fifth floor, stepped off, and headed in the opposite direction of her office.

"Hi, Joanne. Is Mark in?" she asked the petite young brunette coming out of the corner office.

"Yep." She scrunched her nose. "He was here before me this morning."

"Really?" Rebecca brushed past her and poked her head just inside the office door. "Hey."

Mark's attention veered from the file on his desk. "Hey."

She slipped in and pushed the door closed behind her. "I missed you this morning."

"I had a few things to catch up on."

Rebecca dropped her bags onto the couch and met him halfway across the office. "What's the point of me not having to rush off in the morning, if you do it instead?" She touched his lips lightly with hers.

"I thought you had meetings this morning?"

She pressed her lips together and shook her head. "No. Now that Daddy's gone, I don't schedule anything before ten."

Mark smiled at her nonchalance. "Isn't that a little inconvenient for the staff?"

"Who cares?" she said with a shrug. "I'm in charge now. I can keep whatever hours I want." She tugged him to her with his tie and let out a short laugh before covering his mouth with hers.

"Mmm…I think I kind of like it when you're in charge," Mark said.

"So why can't I just tell her about us?" Rebecca repeated the same question she'd been asking for the last two weeks.

"You know your mother has plans for you, and they don't include me." He stroked her. "And I don't think you want to be disinherited, unlike your sister."

"I'm tired of all these secrets." She sighed, letting her head drop against his chest. "I want to go out to eat in public again and take you home to Sunday dinner. I want to sleep over whenever I want." Rebecca was tired of sneaking around. She was used to being shown off, not hidden like someone's dirty little secret.

He cupped her face in his hands. "Your father left you well cared for in his will, but until I take care of all the legal details, we need to be careful." He brushed a stray strand of auburn hair from her face. "Just keep quiet for a few more weeks, and I'll make sure you don't have to worry about anything."

"What makes you so sure my mother isn't going to like you?" She stared into his pale, gray-flecked eyes as she snaked a finger lightly across the front of his powder-blue silk shirt.

Mark's hands dropped to hold hers. "It's not about me, Rebecca. It's about who your parents may have envisioned in your future."

"We should've told my father. He would've been thrilled." She twisted her hands free, crossed her arms, and puffed her lips into a pout.

Mark raised an eyebrow in a gesture of uncertainty. "I'm not so sure about that."

"Of course he would've. You're an excellent attorney."

"An excellent attorney who worked for him."

"So what." She flopped onto the couch. "It's not as if you're some stable hand like Kathryn's wife."

"You're going to have to let me ease into the picture. Your mother has to believe I'm as much her choice as I am yours."

"My mother would never disinherit me. Who would run the company?" She sprang up and paced the office. "Even if she did, I have enough stock for us to live very well for a very long time." Rebecca had made some wise decisions with her money and was already a millionaire in her own right.

Mark trailed her across the room and spun her around. "Come on now. Settle down. I know we could do just fine without anything from your mother." He pinched her chin softly between his thumb and finger. "But that's not what you want, is it?" His lips brushed across hers. "You like all the perks of living in high society," he mumbled, his mouth continuing down her neck.

"After everything's settled with Daddy's will, I'm going to tell her about us." She pouted, standing nonresponsive to his coddling.

"You love me, don't you?" Mark's mouth made its way to hers, teasing her lips lightly.

"You know I do." She did love him, but she didn't like hiding her feelings from everyone.

"Then trust me."

"I'm trying." She turned, picked up her purse, and slung it over her shoulder.

"I'll walk with you." He took her valise from the couch and

motioned her to the door. "How long has it been since you've spoken to Kathryn?" He opened the door and followed her out.

"Not since the day she left." She glanced at him curiously. "Why?"

"I suggest you contact her as soon as possible." He smiled and nodded at a familiar face passing in the hall. "With your father gone, your mother may try to convince her to come back to Austin."

"After all these years?" Rebecca couldn't imagine why her mother would bring Kathryn into the business. Her father had been more than clear about his wishes when she left.

"You know she's always had a soft spot for her."

"Good morning, Jenny," Rebecca said, stopping at the desk just outside her office.

"Good morning, Miss Belmont, Mr. Hamilton." The tall, slender woman handed Rebecca a stack of mail.

She thumbed through it, dropped a few pieces of junk mail onto the desk, and then went into her office. "You really think my mother wants Kathryn here in Austin?"

"It would be wise to cover all your bases."

"I thought that's why I had you." Smiling coyly, she dropped the mail onto her desk and moved toward him.

He held her at arm's length. "Go see your mother and find out if she's up to anything."

"You're no fun anymore."

"I'm just looking out for you." He kissed her on the forehead before backing out the door. "See you tonight."

As Mark headed to his office, he took his cell phone out of his pocket and punched in a number.

"Jumpin' J, George speaking," the voice on the other end said.

"What's going on out there?" Mark entered his office and went straight to the mirror in his private bathroom to look at himself. He mussed his short, jet-black hair with his fingers and straightened his tie before he turned away, satisfied with his appearance.

"She's had a visitor for the last couple of days, some chick by the name of Callen."

He looked over his shoulder and shifted the phone to his other ear. "Is she still there?"

"She was this morning but left around eight."

"Any idea where she went?"

"No, but she didn't take her bags."

"Damn." Mark paced the office.

"I'm sure she'll be back. She and Kat seemed to be getting pretty cozy the last few days."

Panic shot through Mark. He hadn't expected this complication. "Get into her room and find out what she's doing there."

"Already did. Found an envelope with Kathryn's name on it."

"What's in it?" Mark heard the sound of clinking glasses in the background.

"Looked like information on her and the ranch." George's voice became quieter, and then Mark heard a door slap closed.

"What'd you say this woman's name was?"

"DJ—"

"Who?" Mark couldn't hear the name over the rushing wind coming through the line.

"DJ Callen."

"Fuck." Mark paced his office. "That's Dani Callahan. What the hell's she doing out there?" This could throw a huge monkey wrench into Mark's plan.

"Looks to be sweet-talkin' the boss lady."

"Find that envelope, make copies of everything in it, and take it over to Victoria. She'll want to see it."

"I'll do it as soon as my shift's over in the kitchen."

"Go do it now. If she's up to what I think she is, she'll be back sooner rather than later. Keep an eye on her when she returns, and let me know if anything changes between them."

"Will do," George said.

Mark spotted Rebecca standing in the doorway and smiled as he wrapped up the call and slid his phone into his pocket.

Rebecca frowned, noticing he'd cut his call short when he'd seen her. "What was that about? You sounded upset."

He smiled and shook his head. "My ten o'clock just rescheduled. A meeting that needed to happen."

"Oh, so you're free for a while?" Rebecca's voice rose as she pushed the door closed.

"Uh-uh," he said, ignoring her advances. "I still have plenty of work to do." He swept his arm across her back and moved her toward the door. "And you, my dear, have someone to see."

"But I'll see you tonight, right?" Rebecca's voice grew lower, and Mark knew exactly what she wanted from him.

He pushed her up against the door and gave her a scorching kiss. "You can count on it." When he was sure he'd placated her, he opened the door and guided her out of his office.

Chapter Thirteen

It was almost noon when DJ reached the Travis County Courthouse. Since it was around lunchtime, she'd been able to find a parking space close to the door, but she didn't know if the lady she'd come to see would still be there. She stopped by the drinking fountain on the way in, dug a few ibuprofen capsules from her pocket, and swished them down with a sip of water. She headed down the hallway, hoping to catch Allison Perkins before she went to lunch.

DJ had met Allison during her days as a law intern. She'd worked in the records department of the county clerk's office for more years than anyone knew and had proved to be an invaluable resource.

Allison had blond hair, pretty blue eyes, and a slender build. She had to be in her mid to late sixties by now, but she kept her age a well-guarded secret. Allison had the most radiant smile she'd ever seen. That, and keeping up with the new clothing styles, gave her an ageless look. Allison knew as much about the court system as any lawyer in Austin and even more about the records. If anyone could help her find the land deeds for the property Victoria Maxwell claimed, Allison could.

"Allison," DJ said in a low, smooth tone as she poked her head just inside the door.

Allison's hands went to her hips. "Well, if it isn't Dani Callahan, in the flesh," she said in her distinct Texas drawl. "I haven't heard from you since you started courtin' the Belmont girl."

"That was short-lived." She never should've considered that fiasco.

"Here I do all those favors for you, and then some sweet young thing comes along, and boom. You're gone like the wind."

"Forgive me?" She leaned over the counter and smiled sheepishly. "I never could resist those rosy cheeks of yours, and where did those adorable curls come from?" Allison's lips curved into a smile, and she flipped the countertop back for her to enter. "Now what's on your mind?" she asked, walking to her desk.

DJ raked her fingers through her hair and followed her across the newly renovated office. She'd forgotten to spike it before she'd come inside. She'd have to remedy that before she saw Elizabeth. "I need to look at a few land deeds."

Allison slid into her chair and began to type, her fingers flying across the keys on the computer keyboard. "What's the current name on the deed?"

"It should be either Belmont or Montgomery."

Allison eyed her sharply as she entered the name. "Francis Montgomery?"

"Yes. Francis James Montgomery."

"The only land in that name was deeded to Kathryn Belmont, who is now Kathryn Jackson." She glanced up at DJ. "I heard you were working for the Belmonts."

DJ stared at the computer screen but couldn't make heads or tails out of the coded information on it. "I only work for Elizabeth."

"You know working for people with that much money can be tricky," Allison said softly.

"Don't worry. I'll be all right." DJ touched her shoulder lightly and smiled at her concern. "Has any land been deeded to Rebecca Belmont?"

"No. There's nothing at all here in Rebecca's name."

DJ rubbed her chin. "It seems odd that Montgomery would deed land to Kathryn and not Rebecca."

Allison frowned. "I've been in this office long enough to say I've seen much stranger things happen in overly affluent families."

"What about the land abutting Kathryn's just to the north?" She slid her thigh onto the corner of the immaculate desk and sat down.

Allison punched the keys rapidly and pressed Enter. A message popped up saying the information wasn't on file. She quickly punched a few more keys, trying a different search, and received the same response.

"There's no information on that land in the computer. It hasn't been transferred yet. I'll have to pull the microfiche." Allison jumped up quickly and walked to one of the large filing cabinets positioned against the wall in the back of the room. After she yanked with both arms, the huge drawer rolled out slowly. She thumbed through the files, turned, and with a slight movement of her hip, she pushed the drawer, which clanged shut. She studied a small sheet of microfiche as she crossed the room to her desk.

Allison held it up to the light. "That's odd."

"What?"

Allison repositioned it. "Something must have happened to the original fiche."

"Why do you say that?" DJ looked it over as Allison held it up in front of her.

"This particular piece isn't very old. We didn't start using this brand until about ten years ago." Allison indicated the markings along the bottom before slipping it into the viewer and turning it on. "This shows the land abutting Kathryn's belongs to Victoria Maxwell. A Bartholomew deeded it to her fifteen years ago."

"You ever heard of these Maxwells?"

Allison shrugged. "No. Can't say that I have."

DJ raised an eyebrow. "How come they own all this land, and you've never heard of them?"

"That's a good question." Allison turned the viewer off and settled into the chair.

"I need one more small favor," DJ said with a smile.

Allison let out a teasing breath. "What would that be?"

"I need access to the vault." DJ knew that's where she'd find all the answers.

Locked up deep in the courthouse basement, the vault was a temperature-controlled room where they kept all the archived paper documents. After many years of humidity, combined with oils that collected on the documents from handling, they began to deteriorate unless kept at a constant sixty-five degrees.

Allison's fine arched brows flew up quickly. "You want to get me fired?" She took the microfiche from the viewer and slipped it into the paper sleeve.

DJ followed her across the room to the filing cabinet. "You said yourself the fiche doesn't look right." She pulled the huge drawer open for her. "All you have to do is unlock the door. I'll slip in and out before anyone notices. I promise."

"And just what do I gain from this?" Allison swung her hip against the file drawer to close it, just as she had before.

"Lunch at the best restaurant in town." DJ flashed Allison her sweetest grin.

"You're lucky you have that gorgeous face, Dani Callahan." Allison gave her a mischievous smile. "If I were just a little bit younger, you'd be in trouble."

"If you weren't already married, that wouldn't even be an issue." The compliment rolled smoothly off DJ's tongue.

Allison shook her head and let out a low chuckle. "Oh my, you *are* quite the charmer." She turned quickly and led her through the door and down the stairs. The temperature dropped suddenly as they entered the brick-encased, refrigerated room. "This should cool you off for a while." Allison's voice held a trace of laughter.

DJ stood speechless, letting her eyes roam across the countless filing cabinets filling the room. This was going to take longer than she'd expected.

"Where do I start?" she asked, her bemused expression giving way to her frustration.

"Don't panic." Allison smiled, apparently entertained by her reaction. "Everything is in alphabetical order. *B*'s are here." She pointed to a row of cabinets at the left end of the room. "And *M*'s are here." Allison pointed to the row directly in front of them. "I'll give you twenty minutes. I'll be ready for lunch by then." She turned and went up the stairs.

DJ started with the *M*'s, and with no trouble at all, she came upon original documents dating back more than fifty years that did, indeed, confirm the land had originally belonged to Elizabeth Belmont's grandfather, who was also Kat's great-grandfather, James Montgomery. The documents also proved the land had been deeded to Kat's grandfather, Francis Montgomery, before it was split and deeded to Kathryn and Rebecca equally.

Kat had been right all along. There was no mention whatsoever of Bartholomew or Victoria Maxwell. Somewhere along the line, without Kathryn or Rebecca's knowledge, someone had forged new documents that deeded the land to Victoria.

She climbed the steps, pushed the door open a crack, and peeked out into the room. When she saw no one else in the office besides Allison, she entered and went straight to the copy machine.

"What are you doing, Dani?" Allison asked, creeping up behind her.

"I need copies of these, okay?" DJ said discreetly, seeking her permission.

Allison took the documents, thumbed through them, and handed them to DJ. "Make it quick." She skimmed the front of the office, making sure it was still unoccupied.

DJ made the copies and then took the documents to the basement, but instead of putting the originals back in the file, she replaced them with the copies. Chances were, once she started poking into the whole thing, the originals would disappear or be destroyed. She had to make sure that didn't happen.

DJ folded the documents into thirds and unfastened the first few buttons of her shirt. She slid the documents inside and tucked them just under the waistband of her jeans before she headed up the stairs. She turned the knob and pushed the door open slightly, cursing as it slammed back hard against her face. DJ could hear a muffled conversation through the door. One of the other ladies in the office had returned from lunch. She leaned up against the cold brick wall, turned off the light, and waited.

Surrounded by the thick, black darkness, she let her thoughts wander to Kat. The deep, throaty resonance of her laughter rang through her mind, and her body produced a pool of wetness. Kat would be thrilled to hear the news about the land, and DJ knew she might possibly reward her in turn. Kat had made it perfectly clear last night that she'd wanted DJ as much as she wanted Kat.

Second thoughts clouded her mind. She let her head rest against the brick. She shouldn't become involved with this woman. Too much was at stake. The façade DJ had built around herself was beginning to crumble and was apt to come crashing down at any moment. Her gut twisted, and suddenly a blazing streak of light blinded her.

"Sorry about that," Allison whispered, rushing her out to the other side of the counter. "Did you find everything you were looking for?"

"Yes. Thank you. I did," DJ said as she patted her hand against her belly and felt the documents. "Now where are we going for lunch?"

"How about that fancy Italian place down on Main Street?"

"Donatello's?"

"That's the one." She took her purse out of the drawer before leaning through the doorway behind her desk. "I'm going to lunch now."

DJ held the door for her as she came around the counter. "One of my favorites."

"You knew it was going to cost you," Allison said, her Texas drawl thick again.

DJ smiled and gave her a wild-eyed gesture. "I wouldn't have it any other way."

After some nice conversation and a filling lunch, DJ dropped Allison off in front of the courthouse before continuing on to see Elizabeth at the Belmont estate. She took her usual route, admiring the beautiful scenery on the way. An abundance of immense oak trees flanked the entrances of the many estates and lined the road. It was hard to believe these kinds of mansions existed only a few blocks from the concrete skyscrapers of downtown Austin.

The sunlight flickered at her eyes like a strobe, and her mind wandered back to the ranch, back to Kat, the feel of her soft, damp skin from their afternoon at the river still fresh in her mind. She relived the memory of holding her against her as she slept, and the heat of her breath upon her chest sent a surge of desire through her.

Last night, when Kat had kissed her with such urgency, DJ had pushed right past the boundaries she'd always kept firm and steady. She had no idea what had come over her in the past few days and wasn't sure she wanted to know. But somehow, in some way, she wanted to be part of Kat's life.

DJ downshifted as she rounded the corner, and after passing through the massive iron gates, she quickly regained speed and continued up the short brick road to the main house of the Belmont estate. She screeched the BMW to a stop, reached into the glovebox, and took a few minutes to spike her hair before she pushed open the door and climbed out of the car. She rang the doorbell and stood waiting between the huge columns flanking the porch. The heavy door swung open almost immediately, and beads of light swished across the marble floor.

DJ grinned at the woman standing in the doorway. "You're pretty quick there, Maggie."

"The sound of that machine is unmistakable." Maggie eyed the BMW as she pinched her lips together. She closed the door and turned toward the kitchen.

"How's Mrs. Belmont today?" DJ asked before heading up the vast winding staircase.

"Cantankerous as ever."

"If she wasn't, we'd know something was wrong," DJ said, her usual caring manner laced with antagonism. She continued up the stairs and down to the end of the hallway. Slowly pushing on the partially open bedroom door, she peeked inside to see if Elizabeth was awake.

Elizabeth's eyes lit with delight. "Danica, what a nice surprise. I wasn't expecting to see you today."

"You know I can't stay away for very long." DJ bussed her on the cheek, then propped herself on the side of the bed. "I don't know what I'm going to do with you." She took Elizabeth's hand in hers and stretched her lips into a warm smile.

"Whatever do you mean, dear?" she said, the innocence in her voice clearly fabricated.

DJ blew out a heavy breath. "You didn't tell me the whole story." It wasn't so much that she'd played into Elizabeth's hands as the fact that DJ hadn't seen it coming.

"Would you have gone if I had?"

"You know I wouldn't have." Her tone was strong and firm.

Elizabeth raised an eyebrow. "Have you become acquainted with Kathryn?"

"Yes. I have." DJ smiled softly, her demeanor changing as the thought of Kat floated through her mind.

She gave DJ's hand a slight squeeze. "I can tell by your expression, you're taken by her."

She nodded. "She is a beautiful woman." *In more ways than one.*

"And very strong-willed."

"Just like her mother." DJ's smile faded. "She doesn't want your money."

"I assumed as much." Elizabeth looked down at her hands, laced her fingers together, and dropped them heavily into her lap.

DJ dropped her chin and stared at her. "I really don't like being put into the middle of your family squabbles."

"There was no other way, Danica. She won't talk to me."

Elizabeth's voice rose uncharacteristically, and DJ saw something in her eyes she didn't recognize. Hurt, despair, loss? She wasn't sure which, but Elizabeth was expressing emotions DJ hadn't seen in her before.

"From what she's told me, I don't blame her." DJ walked across the room and picked up a picture of Kat from the bureau.

She'd seen the photo of Kat sitting on the fence rail many times before. Now, after her trip to the ranch, DJ knew exactly where it had been taken. She could just barely make out the double-J emblem on the barn in the background. She'd never paid much attention to the letters before because she'd always assumed it had been taken at the Belmont ranch.

"This picture was taken at the Jumpin' J." DJ let her bewilderment show in her voice.

"Yes. I believe it was." Elizabeth reached into her bureau drawer, drew out a small photo album, and handed it to her.

DJ cocked her head curiously. "What's this?"

"Open it."

She lifted the cover and thumbed through the first few pictures. Her curiosity quickly turned to understanding. "You've been keeping track of Kathryn all along, haven't you?"

Elizabeth nodded. "She looks happy there, doesn't she?"

DJ flipped through the sequential pictures of Kat and Arizona leading the horses into the corral, all the while stealing glances at each other and smiling.

DJ hesitated for a moment as she studied a picture of them sitting on the front-porch swing. Kat looked perfectly content leaning up against Arizona with her legs outstretched across the swing. A flash of jealousy shot through DJ as she noticed Arizona's arm wrapped around Kat's waist and their fingers intertwined. Sadness replaced the jealousy as DJ realized she could compete with any living, breathing female but never replace the memory of a lost love.

She quickly flipped to the next set of photos and stopped again. She found one with Kat leaning against the very same tree she and DJ had picnicked under the day before. No smile lit her face in these pictures. Her eyes were dark and her cheeks hollow. She looked empty somehow, locked deep in thought as she stared at the river. Her heart hammered unexpectedly at seeing Kat so sad.

"These were taken after Arizona died," she said softly as she tried to purge the sadness from her heart. DJ was slowly realizing that what she felt for Kat had turned into much more than physical attraction.

"A few months after." Elizabeth let out a ragged sigh as she took the pictures from DJ's hand. "As you can see, her world has changed," she said, dragging her fingers across the shot. "They fell in love the summer after Kathryn's senior year of graduate school. She received a master's degree in finance at Baylor University. Charles had planned for her to go to work for him at Montco Oil immediately after graduation."

"I see that didn't happen."

"No. It didn't. Somehow Kathryn convinced Charles to let her have one last summer free of responsibility. A decision he always regretted," she said wryly, the edges of her mouth tipping up slightly. "Kathryn spent every waking moment of that summer at the Belmont Ranch." She touched DJ's hand lightly. "Arizona was one of the horse trainers there, you know. Charles had always praised her for her expertise." Her eyes narrowed. "But when he found out Arizona and Kathryn were connecting in ways other than equestrian training, his opinion quickly changed." She flipped her hands up in disgust. "He didn't mind her running the stables or even the fact that she was a woman, but Charles had no intention of letting the hired help into the family."

"Kathryn didn't agree, I take it."

"I don't think what her father thought was even an issue for Kathryn. In her eyes, Arizona was the perfect mate." Elizabeth's face lit as though it were she who had been in love. "I understood fully. She was gorgeous. At an even six feet tall, with big brown eyes and dark hair, the young woman had a heart bigger than Texas. Virgil, Arizona's stepfather, a long-time Belmont horse trainer, had raised her on the ranch. Kathryn saw Arizona frequently when they were children." She let out a throaty chuckle. "I clearly remember the look on Kathryn's face. She fell hopelessly in love with Arizona at the mere age of fourteen. I don't even think she knew she was a lesbian yet."

DJ's brow rose quickly. "But you knew?"

"Yes. I saw it. The sparkle in her eye, the excitement whenever Arizona was around. It was very obvious to anyone who watched them."

DJ stared across the room at nothing in particular. "So they started dating when she was fourteen?"

"Certainly not." Elizabeth patted DJ's hand. "Arizona always kept her distance from Kathryn. She was older, and, of course, Kathryn had a few others in her life along the way. I think Arizona was about twenty-one or twenty-two the first time she really saw Kathryn as a woman." Elizabeth took in a deep breath and let it out slowly. "But when Kathryn came home from college that summer after graduation, she saw her very differently, and Kathryn's dream finally came to fruition. I knew she wouldn't give Arizona up no matter what her father had planned."

"Charles gave her an ultimatum?"

"Yes. Charles fired both Virgil and Arizona, and ordered Kathryn to stop seeing her. I wasn't at all surprised when she defied him. Since she was a child, Kathryn has always been a very strong-willed young woman. After they ran off and were married in California, Charles made sure she was cut off from the family completely. Financially and personally. All she had was the land my father had deeded her in his trust."

"Why didn't you stop him?" DJ asked, trying not to judge but to understand how Elizabeth could let her husband force her daughter to walk out the door without a place to live or any money to start out on her own.

"It was a bittersweet moment for me when Kathryn left the family for the woman she loved." She closed the photo album and carefully placed it in the drawer. "I only wish I'd been that strong in my youth."

DJ stood motionless, staring out the window into the rose garden where the gardener was trimming away dead flowers, making way for new buds to bloom. "Forgive me, Elizabeth, but I don't quite understand why you would let Charles make a decision like that." She turned and gave Elizabeth her full attention again. "I can't recall you being silent about anything since I've known you."

"It's fairly common knowledge that at the age of sixteen, through no choice of my own, I was wed to Charles. It was an arranged marriage." She shifted slightly, raising her hand to DJ when she attempted to help her adjust the pillow behind her. "It may come as a shock to you, but I'm not as young as I may seem." Elizabeth pinched her lips together. "That's the way things were done in my day, and it wasn't considered proper to protest your parents' wishes."

DJ was tickled but not surprised at her vanity. Elizabeth Belmont was a beautiful woman, and she was absolutely right. She had no idea how old she was.

"It was difficult at first, but the Belmont family was very good to me. Even though I hadn't married for love, Charles was a very handsome and quite charming man. Being young and naive, I thought as time went on, perhaps we would grow to love each other."

"And that never happened," DJ said sadly. During the years she'd known Elizabeth, her relationship with Charles had been cordial at best. She hadn't known exactly how far the history went.

Elizabeth sucked in a breath and let it out slowly. "No, it didn't."

"Then why did you abandon Kathryn?"

"I believed Charles when he said she'd be back for the money." Her eyes lowered. "Deep down inside, I knew he was wrong." She looked up at DJ, her eyes beckoning for some sort of understanding. "Kathryn isn't like me. She's not the kind of woman to sacrifice her dreams for money."

"Why don't you just tell her all this?"

"It's hard for an old woman to swallow her pride, Danica," Elizabeth admitted. "Whether Kathryn knows it or not, she's already had more in her lifetime than I ever did."

"Then why are you trying to force her to return?"

"I gave birth to *two* beautiful daughters, Kathryn and Rebecca. I've always assumed both of them would carry on my family's place in Austin society."

DJ raised an eyebrow. "I think there's more to it than that, Elizabeth," she said, flattening her lips.

"Fine." Elizabeth slapped her hands to the bed. "If you must know, I'm not sure Rebecca can run the company on her own," she said, seeming to corral her emotions.

"Why not?" DJ was surprised Elizabeth didn't have more faith in Rebecca. "She has the education, and she's worked closely enough with Charles for the past few years to know exactly how he's been running the company."

"That's what worries me." Elizabeth shook her head. "In the past, Charles has done some things that may have been legal, but not necessarily ethical." She sat up straight, squaring her shoulders. "I'm tired of the Montgomery name being dragged through the mud along with the Belmonts'."

DJ knew Rebecca could be an astute businesswoman when needed, but she'd never known her to do anything illegal.

"Right or wrong, Rebecca never questioned him. When Charles told her to do something, she did it." She blew out a heavy breath. "She was always trying to please that unbearable tyrant, thinking in some way it might make him love her more, I suppose." Elizabeth's hands shook in apparent frustration. "I shudder at the thought. My father would turn in his grave if he knew some of the things they've done."

DJ shook her head. "She can't be all bad, Elizabeth. She's your daughter too."

"Yes, but maybe she's become a little too much like Charles." Elizabeth gave her an impenetrable stare. "You know exactly what I'm talking about, Danica."

DJ whirled around to look out the window. "Yes. I do," she said, knowing Elizabeth's gaze would still be fixed on her when she turned around.

"Do you love Rebecca?"

"Rebecca is a very beautiful woman." She stared blindly out into the hazy blue horizon. "You know, I've always thought the world of her."

"But?"

"She and I have some things to work out." The poorly constructed ruse Rebecca had convinced her to participate in to keep her mother at bay had been appealing at first, thinking she might have a little fun with Rebecca while it lasted. But Rebecca was a high-maintenance woman, and DJ wasn't up for catering to her needs.

Elizabeth sighed. "Rebecca doesn't know what it's like to do without."

"You don't have to do without to appreciate what you have," DJ said.

"Maybe so."

DJ swung around quickly and grabbed the top of the chair firmly. "Who is Victoria Maxwell?" she asked, abruptly changing the subject.

Elizabeth's brows drew together slightly. "I don't know anyone by that name."

"You've never heard or seen her name on any legal documents you may have signed?"

Elizabeth looked thoughtful for a moment. "No. I don't believe I have."

She narrowed her eyes. "Are you sure, Elizabeth? I need you to be truthful with me."

"The name is not familiar to me, Danica, and I don't appreciate the interrogation or your tone," she said adamantly. "Now what's this all about?"

DJ relaxed her grip on the chair. "Apparently, she owns some land just north of Kerrville." She observed Elizabeth's reaction for a moment. "Land that I believe belonged to your family."

Elizabeth shook her head. "I wouldn't know anything about that. Charles didn't involve me in any of his real-estate dealings."

"Seeing as how the Montgomery side of the family originally owned this particular piece of land, I thought you might know something about the transfer."

"What land are you talking about?"

"The land abutting Kathryn's ranch."

"That's impossible," Elizabeth insisted. "That land was to be deeded to Rebecca from her grandfather's trust when she turned twenty-one. Just as Kathryn's land was deeded to her."

"Somehow that land was deeded to Victoria Maxwell instead of Rebecca, and it looks to me like someone has gone to great lengths to cover up the transaction." DJ absently rubbed her hand across the back of her neck. She could tell Elizabeth was disturbed and had no idea the land had been deeded to Victoria. "From what I can tell, it looks like an attorney by the name of Mark Hamilton took care of most of your husband's real-estate deals."

Elizabeth's gaze snapped to DJ. "Did you say Mark Hamilton?"

"Yes. Do you know him?" DJ had rarely seen Elizabeth lose her composure, but she could see she was rattled. "What's the matter? Why are you so upset?"

"I'm sorry you had to find out this way, Danica, but I believe Rebecca and Mark are personally involved." Her words were slow and cautious.

DJ drew her brows together. "How long has she been seeing him?" DJ's only worry was whether the man could be trusted.

"Six months, at least. She doesn't think I know about him, but the two of them have been sneaking around for quite some time."

"Not real tall, but lanky, with jet-black hair?" DJ guessed his height to be only about five foot ten, but his lean, sculpted frame hinted that he took more pride in his looks than the average Joe.

"I've only seen him once or twice, but that sounds like him."

"Humph." DJ threaded her fingers through her hair. When Rebecca had introduced her to Mark at the company Christmas party last year, DJ had told her to be careful. The man was just a little too smooth, but apparently she'd ignored DJ's advice. "Didn't take her long to move on with her life, did it?"

"And you?" Elizabeth hesitated. "Your heart belongs to someone else now as well, doesn't it? Someone who is beautiful inside *and* out," she said, not waiting for DJ to respond.

"Don't you worry about me, Elizabeth." DJ skirted the issue, knowing full well she'd planned for it to happen all along.

"If I don't, who will?"

"So, how about you pay off that mortgage we spoke about."

"As soon you complete your task, it'll be done."

DJ shook her head, knowing it was useless to protest. "Is Hamilton's office in the Montgomery Building?" She headed for the door.

"I believe it is."

"Oh, and Elizabeth." She turned momentarily. "Please don't mention anything about our conversation to Rebecca until I have all the facts straight."

Elizabeth nodded. "Danica," she called before DJ went out the door. "Is this about Rebecca or Kathryn?"

"This is about both your daughters, Elizabeth," she said, closing the door behind her.

DJ slid down into her BMW and drove the short distance from the Belmont estate to the Montgomery Building. She didn't like the way things were beginning to sound regarding this land deal. Learning that Rebecca was personally involved with Hamilton would make finding the truth more difficult. Maybe Rebecca wasn't involved in any of the dirty deeds. Either way, the fallout would have an impact.

After passing the security desk, DJ stopped to check the building registry. She located Hamilton's office, boarded the elevator, and rode straight up to the twenty-fifth floor. As she rounded the corner past her own office, DJ wondered why she'd never seen Mark in the hallway before. Then the thought crossed her mind that he might have been purposely avoiding her.

"Is he in," DJ asked the woman sitting at the desk just outside the office.

"Yes. Your name, please?"

"Danica Callahan. Mrs. Belmont's personal attorney."

The woman pushed the intercom button. "Mr. Hamilton? There's a Danica Callahan here to see you. She says she's Mrs. Belmont's personal attorney."

"Send her in." The voice rang through the intercom.

Mark met DJ halfway across the office with his hand extended.

"I appreciate you seeing me," DJ said and shook his hand.

"No problem. I always have time for Mrs. Belmont. What can I do for you, Ms. Callahan?"

"I have a few questions concerning a land deal involving Mr. Belmont and a woman by the name of Victoria Maxwell."

"I'm not aware of any such recent deal." Mark turned and walked behind his desk.

"It wasn't a recent transaction. It would have been about eight years ago."

"I can check my files." He slid down into his leather chair. "But it doesn't ring a bell."

"I'd appreciate that." DJ took a business card out of her wallet and handed it to him. "If you come across anything, please give me a call."

DJ had the feeling the man knew more than he was saying, but she wasn't ready to push him until she knew just how involved he was with Rebecca. Besides, it was close to six o'clock, and DJ needed to get moving if she was going to make it to the ranch in time to see Kat tonight. And she *wanted* to see her.

CHAPTER FOURTEEN

K at settled into the arms of her surrogate, wishing she was dancing with someone else. Her head fogged with thoughts of DJ, and heat rushed her system as visions of last night overwhelmed her. First, the seductive, mind-blowing kiss. She'd wanted DJ so badly, she was ready to give her everything. All she had to do was ask. Maybe that was wrong, but DJ did something to her that she couldn't deny. Thoughts of the fire shot through her, and she shuddered. She didn't know what she would've done if something had happened to her before she'd had a chance to be with her, touch her, love her. *Love her? Oh God, am I falling in love with her? That can't be. Can it happen in only a matter of days?*

That adorable grin of DJ's popped into her head, and she knew how it happened. Kat couldn't suppress the smile spreading across her face. When DJ came back, *if* she came back, Kat wasn't going to deny her feelings anymore. She wanted another chance at happiness, and she wanted it with DJ. Kat knew well enough that life was too short. A rush of panic flew through her. God, she hoped DJ was coming back. She clamped her eyes closed, thinking only of DJ as she danced.

"Now this is the kind of dancing I like," Cody whispered.

She slung her head up and stared into Cody's puzzled eyes. They weren't the eyes of the woman she'd been thinking of. *She* was gone, and with the way Kat's luck ran, she'd probably never see her again.

"I'm sorry, Cody. I'm gonna have to sit this one out." Kat turned and left her standing solo on the dance floor.

"Hey, what'd I do?" Cody followed her to the table.

"Nothing." Kat shrugged as she sat down. "I just need to take a break." Kat gave her a polite smile, then pressed her fingers to her forehead as thoughts of the woman who'd been inching her way into her heart for the past several days whirled through her mind. Interrupted by scattered images of Arizona, her head ached as the two women battled for her heart.

"How about a drink?" Cody asked.

"Just water, thanks."

Kat was staring off into space, still sorting through her thoughts, when the waitress set a shot glass full of amber liquid in front of her. "Wrong table." She looked at the drink. *Tuaca.*

"It's from the woman sitting at the end of the bar." She motioned behind her. "The one with the curly-blond hair."

The seat at the end of the bar was empty. "What woman?"

The waitress glanced over her shoulder and shrugged. "She asked if there was somewhere quiet where she could make a call. I told her the best place was probably the hallway." She set a lavender rose on the table. "She sent this too."

Kat picked up the rose and held it to her nose, slowly taking in its delicate scent. It filled her senses, and she tingled all over. She knew who'd sent this. Kat looked up quickly, searching the room, and caught a glimpse of her as she rounded the corner into the hallway. Her pulse quickened.

"Thanks." She gave the waitress a quick smile and shot up to follow.

Her heartbeat doubling with every step, she fought her way through the guests and locals, smiling politely and not stopping when each one spoke to her as she passed. By the time she reached the hallway, no one was there.

Kat tossed her hair across her shoulder and cursed as she looked to the bar and scanned the crowd. *Where could she have gone?* She heard the faint creak of the office door opening behind her, and before she could turn, someone took her hand and pulled her inside.

The door slammed shut, and she was pressed up against it in the darkness, being sucked into the most urgent, wanting kiss. Trying to adjust to the sudden darkness, Kat struggled until the familiar taste filled her mouth. She'd kissed DJ only a few times before, but her essence had been embedded deep within her memory. She *had* come back. Rippling emotions rushed through Kat like a rampant river. It had been a long time since any woman had excited her so completely. Kat's hands, pressed firmly against DJ's chest, quickly lost their strength as they felt their way up and across the fuzzy remnants of hair on her neck. She let out a soft moan and melted into her, wanting to be so much closer as she returned DJ's kiss fully.

"I thought you'd never stop dancing." DJ broke away just enough for her lips to form the words.

"And I thought I might never see you again." Kat uttered softly. Her eyes adjusted to the darkness and sought DJ's. Kat could see her in the faint glow of the security light shining through the window.

"I had a few things to take care of in Austin." DJ's voice was soft and low.

Kat thought for a moment about the name DJ had mumbled in her sleep. "You're not going to tell me you have a wife and kids waiting for you there, are you?"

The corners of DJ's mouth curved up. The only woman she'd ever thought about getting attached to was in her arms right now. She shook her head. "No wife. No kids." Just one other unforgivable thing that DJ would keep to herself for now.

Kat drove her fingers into DJ's soft, blond curls.

"You like those?" She'd stopped by her penthouse to shower and had left them loose again.

Kat cupped DJ's neck in her hands and drew her in. "Uh-huh." She tugged at DJ's bottom lip and then let her tongue slowly make its way inside her mouth.

The result was a long, slow-kissing inferno that needed to be either doused or stoked. DJ dragged her mouth away. "You want to dance more?"

"Not really." Kat locked DJ's gaze and touched her lips softly with her own again.

DJ trailed her thumb down Kat's neck and felt her pulse skitter beneath it. Kat let out a groan, and DJ almost lost it as Kat's heated breath lingered on her neck and her soft breasts melted into her chest. Kat's body trembled against her, and her need multiplied. Every inch of DJ's body pulsed. The slightest touch would trigger an explosion. Kat stared up at her through thick, fluttering lashes. There was no mistaking the plea in her eyes tonight. Kat was begging her to explore.

"Are you sure?" DJ offered Kat one last out but hoped to God she didn't take it.

Kat pressed her thigh against the apex of DJ's legs, and her stomach flip-flopped.

"Positive." Kat's eyes were dark and wanting.

"We'd better go to the house." DJ needed her now, but quick-and-dirty here in the office wasn't how she wanted it to happen with Kat. She took her by the hand and led her out through the crowded bar. When Kat's hand slid out of DJ's, she turned to see the woman Kat had been dancing with earlier blocking her path. She couldn't hear the conversation, but the woman had grabbed Kat's arm, which was *not* okay.

"Is everything all right?" DJ slipped in beside Kat.

The woman's lip hitched up, and she cocked her head. "Oh, I see. Your bed's already taken tonight."

Kat must have seen the anger flare in DJ's eyes. She quickly wedged herself between the two women. "Please don't," she pleaded, forcing DJ to look at her. "Not here. Not now."

DJ sucked in a deep breath, backed up, and moved Kat in front of her. Kat led her out the door. The cool night air whisked across DJ's neck. She noticed Kat cross her arms and rub her shoulders briskly to fight the chill. DJ took off her jacket, put it around Kat's shoulders, and felt the masses of tiny goose bumps prickling at her skin.

"I'm sorry about that," Kat said with a twinge of embarrassment in her voice.

"She's the one who should be sorry." DJ put her arm around Kat and rubbed her shoulder as they walked. "The woman should thank her lucky stars you ever gave her a second look."

She shook her head and stared at the ground. "DJ, I've done some things in the past that I'm not very proud of."

"Haven't we all?"

"I mean I've made more than just a few—" DJ stopped, blocked Kat's path, and took her by the shoulders. "Mistakes from the past don't matter to me, Kat." Kat's vivid blue eyes glowing in the moonlight had DJ mesmerized until the wind began to blow wildly, sending Kat's loose onyx hair flying into the air.

"Come on. We'd better get you inside. It looks like we're going to have a storm tonight." DJ clasped Kat's hand in hers and led her across the grounds.

"I just need to know one thing." Kat moved closer, shortening the distance between them.

"What's that?" DJ stopped and turned.

Kat curled her fingers into DJ's shirt. "Are you going to stay tonight?"

"I could never walk away from you twice," DJ said, brushing her lips lightly with her own. Seeing her in the bar tonight, dancing with another woman, had made DJ realize she didn't want to resist the force between them any longer. She let out a low, rumbling growl, took Kat's hand, and settled her up under her arm. Kat tucked her thumb into DJ's waistband and let her fingers drift across her ass, sending a completely new array of hyper-erotic sensations surging through DJ.

As they approached the house, they could see a light in the horse stalls. "I'd better go check that out," Kat said, noticing the wide-open door. "I only want one kind of blaze going on tonight," she said with a suggestive smile.

DJ grinned. "It's probably just Virgil. Why don't you go on in the house, and I'll see what he's doing." DJ kissed her softly and pushed her toward the steps.

"Don't take too long," Kat chanted seductively from the bottom step of the porch.

"I'll be right there." DJ peeked over her shoulder and felt the familiar flutter in her stomach.

DJ was almost to the stable when the light went out, and Virgil came through the doorway.

"Ah, Ms. Callahan. You're back. Or is it still Callen?"

"Let's just keep it at DJ for now," DJ said, ignoring the disapproval she saw in Virgil's eyes. "I was walking Kat home, and we saw the light."

Virgil looked to the house and waved at Kat. "Had to close all the windows and shutters. It's fixin' to storm tonight."

DJ looked up and watched the clouds roll across the darkened sky. "Looks like it could be a big one." She heard the clatter of the wooden screen shutting and returned her attention to the house for a moment. "Any word on what caused the fire?" DJ had a feeling it wasn't an accident.

"Not yet. Fire inspector came through and took a few things." Virgil walked to the rubble. "Looks like it started in this corner."

"Electrical?"

"Doubt it." Virgil pushed a burned timber with his foot. "No electricity on this side." He flattened his lips. "We'll know more tomorrow."

"Let me know what you find out." DJ turned toward the house.

"Not so fast, young lady," Virgil said, and DJ whirled around. "Did you tell her who you are yet?"

"No, but I will. I promise. Just give me a little time."

"I may have told you this before, but I'm gonna say it again." Virgil stood nose to nose with DJ and moved closer, narrowing his eyes in what DJ took as warning. "That girl is very special to me. In fact, you could say she's like a daughter. So you'd better be very careful with her. Understand?"

"Yes, sir," DJ said without flinching, then turned and walked to the house. She didn't want to hurt Kat, and she knew it would sting when Kat found out why DJ had really come to the ranch.

She quickened her stride as she tried to outpace the huge raindrops beginning to fall. DJ could see Kat in the kitchen staring out the window as she took the last few steps to the porch. Her mood had changed.

DJ touched Kat's shoulders lightly as she came up behind her. "What's wrong?"

She turned her stare to the message machine on the counter, prompting DJ to reach over and push the Play button. DJ was surprised to hear Mark Hamilton's voice spewing some sort of legal jargon about her father's estate. *Why the hell is he calling Kat?* Her visit today must have stirred up something.

DJ let out a heavy breath and let her arms snake around Kat's waist. "You know you're going to have to take care of that."

"I thought I hated that man." Tears streamed down her face.

It seemed they had something in common. DJ didn't know if she could advise Kat to forgive her father when she hadn't had it in her to forgive her own. She just knew she regretted not doing it. "You can't deny he was your father."

"God. I wish I could." Kat wiped a tear from her cheek and moved into the living room.

DJ took Kat's arm and swung her around to face her. "Please

don't shut me out." Kat flinched when a sudden clap of thunder rolled powerfully in the distance. Her eyes were a deep sapphire blue now, more tears threatening to spill out again at any moment. DJ could see that the break from her family wasn't as clean as Kat had forced herself to believe. She must have locked her feelings away, hidden the pain, and buried it deep. It seemed to be simmering inside, threatening to resurface at any time.

Kat fell against DJ's chest. "Why couldn't he just love me?"

"Sometimes people do things for reasons we don't understand until it's too late." DJ hugged Kat close, wishing she could take it all away, that they'd met under different circumstances. DJ had come to the ranch to seduce her, to lure Kat to Austin. She'd never expected such a powerful connection or feelings like this to explode inside her.

Kat pressed her mouth urgently to DJ's, and the desperate need to touch her surged through her again. DJ had been with many women before, never looking past the one brief moment of gratification, but Kat was unlike any woman she'd ever known.

Kat stared into DJ's gentle, caring eyes. Was DJ really a woman she could depend on? It didn't seem possible to find someone who didn't care about her past, someone that made her feel innocent and pure again. There had been so many before, when she'd tried to return to a normal existence after losing Arizona. So many that sometimes it seemed like an endless game. Becoming this wrapped up in DJ was a mistake, she thought, resting her head against her chest. She pulsed with anticipation as DJ's fingers tormented her with soft, heated caresses. She'd forgotten what it was like to let someone else take control, to let everything play out naturally instead of knowing how and when it was going to end. This particular feeling of domination was overwhelmingly intoxicating. Being this close to DJ made her feel alive again, as though nothing else mattered.

The thunder clapped again. Kat stiffened and pushed DJ away. "I can't do this." She hated thunder. It reminded her of something she'd lost. Something very precious.

"You missed me, didn't you?" DJ held Kat firmly with one hand while the other slowly traced up and down her spine.

"More than you'll ever know," Kat murmured, staring into her eyes intensely, searching for some sort of reassurance.

"I don't know how I ever thought I could resist you," DJ said, her mouth making its way to Kat's.

Kat met DJ's mouth in a heated frenzy, touching and baiting as she grabbed at the fabric left between them and the pearl snaps of DJ's shirt popped open. Kat needed to feel her skin—now. She stopped for a moment and looked at the woman before her. Pinked cheeks and chest heaving, DJ was more stunning in this moment than Kat had ever imagined. She slid her hands across the soft skin of her chest before she pushed the shirt from DJ's shoulders and let it fall to the ground. DJ tugged the cotton T-shirt loose from Kat's belt, her hands making their way underneath, gently touching, caressing. Completely unprepared for the barrage of sensations coursing through her, Kat gasped as DJ's hands skimmed her rib cage. Her thumbs swept up and under the fabric of Kat's bra, and Kat's nipples immediately stiffened. She let a throaty moan escape her lips before she pulled her shirt over her head, and tossed it aside, leaving her black, silken bra still intact. She urgently returned her mouth to DJ's as DJ fumbled awkwardly with the clasp. Kat slid her hands across DJ's tense muscular arms before she reached around and popped it open easily. One by one, Kat slid the straps slowly from her shoulders, revealing the breasts trapped just behind the cups.

Wanting blindly, they fell across the end table and onto the couch, knocking the lamp on its side and catapulting the throw pillows off onto the floor.

Kat shifted on top and straddled DJ, clumsily trying to unfasten her jeans. "Damn."

DJ took Kat's hands in hers. "Slow down, darlin'. I'm not going anywhere." DJ sat up and removed her bra before she took Kat in her arms and traced the line of her shoulder with gentle kisses. Kat shuddered out a breath and pressed herself into DJ. The touch of DJ's soft warm breasts against hers made reckless desire echo through her, and wetness gushed to her panties. The long-forgotten sensation only added to the intense confinement of her jeans.

DJ lifted her from the couch, and Kat wound her legs around her waist as she carried her down the hallway. She pushed the first door open, backed out, and went into the next room. "Fuck. Which one is it?"

Kat smiled at DJ's urgency. "Last one on the right," she said, eager to feel DJ's hot mouth on her already blazing skin.

After finally making it to the bedroom, DJ laid Kat on the bed and shed the rest of her clothes. Kat kept her gaze glued to DJ until she removed the last piece of clothing. She blinked at the sight. Long legs, muscular body, and small, perky breasts with nipples standing at attention. How could a body look so perfect? Kat swallowed hard and began tugging off her jeans.

"Wait," DJ said, moving Kat's hands. "I want to do that." Her strong yet gentle hands swept across Kat's thighs, slowly sliding the jeans off before returning up her legs.

Kat's skin sizzled with each fleeting touch. DJ slid the remaining underpants down Kat's thighs before she let her tongue move urgently between Kat's folds, sending a sudden gasp of pleasure through Kat's lips. The anticipation had gotten the best of her, and she couldn't stop the thundering orgasm. Her mind spun into colors of pure bliss as she was instantly and completely consumed. Her muscles contracted with unimaginable strength, and the electricity pulsing through her made her tremble uncontrollably. The turbulent sounds of the storm were lost in the distance as sensations rocketed through her, each never fading completely before the next began. DJ took her to the very edge and back again. Her tongue moved exquisitely in rhythm from inside her to her intensely sensitive clit. Then she suddenly stopped, leaving Kat yearning for final surrender.

Kat grabbed at DJ's curls and growled. "Jesus. Don't stop now." She heard a soft chuckle and felt a quick breath on her center before DJ's mouth went to work and pushed Kat over the edge into another surging orgasm.

Kat was still reeling when DJ crawled up and sucked a nipple into her mouth. Kat motioned her up farther and met DJ's mouth and tongue eagerly. Kat's senses heightened as her need to touch DJ increased. She shoved DJ onto her back and straddled her as she took a breast into each hand, flicking the nipples with her thumbs and then her tongue. Kat felt DJ's hand move between her legs and quivered as more than one finger explored her. *Oh, my God. What are you doing to me?* She rocked against DJ's hand, stiffening as two fingers penetrated her, and she stopped before fully engulfing them.

"Are you okay?" DJ asked.

Kat shifted forward, blanketing DJ's body with hers. "It's been a while," she whispered.

"We'll take it slow." DJ sat up and held Kat closely to her as she eased farther onto DJ's fingers, lifting her slightly when Kat let a gasp escape.

Kat lowered and rose in a slow, steady rhythm until DJ's fingers were fully inside, and then she let Kat manage the pace. She gradually adapted and quickened her pace as she indulged in the intensity of each thrust, plunging DJ's fingers deeper inside. A jolt shot through her when DJ's thumb pressed against her clit. She had to slow down.

"Not yet," Kat murmured as she stilled and stared into DJ's dark-green eyes. Kat was incredibly wet, and DJ was taking her with such intensity, such hunger, her body was about to explode…again. She covered DJ's mouth with hers and continued her rhythm. The taste of herself on DJ's lips only ignited her desire more. One, two, three thrusts, and Kat was thrown into another staggering orgasm. She clenched DJ as she rode out the mixture of wildly intense emotions and sensations. She had no idea an orgasm that deep was even possible. When Kat collapsed against her, DJ withdrew her fingers and lowered Kat on top of her.

Kat waited only a few moments before she pressed her mouth to DJ's and kissed her again. She wanted to touch her all over, to taste her, to make DJ hers. She held one of DJ's breasts in her hand and pinched the nipple before she took the other nipple into her mouth and circled it with her tongue. She lingered, toying with their pointed peaks, causing them to pebble hard. She moved her mouth slowly down across DJ's stomach and felt her belly tighten. She went lower, trailing across her hip, then gently weaving back and forth, in and out of every crevice lightly with her tongue. She stopped and hovered just above the blond patch of curls that led to what Kat knew would be her own undoing. She took in her scent, and the heady haze it threw her into spun into insatiable desire. She had to taste her.

She looked up across DJ's stomach and took in the beautiful view before she dipped her tongue between the folds. She heard DJ's breath catch, and she arched into her. Kat grabbed her ass and held her steady as she moved her tongue up and down, stopping to suck and nibble with each pass. She tasted incredible, which only succeeded in making Kat more wet. She plunged her tongue deep inside, and DJ responded with a low moan. She slid a finger in and then another as she focused her tongue on DJ's clit, which hardened with each stroke. It wasn't long before DJ's breathing quickened and Kat felt her constrict around her fingers. DJ grabbed at the sheets and clamped her legs together as indecipherable words rumbled out of her mouth. Kat was totally turned on *again*.

Her nerve endings still on fire, Kat lay in the crook of DJ's shoulder, her face nestled into her chest, trying to keep her eyes open. They'd made love several more times during the night. The igniting passion that had coursed through her only a few moments ago had drained her to her very core. As her pulse finally began to slow, she thought about how gentle DJ had been with her, calming her, bringing her to a level where she could let go and enjoy the sensations spiraling through her. Arizona had been the only other woman who could do that.

Kat looked up and watched DJ's beautiful face as she slept. There was only one other woman she'd given herself to or taken so completely. She'd had sex with an array of women since Arizona died, but she hadn't been this intimate with anyone. It was too close, too personal, but the connection between her and DJ was unmistakable. Kat had wanted to be as close as she possibly could to DJ. She took in a deep breath and hoped she hadn't made a mistake.

Having one true love in her lifetime had been a blessing, and now to have another come along was unbelievable. The storm had passed, and she was safe in DJ's arms, completely and utterly content.

Chapter Fifteen

As the sun came up the next morning, DJ thought about the woman in her arms. She'd wanted to take her time pleasing Kat, but her control had weakened with each sensual sound Kat had uttered. Kat's fingers had tangled in the curls of her hair, moving through them, tugging urgently as DJ continued to roam Kat's body, exploring every crevice over and over again.

DJ remembered how her body had quivered as she nipped at the flesh of Kat's breasts, savoring the taste, teasing her nipples. When, with a groan of utter need, Kat had begged her for release, DJ had plunged her tongue deep inside. Kat had responded even more urgently than the first time, letting out a soft shudder as another wave of staggering sensations rolled through her. Kat was hot, steaming with desire beneath her, which made DJ want her even more than she'd thought possible.

DJ touched her nipple. It was agonizingly sensitive. Kat had done that. She clamped her eyes closed. *What the fuck am I doing?*

She slid her arm out from under Kat and moved to the side of the bed. How had she gotten here? She'd tried to keep her distance, but apparently not hard enough. Commitment had never dared cross her mind before, but Kat could complete her in many ways. The connection she'd felt with her was stronger than she'd ever felt with any woman. Was having a life with Kat possible? Could she bury all the pain she'd endured after leaving her family farm when she was younger? Would her family forgive her for the distance she'd put between them?

"Where are you going?" Kat looked up at her through thick, sleepy lashes.

"Shh. Go back to sleep." DJ kissed her softly. "I have a couple of things to take care of this morning. Be back this afternoon."

"You're not escaping that easily." Kat tugged her closer.

As she fell into bed, it hit DJ again how wonderful it felt to be with this woman—to kiss her, to touch her, to spend the night in her arms. Fear fleeted through her. This wasn't just for fun anymore. DJ was getting attached.

Kat must have seen her expression change as she stared up at her. "Oh, no, you don't. We're way past second thoughts." Kat buried her face into DJ's neck, tickling her until she couldn't stand it anymore.

"Stop," DJ squealed in a breathless laugh.

Kat sat up and held her tight, pressing her forehead to DJ's. "No second thoughts."

DJ let out a long, slow breath. "No second thoughts."

She fused her lips to Kat's in a long, slow kiss. The overpowering heat washed through her again. This was crazy, but she never wanted to move from this moment in time.

"Kat," Virgil shouted, pulling open the screen and pushing through the door. Like every other day, he took a cup out of the cabinet and went straight to the coffeepot. After pouring himself a cup, he wrinkled his face in disgust as he swallowed the cold, day-old coffee. He dumped the liquid into the sink, rinsed the pot, and then set it on the burner before crossing to the refrigerator for the can of coffee.

He glanced into the living room as he opened the refrigerator door and panicked. When he saw the lamp on its side and the couch pillows strewn across the floor, he rushed down the hallway, slowing only when he noticed the trail of clothes on the floor leading to Kat's bedroom.

"Kat, you okay?" he shouted.

"Be right out," she said from the other side of the door.

Virgil let a wide grin spread across his face as he gathered the scattered clothes and turned into the living room to straighten up. DJ hadn't told her why she was here. If she had, Kat would've already been up and in the kitchen spittin' fire when Virgil came in this morning.

"You feelin' all right?" Virgil asked when Kat came through the doorway into the kitchen.

"I'm fine, Virgil. Why?" She took a seat at the table and tugged a boot on.

"You just seem to be running a little late this morning."

"I must have forgotten to set the alarm."

"You haven't used that alarm clock in years. What's going on, Kat?" he asked calmly, observing her uneasiness.

Kat let out a deep breath and sank into the chair. "You know DJ came back last night."

"You and she...?" Virgil stopped without finishing his question.

"Yeah." Kat averted her eyes as the response blew softly out of her lips. She bit her lip nervously as she shifted to tug her other boot on.

In her heart, Kat knew she shouldn't feel guilty. Arizona would want her to be happy, but Virgil was Arizona's father, and his opinion mattered. Life had been pretty rough after Arizona died. At times it had seemed unbearable. In a few of her weaker moments, Kat had thought seriously about crawling back to her parents. Whenever she began to question herself, Virgil would point out all that she'd accomplished, reinforce her confidence, and give her the strength to go on. If it weren't for him, Kat never would've made it.

The screen door swung open, and Victoria Maxwell strolled into the kitchen.

Kat bolted to her feet. "Get the hell out of my house."

"Settle down. I just came to give you a little information." She looked around the kitchen. "Place hasn't changed much. Bedroom still the same?" Victoria asked as she raised her brows.

Kat narrowed her eyes and gave her a hard stare. "It's been disinfected twice since you've been here." She slid down into her chair. She knew her remark was juvenile, but the woman provoked that type of reaction in her.

"Now that hurts, Kat. All I was trying to do was help you out, just like I am now." Victoria moved closer, took a swag of Kat's hair, and rubbed it between her fingers. "Did your new girlfriend tell you why she's really here?"

Kat slapped at Victoria's hand as she reared her head, jerking her hair from her fingers. "Who are you talking about?" She knew perfectly well who she was talking about.

"DJ Callen." Victoria glanced at Virgil.

"She's not my girlfriend. She's here on vacation." Kat slapped her foot to the floor, seating her heel into the boot.

"Not according to these, she's not." Victoria dropped a manila envelope on the table in front of her.

Kat drew her brows together. "What's this?"

"I found it in her room."

"What do you think you're doing going through my guests' things?" Kat flipped her stare to Virgil. They'd just had all the codes to the rooms changed. Now they'd have to do it again.

"When I read it, I found out all kinds of new things about you. Next time I see her, I'm gonna have to thank her." Victoria pressed her lips together into a smile that sent a shiver through Kat.

What kind of things is she talking about? Kat picked up the envelope, turned it over, and saw her name on it. *That doesn't mean anything. Victoria could've written that.*

Hesitating a moment, Kat tossed it onto the table, then reached down and continued lacing her boots. "Get out."

"Okay." Victoria gave her a wink. "Don't worry. I won't hold it against you when you find out I'm right." She pushed open the screen door and stepped out. "You know where I'm at."

"It'll be a cold day when I ever set foot in your place again," Kat said, and she meant it.

"Winter's comin' sooner than you think." Victoria gave her a wicked smile that made Kat's stomach clench and let the door slap shut.

"Oh boy." Virgil frowned and rubbed his forehead. "Are you gonna open it?" Virgil pushed the envelope closer to Kat.

"It's not my business, Virgil."

"It damn sure is. It's got your name on it." Virgil picked it up and let the contents slide out into his hand. After reading the first page, he shook his head. He flipped through the rest of the documents before slipping them into the envelope and dropping it onto the kitchen table. He eyed it for a moment before he went back to making the coffee.

Kat planted her hands firmly on her knees and stared at the envelope. "I told her how much trouble Maxwell's been giving us. She probably just did some checking when she went to Austin yesterday." She sucked in a deep breath and pressed her lips hard together.

"Why don't you just take a look and find out?" Virgil slid the envelope over to her.

She picked it up and ran her finger under the flap. Still undecided, she let the documents slide slowly out into her hand. As she focused on the first few lines, all that registered in her mind were the words Montco Oil and stock transfer. She suddenly found it hard to breathe. She felt like someone had punched her in the chest. The documents weren't about Victoria at all. They pertained to Montco Oil Incorporated.

She read further. It appeared that Elizabeth was willing to sign over one third of her interest in the company to Kat, free and clear. The one catch was that she take an active position in the company and attend all board meetings in the future.

She didn't understand. These weren't even copies. They were original documents. DJ had acted like she didn't know her family. Why would she have them? She scanned each page from top to bottom as she flipped through the rest of the papers, and pain stabbed her heart. They were all about her. It was a well-composed dossier of her life, including everything from early childhood to the present.

She felt the warmth of the tears streaming down her face as she continued to read. Her whole life story was right there in one neat little package. No wonder she was so attracted to DJ Callen. She had prepared herself well. She knew more than enough about Kat to seduce her.

She scattered the documents across the table. "Damn her."

"I'm sorry, Kat." Virgil stood in the doorway, concern clear in his eyes. She wished she could lose the last half decade of her life, fall into his protective arms, and let him comfort her as she had when she was younger, but she'd made this mess, and her pride wouldn't let her.

"I should've known better," Kat said, storming past him. "Are all women like this?" she asked, without needing an answer.

DJ Callen was no better than Victoria Maxwell. She might not be quite as transparent, but she was just the same. Kat had let her guard down and trusted her. Now she'd abused that trust.

"Where are you going?" Virgil shouted after her.

Kat threw the screen door open. "Out on the range. I have work to do," she said and sprinted toward the stable.

Chapter Sixteen

When DJ arrived in Austin, she went straight to see Mark Hamilton to find out why he was calling Kat. The door to Mark's office was open, and his assistant was away from her desk. She stepped into the office and found it empty, an opportunity DJ couldn't pass up. She beelined it across the room to the cherrywood desk.

She set her briefcase on the desk, sat down in the high-backed chair, and shuffled through the neatly stacked papers. Nothing here DJ hadn't already seen. She opened the right-hand file drawer and thumbed through the file folders. Nothing that pertained to Kat or the Montgomery land. She yanked open the other drawer, but it seemed to hitch before sliding all the way out. DJ examined it before she slid the other one out again. The one on the left wasn't as deep as the one on the right. She gave it another tug and it didn't budge. She reached into the right-hand drawer and shoved all the files to the front. After feeling the back panel of the drawer, she knocked on the wood—solid. She did the same in the left-hand drawer, but the sound was hollow. She tried to pry it free with her fingers but couldn't. She opened the middle drawer, searching for something to force the wood loose. Coming across a silver letter opener, she jammed it into the joint and pried the panel loose. *Empty.* Nothing in the six-inch space.

"Damn!" DJ tossed the letter opener onto the desk. The man wasn't stupid enough to keep anything in his office. DJ heard voices coming toward the office, so she quickly slammed the drawers shut and hurried to the wet bar embedded in the wall of every executive office in the building. She dropped a few ice cubes into a glass, reached into the compact refrigerator, and filled it with orange juice.

"Good morning," she said, surprising Mark as he came through the doorway.

"Who let you in here?"

"Door was open," DJ said as she sipped her juice.

Mark rounded his desk and sat looking at his files as though he could tell things were a little askew. It really didn't matter. She was putting the man on notice today.

"I received a call from Kathryn Jackson." She swirled her glass, letting the ice clink against it. "She said you tried to contact her."

Mark picked up the letter opener and put it in his desk. "As a matter of fact, I did."

"What for?"

Mark popped up out of his chair but remained behind the desk. "I've been researching the property you asked me about."

DJ kept her stare still and even. "I asked you about the property abutting hers."

Mark stared down at his desk, his confidence faltering. "I'm just trying to find some history on the whole area."

"What could you possibly find out from Kathryn?"

Mark narrowed his eyes. "You said she thought that her grandparents owned it, right?"

"Uh-huh." DJ scanned the office, noting the lack of anything that might connect Mark to Rebecca. She relaxed, thinking perhaps it was a sign they weren't as close as Elizabeth had thought. Then again, other than the framed law degree hanging on the wall, the room seemed to be void of any personal items.

"I was trying to find out where she'd gotten that impression." After straightening the pile of papers, Mark slapped them to the desk. "Then at least I'd have a place to start."

"Why didn't you start with Rebecca?"

"Rebecca has nothing to do with this."

"Actually, she does, and that's why you couldn't go to her." DJ studied him for a minute before slapping her briefcase onto the desk. "If you had, she'd know what you've done." She set her glass on the desk, took out a copy of the forged land deed from her briefcase, and floated it across to him.

"That is your signature, isn't it?" DJ could see the look of surprise on Mark's face as he picked it up.

"Where did you find this?" Mark's voice was shaky and uneven.

"That's not important."

"It certainly is," Mark said, clearly agitated. "I didn't sign this."

DJ ignored his claims of innocence. "I think you did. How was Rebecca's land deeded to Victoria Maxwell?" She moved around the desk, prompting Mark to roll the high-back leather chair between them.

"I don't know. Maybe Rebecca didn't want the land and sold it herself." Mark kept a firm grip on the chair and pointed to the date on the document. "This happened long before I started seeing her."

DJ pointed to the scribbled line across the bottom. "That still doesn't account for your signature."

"That's not mine."

"Okay. Let's say it's not. Why would the county records show that Maxwell's father originally owned the land?" DJ wasn't going to let up. Mark had a hand in this. She just didn't know exactly where.

"I have no idea," Mark said, keeping a tight grip on the chair.

"All the documents filed at the county show that everything in that area *is,* and *has been*, owned by the Maxwell family for quite a long time."

Mark made a wide-eyed gesture at the pile of documents on the desk. "I'm aware of that."

"Someone has gone to a great deal of trouble to make these documents look authentic, and your signature is on all of them."

"I don't like what you're implying." Still keeping his distance, Mark moved around to the front of his desk. "I think it's time you left, Ms. Callahan."

"I don't really care what you don't like." DJ reached for the copy of the deed on the desk and slid it into her briefcase. "You leave Kathryn Jackson alone."

"Is that some kind of a threat?"

DJ's narrowed her eyes as she moved closer. Mark didn't flinch this time.

"Threat. Warning. Advice. Take it whichever way you want. Just stay away from her." She took her case from the desk and headed out the door.

❖

Elizabeth's private nurse was in the room checking her blood pressure when DJ arrived at the Belmont estate.

"Is everything all right?" DJ asked the nurse as she entered.

The nurse smiled. "Everything's fine. Just checking vitals."

"Back so soon?" Elizabeth said in her usual sweet manner.

She waited for the nurse to finish up and leave the room. "We need to talk."

Elizabeth pointed to the chair next to the bed. "Come. Sit down."

DJ remained standing as she glided a hand across her stiff, spiked hair and felt it tickle her palm. "I can't help you anymore, Elizabeth. If you want Kathryn involved in Montco Oil, you're going to have to find some other way to convince her."

"Having a sudden attack of conscience?"

"I guess I am."

"What about your family and their farm? Have you lost all loyalty to them?"

A wave of guilt filled her. "I'll have to find another way to resolve that issue. Kat loves the life she's built for herself at the ranch, and I'm not going to help you take it away." DJ knew that once Kat discovered her original motive for coming to the ranch, she'd never forgive her. In any case, DJ couldn't deceive her any longer, not even to save the farm.

"Even if you can't share it with her?" Elizabeth's voice softened. She must have caught the uncertainty in DJ's eyes. "You're in love with her."

A shot of heat flashed through DJ. Could she be right? Was she in love with Kat? After only a few days? She shook her head. "No. That's not possible." It certainly couldn't be her moral sense making her second-guess the task. DJ had always led Elizabeth to believe she was a woman who lived life without regret. She'd never revealed any of the torment from her past that she kept locked inside.

"You may not realize it yet, but I can see that you are."

"But Rebecca—"

"You and Rebecca have put on quite a show to make me think you're involved, but we both know that's not true."

"You sent me out there, knowing full well she'd intrigue me." DJ's voice rose, and she tried to suppress her anger. "That was your plan all along, wasn't it?"

"Of course," Elizabeth said matter-of-factly, obviously indifferent to any consequences she might have created. "I sent someone I knew could bring her to Austin."

DJ shook her head. "Don't count on that, Elizabeth."

"Would that be so bad, Danica? Sporting Kathryn on your arm at all those boring society parties?" Persuasion rang clearly in Elizabeth's voice.

"She wouldn't be happy here." DJ shrugged as she turned toward the door. "You'd know that if you'd ever taken the time to visit her."

"Are you sure about that? Not even with you?" Elizabeth's voice rose sharply.

"I'd rather let her go than bring her here to be a pawn in your games." DJ didn't look back as she closed the door behind her.

After clearing the gates, DJ sped down the road past the cabins to Kat's house. She glanced at her watch and saw it was already close to six o'clock. Virgil met her at the door and handed her the duffel bag she'd brought, the manila envelope containing her initial research on Kat and Montco Oil sticking out of the top. Her world spun as panic rushed her, and she grabbed the porch railing for balance.

"She doesn't want to see you," Virgil said firmly. "And I can't say I blame her."

DJ took the envelope from the top of her bag. "Did she read these?"

"Yep. Every one of them."

"Damn," DJ said, jamming it into the bag. "Where is she?"

Virgil narrowed his eyes. "I think you should just leave her alone."

"Please, Virgil?" DJ's voice deflated. "I need to explain this to her." Forgiveness was a long shot. She hadn't been honest with either of them.

Virgil eyed her for a minute as he twisted one end of his mustache. "She's out on the ranch somewhere. I'd check that tree by the river first."

"Thanks." DJ turned and headed for the farm truck.

"You'll make it there faster if you take a horse," Virgil shouted after her.

She nodded and veered off toward the stable.

❖

Pain shot through DJ's fist as she smashed it against the walnut tree. She'd been certain Kat would be here. She walked over and plunged her hand into the river, soothing it in the icy-cold water. After wrapping it in a handkerchief, she dropped down by the tree and shook her head. Her stomach rolled as the mixed bag of emotions assaulted her. She was thoroughly disgusted with herself for being such a fraud. Kat had been truthful with her from the very start, and she'd deceived her in an unforgivable way. DJ had experienced deceit herself and knew how hurtful it was.

As a young girl, DJ had spent most of her free time at the small rodeo arena in her hometown, practicing, making sure her timing was perfect enough to compete on the professional rodeo circuit. Becoming a rodeo star was her dream, a dream that someone she loved dearly had shattered. DJ would never forget that day her father made her leave the farm and forced her to take a path she didn't particularly want to travel. She'd given up her rodeo dreams to go to college, then to law school to help support her family, only to lose her father years later before she could find it in herself to forgive him.

She didn't blame him anymore. Her father had only wanted a more secure future for her. He might have been right, but it took DJ a long time to forgive him. He had purposely broken DJ's spirit with good intentions. DJ had never realized how hard it must have been for him until now. She'd let Elizabeth seduce her with the promise to save her family's farm from foreclosure. She'd had good intentions as well, but DJ had betrayed Kat in the process.

Her mind strayed to thoughts of the night before, thoughts of making love to Kat and of Kat making love to her. Waking in the morning with Kat's body molded to hers. She was in love with Kat. Sadness filled her at the thought of never holding her in her arms again. She hauled herself to her feet and searched the hillside, hoping to catch a glimpse of Kat. When she didn't show herself, DJ climbed on her horse and rode farther down the trail.

After searching the trails endlessly, DJ returned to the stable and settled the horse into her stall before walking over to Kat's house.

Virgil sat on the front porch, slowly teetering back and forth while he sipped on a beer. "No luck, huh?"

DJ flopped down into the chair next to Virgil. "She hasn't come in yet?"

"Give her some time. She'll talk to you when she's ready." Virgil's protective manner had softened measurably from their last conversation. "You gonna explain any of this to me?"

She was legally bound not to disclose her conversations with Elizabeth Belmont, but DJ seemed to have found an ally in Virgil. Holding back now would be a mistake, but confiding in Virgil could jeopardize any promise of redemption that Kat might offer in the future.

DJ blew out a short breath. "It's complicated."

Virgil nodded. "Most everything is when it comes to the Belmonts."

DJ shook her head and said, "I've never had this much trouble dealing with a woman before in my life."

Virgil chuckled. "Kat's not just any woman."

"You're right about that." DJ tugged her lip up to the side.

"You want a beer?" Virgil asked, drinking down the last of the one he'd been holding.

"No thanks. I need to take a shower and clean up." DJ picked up her bag and went down the steps. "You didn't change the lock on my room, did you?"

"Not yet."

"When she gets here, tell her I'll be in the bar," DJ shouted, walking across the grounds to her cabin.

Chapter Seventeen

Kat watched from the barn as DJ sat on the porch talking to Virgil. She grabbed hold of the wood as the raw pain spiked. Her heart physically ached. She waited and watched as DJ walked across the grounds to her cabin. Kat didn't want to…couldn't see her right now. Her head was too scattered, and her heart might never forgive her. Once DJ was out of sight, she came out of the barn, dashed around the corral to the back of the house, and snuck in through the screen door.

"Come on out here and talk to me," Virgil said quietly as he rocked. "I know you're in there. I heard the door squeak when you came in."

Kat stood just inside the screen door without saying a word.

"Why don't you let the girl explain?"

"I'm too angry right now, Virgil."

"You can't avoid her forever."

"I know." Kat pressed her forehead against the mesh of the screen door. "Can you take care of things around here for a few days?"

"Where you goin'?"

"Austin. I think it's time I had a chat with my mother."

He looked over his shoulder at her. "You sure you wanna do that?"

"I don't want to, Virgil, but I have to find out what this is all about."

"Okay. I'll take care of things here."

"Thanks." She leaned out the door, kissed him on the cheek, and then went inside to pack.

Kat had been propped up against the tree, captivated by the red glow of the river as the sun dipped lazily down behind the treetops.

She'd always felt safe and closest to Arizona in that particular spot by the river. The two of them had spent many an afternoon fhere in the past, dreaming about their future, forgetting their past, and making love.

Kat had been angry at Arizona for leaving her. So angry, she'd stayed away for a long time after she'd died. She'd promised to be here forever, and then suddenly Kat was left tending to the dream they shared all alone. She'd made many mistakes after Arizona died, searching endlessly for comfort, for some way to dull the pain, and hit rock bottom with Victoria Maxwell. Finding her way back to a balanced physical and emotional existence wasn't easy. Kat had finally realized she wasn't trying to punish Arizona. She was punishing herself for letting her go out alone that day.

Since day one at the Jumpin' J Ranch, checking the trails had been a daily ritual they'd always enjoyed together. The morning Arizona died, they were both angry. They'd fought about something Kat couldn't even recall now. Arizona had gotten on her horse, leaving her behind, and Kat hadn't followed. She couldn't help but think Arizona would still be alive if she'd gone after her.

The dream she'd had of Arizona today had been as real as an IMAX movie. She hadn't had one in days, but when she'd been at the river earlier, Arizona was right there propped up next to her. A long piece of straw hung from the corner of her mouth as her lips curled into the cocky grin Kat adored.

"I sure know how to pick 'em, don't I?" Kat shook her head.

She heard Arizona's soothing voice. "You're gonna be all right, Kat."

"What's the matter with me, Arizona?" She sighed. "I've fallen for a woman who isn't at all who she said she was."

"You're not gonna find another woman like me, darlin'." Arizona took the straw from her mouth and flicked it into the dirt.

"I know." Kat's voice hollowed as she reached to touch Arizona's face.

"You'll always love me, Kat, but you have to let me go." Arizona stood up and walked toward the river. Turning back momentarily, she smiled. "Your heart has the right idea. Let it lead you."

Arizona's message was painfully clear. It was time to move on.

Whether that included DJ was yet to be seen. Her heart sure felt like it did.

The rhythmic sound of hooves hitting the trail had slowly brought Kat out of her drowsy state. She hadn't been able to see anyone in the distance, but the sound had continued to amplify. The horse had been coming her way, and she didn't want to see anyone, especially DJ. Kat had mounted Minow and galloped up the hill into the trees. When DJ rotated, stared up into the trees, and shouted her name, Kat had led Minow along behind her and ducked farther into the wooded area. It seemed as though, somehow, DJ knew exactly where she was. She'd wiped the tears from her cheeks and rubbed her hand across Minow's side as the horse stood motionless, huge brown eyes staring at her. It was time to go to Austin and settle some things. She'd patted Minow lightly before climbing into the saddle and riding to the house.

Kat opened the door and entered the massive foyer of the Belmont estate. The door was unlocked, so she hadn't knocked. The heels of her rarely worn leather pumps clicked against the marble floor as she crossed the foyer. She slowed and inhaled the aroma of fresh-baked cornbread in the air. Warmth filled her body. As she stood at the foot of the winding staircase, memories rushed her as though she'd left only yesterday.

Kat noticed the elevator that led to the floor above, a new addition since she'd lived here. She smiled, thinking of the playroom where she and her sister had spent most of their time as children. She doubted it looked anything like it had when she was young. The toys and dolls had probably been long since discarded. The rest of the floor was all bedrooms—hers and Rebecca's at one end of the house, and each of her parents had a room at the other. Separate rooms didn't seem odd to Kat as a child, but by the time she was twelve, she knew things were strained between her parents. All her friends had parents who ate together, laughed together, and slept together. Her parents shared locked doors, disconnected lives, and separate bedrooms. The only thing they seemed to agree on was their decision to cut her out of the family.

She remembered the harsh words she and her father had spoken and stiffened. The warmth she'd felt vanished. She trembled as the argument still echoed clearly in her mind. The ultimatum, her defiance, and the sadness that had ripped through her as she'd left the only home she'd ever known.

Her stomach rolled. *Coming here was a mistake.* She had just turned to leave when she heard a voice through the doorway behind her. "Most people ring the bell and wait to be invited in." Kat whirled around and smiled broadly at the sound of the strong, velvet-edged voice. "Oh, my Lord. Is that you, Miss Kathryn?" Maggie asked, grabbing Kat's hands and holding them tightly. "Look at how beautiful you've become." She beamed.

"Flattery will get you everywhere, Maggie." Kat kissed her on the cheek, and the woman threw her arms around her, holding her as if she would never let go.

"Now you know, I'm nothing but truthful," Maggie said into her ear.

The warmth returned and Kat smiled. "You're too kind."

"Let me look at you." Maggie sighed. "We have greatly missed your smile in this house."

"I've missed you too." Kat leaned forward, reached into the pocket of Maggie's apron, and took out a piece of hard candy. "I see you still have that sweet tooth."

"But no one to share with anymore." Maggie's voice lulled her.

Kat unwrapped the butterscotch disc and popped it into her mouth before stepping into the living room. She took in a deep breath as she beheld the many things she remembered from her childhood. Dark cherrywood tables and authentic Tiffany lamps still accented the perfectly placed paisley cream furniture.

"Everything is exactly as I remember." Kat cut quickly across the room and through the doorway to the sitting area that housed the baby-grand piano she'd spent so many hours playing. *Yes, exactly the same.* She turned to look at the huge rock fireplace and smiled. On gloomy, wet days when she couldn't go to the ranch, and she'd already played her fingers numb, she would sit in the oversized love seat in front of the roaring fire and read. Kat had loved this room.

"Do you still play, Miss Kathryn?"

She slid onto the piano bench and lifted the cover from the keys. "Not really." A piano was a luxury she couldn't afford at the ranch. She stroked the smooth ivory keys before spreading her fingers, dashing off a piece of Mozart's Sonata Number 15. "It's something you never forget."

"I've missed that beautiful music flowing through the halls. It kept this house alive."

She slid the cover back across the keys and let her hands drop to her lap. "Why did she keep it?" Kat said softly, the pain in her heart deepening just a bit.

"You know your mother. She doesn't like change," Maggie said under her breath.

Kat laughed and slid off the bench. "Is she still eating oatmeal and brown sugar for breakfast?"

"Every day." Maggie chuckled along with her.

Kat's laughter faded with a tentative look through the doorway to the set of portraits of her parents hanging on the living room wall. "Is she all right? I mean, after the accident."

Maggie took Kat's hand and led her out of the room, commanding her attention away from the daunting portrait of her father. She gave her a cheerful smile. "She still spends quite a lot of time in bed, but she's moving around much better now."

Kat knew she was trying to lift the cloud that darkened the room. Maggie had witnessed the whole excruciatingly final event. It had been just as hard for Maggie to watch as it was for Kat to walk out that door ten years ago.

"That's good to hear," Kat said, returning her smile as she held the tears threatening to drown her eyes.

"The doctor insists that she stand up and walk the hallway at least twice a day. He told her if she didn't, she might as well just resign herself to using a wheelchair for the rest of her days. And you know she's too stubborn for that."

Kat rolled her eyes. "I *do* know that." She straightened her skirt. "Well, I guess I can't put this off any longer." She took in a deep breath and headed to the staircase.

Maggie gave her an encouraging smile. "It'll make her happy to see you, Miss Kathryn."

Kat turned briefly before starting up. "I'm not so sure about that, Maggie."

After reaching the top of the stairs, Kat continued down the corridor to the last door on the right. Her mother's bedroom. She hesitated for a moment before opening the door and poking her head inside, detecting the same sweet-scented perfume she remembered as a child. After she crept quietly into the room and slid her handbag onto the dresser next to a few framed pictures, she picked up one and was surprised to find it was her college graduation picture. She picked up the other. It was her sister, Rebecca. She'd grown into a beautiful woman. She returned it to its place and crossed the room to sit in the chair next to her sleeping mother.

Elizabeth's face was stripped of all makeup, and her fingers were devoid of nail polish. Her mother had aged so much since she'd seen her last. Kat watched her chest rise and fall. Elizabeth had become small and frail. She'd always been a delicate woman, and now she looked as though she'd lost quite a bit of weight. Probably due to the accident. Kat had seen her picture in the society pages a few times in recent years, but touched-up black-and-white photos didn't represent anything close to reality.

"Maggie," Elizabeth mumbled, rolling over and pushing the button on the intercom. Apparently, when she woke, she hadn't seen Kat sitting in the chair.

Maggie's voice rang through the speaker. "Yes, Mrs. Belmont."

"Coffee, please." Her hand swept the mattress until she found the remote and raised the top of the bed into a sitting position. "Did I hear someone playing the piano?"

"Even flat on your back, you're still in command," Kat said with a twinge of laughter in her voice.

Elizabeth's eyes lit with a smile. "Oh. I didn't see you there, Kathryn."

Kat hadn't anticipated her mother's warm welcome, and emotion stilled her as she searched for words. "I'm sure I'm the last person you expected to see." Kat folded her hands neatly in her lap.

"You're looking well," Elizabeth said, politely surveying her. "Country life seems to agree with you."

"Yes, it does."

Maggie came through the door with a tray of coffee. After setting it on the table, she poured Elizabeth a cup and handed it to her.

"Thank you, dear."

"You're welcome." She returned to the pot. "Would you like a cup, Miss Kathryn?"

"Thanks, Maggie. I'll get it in a minute."

"Isn't it wonderful to see Miss Kathryn again?" Maggie said, giving Elizabeth a pressing look.

"Yes. It certainly is," she said, with what seemed like a genuine smile.

"Let me know when you're ready for breakfast," Maggie said as she moved across the room.

"I'll have oatmeal and brown sugar today."

Kat laughed at her mother's unvaried breakfast choice as she went to the silver decanter and poured herself a cup of coffee. She doused it with cream and took a sip before sitting down.

"Let's cut to the chase, Mother. What do you want?"

Elizabeth raised her cup to her lips, let a small amount of the steaming liquid flow into her mouth, and then set it on the table next to the bed before responding. "I want you to be part of the family again."

Kat couldn't believe her mother's audacity. "It's a little late for that, isn't it?"

"I know it's been a long time since we've spoken, Kathryn, but I want you to know, I've missed you." Elizabeth's voice was soft and loving.

Kat stirred at her mother's sweet, subtle tone, remembering the many times she'd used it to soothe her as a child. She fought to ignore the emotions it provoked. "Mother, let's be honest, shall we?" The delicate china cup clanged against the saucer as Kat slid it onto the table. "If you'd really missed me, you could've come out to the ranch any time."

Elizabeth peered through thinning lashes, and her pale-blue eyes looked uncharacteristically timid. "I thought about it many times, but I wasn't sure how I'd be received."

Kat gave her a slight nod before shifting in the chair and crossing her legs. "I have to admit, I can't honestly say you would've been welcome."

Her mother's forehead creased with a sincere look of uncertainty. "It would have been your right to turn me away."

"Yes. It would have. But I doubt I would've done it." Kat fidgeted with the material on the arm of the chair for a moment. "You are still my mother."

Elizabeth closed her eyes and shook her head. "You're much more forgiving than I, Kathryn."

"I didn't say anything about forgiveness, Mother. I've just moved on with my life." Kat retrieved her cup from the night table and brought it to her lips again. "Now, let's get to the reason I'm here. Why do you need me here? Isn't Rebecca running the company?"

"Your sister still has a lot to learn about the business world."

"And you think I can teach her?" Kat laughed. "I'm sure she knows more about Montco Oil than I ever will."

"She may have the business knowledge, but you have the maturity. Working together, the two of you would be just the right balance." Elizabeth laced her fingers in her lap. "And with Charles gone now, she's going to need some guidance."

"I'm sure Rebecca would resent any guidance I would presume to give her. If the situation were reversed, I certainly would."

"But the two of you used to be so close."

Kat lowered her eyes. "That was a long time ago."

Elizabeth took a deep breath. "If you don't agree to come to Austin, I may have to take control myself."

Kat glanced up to meet Elizabeth's gaze. "That would be a *wise* decision." Her voice was thick with sarcasm. "I'm sure you haven't set foot through the door of that company in at least twenty years.

"That doesn't mean I can't, or won't," Elizabeth said coolly, sliding her cup and saucer onto the night table. "Can I count on your support?"

Kat shook her head. "I'm not coming back, Mother." She raised the delicate china cup to her lips and took one last drink of coffee. "Now, if that's all you wanted, I'll be on my way."

Elizabeth threw up the blanket and then fastened it tightly across her legs. "I can't believe you have no interest in the company at all?"

"None whatsoever." Kat pushed out of the chair and stood briefly at Elizabeth's bedside. "But I am glad to see you're doing well," she said softly, her voice cracking. Her emotions surfacing, Kat picked up her bag and rushed to the door. As she reached for the knob, the door flew open, flattening her against the wall behind it.

The door swung closed again, and she watched Rebecca sail

into the room. Apparently, her little sister had discovered the perks of femininity while Kat was away. Blessed with long legs and a curvy body, she had the kind of shape any woman would envy. Kat was sure those assets came in handy when negotiating a business deal.

"Good morning, Mother," Rebecca chanted, crossing the room and dropping a pile of magazines into Elizabeth's lap. "I think that should be everything you asked for." She turned and dropped her purse on the nightstand before kissing her on the cheek.

"Look who's here, dear." Elizabeth motioned behind Rebecca, where Kat stood against the wall motionless, still stunned from the impact of both the door and seeing her little sister all grown up.

"Well, if it isn't my long-lost sister." Hard and vindictive, Rebecca's voice didn't even shudder.

"Hello, Rebecca," Kat said uneasily. "How've you been?"

Rebecca's gaze swept across her, scrutinizing Kat from head to toe. "I've been absolutely wonderful. As if you care."

Kat ignored the glare and nasty tone, yet still fumbled for something to say. Anxiety stifled any semblance of words that came to mind. Rightfully so. She didn't know the first thing about her sister. It had been ten years since she'd seen Rebecca. Kat had no idea how to interact with her, let alone deal with this prim-and-proper ogre hurling attitude at her.

"I was hoping you might come stay with me at the ranch sometime," Kat finally managed as she crossed the room.

"Why would I do that?" Rebecca flipped her hair onto her shoulders. "Herding cattle is not my idea of fun."

"You wouldn't have to do any of that." She put her hand on Rebecca's arm, letting it drop quickly when she recoiled. "I just thought maybe we could get to know each other again."

"I'm not sure I want to do that either."

"Well, you're always welcome." Kat's voice withered as Rebecca's words stabbed at her heart. She'd never meant to hurt her sister. She'd only wanted her freedom. Apparently she'd alienated Rebecca in the process. Elizabeth and Charles had probably done everything they could to poison Rebecca's mind against her over the years.

CHAPTER EIGHTEEN

It was a little past seven a.m. when DJ wandered across the road to Kat's house. She'd meant to be up earlier but hadn't had much sleep last night, and she'd had more than a few drinks while she'd waited in the bar hoping Kat would show up. She hadn't shown, and it was close to midnight before DJ had left. She'd stood in front of Kat's house, wanting an opportunity to talk to her, but didn't see a light on in the place.

DJ had made a mistake. A phenomenally huge fuckup. If Kat would just give her a chance to explain, DJ would make her understand that she'd never intended to hurt her. She certainly had never intended to fall in love with her. Did Kat even know she'd captured her heart without trying?

As she'd stood staring, looking for some sign of Kat in the darkness, all she'd wanted was go inside, crawl into her bed, and make love to her. She'd even thought seriously about doing it. She'd knocked on the door but had no answer. She'd wanted to settle everything right then and there. But aggressive wasn't the way to go with Kat, so DJ let her be for the night. Maybe she would be willing to listen this morning.

"Kat," she said as she knocked on the screen door.

Virgil pushed the door open. "She's not here."

"Where is she?" DJ walked past him, searching the house.

"Left for Austin before sunup."

Fuck! DJ slammed the screen door open and ran across the grounds to her car. She slid into the driver's seat of her BMW and fired the engine. After jamming it into gear, she spun out in the gravel before picking up her cell phone and punching in Elizabeth's private number.

The phone remained silent, and she pulled it from her ear and saw the no-service message on the screen. She cursed and tossed it onto the passenger seat as she headed out the main gate.

It had never entered DJ's mind that Kat would actually go to Austin. All she needed was Kat, Elizabeth, and Rebecca in the same room together—discussing her. She didn't think things could get much worse, but if Kat got to them first, Elizabeth would manipulate the situation. Her current relationship ruse with Rebecca would complicate things even further.

DJ was just entering the Austin city limits when she tried to call again. The phone rang twice before Elizabeth answered. "Hello," she said pleasantly.

"Hello, Elizabeth. How are you feeling today?" DJ asked calmly. She didn't want to let on that anything was wrong.

"I'm doing much better, thank you," Elizabeth said.

"Is Kathryn there with you?" DJ suspected she was. It was unusual for Elizabeth not to call her by name when they spoke.

"Yes, darling." Elizabeth hesitated. "She's right here. Would you like to speak with her?"

"No. That's not necessary. I'll be there in a few minutes. Please don't let her leave."

"I'll see you then," Elizabeth said sweetly.

After DJ burst through the door, she fixed her gaze on Kat, standing in front of the window looking out. DJ almost didn't recognize the woman with whom she'd become so intimately acquainted. Dressed in a light-blue skirt and jacket, Kat wore her long, velvety hair twisted up and fastened neatly in a clip. She followed the line of Kat's long, slender legs as they crept up under the mid-calf length skirt clinging to them. She was stunning.

"Dani, darling," Rebecca cooed, barely touching her cheek with her lips. "I wasn't expecting to see you today. Mother said she'd sent you off on some sort of adventure." Rebecca snaked her arm around DJ's and led her across the room. "Come. I have a surprise for you. This is my sister, Kathryn." She tugged DJ closer. "Dani's my fiancée."

Kat turned, and her tentative smile dropped the instant she saw

DJ. Shock evident in her eyes, she offered her hand reluctantly. "Hello, DJ." Her voice was cordial but cold, and it stung.

"It's nice to see you again, Kat." DJ took Kat's hand gently. Kat gave her absolutely no physical response, but she could see the fury smoldering in her eyes. DJ would settle for anger at this point. If Kat was angry, she was feeling something deeper inside.

"Oh, you've already met?" Rebecca asked, apparently observing the tension between them.

DJ didn't take her eyes from Kat's angry stare. "Yes. We've met."

"When?"

"Just this past week." Kat slowly slipped her hand from DJ's and squared her shoulders. "Didn't Mother tell you? She sent her looking for me at the ranch."

Rebecca gave her mother a peculiar look. "That was the adventure you sent her on?" Her gaze snapped to Kat. "I had no idea."

"Kathryn, why don't you and Danica have lunch today?" Elizabeth suggested. "You can get to know each other a little better."

"No need for that, Mother. I think I'm familiar enough with Ms. Callen."

"Callen?" Rebecca's brows drew together.

"It's actually Callahan," DJ said in a low, rumbling whisper.

"My mistake." Kat narrowed her eyes and gave her a fuck-you smile. "I'm sure Ms. Callahan has some other unsuspecting woman to prey on."

"Kat, let me explain," DJ said softly.

"What's to explain? My mother sent you in to close the deal." Kat kept her distance and choked out a cynical laugh. "And you almost did it."

She moved toward her. "Kat, you know it wasn't like that."

"Do I?" She threw her hands up in front of her, gesturing for DJ not to come any closer. "I'm not sure what it was exactly. But I *do* know it's over."

Kat's words sliced deep in DJ's heart. "Let's go somewhere and talk."

"Yes. Why don't you two go down to the study," Elizabeth interjected. "You can have a private conversation there."

"No. I can't do this right now." Kat patted her sides looking for pockets. "Where are my keys?" she said absently, then brushed past DJ to grab her purse from the chair. She searched through it, found her keys, and hurried through the doorway to the stairs.

"Kat, wait," DJ shouted, then turned to Elizabeth. "Do you have any idea what you've done?"

"I haven't done anything. Rebecca just told her the truth, didn't you?" She looked over at Rebecca, prompting her to let out an annoyed breath.

"I'm sorry, Dani. I didn't know."

"Damn it, Elizabeth!" She took off out the door after her.

Rebecca had no idea what had happened, but evidently her mother had set it up. The only questions now were why her mother had sent DJ to see Kat at the ranch and what had happened between them while she was there.

"Mother, what the hell is going on here?" Rebecca stood next to the bed waiting for an answer.

A sneaky smile crept across Elizabeth's face. "Apparently, Danica and your sister have become rather close in the past week."

Her hands went to her hips. "You sent Dani off to have an affair with my sister?"

Elizabeth nodded. "Yes. I did."

Rebecca raised an eyebrow. "Fully aware that she's my fiancée?"

Elizabeth frowned. "We both know that's just a fraudulent attempt to keep me out of your affairs."

Rebecca crossed her arms and shrugged. The old bird was smarter than she thought. "You sent DJ there, knowing exactly what would happen." Rebecca spread her lips into a half-smile.

Elizabeth's smile was wide, as if she was satisfied her plan was playing out the way she'd hoped. "I had a suspicion."

"And now your scheme has backfired on you."

"It hasn't completely gone bad." Elizabeth's brows drew in, defining the lines on her forehead. "Did you see Kathryn's face? She's fallen in love with Danica." She tugged on the sheet and folded it down neatly over the blanket. "Now she'll move to Austin to be with her."

"I wouldn't count on that, Mother." Rebecca plucked her handbag from the nightstand. "Right now, because of you, she thinks Dani's a cheating liar."

"That will pass."

Rebecca moved toward the door. "And when it does, what makes you so sure she'll come to Austin?"

"She'll come. She loves her," Elizabeth said confidently.

Rebecca stopped and turned momentarily. "You know Dani grew up on a farm in Johnson City?"

"Yes. I'm aware."

"She wanted to be a rodeo star when she was a kid."

"She never told me that."

Rebecca shook her head and smiled lightly as she turned to go out the door. "You should've done a little more research, Mother. You may have just lost your star lawyer."

Kat rushed down the stairs and out the front door. When she'd realized who DJ actually was, Kat had suddenly felt very foolish. It was just like a scene from a bad movie, only the audience of two was on the edge of their seats taking in every word she'd said. She had to get out of there before she lost it.

DJ caught up with her and took her arm before she could start down the front steps. "Wait a minute."

Kat yanked her arm, trying to break free. "It all makes sense now. That's why you left me standing there that night on the porch."

DJ held firm, swinging Kat around to face her. "Just let me explain."

"What's to explain? You're engaged to my sister." Kat's voice wavered as she tried unsuccessfully to disguise the pain crushing her heart. "Have you told her you slept with me?" she continued, desperately trying to hold back the tears.

DJ shook her head.

Kat mustered up all the venom she could. "You're a liar and a cheat, and now you've been caught."

"I'm not cheating on her."

"Then why doesn't she know about us?"

"How could she know? *I've* only known about us for a few days."
DJ let out a heavy breath and released Kat's arm. "Rebecca and I did go
out a few times." She rubbed her neck. "But it wasn't serious."

"You're engaged. If that's not serious, I don't know what is," Kat
said as she spun toward the steps.

"We're not engaged. Elizabeth just thinks we are."

Kat whirled back around. "Why would she think that?" Kat's
voice softened. She didn't know what to believe.

"You know your mother as well as I do. She likes to make other
people's decisions for them. Rebecca and I decided it was easier to let
her think we were, so she'd stay out of our love lives."

Kat knew her mother was *very* controlling. It didn't surprise her.
"Meaning?" Her tone spiked again.

"Meaning, we're *not* engaged." DJ threw up her hands.

"Apparently, Rebecca doesn't know that."

"She knows. Believe me, she knows." DJ closed her eyes and
shook her head. "She doesn't want to be with a woman."

"You sound disappointed."

DJ's eyes snapped open, and her gaze returned quickly to Kat's.
"No. Not at all."

"So, you thought you'd give the older sister a try?" Kat was on an
emotional roller coaster as her anger spiked again. "God, I can't believe
this. I should've known it was too..." Kat's voice cracked.

"Too what, Kat?"

Kat could see the question in DJ's eyes, and her heart hammered.
"Too fucking good to be true."

"But it is true, Kat." DJ wrapped her arm around Kat's waist and
inched her closer. "You've done something to me I can't explain." Her
voice was a whisper, emotion spilling out in her words.

Kat pushed out of her arms. "Jesus, DJ. I didn't even know your
real name until a few minutes ago. How am I supposed to know who
you are?" Her mother had called her Danica, Rebecca had called her
Dani, and Kat knew her as DJ. Her name was as phony as the woman
she'd proved to be.

"What about you? The makeup, the suit, the hair. I almost didn't
recognize you."

"Isn't this what you want?" Kat's lips trembled as she fought to
keep her voice steady. "A corporate woman?" Kat motioned down the

front of her with her hands. "Well, take a good last look, because this woman is not moving to Austin."

"God, no, Kat. This isn't what I want. This isn't you." DJ removed the clip from Kat's hair and let it fall to her shoulders. She moved closer, and Kat sank into her arms as DJ touched her lips gently with her own. Kat reached up, took DJ's face in her hands, and plunged further into the kiss. The familiar bounce in Kat's belly surfaced as DJ's tongue joined Kat's in the erotic dance she'd had the pleasure of performing only a few times but had come to crave.

Kat ripped her lips away and stared into DJ's eyes. "You know, that right there, and that wonderful thing we did the other night?" Kat waited for DJ to nod. "There was so much more." She shook her head. "That was just a taste of what we could've had, you and I."

"We can still have it, Kat." DJ pressed her lips to Kat's again.

The kiss had been bittersweet. Her strength was weakening as emotions battled between what she wanted to do and what she couldn't. What she'd *already* done. Kat couldn't continue to have these feelings for a woman involved with her sister. *What the fuck was I thinking? Sleeping with someone after knowing her for only a few days.*

Kat heard footsteps on the porch and pushed out of DJ's arms. She looked up to see Rebecca staring, her vivid blue eyes burning through her like lasers. She was clearly letting Kat know she'd crossed the boundaries. Kat scrambled down the steps and climbed into the huge dually truck she'd parked in the drive. The starter whined momentarily before it caught, and then she threw it into gear and let the tires squeal as she sped down the road and out the gates.

Rebecca had stood in the front doorway and watched the reunion unfold, and it oddly tugged at her heart. Her sister and her ex-lover kissing right in front of her, and she didn't have the slightest twinge of jealousy. She must be going soft. Kat had clearly been shaken at the sight of her watching. Rebecca didn't know by which—the kiss or because she'd been caught.

Rebecca took a step down the stairs. "Comparing sisters?" she said, raising an eyebrow. "That was some fireworks show upstairs."

DJ held up a finger in warning. "Don't start."

"I didn't start anything…DJ. Is that what she calls you?" Rebecca laced her voice with sarcasm. "But apparently *you* have." She continued to tease, ignoring DJ's commanding tone, which she'd become familiar with over the past few years.

DJ dropped down and sat on the steps. "Don't tell me you're jealous."

Rebecca shook her head and smiled. "Not in the slightest."

DJ rubbed her face. "Then why did you tell her we were engaged?"

Rebecca lifted her shoulders. "I didn't know you knew her. I was just keeping with the ruse." She touched DJ's shoulder and sat down on the step next to her. "And I had no idea the two of you were *involved*."

"Well, now you know." DJ let out a heavy breath. "That is, if she'll still have me."

Rebecca let a quiet laugh escape her lips. "Wow. You really are smitten." She put her hand on DJ's back and traced the Western outline of her shirt before stroking her hand across it. "What happened to never settling down?"

A slow smile crept across DJ's face as though she were reliving a memory. "Kat's different. She's not like any woman I've ever known."

Rebecca rested her head against DJ's shoulder. "Any woman?" She'd thought she might have made some impact on DJ. She let out a sigh and wrapped her arm around her.

DJ twisted to look at her, and her brows drew together. "You made the break with me, remember?"

"Well, I certainly wasn't going to let a woman with a reputation like yours break my poor little heart."

"Break *your* heart?" DJ chuckled. "You always have to be in control, don't you?" She brushed the hair from Rebecca's face. "It never would've worked out for us."

"You mean the penis thing?"

"Exactly."

Rebecca rocked her body against DJ's. "But we sure had fun, didn't we?"

DJ smiled and nodded. "Yes, we did."

Rebecca played with DJ's soft curls and then tugged on the collar of her shirt. "This look suits you. Maybe Kat does too."

DJ stared at the ground in front of her. "I don't know how it happened…I think when you finally meet your other half, you understand why you let all the others go."

"You don't owe me any explanations." Rebecca curved her lips into a soft smile. "She's in love with you, Dani."

DJ's head flew up, and her gaze snapped to Rebecca. "You think so?"

"It's pretty obvious." Rebecca propped her chin up on DJ's shoulder. "And you're in love with her."

DJ nodded. "God help me, I am."

"Well then, if you can remove Mother from the middle, maybe it will all work out," Rebecca said, being careful not to show any jealousy in her voice.

"You're being remarkably gracious about this."

Rebecca shrugged. "If it were any other woman, I'd probably be upset."

"Is it because she's your sister or because you've found someone new to occupy your time?"

"Now who's jealous?" Rebecca said, giving DJ a light slap on the shoulder.

"Would it matter if I were?" DJ asked, leaning back on the heels of her palms.

Rebecca shook her head and smiled. "Not really."

"You're something else, you know that?" DJ laughed lightly, stood up, and offered Rebecca her hand. "I need to find Kat."

"She's probably gone to Montco," Rebecca said as she took her hand and DJ helped her up off the step. "I'm not sure, but I think she may still have a small interest in the company." She swept her hand across the back of her skirt. "There's a board meeting next month, and now that Daddy's gone, she may want to see how things are being handled."

"You may be right." DJ slapped Rebecca on the butt as she started down the steps.

"Hey!" Rebecca stopped abruptly and gave her a stinging glare.

"What?" DJ's eyebrows rose. "You can't go into work looking like you've been sliding around in the dirt." She smiled, took her hand, and led her down the steps. "Why couldn't we ever work things out?"

Rebecca bumped her shoulder against DJ's playfully. "I don't like to battle for control."

"You're right about that." DJ chuckled, swinging her arm around Rebecca. "Come on. I'll give you a lift."

Rebecca turned and placed a finger on DJ's chest. "Why don't you let me talk to her first?"

DJ narrowed her eyes. "You're going to help me, right?"

"I promise." Rebecca kissed her on the cheek. "Go home. I'll call you later." She opened the door and slid into the driver's seat.

"You'd better." DJ didn't smile as she gripped the top of the door panel with her hand.

Rebecca started the car, looked up at DJ's seriously pained face, and laughed. "Don't worry. I won't let you down." She patted DJ's hand, prompting her to move it, and drove off.

CHAPTER NINETEEN

K at found herself sitting in the lobby of the Montco Oil Building, one of the oldest buildings still remaining in the downtown area. Frances Montgomery had purchased it to accommodate his growing company, Montco Oil, during the oil boom in the early seventies. She thumbed through a news magazine, looking absently at the pictures as she ran through the scene at her mother's house.

Staring out the window into the garden, Kat had blocked out her mother's rambling voice as she listened to the whoop of the whippoorwill nesting in the tree just outside. She'd been so entranced by the melodious bird she hadn't heard the door open or DJ's voice when she walked into the room. She'd only emerged from her thoughts and turned around when Rebecca had touched her on the shoulder. When she'd seen Rebecca with her arm snaked around DJ, Kat's stable world had shifted. And with the introduction of DJ as her fiancée, the back of her neck had burned, and the room suddenly grew smaller.

She should've bolted when Elizabeth had announced to Rebecca the phone call was from her betrothed and she'd shown her the ring. Kat had forgotten just how soft a society woman's hands could be as she took Rebecca's hand in hers and looked at the huge diamond sparkling on her finger. A gem that big had probably cost enough money to keep her ranch running for at the least a few years.

Rebecca had smiled as though she'd just won the lottery, and Kat had just assumed it was from some man who belonged to another wealthy family in Austin. Her mother had reminded her of the perks that went along with high society and told her she could have it back in an instant if she'd just come home. Kat remembered why she'd purposely blocked those perks from her mind. She wasn't prepared to pay the price that came with them, *ever*. She should've taken the cue to leave at that point, but she'd needed just a little more time in the comfort of her childhood home and ended up enduring the whole fucked-up show.

To make matters worse, when Rebecca had seen her kissing DJ on the porch, pure humiliation had rushed through her as she ran down the porch steps and climbed into the truck. She didn't wait the usual few seconds for the diesel battery to charge and clicked on the ignition. She'd prayed it would start, and thank God it had. She couldn't stay there another minute.

"What are you doing down here?" At the sound of Rebecca's voice, Kat shook herself out of the memory and fanned herself with the magazine. Rebecca gave her an odd look.

"They wouldn't let me go up." Kat tossed the magazine onto the table and stood. "Apparently, I don't have the proper security clearance."

"Oh. I'll take care of that right now." Rebecca led her over to the security desk.

"Good morning, Randy." Rebecca smiled at the handsome young security officer.

"Good morning, Miss Belmont," he said, returning her smile.

"This is my sister, Kathryn Jackson."

"Nice to meet you, Miss Jackson."

"Mrs.," Kat said, politely.

"Mrs. Jackson." He offered his hand.

"You also." Kat smiled, shaking it.

"Anything she wants, she gets. She's to have full clearance. Understand?"

Full clearance. Was that show for my benefit? Kat kept her smile friendly. She guessed Rebecca would change that stipulation later, when she found out why her mother wanted Kat in Austin. *Trust breeds trust, even if it's false.*

"Yes, ma'am. I'll take care of it this morning."

"Send her security badge up to my office."

"Will do."

"Come on," Rebecca said without a glance as she headed to the elevator.

"He looks pretty young to have so much responsibility." The boy couldn't be more than twenty years old.

"Who? Randy? He's just one of many young ones we have here. New ideas spring from new blood. He's not very high up in the scheme of things, but I try to make them all feel important. It produces a better work ethic."

Kat smiled, thinking about what her mother had said. If Rebecca was as ruthless as she thought, why would she take the time to motivate any of her employees, least of all the security staff?

Elegantly decorated in French provincial, Rebecca's office was on the twenty-fifth floor overlooking downtown Austin. Rebecca clearly had her mother's taste for the finer things.

"This is beautiful, Bec." Kat let Rebecca's nickname slip out and hoped she didn't protest.

"Thank you. I decorated it myself." Rebecca leaned against the front of her desk. "You want some coffee?"

"Sure."

"Still cream, no sugar?"

"Uh-huh." Surprised that Rebecca remembered, Kat let her stiff veneer crack a little. She'd never meant to hurt her sister. Rebecca's lack of communication after she'd left was a clear sign she had. Hoping to keep the fragile splinters hidden, Kat turned and picked up the antique vase centered on the small meeting table in the corner of the office. She traced the small, delicate veins of gold snaking through it. It was probably worth a few thousand dollars at the least.

Rebecca pushed the button on the intercom. "Jenny, could you bring coffee for two with cream, please."

"Be right in." Jenny's voice rang through the intercom, and within minutes she came through the door carrying a tray of coffee and croissants. "Anything else?" she asked as she transferred them from the tray to the coffee table.

"No. That's all for now. Thanks, Jenny." Rebecca smiled and sat down on the couch. She motioned to Kat. "Come sit. Tell me. What's brought you to Austin after all these years?"

"I'm here to find out why Mother is trying to drag me into this company."

As Rebecca reached for the coffee decanter, her finely arched brows drew together. "What exactly are you talking about?"

"She offered to give me a fair amount of company stock if I'd agree to come."

"How much stock?" Rebecca clanged the decanter onto the tray, clearly unaware of her mother's plans.

Kat contemplated what to tell her. She wanted to tread lightly but couldn't think of a way to do so. "Enough so that if I teamed with her, I'd have a controlling interest."

Rebecca hopped up from the couch and shot across the room. "Why would she do that? She knows you've never had any interest in Montco."

"You tell me." Kat lifted her cup, took a sip, and stared over the top of it at Rebecca as she seemed to process the information. "Why does she need someone to keep tabs on you?"

"She doesn't." Rebecca paced, gathering her thoughts. "She wouldn't do that." She seemed to be growing angrier by the minute. "Now that Daddy's gone, you're going to try to push me out."

Kat's cup rattled as she pushed it onto the coffee table. "Wait a minute." Kat jumped to her feet. "Let's get something straight here. She called me. I don't want anything to do with this company."

"If that were true, you wouldn't be here."

Kat held her tongue. Taking in a deep breath, she slid down onto the couch again. This wasn't the way she'd wanted this conversation to go. She'd come to Austin only to find out why her mother was offering her the stock. She hadn't planned to have a face-off with her sister in the process. In fact, she hadn't even planned to tell Rebecca about her mother's proposition. Kat was fully prepared to sign any stock she received directly over to Rebecca, no questions asked. She didn't intend to take anything away from her sister and definitely didn't want to become her enemy. They were very different women now, but Kat couldn't forget how close they were as children. Even though it wasn't under the best of circumstances, she was still hoping to regain some of that closeness.

Kat watched her continue to pace. She'd forgotten how emotional Rebecca could be. It had been a long time since they'd had any kind of rapport.

"I had a little time to chat with Mother this morning before you arrived." Kat picked up her cup, took another sip of coffee, and then calmly slid it onto the table.

Rebecca's stare snapped to Kat, and she narrowed her eyes. "Setting your plan into motion." Her tone was filled with accusation.

"She wants me to squeeze you out." In one smooth motion, Kat took a croissant from the tray, tore it apart, and stuffed a small piece into her mouth.

"What?"

"You heard me. Mother's the one who wants you out. Not me." Kat took another bite of her croissant and washed it down with her coffee. "Think about it, Bec. Why else would she give me the stock?"

Rebecca stood by her desk, her gaze fixed on Kat, measuring her carefully.

Kat dropped the remaining piece of roll onto her plate and dabbed her fingers with one of the cloth napkins on the tray. "I told her I wouldn't do it."

Rebecca's angry expression melted into one of uncertainty.

"Don't be so surprised. No matter how nasty you are to me, you're still my little sister. I would never do anything to hurt you." Kat relaxed into the couch and crossed her legs. "But tell me something, Bec. Why do you hate me so?" Kat watched as Rebecca crossed her arms and fidgeted like an angry child sifting through her thoughts.

"You left when I was sixteen." Rebecca's voice cracked as it rose. "I came home to an empty room with a scribbled note on the dresser." She reached into her desk, took out an old crinkled piece of paper, and dropped it in Kat's lap. "I couldn't believe you'd just leave like that without talking to me or at least telling me where you were going. When I realized you weren't coming back, it became simpler to hate you. It was difficult at first, but it was much easier than missing you." She looked away and blinked. "For God's sake, Kat. I didn't even know where you were until I was twenty."

Kat's stomach clenched as she flattened the creases in the note while she read it. She'd made so many bad decisions when she'd left, but this was clearly the biggest. She vividly recalled the day she wrote it. Leaving her sister to live alone in a household that was void of any type of love or affection was one of the hardest things she'd ever done. Everything she'd written was there, except the portion containing the address and phone number of the small house she and Arizona had called home while they'd built their ranch. It had been neatly cut off the bottom, so Rebecca never knew it was there. Rebecca couldn't possibly have contacted her.

"And by then, I'm sure you'd heard enough negative things about me from Mother and Daddy," she said softly.

"No. That's not true. They never said a word about you," Rebecca choked out. "And I wasn't allowed to ask, which made it even worse."

"When you found out where I was, why didn't you come see me?" Kat asked calmly, desperately trying to hold her emotions at bay.

"I tried once. I barely made it past the front gate." Rebecca grabbed the note from her and threw it into the drawer. "I saw what you and Arizona had. Your perfect life."

Kat shook her head. "Believe me, Bec, my life has been far from perfect." She bolted off the couch and shot across the room to the window. "And I refuse to complicate it any further by coming into this snake pit."

"Then why are you here?" Rebecca hurried around the desk and flopped down into the chair. "You should've just told her no."

"I've been telling her no for weeks. She won't leave me alone." Kat threw her hands up in the air and let out a growl of irritation. "My life was going just fine until she decided to meddle in it."

Something must have clicked because Rebecca's eyes grew wide. "That's why she sent Dani out after you."

Even though Kat was relieved that Rebecca knew her mother *had* set up the whole thing, the thought of DJ made the knot in her stomach tighten again. "I suppose," Kat said, turning to the couch.

"And something besides the kiss I saw has happened between you two?"

Kat took in the huge diamond on Rebecca's finger as she sat down on the couch again and quietly debated what, if anything, she should tell her. Coming clean about the whole torrid mess would be the right thing to do. Not the easiest, but probably the best. If DJ was her fiancée, Rebecca should know she'd been unfaithful. Then again, she was her little sister, and Kat really didn't want to hurt her any more than she already had.

"No. I was just surprised to find out that the two of you are engaged," Kat said, deciding to keep the information to herself for the time being.

Rebecca twisted the ring around on her finger and shook her head. "We're not engaged. That's just something Dani has helped me with in order to keep Mother out of my personal life." She twisted the ring off her finger and tossed it into the desk drawer as though it were an unneeded binder clip. "I only wear it when I visit her. Apparently the jig's up."

Kat's heart pounded. "So you and DJ aren't…?"

"Engaged?" A faint sound of laughter shuddered from Rebecca's lips. "Definitely not."

The knot in Kat's stomach eased when she realized DJ had been telling her the truth.

"But something did happen between you two." Rebecca must have observed the ambivalence in Kat's eyes.

"Right now, I'm not sure how I feel about her." Kat sighed, pressing her fingertips to her temples, kneading the dull pain beginning to erupt in her head. "She's not the woman I thought she was." Even if she wasn't engaged to Rebecca, DJ had still lied to her about everything else.

Rebecca moved from behind her desk to sit on the couch next to Kat. "Listen, Kat. I've known Dani for a long time. I've never seen her upset about any woman before."

"Is she upset about me or because she's been caught?" Kat's words tumbled out, tired and weak. "Do you have any aspirin?"

Rebecca went to her desk, opened the drawer, took out a bottle of ibuprofen, and then went into the bar for a glass of water. "I think you already know the answer to that," she said, coming out and handing the water and pills to Kat. "You don't need me to tell you what kind of woman she is. You already know that in your heart." Rebecca touched Kat's arm gently.

"Everything she said to me was a lie." Kat shook her head. "She even told me some story about growing up on a farm."

"That's true," Rebecca said eagerly. "She grew up on one just outside Johnson City. Her brother manages it, but her mother still owns it. She would've still been there today if her father hadn't insisted she go to college." She reached across to the end table and picked up an antique silver frame with an old black-and-white picture in it. "See?" she said, handing it to Kat. The picture showed a smiling little girl sitting on a horse next to a man dressed in overalls.

"Is this her father?"

"Uh-huh."

"She looks just like him." Kat smiled, lightly dragging her fingers across the picture.

"She's in love with you," Rebecca blurted.

Kat took in a deep breath. "Well, that's kind of a moot point now." She leaned forward and set the picture on the table in front of her.

"She's a good person, Kat," Rebecca said as she picked up the picture and put it back in place. "Don't get me wrong." She crossed her arms and melted into the huge, overstuffed, leather sofa. "What she did wasn't right, and you should make her suffer a while for it." Her lips twisted into a smirk. "But after that, you should give her another shot. For your own good."

Kat looked away, wondering if Rebecca was guessing or if the chemistry between her and DJ had been that obvious this morning. Either way, the pangs plaguing her heart were becoming more difficult to disguise.

"Let's face it, Kat. *You're* in love with her too."

"Is it that obvious?"

Rebecca nodded.

"I'm so sorry, Bec. I should've taken you with me when I left," Kat said as the tears streamed down her face. She couldn't hold them in any longer. Rebecca could still read her, just like when they were kids.

Rebecca threw her arms around her and held her tight as she sobbed into her shoulder. This was the moment she knew Rebecca had wished for since the day Kat left, just as she had. She couldn't pretend anymore. They were sisters again. As she held Rebecca in her arms, a feeling of contentment rushed through Kat, making her earlier apprehension vanish. After so many years, they'd never really lost the closeness they'd once shared. Even though many changes had occurred in both their lives, molding them into two very different women, their unbreakable bond still remained.

"When I came here, I didn't want to be involved in Montco business," Kat said as she wiped the tears from her face. "But now, I can see I'm going to have to help you rein in our mother."

Rebecca reached for the box of tissues. "I'm going to need it. That won't be easy."

❖

After closing and locking all the pasture gates, Virgil went into the stable to tend to the horses. He performed the ritual nightly, making sure all the tack was put away properly and the horses had feed, water, and hay.

He'd checked all the stalls, latched the gates, and was heading out the door when Victoria Maxwell trotted up on her horse with a few of her ranch hands following. He scanned the grounds looking for backup, but it was Saturday night, and most of the guys had gone into town.

"What do you want, Victoria?" Virgil asked. She didn't come around unless she wanted something.

"I came to see that lovely boss of yours." She slid off her horse.

"You mean my daughter-in-law?"

"Technically, I don't think she's your daughter-in-law anymore, since your girl's dead." Victoria laughed. "You ain't gonna be nothin' to her once we're married."

Virgil clenched his fists. He'd never hit a woman, but this particular woman might just make him do it. "She'll never marry you."

"We'll see about that." She twisted her head to look at the house. "Where is she?"

He slid the door halfway closed behind him. "You're out of luck."

"You sure she's not hiding around here somewhere?" Victoria circled around him and looked inside the stable.

Virgil stepped between Victoria and the door. "She's in Austin."

"What's she doing in Austin?" Victoria's voice held more than a hint of annoyance.

"That's none of your business. Now leave."

Victoria motioned for one of her men to shove Virgil against the door, forcing him into the stable. "You'd better be careful, old man, or you're gonna wind up just like that daughter of yours."

Virgil stumbled backward. "You shut up about my daughter."

Victoria's face twisted into an obscure smile. "Arizona didn't turn out to be such a tough girl after all, did she?"

Virgil narrowed his eyes. "What the hell are you talking about?"

"I really felt bad about her." Leaning against the railing of

Minow's stall, Victoria frowned. "I actually kind of liked her, but she started digging into things that weren't her business."

When Virgil realized what Victoria was saying, he lunged at her. The railing broke behind them, and Victoria's men rushed to drag Virgil off her.

Victoria scrambled to her feet. "Now with you out of the way, Kat won't have anyone left to help her."

Virgil struggled to break free. "She won't ever be yours."

"We'll just see about that." Victoria tossed a piece of the broken railing to one of the men. "Make sure he can't do any talkin'." She brushed hay from her shirt as she looked around the stable. "And move all these horses out of here before you torch it this time. I don't wanna have to spend any more money than I have to when I take over this place."

CHAPTER TWENTY

DJ sat behind her desk, trying to focus on the file in front of her. She couldn't concentrate, not after what had happened today. DJ could see in her eyes that Kat had been devastated. Her insides had twisted when she'd tasted the tears on Kat's lips. The kiss had been filled with pain and anguish. DJ had never expected to experience anything like that with Kat. She understood why Kat had said the things she had and couldn't help thinking it was all true. She deserved everything Kat had thrown at her. Could DJ make Kat forget it all? She had to find a way to make her see past her deception, or she would never be a part of her life.

She slapped the folder closed, shot up, and headed across the room. She couldn't just sit around and do nothing. DJ needed answers, and she was going to get them out of Mark Hamilton, one way or another. She marched through the doorway and down the hallway to Mark's office. The door was open, but the only person in there was one of the cleaning crew that came through nightly. She glanced at her watch. Eight o'clock.

"Damn." DJ took off down the hallway and barreled into Marcia, practically knocking her off her feet. "What are you still doing here?"

"I thought you might need me for something."

"Could you find Mark Hamilton's home address for me, please?" DJ went into her office for her briefcase.

When she came out, Marcia glanced up from her desk and handed her a slip of paper. "Here you go."

"If anyone asks, you don't know where I went."

Marcia lifted her eyebrows. "Do I ever?"

"Thanks, Marcia." DJ looked at the paper she'd handed her and hesitated. "You'll let me know when you need some time off, right?"

"Of course." Marcia smiled. "And I'll expect it with pay."

"And you'll get it that way." DJ laughed and headed down the hallway to the elevator. Marcia might be a thorn in her side sometimes, but DJ could trust her.

DJ screeched out of the parking garage and headed toward Mark's loft. She needed some answers, and if it was going to take another face-to-face with the man in his own territory, so be it.

DJ parked her BMW in the lot next to the Waterstreet Lofts and hurried around to the front of the building. After climbing the stairs to the third floor, she was a little winded. She found the door and gave it a swift succession of raps—no answer. She twisted the knob—locked. The door had a deadbolt, but maybe Mark wasn't a stickler for security. She slid a credit card into the doorjamb and shoved hard with her shoulder. The door flew open.

She rubbed her arm as she stepped inside and took a minute to survey the condo. The place wasn't very big. One bedroom with a small loft. She spotted a desk upstairs and went straight to it, passing the bedroom and kitchen to the narrow, small, metal spiral staircase. The top of the desk was spotless. She opened the drawers but found nothing. This place was just as clean as his office. DJ hurried down the steps and hit the bedroom next, checking the dresser, closet, and mattress—still nothing. It didn't look like he even lived there, or he wasn't planning to stay around much longer. Maybe he was planning to move in with Rebecca. She heard voices in the hallway but didn't balk. At this point DJ didn't care if Mark caught her. She rushed to the kitchen and scanned it.

Where would I hide something in this place? A few plates and glasses sat in the drain board. She opened the dishwasher door. The packing tape was still on the rack. *Why wouldn't he use the dishwasher?* She squatted down and looked inside—nothing. She closed it and felt around the plate covering the electrical wiring at the bottom. Some of the screws were missing. She pinched the piece of metal between her thumb and index finger, and it popped off. *Bingo!* A small manila envelope had been hidden in between and under the wires.

The envelope wasn't sealed, so DJ had no trouble sliding the documents out to see what they were. As she read through them, she realized Mark's predicament. Mark did know Victoria Maxwell. In fact, he knew her very well, and the parasite was putting the screws to him big-time. It looked like Mark's get-rich-quick scheme had backfired. DJ slid the papers into the envelope and pushed it into her coat pocket. Someone else needed to see these.

It was past ten when DJ knocked on the front door of Rebecca's condo.

"Who is it?" DJ recognized Mark's voice through the door.

"Dani Callahan."

She heard the deadbolt flip, and Mark opened the door slowly.

DJ didn't wait for an invitation. She pushed her way inside. "I thought I might find you here."

Mark turned, still standing in the doorway. "What do you want, Dani?"

"We need to talk about that little land deal you took care of for Mr. Belmont."

Mark closed the door and lowered his voice, "I told you, I didn't have anything to do with that."

DJ gave him a look of warning. "Don't dig yourself in any deeper, Mark." She reached her hand under her coat and let him see the envelope. "I know exactly what you did, and now I have the proof."

Mark reached for the envelope. "You broke into my loft."

"Door was open. I just looked around a bit."

"You don't know what you're doing, Dani."

"Why don't you fill me in?"

Mark kneaded the back of his neck roughly with his fingers and paced the room until he seemed to drop his shoulders in relief. "I was caught in the middle of this mess and couldn't find a way out." His eyes shifted nervously. "I only did what Charles told me to."

DJ saw what seemed to be a twinge of remorse, and she didn't know what to think. "But you knew it was illegal."

"You're an attorney. You know there's a fine line between legality and loopholes."

"At the very least, it was unethical." DJ looked toward the bedroom. "How'd you convince Rebecca to sign the papers?"

An arrogant smile crept across Mark's face. "It's amazing what you can get a woman to do by just paying attention to her."

"You seduced her so you could manipulate her?" DJ knew Rebecca was the one who was going to be hurt here.

"Seriously?" Mark let out a short breath. "You're doing the same thing to her sister, and you have the nerve to question my motives?"

DJ sucked in a deep breath and let it out slowly. Mark was right. When DJ had started this whole thing, she wasn't much different from him. Somewhere along the line, DJ had developed a conscience and fallen in love. Which came first she wasn't sure, but knowing what she'd done to Kat made her stomach turn.

"Don't be so hard on yourself. It's not like either one of them wasn't willing." Mark gave her a sly grin. "What's wrong with mixing a little pleasure with business?" He let out a chuckle.

Mark's eyes flew wide as DJ hit him hard across the chin, sending him flying over the couch. It was much more than pleasure for DJ. Mark touched his lip, and his eyes narrowed when he saw the blood on his fingers. "If her wife hadn't died, you wouldn't even be in the picture." He wiped the blood on the bottom of his shirt and stood up. "I'm surprised she isn't already shacked up with Victoria Maxwell."

DJ went after him again. She pushed him up against the wall and held him there. "That's enough about Kat."

"What's going on out here? I can hear you two all the way in the bathroom." Rebecca emerged from the bedroom in her robe. "Dani, what the hell's the matter with you?" She wedged herself between them.

DJ stared past Rebecca at Mark. "Your boyfriend and I were just having a little discussion."

"Doesn't look like much of a discussion to me." She planted her palms on DJ's chest and shoved her so Mark could slide out from behind her. "You'd better leave."

"I not going anywhere until you and I have a talk," DJ said, ignoring the cell phone ringing in her pocket.

"She's not your business anymore," Mark spouted.

"Oh yes, she is." DJ kept her gaze firm and steady.

"Isn't that your phone, Dani?" Rebecca reached into DJ's coat.

DJ took the ringing phone from her hand and dropped it back into her pocket, unanswered. "You need to know a few things before you become any more involved with this man."

"Just what exactly does she need to know, DJ?" Kat said, appearing in the doorway of the spare bedroom. "And why should she believe anything that comes out of your mouth?"

The venom in Kat's voice caught DJ off guard. She deserved every bit of her wrath, but for whatever reason she hadn't expected it to cut so deep.

"Well?" Kat crossed her arms and waited for her response.

DJ searched her eyes for some glimmer of understanding. "I didn't know you were here."

"This isn't about business, Kathryn. It's about you and your sister," Mark said, pointing a finger at her and then at Rebecca.

DJ moved toward Mark again. "You're damn right it's about them."

"Back off, Dani," Rebecca said, still standing between them.

With her eyes fixed on Mark, DJ slowly withdrew. "I guarantee there will be another time for this."

Rebecca pushed DJ to the door. "You need to go now."

"We have to talk, Rebecca."

"Not now." Rebecca opened the door, pushed DJ out, and closed it before she could say anything else.

Before DJ reached the elevator, her cell phone rang again. She fished it out of her pocket, touched the screen, and pressed it to her ear. "What!"

"Is this Danica Callahan?" the voice on the other end asked.

"Yes."

"Ms. Callahan, I'm a medical flight nurse out of Austin General."

Her stomach clenched. She immediately thought something was wrong with Elizabeth. "Yes."

"There's been a fire at the Jumpin' J Ranch."

"Fire?" She was barely able to hear the man's voice over the swishing helicopter noise in the background.

"It looks like it started in the horse stable."

"What happened? Is everyone all right?"

"The fire chief isn't sure how it started, but it looks as though Mr. Jackson may have been trampled by a horse. Someone found him on the ground in one of the horse stalls and carried him out before the fire burned out of control. He's unconscious now, but before we sedated him, he took your card out of his pocket and asked me to call you."

Fear flashed through her. "How long till you arrive at the hospital?" Virgil was the only person Kat was close to in this world.

"About thirty minutes."

"I'll be there." She slid her phone into her pocket and rushed down the hallway to Rebecca's door.

❖

Kat had almost reached the bedroom when she heard the banging on the door. She leaned against the wall and closed her eyes. She needed time to think, and it didn't look like DJ was willing to give her that. She pushed off the wall and went to the living room.

"I told you to go home, Dani," Rebecca shouted without opening the door. "She's not up to dealing with you right now."

"Something's happened at the ranch," DJ shouted, urgency vibrating in her voice.

Panic surged through Kat as she rushed across the room and yanked open the door. "What?"

"Virgil's been hurt. They're not sure exactly of the circumstances, but there was another fire in the stable. One of the hands found him on the ground inside and carried him out."

"Another one?" Her mind spun in a million different directions. "Oh my God, is he all right? Where is he?"

"He's being flown to the emergency room at Austin General. They should be there in about thirty minutes."

She pushed by DJ and headed for the door. "I have to go."

"Kat." Rebecca grabbed her arm. "You should put some other clothes on first."

"Right." Kat held her head, trying to settle herself as she rushed into the bedroom to change.

DJ followed her in. "I'll take you."

Kat ripped off her pajamas and pulled on a T-shirt and wool field shirt. "I can drive myself." Her hands trembled as she grabbed her jeans off the chair and slid them on. "Damn it," she said, her voice slipping into a fragile shakiness she hadn't wanted DJ to hear. *I can't lose Virgil.*

"Kat, I'm sure he'll be fine," Rebecca said, trying to calm her.

"He has to be." Kat yanked her boots on and rushed past her.

"I'll be right behind you," Rebecca said.

"Thanks." Kat turned, giving her a quick hug before continuing out the door.

DJ quickened her pace, following her out the door and into the elevator. "You're in no condition to drive. I'm going to take you."

She didn't argue as she pressed the elevator button repeatedly. "Did they say how badly he was hurt?"

"No," DJ said, hesitation in her voice. "I'm sure you've seen accidents like this before."

Kat punched at the elevator button again. "If they're flying him in, it can't be good." DJ was trying to prepare her without alarming her too much. It was serious.

DJ took her hand. "Kat, all I know is what I told you."

She tugged her hand from DJ's as the elevator doors opened and headed for her truck.

DJ grasped Kat's hand again and towed her along behind her. "You're as stubborn as a mule. I told you, I'll drive."

When they reached the road, Kat sat motionless, staring at the white line on the pavement in front of them. "How could something like this happen?"

"You never know with horses. They can be pretty temperamental."

"Those horses are all harmless, and Virgil's the best trainer I know. It must have been the new filly." *Why would he be messing with the new filly?* She had to call the ranch and hear the whole story. "Can I use your phone?" she asked softly. "I left mine at Rebecca's."

DJ took her phone from her pocket and handed it to her. Kat punched in a number and waited for someone to answer. When the cook finally did, she kept a calm, even tone as she shot off the beginning of a string of questions. "What the hell happened out there?"

"I don't know. I was cleaning the kitchen when I heard the commotion. No one knew Virgil was in there until George carried him out. He was in Minow's stall."

Another flash of panic hit her. "Is Minow all right?" she said urgently.

"She followed him out."

"Thank God George was there. How in the world did we have another fire?"

"They don't know yet. They're still here looking things over."

"What about the horses?" Her voice settled into the calm tone she'd started with.

"They're all okay. Someone let them out into the corral." Kat suspected that person was Virgil. Probably the reason they found him in the stable.

"Okay, thanks. Let me know if you find out anything." She hit the end button and held the phone to her chest. Everything was falling apart. DJ, the ranch, Virgil. How had her life suddenly gone to shit?

DJ reached over and glided her hand across Kat's leg before curling her fingers underneath her thigh and letting it settle there permanently. The warmth sizzled through Kat, and her system jolted. Suddenly the confines of the car seemed very intimate. What the hell was wrong with her? The man she respected most in the world was seriously hurt, and all it took was a single touch from DJ to scatter all her thoughts.

"This doesn't change anything between us, DJ," Kat said, offering her the phone and hoping she'd remove her hand. She did, and after sliding the phone into her pocket, DJ let her hand rest on the gear stick. Kat shifted in her seat, thankful for something besides her leg to occupy DJ's hand.

"How did it happen?" DJ asked.

"They don't know." She stared out the window through the droplets of rain into the darkness, trying to envision what had gone on. "George found Virgil in the stall with Minow."

"With Minow?" DJ's voice rose.

"Apparently this storm went through there tonight too. Maybe the lightning started the fire and spooked her."

"Stranger things have happened."

"That's crazy." Kat shook her head. "Minow doesn't spook. I trained her myself. She's the gentlest horse I have."

"Do they know when it happened?"

"No. They're not sure how long he was lying there before they found him. My guess is it wasn't too long ago. Virgil checks the stable every night about nine o'clock?" She sat in silence for a moment. "Damn it." She shook her head.

DJ looked over at her. "What?"

"Something strange is going on." Kat twisted in her seat to look at her. "If a storm was coming, Virgil would've already had the stable locked down with the horses in it. Right?"

"Right."

"They said all the other horses were out in the corral when they showed up." The timing was all off.

"Maybe the storm came up quicker than he thought."

"No." She shook her head. "Virgil can smell a storm coming. There's no way he would've left the horses out." She slapped her hand to the dash. "I don't think this fire was an accident." Only Virgil could tell them what really happened. She just hoped he was all right.

DJ pushed the accelerator pedal to the floor, sending the speedometer shooting up past the speed limit.

After entering the emergency room at Austin General, they found that the medical flight helicopter had already arrived. The two of them went straight to the nurses' station.

"Can you give me any information on Virgil Jackson?" DJ asked.

The clerk spun around in her chair to speak to the nurse behind her. "You have any info on Virgil Jackson?"

The nurse looked up from the chart she held. "They just brought him in. Are you a family member?"

"I'm DJ Callahan, Virgil's personal attorney, and this is Kathryn Jackson, his daughter-in-law."

"Well, Ms. Callahan, I don't have a status yet, but if you'll follow me, we can check with the flight nurse that transported him."

Kat followed with DJ firmly in tow.

"Only one at a time, please. This is a trauma center," the nurse said before going through the double doors.

DJ turned to Kat. "Wait here a minute. I'll be right back."

"But—"

"You're too emotional now, Kat."

"Emotional, my ass." Kat pushed past DJ and through the door. "*You* wait out here."

DJ rushed up next to Kat as the nurse led them through the doors and down the hallway to the exam rooms.

"I said only one of you." The nurse stopped and blocked the doorway with her arm.

DJ flashed the nurse a disarming grin. "Can you make an exception, just this once?"

Kat blew out a quick breath of air through her nose to let DJ know she was disgusted with her tactics, but DJ didn't seem to care.

The nurse pointed to the woman in uniform, packing supplies into a medical kit. "There's one of the flight nurses that flew in with Mr. Jackson. She might be able to answer some of your questions."

"Thank you so much." DJ took the nurse's hand between hers and held it momentarily.

Kat clenched her hands into fists and swallowed hard. "That smooth charm certainly comes in handy, doesn't it?" She didn't know what she expected. DJ had used her good looks and charisma so often, it was probably second nature.

DJ reached for her. "Kat…"

She threw her hands up. "Not now, DJ."

Without argument, DJ whipped around and headed into the exam room. "DJ Callahan, Mr. Jackson's personal attorney," she said, extending her hand. "And this is his daughter-in-law, Kathryn Jackson." She motioned to Kat. "How's he doing?"

"I'm afraid there's not really much to tell yet. They just took him up to surgery." The nurse shook DJ's hand, gave Kat a nod, and continued to pack the kit. "He has multiple chest contusions. I saw that when I hooked him up to the monitors."

Kat looked at the bloodied gauze on the floor. "Is all this from him?" she asked and sucked in a deep breath, trying to keep the queasy feeling at bay. Her stomach felt as though it might erupt at any minute. She didn't know why it bothered her. She saw more blood than this during the animal births she handled at the ranch.

"I'm afraid so," the nurse said.

"How serious is it?" The thought of Virgil lying helpless, tubes running from various parts of his body, and machines hovering next to the bed swept through Kat's mind, and she felt scared and very much alone. Virgil wasn't a young man, but he always took pride in his virility. An immovable fixture in her life, he would by no means be considered frail or weak. He was the rock she'd held onto so many times when things got tough. He had to be okay.

"It's serious." The nurse looked up momentarily and seemed to take note of Kat's fixed gaze on the blood-soaked gauze strewn across the floor. "He could have broken ribs and internal bleeding."

"Did he regain consciousness at all?" Kat asked, her voice weak.

"Just for a few minutes. As I told Ms. Callahan on the phone, he gave me her card."

Kat's body heated, and her vision went fuzzy. The nurse ripped open a pack containing a wet cloth and moved quickly to her.

"Here. This should help." The nurse blotted Kat's face with the cool cloth and then slid it across the back of her neck.

The double doors swung open, and Rebecca came into the room with Mark following her. "Any news?" Rebecca asked as she wrapped her arm around Kat's shoulder.

"Nothing current." Kat sank into Rebecca and closed her eyes to combat the light-headedness.

"She needs to sit down. Would you please take her outside while I finish up here?" DJ said.

Rebecca nodded and led Kat to the door. "Come on. Let's go out here where it's a little cooler."

"I'm fine," she said, fighting the darkness blurring her mind. She didn't want to leave. She didn't like being handled. She wanted firsthand information about what had happened, but the blood had done her in. Heat pricked her neck, so she went with Rebecca to the waiting room.

Chapter Twenty-One

DJ didn't want to send Kat with Rebecca, but she looked like she might pass out any minute, and DJ wouldn't be able to gain more information from the nurse if she had her hands full with Kat. Virgil might have said something to the nurse while he was being transported.

DJ waited for the door to close behind the two women before she turned to the nurse. "Were there any other injuries?"

"It looks like he took a pretty good blow to the head. He could have a skull fracture."

"Damn." DJ rubbed her hand across her chin. "Did he say anything else to you besides asking you to call me?"

"Nothing coherent." She stopped packing for a minute and looked at DJ as though she was trying to remember. "After we talked, he did regain consciousness for a few minutes. He started mumbling something over and over."

"What was it?"

"Something about someone named Victoria." She continued to sort through the supplies.

DJ reached over and closed the medical kit she was packing. "Listen. It's really important that you try to remember exactly what he said."

She let out a sigh. "I don't know. It was so loud up there." She shook her head. "I think he must have been delirious. He said something about a cat and keeping it away from her."

"Is that it?"

"Yeah. After that he was in and out of consciousness. The monitors were topping out, and his blood pressure was going through the roof."

"Thanks," DJ said, and her mind began to spin. Could Victoria have possibly caused this accident? Did she want the land so badly she would destroy the ranch for it? Or did she just want Kat?

"Sorry I couldn't be more helpful. You might want to talk to the other guy we brought in." She zipped up her kit and slung it over her shoulder.

"What other guy?" DJ asked, snapping out of her thought.

"The guy who carried him out. He's in the next room." She pointed through the glass window.

Even though his shoulder-length hair had been fastened into a ponytail away from his soot-smeared face, DJ immediately recognized George, the bartender from the ranch.

"How's he doing?"

"I don't know. Why don't we ask the doc?" The nurse knocked on the glass and waved the doctor over. "How's the hero, Doc?" she asked as he came through the doorway.

"He's doing pretty well. Just a few minor burns and a little smoke inhalation." The doctor was busy making notations on the chart and didn't look up. "If he hadn't been there, the guy they brought in with him would probably be dead."

"Can I talk to him for a minute?" DJ asked.

"That depends on who you are?"

"DJ Callahan, legal representative for the Jumpin' J Ranch." She handed him her card. "I'm also a friend."

The doctor read it and handed it back. "Okay, but only for a few minutes."

DJ pasted on a big smile and pushed through the door. "Hey, buddy. How ya doing?" She fought to hold her smile as the overwhelming smell of burnt flesh penetrated her nostrils.

"I'll be all right. It looks worse than it is." George lifted his bandaged arm. "Other one's okay, but all the hair's gone." He lowered his eyes. "How's Virgil?"

"Don't know yet. They're still working on him." DJ propped herself up on the end of the gurney. "It's a good thing you were there."

"That's what they tell me."

"How did you find him so quickly?"

"It's my night off, and I try and stay away from the bar when I'm not workin'. I was out taking a walk when I saw the smoke coming from the stable." He rubbed his face nervously. "My first thought was the horses, but when I opened the gate to Minow's stall, I saw Virgil on the ground."

"So you carried him out first and then set the horses free?" DJ asked, trying to figure out the sequence of events.

"No. I didn't have to let the horses out." George looked a little confused. "Minow was the only one in there, and she followed me out when I picked up Virgil."

DJ rolled her lips together. "The fire chief said the horses were in the corral when they arrived."

"If he says they were, then they were." He stared down at the floor. "But I didn't put them there."

"You have any idea how the fire started?"

George looked at the door and hesitated. DJ turned and saw Mark watching them through the glass. "Must have been the lightning." He slapped at the soot covering his pants.

"Well, anyway, it's a good thing you found Virgil when you did." DJ gave him an appreciative smile, but she got the feeling George knew more about this fire than he was saying.

"Tell Kat I'm sorry I didn't get there sooner," George said, a sad sort of sincerity ringing in his voice.

He peered up at DJ, then to the floor quickly. If George was involved, he seemed to be regretting it now.

"I will." DJ patted him on the shoulder and headed into the other exam room.

"Who's that?" Mark looked through the glass.

"You don't know him?" DJ asked.

"No. Why would I?"

"He's one of the bartenders at the ranch." DJ looked at George momentarily. "You should be very thankful he found Virgil when he did."

Mark stepped in front of DJ, blocking her way. "Why do you keep insisting that I'm involved in all this?"

"Just following the trail, and right now it seems to be leading directly to you." She pushed by him.

DJ went through the double doors and met Kat in the hallway. "He's going to be in there for a while." She took Kat by the hand and led her into the waiting room. "How are you doing?"

"I'm fine. Just a little overwhelmed by the blood. What did she say?"

"It looks like, along with the multiple chest contusions, Virgil may also have a skull fracture."

"Oh, my God!" Kat said, and her knees seemed to buckle beneath her again.

"You have to stay positive, Kat."

Kat began to sway, and DJ held her close. "This is my fault. I should've never left him out there alone." She pressed her face against DJ's chest and began to sob uncontrollably.

"He wasn't alone. You have twenty or more ranch hands on site." DJ felt the warmth of Kat's tears through the cotton T-shirt she wore as she held her tight.

"But they don't look after him like I do." She sobbed, tears choking back the words.

"He's going to be all right, Kat. You have to believe that." DJ stroked her hair lightly. Believing Virgil was going to survive this was the only thing helping Kat through this right now.

Unsettled by this place where people teetered on the brink between life and death, DJ heard her stomach rumble. She knew from experience that anyone could easily lose that balance in a split second. She could handle the blood, but the antiseptic smell stinging in her nose brought back painful memories of her father's death. The heart attack. The tractor. The reality that his body could've withstood the coronary, but the damage done by the tiller was too much. DJ should've been stronger. If she hadn't left the farm, she would've been on the tractor. There would've been no heart attack, no accident, and her father would still be alive. She stared down at Kat, huddled closer to her, and took in a slow, deep breath. The warmth of Kat against her soothed the feeling of helplessness inside. Kat didn't know it, but she was comforting DJ as much as she was comforting Kat.

The double doors flew open, and the commotion revived the waiting room full of sleepy-eyed people. A man dressed in pale-green scrubs appeared. "I'm looking for the family of Virgil Jackson."

Kat shot out of DJ's arms. "I'm Kathryn Jackson, Virgil's daughter-in-law."

He extended his hand. "Hi, Mrs. Jackson. I'm Steven Kane."

"How is he?" Kat asked softly, a slight waver in her voice.

"Well, Mrs. Jackson, he took a pretty good beating, but your father-in-law is a tough guy." The doctor smiled. "It's going to take some time for him to recover, but I think he'll be all right."

She let out a sigh of relief. "Thank you, Dr. Kane. Can I see him?"

"He's in recovery now. You can see him as soon as he's settled into intensive care." The doctor turned to the nurses' station. "One of the nurses will take you to him in just a little while."

"Thank you again, Dr. Kane," Kat said.

He nodded and headed to the double doors, stopping just before he entered. "Mrs. Jackson," he called to her. "Don't be alarmed when you see him. He has a few facial lacerations, but they look a lot worse than they are."

"There, you see?" Rebecca smiled. "He's going to be just fine."

Kat crossed her arms and paced the waiting room. "I still can't figure out what happened."

Rebecca stood in Kat's path and made her look at her. "That's not important now. I'm sure Virgil will fill you in when he feels up to it."

She glanced at her watch. "It's after three, Bec. You should go on home. I'll be all right."

"Are you sure? I don't mind staying."

Kat tensed and stared across the room at DJ. "I'll be fine."

Rebecca put her arm around her big sister. "She cares about you, Kat. Let her help."

"I know." Kat felt the familiar twang in her belly, and her weary voice faded. Even with her anger, the connection she felt with DJ hadn't diminished. Rebecca's confirmation of it didn't help matters.

After speaking to the nurse, DJ went to Kat and Rebecca. "I'm sorry to interrupt, but they're ready to take us up now." She led them to the elevator and held the door as they entered.

"Call me if you need me." Rebecca kissed Kat on the cheek before stepping out.

DJ put a foot into the doorway, making the metal doors bounce into the channel. "You're not coming up?"

"No. Mark and I are going home." Rebecca touched DJ's arm. "You take care of her, all right?"

DJ glanced at Kat, and she gave her a tentative look. "I will." She nodded and backed up to let the doors close.

After exiting the elevator and walking a short distance past the nurses' station, the two of them quietly followed the nurse into Virgil's hospital room.

"He'll probably be unconscious most of the night. He's still heavily sedated," the nurse said, checking the monitors.

DJ could see Kat was shaken at the sight of him, and to be honest, so was DJ. Virgil had a large gash across his cheekbone and another small cut above his eye. Both had been neatly stitched and dressed with some sort of ointment.

Not taking her eyes from Virgil, Kat worked her way around the bed to his side and grasped his hand. "I'd like to stay, if it's all right."

The nurse looked over at DJ. "I'll have housekeeping bring up another recliner."

DJ watched Kat closely as she sat with Virgil, holding his hand. She knew how seeing him incapacitated would make her feel. The sight of Kat sitting there helpless stirred memories and emotions within DJ she'd kept locked away for years. She closed her eyes and forced herself to keep it together. She wanted to help, but she couldn't do anything to take away Kat's pain or worry.

Chapter Twenty-Two

Awakened by the creaking door, Kat watched through slitted eyelids as her mother glided quietly across the room. She kept her eyes closed and remained motionless while she enjoyed the remnants of the dream she'd been having. A minor indulgence before dealing with her mother.

Elizabeth stood next to the bed and touched Virgil's face lightly. His eyes slowly fluttered open, and he began to stir.

"Don't try to move," Elizabeth said softly, moving her hand to his shoulder. "You gave us quite a scare."

Why is she being so nice? He and Arizona were the hired help at the Belmont Ranch before Daddy fired them. Virgil was no different from the driver he'd fired for using one of the Belmont cars to take his mother to the hospital. It didn't matter to her father that it was an emergency and the woman would've died if he hadn't. The man had done it without permission. Kat lifted her lids slightly. Dreaming was impossible now with this odd conversation filling the room.

Virgil gawked around the room, seeming disoriented until his gaze fixed on Kat. She clamped her eyes shut. "What time is it?" he asked.

Kat cracked her eyelids again to see Elizabeth squinting at her watch. "Close to two."

"In the morning?"

"Afternoon. You've been out for quite a while"

He tipped his head toward Kat. "Has she been here all day?"

"And all night." Elizabeth's voice was soft and low. "Stubborn and thickheaded, just like you."

"But still beautiful. Just like her mother," Virgil managed to say, his voice weak and gravelly.

Kat opened her eyes just a smidge more as she processed the sentence she'd just heard.

"It's a good thing too." Elizabeth touched his hand and let the corners of her lips curve into a warm, generous smile. "It would've been tragic if she'd looked like you."

Kat bolted up. "What did you just say?"

"I'm sorry. I didn't mean to wake you, dear." Elizabeth's voice was effortlessly even.

Kat gave her a piercing glare. "Why in the world would you think I could look like Virgil?"

She shook her head. "That's not what I said." Her voice rose slightly. "You must have misunderstood."

"Mother. I did not misunderstand. First you said I'm stubborn and thick-headed, just like Virgil." She tripped as she tried to get up, fumbling with the blanket tangled around her feet. Kicking it from her legs, she let out a frustrated growl and threw it into the chair. "Then you said it would have been tragic if I looked like him."

Elizabeth took in a deep breath and propped her cane against the bed before leaning forward and tucking the sheet up under Virgil's arms. "We should talk about this later. Perhaps you can come out to the house for dinner?"

Kat stood at the end of the bed, hands planted firmly on her hips. "I'm not coming to the house, Mother. Just tell me what you're talking about."

"Oh dear," Elizabeth said, letting out a sigh with which Kat was very familiar. "This isn't the way I'd imagined telling you." She let out another heavy breath. "Kathryn, your father and I never professed to have a perfect marriage." Her eyes were still and focused. "Charles had many indiscretions." She smiled at Virgil and spoke in a voice of contentment that Kat had never heard from her before. "I had only one."

"Virgil?" Kat sank down into the chair feeling as though she'd just taken a blow directly in the gut.

"You see, darling, in my younger days, I had a fondness for horses, just like you. I spent many hours at my father's horse ranch, which is now the Belmont ranch. Virgil and I became very close, just as you and Arizona did."

Kat couldn't imagine her mother having the same sort of feelings for Virgil as she had for Arizona—being so in love with someone you couldn't imagine life without them, someone you'd give up everything to be with. If that were so, her mother would've had no choice but to leave her father.

Elizabeth smiled lightly as she reached over and held Virgil's hand. "Charles was never concerned with what I did or with whom I did it. To him I was just part of a business deal between affluent families." She returned her attention to Kat. "Until I became pregnant with you."

"He knew?"

"Of course he knew. There was no question. We never shared the same bed." She let out a short, maddening breath. "Charles only slept with his secretaries and tennis partners."

Kat sat motionless, her mind spinning as she tried to absorb the flaming ball of information Elizabeth had just hurled at her.

"I know, I should have told you sooner," Elizabeth said. "But with the way things were between us—"

"And Rebecca?" Kat cut her off mid-sentence. "Who's her father?"

"I've had only one love in my lifetime." Elizabeth attempted to move closer, but Kat launched herself from the chair. "Please, Kathryn. You have to understand that life was different then."

Kat stood at the end of the bed, giving Virgil an unbreakable stare. The man she trusted more than anyone else in the world had lied to her. "You knew about this all along?" Her voice wavered, barely rising above a whisper. Her heart pounded in her ears, and she could hardly speak.

"Your mother didn't tell me until after you and Arizona were married and had built the ranch. The two of you weren't blood-related, so there was no reason to keep you apart." Virgil winced, trying unsuccessfully to shift his body. "She asked me to look after you because she couldn't anymore."

DJ came through the door with a cardboard drink holder containing three cups of coffee. "You're awake." She looked at Virgil with a huge smile, but he didn't return it.

Kat glared at her. Another unforgivable lie. "You knew about this too. Didn't you?"

DJ's forehead crinkled and her face went blank. "Knew about what?"

Kat narrowed her eyes as her anger bubbled inside. "Of course you did." The words flew out quickly as the wave of betrayal rushed through her. "You know everything about me. It's all in that little file of yours." She swallowed hard, forcing back the tears, and her voice became low and unsteady. "You knew Virgil was my father all along."

"What…*no*," DJ said. She seemed honestly confused, but Kat had already learned she was a very good liar.

"I have to get out of here." Kat rushed by her, splattering the tray of coffee across the front of her shirt.

The hot liquid burned DJ's face and chest. She had no idea there was any question about who was Kat's father. Elizabeth had done it to her again. "What the hell is going on here?" She dropped the empty tray into the trash can and swiped her sleeve across her face.

"Danica, go after her," Elizabeth pleaded.

Totally befuddled and still feeling the sting of hot coffee, DJ rushed out the door. She searched the hallway and caught a glimpse of Kat entering the stairwell. She bolted in after her and caught up with her on the ground floor.

DJ reached over her shoulder and pushed the door closed as Kat tried to pull it open. "Wait a minute."

"Just leave me alone, DJ. You're as bad as they are."

DJ held the door firm as Kat struggled to open it. "You can't really believe I knew about that."

Kat yanked hard at the door again. "Why not? You knew about everything else."

"Kat, I swear, I didn't know. You have to believe me." She'd given her no reason to trust her and plenty of reasons not to.

Kat jerked around to face her, and DJ saw the pain in her eyes. She pounded her fists hard into DJ's chest, then pushed her and tried to open the door again. "Let me out of here, damn it," she said, her voice cracking.

"You're not going anywhere like this." DJ would never forgive herself if something happened to Kat.

DJ held her hand up to her shoulder and let it hover momentarily. She wanted to console her but wasn't sure how.

Kat pressed her forehead against the door. "It all makes sense now. I always knew I wasn't anything like him growing up." She lifted her head and let out a short laugh. "All along the only man I ever considered any kind of a role model in my life turns out to actually be my father." She stood rigidly as though contemplating her next protest.

DJ waited, bracing herself for another flailing-fist attack. She was at a loss as she rubbed her face absently, trying to figure out what Kat needed right now. Comfort, support, space. She didn't know if any of those would help.

"It looks like Virgil is going to be all right." DJ hesitated before touching Kat on the shoulder lightly. "Why don't you come home with me and rest?"

"I'm going to the ranch." Kat turned to face her, revealing the just-try-and-stop-me look burning in her eyes.

"You can go anywhere in Austin you want." DJ removed her hand from the door. "I'll even find you a hotel room. But there's no way in hell I'm letting you on that highway today." Her stomach knotted at the thought of letting her go. She wanted to hold her, to help her through this, to just make it all go away somehow.

"Then I'll take the hotel. And make it an expensive one." Kat whirled around and yanked the door open.

CHAPTER TWENTY-THREE

K at took off through the door and into the garage, leaving DJ behind, following her to the car without trying to keep pace. The car chirped, and the doors unlocked. She didn't wait for her but slid into the passenger seat and waited.

"How about the Governor's Suite at the Four Seasons?" Kat would make the lying big-city lawyer pay for this mistake.

"If that's where you want to go," she said as the car squealed out of the garage.

Kat waited for DJ to talk her out of it, but she didn't say a word to convince her otherwise. When they parked in front of the hotel, Kat threw open the door and leapt out of the car. She waited for the sliding-glass doors to open and then watched as they fell into place again. She suddenly felt very much alone. She didn't want to stay here, but she had nowhere else to go. She just didn't have the energy to fight anymore. In only a matter of weeks her life had been flipped upside down. When she turned and found DJ right behind her, she fell into her arms and wept.

"Come on. Let's go." DJ tucked her under her arm while they walked to the car. She opened the car door and offered Kat her hand. Kat ignored DJ's gesture as she slid into the seat, grabbed the handle, and jerked the door shut.

"Do you like Chinese food?" DJ asked as she weaved the car into traffic.

"I'm not hungry."

"You have to eat something." DJ picked up her cell phone and punched in a number. After rattling off an order, she dropped the phone into the cup holder between the seats.

Kat stared out the windshield, watching the droplets of rain fall and the wipers slap them away. The sky had darkened. Another storm. Just what she needed to keep her nerves on edge. It had turned out to be a rocky month in more ways than one. DJ downshifted and stopped at a red light. Pedestrians hurried across the water-covered street to the other side. The light turned green, and familiar street names flashed in the headlights as they passed. It seemed she would never be rid of this city.

"Here we are," DJ said, slowing as they rolled up in front of the restaurant.

"I'll wait here, if you don't mind," Kat said, staring at the taillights of the SUV in front of them.

DJ double-parked and left the car running, and Kat watched her rush through the rain, into the restaurant. Had DJ really not known the truth about her parentage? She couldn't believe it herself. How could her mother have let her grow up thinking her father hated her, always trying to please him but never doing things quite the way he wanted? The long-forgotten feeling of constant rejection rang through her bones once again. Her life was a colossal clusterfuck right now. And what about her mother's life? Apparently, she'd had a long-running affair with Virgil. If she hadn't loved Charles, why had she stayed with him all these years? What did her father have on Elizabeth to make her stay?

Startled by a tap on the window, she ran her hand along the armrest and found the switch for the window. The motor whirred as the glass zipped down. DJ passed her three large brown paper bags through the window.

Kat scowled as she peeked over the bags at her. "My God. What did you order?" There was enough food to feed a dozen people.

DJ rounded the car and slid into the driver's seat. "You wouldn't tell me what you liked, so I ordered a little of everything."

After they entered the elevator, DJ slid her key card in the slot and pushed the penthouse button, sending the car directly to her apartment.

Kat was impressed. "My mother must pay you well."

Her lips thinned. "Elizabeth's not my only client."

"But she keeps you on retainer, doesn't she?" Kat shot back, ready to blast her with everything she'd kept inside for the past few days.

DJ clenched her jaw and sliced Kat a sideways glare. "She and a few other people."

The elevator doors opened, and Kat entered the penthouse. She took in the faint scent of the lavender roses flowing from the vase in the foyer, and her body filled with warmth. The subtle fragrance reminded her of the rose DJ had given her just a few nights before, a night Kat would never forget, no matter how hard she tried. She quickly shrugged it off. She didn't want to feel warm and snuggly with her. Kat had let DJ into her heart, and she'd lied to her. She wasn't ready to forgive that betrayal yet. Focusing on the decor of the living room, she followed DJ as she led her through it into the kitchen. From the Italian leather sofa to the Steinway piano, she could see by the elegance of the furnishings and the originality of the artwork that she probably wasn't the one who'd decorated it.

She spied a picture of DJ and Rebecca on the end table, and her stomach knotted. Even if it was over, she could see that what they'd had together was more than just a casual affair. Another reminder that she had no idea who this woman was.

"Rosa, I thought I told you to take a few days off." DJ set the bags of takeout on the kitchen counter.

"I did, but now I'm back. I bought groceries." She took a bag of fresh, multicolored bell peppers out of the refrigerator. "Fajitas?"

"You don't have to cook."

"Don't tell me you picked up Chinese food again." She snapped her lips together and dropped the vegetables into the sink. "I'm beginning to think you don't like my cooking."

"You know that's not true." DJ chuckled and kissed her lightly on the cheek. "You're the best cook in Texas."

Rosa's irritation seemed to fade quickly, and her interest was clearly piqued when she saw Kat enter the kitchen.

"You have a guest?"

"Rosa, this is Kathryn Jackson."

Rosa smiled curiously. "Nice to meet you, Miss Jackson."

Kat extended her hand. "Please just call me Kat."

"Kat." Rosa's smile widened as she assessed Kat briskly before returning her attention to DJ. "It wouldn't take long for me to fix the two of you a very nice lunch."

"I've already bought Chinese food."

"Then I'll fix dinner," she said adamantly, taking out a package of meat. "I'll put the meat in to marinate, and it will be better by then."

"I appreciate it, Rosa, but we didn't sleep much last night. We'll probably crash right through dinner."

"Okay then." Rosa raised an irritated brow before slipping the peppers and meat into the refrigerator. "I'll see you tomorrow. Around noon, okay?"

"That's fine." DJ smiled slightly.

Rosa picked up her purse and went to the door. "It was nice meeting you, Miss Jackson."

"You too." Kat smiled lightly as she watched her walk to the foyer. Unable to resist, she went to the table there, plucked a single lavender rose from the vase, and brought it to her nose. Thoughts of DJ naked beneath her overwhelmed her and made her react in ways she wished she wouldn't. Damn, she wanted to erase that memory, but she couldn't forget what had become one of the best nights of her life in recent years.

"Food's getting cold." The sound of DJ's voice sent a chill through her.

You have to stop this right now. She took one last whiff of the rose, slipped it into the vase, and went into the kitchen.

DJ had unpacked the containers of food and opened them. "Would you grab a couple of plates out of the cabinet?" she said, pointing to the corner of the kitchen.

Kat set out the plates and opened a few drawers to find the silverware before sliding spoons into the first few containers.

"Which of these do you like?" Kat asked.

"I like it all." DJ took a bottle of California chardonnay from the refrigerator, opened it, and poured them each a glass.

Kat filled the plates and carried them to the table. "How long have you lived here?" Kat asked, trying to overcome the uneasy silence.

"About five years." DJ dipped an eggroll into the hot mustard and then bit a chunk off.

Kat lifted the wineglass to her lips. "Have you always lived alone?" She took a sip and looked over the rim at DJ.

DJ blotted her mouth, her lips easing into a smile. "The only women I've ever lived with are my mother and my sister."

Kat didn't let her gaze falter. "I'm sorry. I don't know why I asked." That wasn't true. She needed to know. She hesitated only a moment before shooting DJ a deliberate jab. "I'm not sure I should believe you anyway." The warm smile Kat had become accustomed to disappeared quickly.

DJ let out a heavy breath, let her fork clank onto the plate, and leaned back in her chair, planting her hands on her knees. "Ask me anything. I promise there will never be another lie between us."

"Did you know about my father?"

"No."

"Were you ever in love with Rebecca?"

"No."

"Was Rebecca ever in love with you?"

"No." DJ took a swig of wine. "Anything else?"

"Not right now. But I—"

"Reserve the right to question the witness again?"

Kat couldn't help but smile as DJ finished her sentence. "Yep." She picked up her fork and raked it mindlessly through the small amount of noodles covering her plate. Her heart ached to forgive and trust DJ again, but no matter what she told her, Kat didn't know if she could forget the damage that had already been done.

"Not too bad, huh?" DJ said, observing Kat's empty plate.

"I guess I was hungrier than I thought." That wasn't surprising. In the last twenty-four hours, she hadn't had anything but coffee and a few bags of cheese crackers from the vending machine at the hospital. She stood up and carried the dishes to the kitchen.

"I'll take those." DJ followed her and took the dishes. "Why don't you go into the living room and relax."

"Thanks. My head is killing me." Kat closed her eyes and let her head drop from side to side. The rain was coming down in sheets on the roof, and she pressed her fingers to her temples. More than one storm was rumbling tonight. The pain in her head pounded in even symmetry, and her neck and shoulders ached from holding it upright. Her mind flashed with bits of information she'd absorbed the last few days. She was tired of trying to sift through it all.

Strong, warm hands brushed across her neck before planting themselves on her shoulders. DJ's thumbs worked the muscles in her neck, and the warmth felt good. The familiar jolt DJ's touch produced in her spread lower. Kat spun around and kissed her hard on the lips. She refused to let her seduce her again. This time it would be on her terms. She was going to show DJ what it felt like to be used.

DJ tore herself from the deepening the kiss. "Why don't I run you a nice, warm bath," she said, hurrying by Kat into the bedroom.

Kat met her at the bedroom door as she came out. "What's your rush?"

"No rush. It should be ready in a minute." DJ motioned to the bathroom. "I'll pour you another glass of wine."

Kat stepped in front of DJ as she tried to move through the doorway. She snaked her arms around DJ's neck and pressed her lips to hers again. The urgency of the kiss and the subtle curve of DJ's waist made Kat want her even more. She hated it, but her need for DJ was all-consuming.

DJ tried to break free. "You're tired. You should rest."

"I'm not that tired," Kat whispered in a low, raspy voice before sweeping her hand across DJ's breast. The nipple beneath the shirt hardened immediately. "And neither are you." She unbuttoned DJ's shirt and kissed the valley between her breasts. DJ closed her eyes and sucked in a deep breath. DJ wanted her too.

"Kat, stop," DJ said, holding her at arm's length.

Kat was stunned. "Fine. You don't want me. I'll find someone who does." She slipped out of her grasp and rushed to the door.

"Oh, no, you don't." DJ swung Kat around by the arm and pushed her into the bathroom. "You're not going anywhere." Her eyes were focused and hard, not the eyes of the woman Kat had made love to only a few nights before.

"Who the hell do you think you are?" Kat's voice rose, spiking with anger.

DJ slammed the door closed. "Someone who cares."

"Let me out of here." She pounded on the securely fastened barrier between them. "You can't keep me in here forever!" She spun around, threw herself against the door, and continued to hammer against it.

Kat blinked the angry tears away and then stopped pounding on the door as she looked around the bathroom. On every ledge, tucked into every crevice, was a burning candle. The room was fully illuminated with them. A profusion of lavender rose petals floated freely on top of the bath water. *She does care.* Kat sank against the counter and cried.

After a few minutes of self-pitying tears, she wiped her eyes and tugged her T-shirt over her head. She slid a drawer out and rummaged through it, looking for something with which to clip her hair. After finding only a few plastic clothespins, she twisted her hair up and secured the strands she could.

She heard the door creak open and caught DJ standing in the doorway gazing at her. Her eyes were soft and gentle again, just as they'd been before. Kat let the remainder of her clothes drop to the floor and stood completely naked in front of her, giving DJ one last shot at failure, a last-ditch attempt to make DJ prove she was no better than any other deceitful woman she'd met.

DJ reached in and fumbled as she set the glass of wine on the basin. "Here's something you can wear when you're done." She handed her a pair of black silk pajamas. "I'll be right out here if you need anything," she said, and closed the door.

DJ had more than passed the test.

DJ took off her coffee-stained shirt and then opened the dresser drawer filled with a variety of neatly folded colored T-shirts. After slipping one over her head, she slid her jeans off and put on a pair of navy-blue yoga pants, then settled down on the bed.

She stared at the bathroom door and saw the flickering light underneath it. Visions of Kat standing naked, tempting her, rushed through her head. Even with angry, tear-soaked eyes, she was more beautiful than any woman she'd ever met. It took everything DJ had not to give in and make love to her right then and there, but she wasn't going to let her own desires stand in the way of what Kat needed right now.

DJ might have originally gone to the ranch to seduce her, but she was the one who'd been seduced. Kat had turned the tables on her. She'd drawn her into her world without DJ even realizing it.

Stop! You can't have her now. Do some work or something, damn it. She hopped up, grabbed her briefcase from the living room, and spread the files she'd borrowed from the courthouse vault out on the bed. As she looked through the documents, she unfolded an old geological surveyor's map and studied it. After a few minutes, DJ realized exactly why Maxwell wanted the land so badly. Sporadic blotches of green ran smack-dab through the middle of Kat's ranch. Charles probably hadn't even realized it until after Elizabeth's father died. He must have found a copy of the map among Montgomery's papers.

DJ chuckled aloud. Francis Montgomery was indeed a smart man. When he gave his granddaughters this land, he knew exactly what it was worth. From the look of it, there was probably enough oil just below the surface to fuel the entire state of Texas. All they had to do was tap it, and they'd be set for life.

Everything was coming together now. DJ had always found it strange that such a strong-willed woman as Elizabeth had let her daughter go so easily. She knew Kat would be taken care of.

The door creaked open, and Kat emerged from the bathroom wearing only the pajama top DJ had left on the bathroom counter. Her milky-white skin glowed against the black silk fabric hanging loosely from her shoulders and across her thighs.

"Where do you want me?"

DJ couldn't divert her gaze. *I want you right here, in my bed, all twisted up in the sheets with me.*

"DJ?"

DJ blinked and looked to the files on the bed. "You can sleep in here. I'll take the couch." She gathered up the papers and rolled off. "Are you okay?"

She nodded. "I'll be fine."

DJ left the bedroom door partially open. It was killing her to see Kat like this and not comfort her. She stood just outside the door debating whether to go back in. When she heard the lulled whimpering sounds of Kat crying, she rushed into the bedroom and took her into her arms.

"I'm fine," Kat said, and quickly wiped away the tears. "Just go away, DJ."

She brushed a strand of damp hair from Kat's face. "Isn't it about time you realized I'm not going anywhere?"

Kat leaned into her and let a huge sob spill out. "What am I gonna do?" she said between short, uneven breaths laced with anguish.

"Baby steps, Kat." DJ pressed her lips to the top of Kat's head. "Just take baby steps." She felt the warmth of Kat's tears on her chest, and her heart constricted, knowing she had been partly to blame for Kat's pain. Slowly, but surely, DJ would prove to Kat she could depend on her.

"Stay with me? Please?" Kat whispered softly, brushing her lips against the soft cotton covering DJ's chest.

"I'm right here," DJ mumbled, trying desperately to keep her feelings in check. She suppressed the sensations that buzzed through her as she immediately responded to the woman she longed for, the woman she loved. This was uncharted territory.

"Make love to me," Kat said, looking up at her through bladed, tear-soaked lashes.

Rejecting her this time would be a mistake. In a matter of days, Kat's life had become as fragile as finely blown glass, and DJ refused to shatter it. She placed her mouth on Kat's, and they fell onto the bed. DJ drew back and looked into her deep-blue eyes. Could she possibly fill the need she saw in them? She desperately wanted to be the one who could fulfill all Kat's dreams, and it scared the hell out of her.

Kat unbuttoned the silk pajama top and let her hands fall to her sides as though giving herself fully. DJ moved closer, took Kat into her arms, and kissed her. Her hands trembled as she skimmed the curves of Kat's waist. She traveled farther, letting her fingers circle around one breast, spiraling up to its peak and pinching the nipple between her fingers. Kat gasped, and DJ was instantly, ridiculously wet. She immediately sucked Kat's other nipple into her mouth, was rewarded with an even more intense gasp. She returned to Kat's mouth and kissed her deeply before she trailed her lips down across the smooth, delicate skin of her belly. The subtle tremors DJ felt in Kat as she journeyed farther made her senses hum. Stopping just below Kat's belly button, she tasted and teased the sweet spot with her tongue.

Kat quivered and reached for her panties. DJ took her cue and moved them slowly down her thighs, grazing each passing spot on her legs with her fingertips. Kat's hands went to DJ's hair, tugging her in for another deep kiss.

She tugged at DJ's shirt. "I want you close when I come."

Kat inched farther onto the bed and stared as DJ removed her clothes with a look that made DJ feel particularly vulnerable. She settled in next to Kat, her body hot against her, and slid a finger between Kat's wet, swollen folds and inside. Kat raised her hips, pressing hard against her hand. She added another finger, and Kat thrust harder. With DJ's mouth fused to Kat's, her fingers deep inside, they were completely in sync. When DJ circled her thumb around Kat's clit, she tore her mouth away, letting a loud growl explode from within as she rode out the orgasm.

She let her legs fall open, and DJ moved down her body and guided each one over her shoulders. She kissed each thigh before she teased her way to her center and buried herself there, letting Kat's wetness cover her. Kat's ragged breaths quickened again with each stroke of DJ's tongue. She slid a finger inside, then another as Kat let out a low, rolling moan.

"DJ, look at me," Kat whispered in a ragged breath. DJ gazed into her dark-blue eyes, took another stroke, and felt Kat tighten around her fingers as she watched her launch into orgasm. What an amazingly beautiful sight. Loving this woman was incredible.

After the aftershocks subsided, DJ crawled up next to her and nestled Kat into the crook of her shoulder. Making Kat come had been the most exquisitely gratifying event DJ had ever experienced. She would do it a thousand times more without ever expecting anything in return.

Without any urgency, Kat had been somehow content to let DJ delve into the warm darkness of her soul, illuminating each of her senses one by one as she trekked into the pure depths of her existence. She'd slowly and methodically explored Kat's body, touching, tasting, and experiencing it as though she'd never done it before. There was so much more of Kat she wanted to discover. DJ had always wondered how anyone could limit herself to only one woman, and now she knew. They didn't speak again. She stayed awake, feeling the warmth of Kat tucked tightly against her until she drifted off to sleep, knowing now just how strong the bond could be. Giving up Kat would be like ripping out a piece of her heart.

CHAPTER TWENTY-FOUR

K at sat on the edge of the bed watching the sunrise as DJ slept. It was a beautiful sight. Not much different here than at the ranch, except the sun fought to peek through the spaces between the high-rise buildings, and at home it filled the sky. She had to admit the burnt-orange mixed with cherry-red colors mirrored in the high-rise windows was a spectacular sight. But nothing could beat seeing those same vibrant colors, sometimes tinged with a bit of purple after a storm, bounce off the scattered clouds as the sun rose above the trees at the ranch.

Just a few hours ago, the storm had been in its fullest fury. Thunder rolled outside, and lightning had flashed through the window as she'd locked herself around DJ and launched into spasms of pure ecstasy. She'd pushed all her insecurities and doubts away and had let DJ explore every part of her. Kat's pure need for her had won the battle between her heart and her head. She'd shuddered as DJ's fingers penetrated her, and she'd reveled in the incredible sensations that coursed through her.

When she was totally spent, Kat had collapsed onto DJ's chest and listened to her heartbeat as it slowly returned to normal. She hadn't wanted to budge. She wasn't ready for the cool early morning air to destroy the lasting heat between them. In the soft glow of the city lights just outside the window, Kat listened to the soft pitter-patter of the rain. Her passion hadn't dissipated nearly as quickly as the storm. Her nerve endings had buzzed with the feel of the hands resting across her. Kat had known if DJ moved a muscle, she'd easily ignite again. Then she'd done it. DJ had slid her hand up Kat's side to her breast, and there was no moving quickly that time. Kat had felt her way across

DJ's body, tasting and touching, memorizing every part of her, every response from her. She never wanted to forget how DJ made her feel, how perfect love could be when an emotional connection bound them together.

It was crazy, but nothing in her life had been so clear as the way she'd felt at that moment with DJ. She wasn't thinking about Arizona anymore. DJ's face was burned into her mind now. She'd lain with her head on DJ's chest listening to the slow, rhythmic beat of her heart, wondering about the woman who she now knew loved her unconditionally. If nothing else, she'd shown her *that* these past few days by taking care of her in her time of need and absorbing every bit of verbal abuse she'd spewed at her without a single word of reprisal. Everything had been perfect…for a night.

DJ had changed her. Kat never thought she'd be able to love another woman as deeply as she'd loved Arizona. Sure, she'd had sex with other women, but what DJ gave her was more than just physical. She gave her intimacy, something she'd been unable to think about, let alone recapture after losing Arizona.

She picked up the file of documents DJ had collected on her and flipped through the pages. Her heart sank. In reality, she still had no idea who DJ Callahan really was, and she couldn't help but want to know everything about her. She watched her chest rise and fall with every breath, fighting the urge to crawl back into bed and make love to her again. She *did* love DJ. Kat wouldn't deny that fact, but everything she'd come to know as truth in her life had suddenly turned to fiction. She was questioning everything from the current life she'd built for herself to the very core of her existence.

Over the years, Kat had constructed an impenetrable shield around herself, preventing anyone who'd ever cared from growing too close. But for the past few years she hadn't really been living at all. Not the way she should've been. In the near future, she needed to make some difficult decisions in her life. But for now, it was time to go back to the only thing she knew was real—the Jumpin' J Ranch.

She dressed and silently crept out of the bedroom into the kitchen, where she picked up the phone and called a cab. As she jotted a note on the pad next to it, a tear fell from her eye, blurring the writing. She tore off the page with a few last thoughts about what life would be like here in Austin with DJ. Kat already knew she could love her for the rest of her life. Living this life in Austin would be the challenge. She almost tore up the note and put it in her pocket, but left it on the kitchen counter instead. She filed the unrealistic fantasy away in a place her heart could easily ignore. Even though DJ continually surprised her with her compassion, Kat resolved that any relationship between the two of them couldn't continue, not in Austin.

After glancing around the apartment, she plucked a rose from the vase in the foyer, held it to her nose, and took in a deep breath. She let a soft smile creep across her face as she headed to the elevator. The scent of lavender roses would always stir memories of the love, contentment, and passion she'd shared with DJ. Kat pressed the elevator button, the doors opened almost immediately, and she stepped inside. Her stomach tightened, and the sudden unbearable feeling of loss rolled through her as she descended to the lobby. Tears streamed down her cheeks as she fell against the elevator wall and gripped the railing for balance. Her usual confidence had dissolved into a chaotic pile of uncertainty. How had she become this attached to DJ in so little time? The elevator stopped, and she held the rose to her nose one last time before she slipped it into the railing and rushed into the lobby.

"Good morning, miss," the doorman said, holding the front door open for her. "Is everything all right?"

"No, it isn't, but it will be soon," she murmured, not bothering to wipe away the tears.

A horn blared and she jumped. Reality hit her. The sunrise might be just as beautiful here, but the ecosystem was very different.

"This cab must be for you." The doorman gave her a charming smile before rushing in front of her to open the car door.

She swiped the moisture from her cheeks. "Thank you," she said, sliding into the cab.

"Where to?" the driver asked.

"Austin General."

Unsure she was up to seeing Virgil, Kat stopped at the nurses' station to get an update on his condition before entering the intensive care unit.

"Can I help you?" the nurse asked, lifting her eyes briefly from the chart where she was making notations.

"Can you give me an update on Virgil Jackson's condition this morning?"

"Are you a relative?"

Kat hesitated and then nodded. "I'm his daughter."

"Let me find his chart." She went to the computer and worked the keyboard quickly. "He's doing much better today. At this rate, he'll be out of here in no time." She clicked a few keys and came back to the counter. "I think he's awake. You can see him if you like."

Kat heard the click of Elizabeth's cane coming down the hall and stepped toward Virgil's room. She stopped and took in a few deep breaths, trying to suppress the overwhelming anxiety that coming face-to-face with her mother provoked.

"Good morning, Kathryn." Elizabeth's eyes swept the length of Kat's body curiously.

"Good morning, Mother." Kat was sure her mother had noted the absence of a change of clothes. Kat fought her instinctive reaction to bolt as she crossed her arms and looked her mother in the eye, summoning all her strength to hold her own ground.

"You're here early."

"I just thought I'd stop by before heading to the ranch."

"Where's Danica?"

"At home, I assume." Kat wasn't in the mood to play her mother's games this morning.

Elizabeth's neatly arched brows rose curiously. "I thought you went home with her yesterday."

"Well, you were wrong, Mother." Kat didn't want to give her the satisfaction of knowing that she'd needed DJ last night. She turned to the nurse. "My number is in the chart. You'll call me if anything changes?"

"Of course," the nurse said.

"Thanks for your help," Kat said, and took off to the elevator without another word to Elizabeth.

"Kathryn, aren't you even going in to see him?" The annoyance surfaced quickly in Elizabeth's voice. Her wooden cane clicked rapidly against the floor as she tried to keep pace with Kat.

"I don't think I'm in the right frame of mind for a visit with Virgil this morning." Kat narrowed her eyes and gave her mother a brief stare as she continued down the hallway.

Elizabeth took Kat's arm and led her into a small waiting area. "Kathryn, he needs you."

"Don't tell me about needs, Mother." Kat jerked her arm free, noting that her mother seemed remarkably strong for a woman who'd been laid up with a broken pelvis for six weeks. "You can't just drop a bombshell like that on me and think everything's going to be exactly the same as it was before."

"Please don't take your anger for me out on Virgil. He's always been very good to you." Elizabeth moved closer and Kat retreated. "I honestly thought you'd be happy to find out he was your father."

"Maybe I would've been, if you'd told me twenty years ago." She couldn't believe her mother's arrogance.

"Things were more complicated then."

"Complicated." Kat's voice rose, bitterness spilling out. "My God, Mother. How could you let me grow up thinking I had a father who hated me?" Kat's head spun. She could have avoided all the insecurities and self-doubt her father had instilled in her. Instead, the negativity she'd cultivated from her father's indifference to her was burned into her very being.

"That wasn't easy for me, Kathryn." Elizabeth hobbled to the window. Her recovering body now seemed strained by the chase. "I tried my best to make up for it."

"How's that?" Kat's anger flared. "By cutting me off when I got married?" Her voice cracked. "By never once trying to contact me?"

"You were better off with Arizona." Elizabeth's clouded expression concealed any emotion she might be feeling. "She loved you. I knew you would be all right."

"You think I was better off without my family? Without my sister?" Kat's voice dropped off suddenly. "Without you?" The feeling of loss crashed through her, and Kat thought she might pass out.

"Oh, Kathryn." Elizabeth's voice wavered. "If you'd stayed, Charles would've made your life miserable. I wasn't going to let him destroy your spirit any more than he already had."

Kat raised her brows and continued to stare. "Why was Daddy so good to Rebecca?"

"Because he thought she was his," Elizabeth said, her voice thick with irony. "But I knew from the moment I saw her, she wasn't." She smiled lightly. "She looked just like you."

"Forgive me, Mother, but I could have sworn you said you and Charles never slept together?"

Elizabeth spun around and lost her balance momentarily. Kat reached to steady her. "Charles wasn't a very nice man, Kathryn, and some things are better left alone."

Kat wasn't expecting to see sadness in her mother's eyes and felt a twinge of sympathy for her. "Are you ever going to tell her?"

Elizabeth squared her shoulders and regained her composure. She let go of Kat's arm and balanced herself with her cane. "I suppose I'll have to now."

"Just what exactly do you want from me?" Kat sank down into a chair, cradling her head. The reality was becoming too much for her. She didn't know how much more of this she could take.

"I was hoping *you* would help me talk to her, and then maybe we could all become acquainted with each other again." Elizabeth hesitated before resting her hand on Kat's head and petting her lightly. "As I recall, when you were younger, we used to be quite close."

She couldn't do this. Not now. "I have to go." Kat jumped up and rushed across the room. "I have to take care of a few more things before I go to the ranch." She stopped in the doorway and turned toward Elizabeth. "Things could have been different, you know." She shook her head. "So much different."

"They still can be." Elizabeth's disposition softened, reminding Kat of the mother she once had.

Kat fought the urge to go to her, be captured in her arms and feel the warmth she remembered. "Maybe so." She dropped her gaze to the floor and continued out the door.

❖

Rebecca was hard at work behind her desk when Kat walked through the doorway. "Boy, you're certainly up early."

Rebecca glanced up momentarily. "Look who's talking."

"Just thought I'd stop by before I leave town."

Rebecca pushed back in her chair. "You want a cup of coffee?"

"Love one." Kat slipped her coat off and tossed it onto the arm of the couch. She needed something to keep her going this morning. She hadn't had much sleep last night, and her eyelids were becoming increasingly heavy.

Rebecca pressed the intercom button. "Jenny, I need—"

"On my way," Jenny said, bustling through the door with a tray of coffee and assorted pastries.

Kat laughed, sliding down onto the couch. "You should give that girl a raise."

"Believe me, she's very well paid." Rebecca handed Kat a cup of coffee. "Finding someone you can trust in this business isn't easy or inexpensive."

"I'm sure." Apparently, her mother paid people very well to keep her secrets.

"How's Virgil?"

"Doing pretty well, considering."

"Good. Did you and Dani work everything out last night?" Her brows eased up curiously, and she leaned against the arm of the sofa.

"What makes you think I was with her?" Kat asked, embarrassed to admit she'd needed DJ more last night than she'd ever imagined.

"Well, you weren't at the hospital and you didn't stay at my place, so I just figured…"

Kat took in a deep breath and slowly shook her head.

"You did." Rebecca's voice rose. "Did you work things out?"

"We didn't really talk," Kat said with a groan as she dropped her hands to the couch and dug her fingers into the cushion. "I don't even know what I'm doing anymore."

"Nobody knows what they're doing when they're in love." Rebecca chuckled. "If they did, it wouldn't be any fun."

"Feeling so confused all the time isn't fun." She took a sip of coffee, and it immediately rolled in her stomach.

Rebecca gave her a smile. "I understand. Sometimes I wonder if it's worth it."

"Are you in love with Mark?"

"I don't know." She brought the cup of coffee to her lips. "I mean, he's really good to me and all. But I'm still waiting for all the bells and whistles to go off."

Kat remembered clearly when the bells and whistles had gone off for her. She shook the thoughts of DJ from her mind. "How long have you been seeing him?"

"About a year."

Kat scrunched her nose. "I hate to tell you, Bec, but if they haven't gone off by now, it's probably not going to happen."

"Yeah, I know." Rebecca dropped onto the couch. "Aren't we a pair?" She laughed. "You have it and don't want it, and I want it and don't have it."

"Yep. Quite a pair."

❖

DJ rolled over and reached for Kat, but all she found were silk pajamas. "Kat." She didn't respond. "Kat." Still no response. "Damn." She hopped out of bed and rushed into the bathroom. Empty. She knew she should've resisted last night, but Kat was in such a fragile state she was afraid to say no. DJ didn't want to complicate Kat's life any more than it already was, but she had. She'd complicated both their lives. She slid on her jeans and headed into the kitchen. There she saw the note Kat had written, and the sinking feeling that hit her was almost unbearable.

DJ,

I'll never forget last night. The comfort you gave me will be forever burned into my heart. But going forward, it will only be a memory. You and I live in two different worlds, and anything between us must remain in the past.

Kat

Kat's words stung deep in DJ's heart, words similar to what she herself had used many times before. Until now, she'd had no idea how devastating they could be. She wadded up the note and hurled it across the kitchen before she sprinted into the bedroom and put on the rest of her clothes. DJ had to find her before she left town.

❖

She rushed by the nurses' station and sped down the hallway to the ICU. She'd found the rose Kat had left in the elevator and knew she'd been thinking of her when she'd left, but waking up alone this morning was not a good start.

She pushed open the door to Virgil's room. "Good morning, Elizabeth."

"Good morning, Danica." Elizabeth studied her, seeming to observe her foul mood.

"How are you today, Virgil?" DJ asked, genuinely concerned.

"Still a bit tender." He touched his ribs gently. "But I'm doin' much better. Thanks."

"Good." DJ nodded. "You want to tell me what happened the other night at the ranch?"

"I was in the stable closing up for the storm when Victoria and her boys showed up." Virgil winced as he shifted slightly. "Can you raise the top of the bed some for me?" He pointed to the buttons on the side of it.

DJ pushed the button, and Virgil rose to a reclining position. "Is that better?"

"Much." He shifted the pillow behind his head. "Victoria made some nasty reference to Kat and pretty much admitted she'd killed Arizona."

DJ snapped her gaze to Virgil and leaned in closer, thinking she might have misunderstood. "She admitted that to you?"

Virgil scratched at the stubble on his chin. "Not outright, but I know that's what she meant."

"Try to remember, Virgil. I need to know exactly what she said."

"First off, she told me, I'd better be careful or I'd wind up just like my daughter. When I asked her what the hell she was talking about, she told me Arizona was diggin' into things she shouldn't."

"Digging into what?"

"I don't know. That's when I went after her. Her boys held me off and gave me a pretty good beatin'. Knocked me out cold." He reached up and touched the bandage on his head. "They must have set the fire after I was out."

DJ raked her fingers through her hair and moved to the side of the bed.

"Oh, yeah. She did say one more thing." Virgil tensed and grabbed the side railing, moving himself forward in the bed before he winced and fell against the mattress.

Elizabeth pushed out of her chair and rushed to his side. "That's enough. You need to rest."

"I'm fine," Virgil said as he raised his hand and grabbed DJ's arm to steady himself.

"What else did she say, Virgil?"

"With me out of the way, Kat would be all hers."

DJ stood at Virgil's bedside gripping the railing as she put all the pieces together in her head. It wasn't just about the money. It was about Kat, a beautiful, unsuspecting woman whose only need in life was to feel loved again. A woman whom DJ had callously taken advantage of.

Virgil collapsed against the pillow. "The woman's deranged. She seems to think if she gets rid of everyone Kat loves, she'll come runnin' to her."

DJ pushed herself from the bed railing. "Speaking of Kat, have either of you seen her this morning?" She didn't want to let on that she'd been with her last night.

"Yes. She was here earlier," Elizabeth said. "I spoke with her briefly before she left."

"Did you explain her sudden change in heritage?" DJ was curious to hear the story as well.

Elizabeth let out a heavy sigh. "I tried, but she wasn't very receptive."

DJ raised her eyebrows. "Perhaps you wouldn't mind explaining it to me. You've put me in a very awkward position, Elizabeth."

"She did it for Kat," Virgil said, his face twisting into a grimace as he shifted again. "When Charles found out about us, he made life miserable for Elizabeth, and he would have done the same for Kat if Elizabeth had gone against him."

"If you were having an affair with Elizabeth, why in the world would Charles let you stay on at the ranch?"

"It was his way of punishing me," Elizabeth said bitterly. "Constantly daring me to tell Virgil about Kathryn."

"Why didn't you tell him?"

"Virgil was no match for Charles and his money." Elizabeth gave Virgil a remorseful look, and her eyes began to well. "He knew the girls were everything to me, and he wouldn't have hesitated to use his money to take them from me if we divorced. I just couldn't bear that."

Virgil took Elizabeth's hand. "It must have been very hard for you."

"Kathryn was a beautiful and spirited young girl," Elizabeth said softly, her face beaming. "She spent every waking moment at the stable. She loved the horses, and Charles couldn't change that," she said. "I tried to shield her from him. But as the years went by, Charles grew more hateful toward her." Elizabeth's voice wavered as her emotions became more evident. "When she fell in love with Arizona, I thought the best thing was to just let her go to experience life with someone who cherished her." She took in a deep breath, smiled, and squeezed Virgil's hand. "I knew Virgil would look after her for me whether she was his daughter or not."

"He sent you all the pictures." DJ now understood the reasons behind Elizabeth's decision to distance herself from Kat. It had been as much a sacrifice for her as it had been for Kat.

"And the only reason I let her go."

"Why didn't you keep in contact with her after she left?"

"It was best not to," Elizabeth said stiffly. "Charles could be a cruel man when something didn't please him."

DJ wandered around to the other side of the bed and gave Elizabeth a soft hug. "Charles didn't know about Rebecca, correct?"

Elizabeth managed a soft smile. "Kathryn has confided in you more than I thought."

She hadn't, but it was obvious to DJ in every way that the two of them were full-blooded sisters.

"Once Kathryn was gone, Charles put all his efforts into Rebecca, molding her into a ruthless business adversary, just like him."

DJ let out a short breath. "He did a pretty good job of that, but I think she has a bigger conscience than Charles ever had."

Elizabeth shook her head. "I certainly hope so."

"I have a few more people to see this morning," DJ said and turned to leave. "I'll be back later."

"Is one of them Kathryn?" Elizabeth asked, apparently pleased her plan to bring them together had worked.

"Hopefully," DJ said, and walked out the door.

Chapter Twenty-Five

Is he in?" DJ asked as she passed the same smiling brunette who'd been outside Mark's office a few days before.

"You can't just go in there." She jumped up and followed DJ inside.

"He'll see me." DJ ignored her protest, continued into the office, and rounded the desk. She pushed Mark's chair away from the desk, spun it around, and gripped the arms in her hands. "Did you know Victoria Maxwell was trying to kill Virgil Jackson in that fire?"

The flustered brunette rushed up and stood just inside the doorway. "I'm sorry, Mr. Hamilton. I couldn't stop her. Do you want me to call security?"

Mark turned his head to the side. "No, Joanne. Just close the door on your way out." DJ could hear the tremble in Mark's voice.

Joanne hesitated in the doorway, waiting until DJ released the chair and backed up.

"Go on. Everything's fine." Mark pushed out of his chair and moved it between them.

"My apologies, ma'am," DJ said as she walked around the desk and planted herself on the edge of it.

Joanne reluctantly turned and closed the door behind her.

"You know, I've been racking my brain trying to figure out just how Victoria Maxwell fits into this picture." DJ fingered through the files on Mark's desk. "The woman who claims to have a master's degree in finance from the University of Southern California has an IQ of about eighty. She seems to be no more than an uneducated thug." She dropped a file onto the desk. "I had to ask myself, what the hell was she doing in little old Kerrville, Texas? And why in the world would Charles Belmont deed all that property over to a woman like her?"

Mark sat down and crossed his arms. His eye twitched nervously as he waited for DJ to make her point.

"But then I started doing a little more checking into her background and found that Victoria isn't really from California after all. She's actually from a small town here in Texas by the name of Everly. Population about five thousand. Coincidentally, the same little town where you grew up. I can see you tried to cover Victoria's lack of intelligence as best you could, but you knew someday, someone was bound to get wise."

DJ wandered around the room biding her time, waiting for the moment when Mark had had enough. The man was a snake, and DJ was going to make him squirm until he admitted it.

She observed the framed diploma from Harvard hanging on the wall. "Graduating with honors at Harvard." DJ's voice rose. "Your parents must have been very proud." She tapped the glass covering it with her finger.

"My mother was. My father died when I was nine." Mark jumped out of his chair to straighten the frame.

"I bet not many classmates from your small farming community fared as well as you and Victoria."

"Not many." Mark's voice was sharp and full of arrogance.

"It was probably quite a hardship on your mother to put you through college, then law school after that." DJ already knew exactly how much Mark's mother had spent on his education. She'd checked into Mrs. Hamilton's financial records and found the farm mortgaged for every penny it was worth. Without financial help, she hadn't had enough money to fund the kind of education Mark received.

"Actually, I paid for most of it myself."

"By working for Charles Belmont, doing things most people can't stomach." DJ's spine stiffened knowing that, without her own father's presence in her life, it would have been easy for her to have fallen into the same circumstances.

Mark raked his fingers through his perfectly placed, jet-black hair. "You don't know what it's like to wonder where your next meal's coming from, working the farm all day, wearing your brother's worn-out clothes." He paced the room. "Having your feet ache every night because his old boots are a size too small. Belmont offered me something I'd never had before."

"What was that?"

"Freedom." Mark rubbed his forehead nervously. "Freedom to have anything I want. Any time I want it."

DJ could hear the determination in Mark's voice, which only confirmed just how desperate the man was to succeed. She understood his want for material objects in life, but not his heated desire to leave his family and the farm.

"Was it worth taking someone else's life?"

"I didn't have anything to do with that." Mark's tone was firm and insistent. "I work the paper, Dani. I don't kill people."

"Victoria Maxwell does, and you brought her here." DJ pointed a finger in Mark's direction. "You're involved, whether you like it or not."

"You don't know how evil that woman can be."

"I know she killed Arizona Jackson, and she's probably responsible for the Belmonts' car accident too. Now that she's tried to kill Virgil, my bet is you're next," DJ said coolly. "Now, if that's not a problem, I'll leave you to her." DJ stood up and headed to the door. "What happens to you doesn't matter to me."

"Wait," Mark said, prompting DJ to stop. "I didn't know about Arizona until after it was done." His hand shook as he rubbed his temple. "And I wasn't about to give up everything I've worked for just because Victoria got greedy." He sank into his chair. "This wasn't the way it was supposed to happen. I was just expected to transfer a few titles. That was all. Nobody was meant to get hurt." He closed his eyes and pinched the bridge of his nose. "But Victoria couldn't settle for just the money. She wanted Kathryn." He threw up his hands. "What is it about her? When it comes to class, her sister has her two times over."

That's where he was wrong. Rebecca had class, but Kat knew how to use it. With her face to the door, DJ grasped the knob without turning it. "What did Belmont have to say about that?"

"He wasn't the kind of father I'd expected. I thought it was just about the money, but he didn't care what happened to Kathryn. He told Victoria to do whatever she wanted with her."

"And you just let it happen?" DJ gripped the doorknob.

"By that time, I didn't have a choice."

"Damn." DJ slapped the door with an open palm and spun around. She'd hoped Belmont wasn't as cold and heartless as Elizabeth had made him out to be, but the man had no conscience.

The door flew open, and two FBI agents came rushing through it. "Everything all right in here?"

"Yeah." DJ shrugged. "He's all yours." She pulled the wire from her shirt and handed it to one of the agents before she turned to look at Mark. "I suggest you start talking, or I can guarantee you'll either be dead or in prison for the rest of your life."

The agents waited calmly as he stood up and put on his suit jacket.

Mark's lips curved into a grin. "Like I told you before, you're not the only cowgirl Kathryn's charmed." His cold, gray eyes squinted as he threw one last jab at her. "She probably would've been dead too, if Victoria hadn't taken such a fancy to her."

As DJ left Mark's office, the thought of telling Kat the truth about Arizona's death had her stomach threatening to spill. Telling her that it was a well-thought-out plan of her father's to gain control of her ranch wasn't going to be easy. The fact that Victoria had also done it because she'd thought Kat came along with the deal would only make her feel more responsible and compound her grief.

Kat heard the light knock on the door before she looked up to see DJ coming into the office. The sight of her brought an instinctive smile to Kat's lips, and it took her a moment to force it away. She and Rebecca both sprang up from the couch and headed in different directions—Rebecca to the door and Kat to the other side of the office.

"I thought I might find you here," DJ said.

"Jenny," Rebecca shouted.

She met her in the doorway. "Yes, Miss Belmont?"

"Would you bring Dani a cup of coffee, please?" Rebecca watched DJ following Kat across the room.

"Sure thing," Jenny said, already turning to the hallway.

"I missed you this morning," DJ said softly, dropping her briefcase on the edge of the desk.

"I had a few things to take care of."

"You went by the hospital?"

"Uh-huh." Kat crossed her arms. This was it. She had to do it now. Even though her heart was breaking inside, she had to do it. She had to make DJ believe she didn't love her.

"Is everything all right?" DJ's gaze locked with hers.

"As well as can be expected." Kat purposely kept her response cold and cynical.

"Your note..." DJ searched her face. "I don't understand."

"What's not to understand?" Kat darted her glance away quickly, afraid they might give DJ a hint of the pain she was feeling. Writing that note hadn't been easy, and this was going to be even harder.

"It'll never be just a memory." DJ lifted Kat's chin to meet her gaze, and her pained expression tore through her. "Last night was the beginning of something, Kat."

Kat shook her head and let out the breath she had trapped inside her chest. Her stomach churned, and tears threatened to gush out. "DJ, you're making more of it than it was." Staring into DJ's dark, wounded eyes, Kat forced the words out. "I just needed to be with someone." She looked away. "Anyone."

DJ grabbed Kat's shoulders. "Damn it, Kat. It was more than that."

Yes, it was. Kat fought to keep her composure. It was much more, but no way could she let DJ know how she felt. She had to break it off now, before it went any further. She saw no point in wanting something she couldn't have and loving someone she couldn't trust.

She tried to break free, but DJ kept a firm grip. The anguish in her eyes stabbed at Kat's heart. Her knees began to buckle beneath her, along with her resolve. This was absolute agony. Kat hadn't thought she could possibly hurt any more than she already did.

"What's up, Dani?" Rebecca came across the room and flopped down into the chair behind her desk.

DJ choked out a cough. "We'll continue this later." After letting her hands drag down Kat's arms slowly, DJ went to the desk, opened her briefcase, and turned her attention to Rebecca. "I did some digging the other day, and I came across some information on Kat's neighbor, Victoria Maxwell."

"What kind of information?" Kat asked, her voice gravelly.

"It looks as though you were right about the land originally belonging to your grandfather."

"I knew it." Kat stared into the briefcase, wondering what was new in the folder bearing her name across the top. "How did you find out?"

"I have a few friends at the courthouse. I convinced one of them to give me access to the vault."

"The vault?" Kat glanced up at her and then quickly back to the folders. She couldn't bring herself to look into the eyes of the woman whose heart she'd just shattered.

"That's where they keep the archives." DJ took a handful of manila file folders from her briefcase. "A friend of mine let me borrow a few documents," she said, laying them on the desk. "I also checked some of the financial records at the ranch." She pulled an additional file out. "It looks as though the Jumpin' J had done rather well the year before Arizona died."

"I'm aware of that," she said impatiently, aggravated that DJ had been able to gather so much information on her.

"From what I could find, it looks as though Arizona was checking into buying the land abutting yours just to the north."

"Victoria's land?"

"Yep."

"I wonder why Arizona didn't tell me?"

"I think she may have wanted to surprise you. For your anniversary, perhaps."

Kat closed her eyes. "That September, we would've been married five years."

"And that's not the end of it. Apparently, before Maxwell ended up with it, your grandfather had left the land to Rebecca in his will."

"Wait a minute." Rebecca hopped out of her chair. "Grandfather didn't leave me any land."

DJ took the map out of the file and unfolded it. "Yes, he did. You were supposed to receive it when you turned twenty-one. Just as Kat received the land where she built the Jumpin' J."

Rebecca leaned across the desk to look at the map. "What's this?"

"A geological surveyor's map," Kat said, looking at it carefully. "But it looks different than the one I have."

"It is different. You see these green blotches running throughout the land?" DJ pressed her finger to the map, circling the area.

"Uh-huh." Kat nodded and Rebecca stared at it, looking confused.

"Those are geological markings," she said as she gave DJ a strange look. "Oil?"

"Yep. Your land is filled with it."

"That's why Victoria wants it so badly." Kat's mind filled with a flurry of still-unanswered questions. "But she already had Rebecca's land. It must be worth millions. Why does she want mine too?"

"That's the kicker. You see, it wasn't really her land. It may have been in Victoria's name, but she was just a front for your father. Somehow, Charles had Mark convince Rebecca to sign the land over to Victoria."

"I never signed any land over to Victoria Maxwell." Rebecca spun the map around to look at it, then flipped it around to DJ. "Mark would never do anything like that without telling me."

"Are you sure about that?" DJ tossed a small stack of papers onto the desk in front of her. "That's your signature on those documents, isn't it?"

Rebecca's eyes widened as she thumbed through them. "I never signed these."

"That's what I was trying to tell you when I came to see you the other night."

Rebecca sank into her chair. "I can't believe he did this."

"Their plan was coming along smoothly until Victoria got greedy. My guess is, when she saw you, Kat, she wanted to be rich *and* married." DJ looked at Kat with soft, warm eyes and it occurred to her that the thought had crossed her mind as well.

"But I...I was already married," Kat stuttered as she pressed her fingertips to her forehead. The confusion filling her mind was overwhelming. She sucked in a deep breath and tried to ignore the staggering urge to bolt from the room.

DJ rubbed the back of her neck. "There's no easy way for me to say this, Kat. I don't believe Arizona's death was an accident."

"What?" Kat snapped her gaze to DJ, who gave her a stare completely void of emotion.

"From what you've told me, Arizona was an expert horseman. It's unlikely any horse could have thrown her." DJ hesitated. "Arizona must have found out that your father had deeded the land to Victoria without Rebecca's consent. I'm afraid she may have paid for that knowledge with her life."

Kat's stomach lodged in her throat as the vivid memory of Arizona's death rushed back as though it had happened only yesterday. "Victoria was there." She stared at DJ. "When I found Arizona…" Her hand shook as she brushed her fingers across her lips. "She even called the ambulance." She reached for the edge of the desk to steady herself. "Why would Victoria do that if she wanted Arizona dead?"

DJ slid off the desk to hold her. "She wanted you, Kat."

Kat stared blankly as the revelation hit her. "She almost had me." She curled into DJ, her face pressed hard against the strength of her shoulder. A sudden chill ran down her spine, and she pushed away. "Until she tried to take over the ranch." Kat paced across the room, ignoring any further attempts DJ made to comfort her. She had to be strong. She couldn't let herself depend on anyone else.

DJ sat on the edge of the desk. "Yesterday, Victoria told Virgil that she and her boys ambushed Arizona on the trail that day."

Kat sank onto the couch. "It would've never happened if I'd been with her."

Rebecca sat on the couch next to Kat and put her arm around her. "You don't know that, Kat."

"She's right, Kat. When it comes right down to it, the whole thing is about money," DJ said, watching her closely. "The thought of having you may have been a perk for Victoria. But if you'd been with Arizona that day, they might have very well killed you too."

Rebecca opened her eyes widely. "You're telling me Mark knew all about this?"

"I don't think he was actually involved in Arizona's death, but I do think he went along with it after the fact. I'm sure both Victoria and Charles promised to compensate him very well."

"And then my father died." Rebecca still seemed uncertain, mulling everything over.

"Mark was suddenly left out in the cold. All the land was in Victoria's name, and Mark didn't have any leverage."

Rebecca's eyes lowered as what DJ told her seemed to sink in. "He did it to himself, didn't he?"

"Uh-huh. Everything Mark did was illegal. Victoria knew if Mark exposed her, he'd be implicating himself too. So for the past month he's been working his tail off, trying to cover his tracks."

Rebecca launched off the couch. "All the while continuing to seduce me, so he could still be in the money. I should've known he had a reason for being so secretive. He had his own agenda from the start."

Kat sprang up after her. "And my father, or the man I thought was my father, engineered the whole thing."

Rebecca spun around to Kat. "What do you mean, the man you thought was your father?"

Kat let out a heavy breath and looked over at DJ, silently imploring her to explain. Kat was still having trouble with her newfound heritage.

DJ seemed to know what Kat was thinking and took the lead. "Elizabeth had an affair. We found out yesterday that Virgil is Kat's biological father."

"What the fuck? Who told you that?"

"Mother told me while Virgil was in the hospital."

"Oh my God, Kat." The words whooshed out softly as Rebecca hauled her into a tight embrace.

"I know. I'm still trying to absorb it." Kat knew she should tell Rebecca the whole truth, but she just couldn't bring herself to put her through the same pain she was feeling.

DJ gathered up the documents. "Your Grandfather Montgomery must have known Charles wasn't your father. He made sure the two of you would never have to do without." She slid the files into her briefcase and snapped it shut. "Charles probably didn't know about the oil until after your grandfather died. I'm sure he must have found a copy of the map among Montgomery's papers." A sly smile crept across her face.

"What?" Kat snapped, noticing her grin.

"It must have irritated Charles no end that Montgomery didn't leave it to Elizabeth." DJ latched her briefcase and stood quietly, giving them a few moments to absorb all the information she'd just delivered.

Rebecca slid down onto the couch, breaking the trance they both seemed to be in. "How did you find out about all this?"

"I went to see Mark this morning, and he told me the whole story."

Kat was silent as she stood staring out the window onto the city. She hated this place—the people, the politics, and everything else that came with it.

DJ grasped Kat's shoulders tenderly and pressed her lips to her head. "I'm sorry, Kat."

"Please don't." Kat shrugged out of her grasp. The warmth of DJ's touch reminded her that everything that existed here was a complete fabrication, including the hurtful words she'd spoken to DJ earlier. Kat wanted her. No, she needed her more than she would admit.

DJ slid her briefcase from the desk. "I'll leave you two alone for a while. Kat, I'll be in my office. I'd like to see you before you leave."

Kat nodded. She knew what she had to do now. The only thing she could do. She had to go to the ranch, away from this madness…Now. She raced to the couch, picked up her coat, and headed for the door.

"Where are you going?" Rebecca's voice rose in what sounded like desperation, and it hit Kat somewhere deep in her heart, in a place she hadn't felt anything in a very long time.

Kat stopped in the doorway. "I'm going to the ranch. I have to check the stable and see what kind of damage the fire caused."

"What about Virgil?"

"He's doing fine. I checked on him this morning."

"What about me?" Rebecca's voice faltered. "You can't just abandon me. Not again. You aren't the only one who's been deceived."

Kat turned to see tears streaming from Rebecca's eyes. *Damn! How selfish can I be? Thinking about only myself when the blow Rebecca received has been just as devastating.* She threw her coat onto the couch and slid down next to her.

"Come here." She pulled Rebecca to her and held her close.

"I don't know why I'm crying." Rebecca sniffed, trying to stop the tears continuing to spill out. "I'm not even in love with him."

"You trusted him, and he lied. That's what hurts." Kat wiped the black streaks of mascara from Rebecca's cheeks with her thumbs.

"One thing you never did was lie to me."

Kat drew in a deep breath and shifted to tuck her foot up under herself. Rebecca was right. Kat had never lied to her before, and she wasn't about to start doing so now. She didn't want to tell Rebecca that Virgil had fathered them both. In all fairness, she should let her mother do it, let Elizabeth experience Rebecca's disappointment as well as her wrath. But Elizabeth wasn't here, and Rebecca was looking at her with the pleading eyes of not a ruthless businesswoman, but a little sister. She had to tell her now.

"There's something else, isn't there?" Rebecca asked.

"Listen, Bec." Kat closed her eyes and pressed her fingers to her temple. Her head was throbbing, and the pain was about to become ten times worse. "Mother has told me some details about her relationship with Daddy that aren't very pleasant."

Rebecca tilted her head. "Like what?"

Kat hesitated, gathering her thoughts. "Did you know they never shared the same bed?"

"I know they had separate rooms as I grew older, but they must have shared one at some point or another. After all, they conceived me."

It has to be done. Stop beating around the bush and just say it.

"No, *they* didn't," Kat said tentatively, tossing her arm up on the top of the couch.

"What are you talking about?" Rebecca's brows drew together. She wasn't fully understanding what Kat was saying. "Oh my God." She sank into the couch. "He's not my father either."

Kat shook her head. "No. He's not."

"I didn't think my life could get any worse. Now the very essence of my existence is being stripped away." She choked as if suddenly remembering to breathe. "How many men were there?"

Kat took her hand and held it tight. "Mother said she had only one love in her lifetime."

"And that was…" Her eyes flew wide and her face twisted. "Virgil Jackson?"

Kat fought to stifle a laugh when she saw the look on Rebecca's face. "Apparently so."

"That can't be true," she said, and jumped to her feet. "The man's a stable hand, for God's sake."

Kat stiffened, instinctively offended. She might be upset with Virgil for keeping the truth from her, but to Kat, Virgil was much more than just a stable hand. He'd been there since she was a little girl, teaching her everything she knew about horses, from stowing tack to breaking the toughest filly. He'd been a kind, gentle man who always took time for her. More time than her father ever had. Virgil Jackson was twice the man Charles Belmont ever was. She had no doubt in her mind now that he was her father in every way.

She watched Rebecca pace the office, rambling on about what people were going to say. Kat let out a slight chuckle and stood up. Only Rebecca would be more concerned about Virgil's status in the community than what kind of man he was.

Kat took her coat from the couch. "Listen, Bec. I really do have to go to the ranch and watch over things."

"Oh, right," Rebecca mumbled, obviously preoccupied.

Kat touched her shoulder lightly. "Why don't you come with me?"

Rebecca closed her eyes briefly and smiled. "Go ahead. I'll be fine."

Kat skimmed the back of her fingers across Rebecca's cheek. "You know who you are, Bec. Don't let what other people say change that." She wrapped her arms around her and kissed her temple. "I'll give you a call tomorrow."

Chapter Twenty-Six

As Kat drove the gravel road to the house, she felt the impact of the destruction deep in her heart. The damage wasn't quite as bad as she'd imagined, but seeing the huge, gaping hole in the side of the stable was a little more reality than she needed right now. She parked the truck and waded through the thick, black muck covering the ground. The stale smell of soggy, burnt embers filled her nose as she stood in the remains of Minow's stall. Terrifying visions of the fire filled her head, and she rushed to the barn. Relief washed through her when she saw the horses in the makeshift stable. Not spotting Minow, she hastened her pace as she made her way to the end stall, where she lay sprawled out on the ground in the corner.

"Oh, baby." Kat slid the gate open and entered the stall. "I'm so sorry I wasn't here to take care of you." She fell to her knees and rubbed the horse's neck gently. Minow let out a grunt. An overwhelming feeling of guilt came over her when she saw the burns on Minow's back, burns probably caused by the falling roof as she stood over an unconscious Virgil protecting him.

Kat sat and stroked her softly, thinking about the day she and Arizona had found her. There were so many horses at the auction that day. Kat had fallen in love with a beautiful palomino, but the bidding went much higher than she'd anticipated. She couldn't justify spending thousands of dollars on a horse she wanted just for her own pleasure.

Disappointed, she wasn't at all interested when they brought Minow out. She was a sad sight compared to the horse Kat had planned to take home. Minow was a two-year-old black Arabian with a tattered mane. Kat could tell Minow hadn't been cared for well. Her ribs were visible through her coat. She wasn't Kat's first choice, and probably not her second either, but Arizona insisted she bid. Arizona had a natural eye for horses and was right about this one. With a little food and special attention, Minow had quickly blossomed into a wonderful companion for Kat.

Kat closed her eyes and thought about Arizona, trying to envision her as she always had in the past. She couldn't see her. The only woman appearing in front of her now was DJ. *Fuck.* How could she forget her one true love for a woman who'd lied to her, a woman who'd joined forces with her mother to fuck up her life?

What the hell was I doing, telling my whole life story to a complete stranger? She let out a sigh and leaned against the wall. A stranger who'd forced Arizona's memory to sink into the shadows of her mind. Kat had known her less than a week, yet she'd invited her into her bed, and DJ had fulfilled her every need, filling her heart, loving her in a way no one else had been able to since Arizona. She'd made her feel as though nothing else mattered. But other things did matter, things between them that hadn't been resolved, possibly couldn't be resolved.

Kat heard the creak of the door opening and jumped to her feet. She wasn't surprised to see Victoria Maxwell strut across the barn.

"Victoria, I don't have time for your crap today."

"I knew if I waited long enough, you'd come home." Victoria crept slowly into the stall. Minow scrambled to her feet at the sound of her voice.

"I didn't think you'd show your face around here again after what you did to Virgil."

Victoria's lips spread into a wide smile. "Isn't there a chance we can work something out together? Form some sort of partnership?"

"You're completely delusional." Kat shielded herself behind Minow. "They're going to put you away for a long time, and I can't wait for the day they do."

"Feisty as ever." Victoria smiled. Her interest in Kat seemed to grow with each insult she threw at her. "You and I were good together." She shook her head. "We could've merged our land and had something really nice here."

"I already have something really nice here without you, Victoria." Kat held her voice steady as she noted the gasoline can just outside the stall. *Jesus. She's going to burn it again.* "You can't possibly be thinking about starting another fire."

Victoria raised an eyebrow. "What makes you think I started the last one?"

"I know it wasn't an accident." Kat didn't dare tell her Virgil had lived to tell her what happened.

"Well, this one won't be either." Victoria slapped the horse on its hip, and Minow bolted out of the stall and through the barn. "Boys, I've got this. Move all the horses and scram. I don't want any of them hurt."

"No one's going to let them take all the horses." There were at least ten ranch hands on the grounds at any given moment.

"I guess they wouldn't if they weren't all off trying to round up the cattle that broke through the range fence this morning."

"You're not going to get away with this." Kat tried to move past her, but Victoria blocked her way.

Victoria moved to her quickly and popped her in the nose with the palm of her hand. "I really wish we could've done this the easy way."

Kat tried to blink away the dizziness as pain wracked her and the taste of metal coated the back of her throat. Adrenaline raced through her system. She refused to die this way. Not now, not after everything she'd worked for. She swung her fists at Victoria as she pushed her, but she absorbed them without flinching. Kat tripped and fell backward, and Victoria was on her instantly. She closed her eyes tight as Victoria pelted her with her fists. The pain in her face became overwhelming. Her vision began to fade as Victoria's fingers wrapped around her throat. She struggled beneath her, scratching at Victoria's face, but she was too powerful.

❖

When DJ came around the corner to Rebecca's office, Jenny wasn't at her desk. She looked at her watch. It was too early for her to have gone to lunch. The door was slightly open, so DJ continued in to find Rebecca, sitting in her chair, turned away from her desk. She was staring out the window just as Kat had been earlier. DJ had wanted to flip Kat around and shake some sense into her, but she hadn't pushed. Kat had a lot to deal with right now, but sooner or later she would have to deal with DJ, whether she wanted to or not.

"Well, this is a first." DJ's voice stung with a mixture of surprise and amusement.

"What?" Rebecca rotated around in her chair with her perfectly arched brows raised inquisitively.

"I rarely catch you taking a moment to relax."

"Relax isn't exactly the word I would use." She tossed the pen she'd been rotating through her fingers onto the desk. "To say the least, it's been a very enlightening day." She leaned forward and let her head drop from side to side. "What's going to happen to Mark?"

"That depends on how much he cooperates."

"Isn't it just my luck?" She twisted in her chair. "At least with you, I knew where I stood."

"Sometimes you have to take chances in life to get what you want." DJ kept her expression still. "Even then, it doesn't always work out."

"Like you and Kat?" Rebecca said.

"Something like that." DJ curved her mouth into a thoughtful smile as she looked around the office. "By the way, where is she?"

"She went to the ranch."

The lump that had remained steady in DJ's stomach for the past few days catapulted to her chest, and her heart rate soared. "Damn!" She spun around and took off for the door. "When did she leave?"

Rebecca focused on the crystal clock on her desk. "About thirty minutes ago. I thought you knew." She shot out of her seat to head her off. "Didn't she come by to see you before she left?"

"No."

"You need to give her a little time, Dani."

DJ stopped just short of her. "Victoria Maxwell's still out there, Rebecca."

Rebecca's eyes widened. "I hadn't thought about that." She reached for her cell phone. "I'll call her."

DJ pushed by her, moving frantically toward the elevator. "I have to get there before Victoria finds her."

"Dani, wait. I'm coming with you," Rebecca shouted as she

followed her down the hallway with the phone pressed to her ear. "She's not answering."

❖

DJ slammed on the brakes, and the car slid across the gravel. She rolled out of the car, ran to the house, and threw open the door. She searched the entire house before joining Rebecca on the porch.

"She's not in there," DJ said as she spied Minow wandering around to the side of the barn. "Where'd the horse come from?"

"I don't know. Wasn't it there when we drove up?"

"No, it wasn't." DJ scrambled down the steps and across the yard. "Find some help." She made her way quickly through the makeshift stable, glancing in each stall she passed until she saw the gas can outside Minow's stall. She raced straight there and found Victoria hovering over Kat.

DJ grabbed Victoria by the collar and threw her up against the wall. Victoria threw a fist to DJ's face, and she knocked Victoria to the ground. She turned to tend to Kat, and when she saw the redness surrounding her dull-blue eyes as they fluttered open, DJ's anger exploded. She turned to Victoria and flew into a brutal frenzy, punching her relentlessly.

"DJ, stop. Please!" Kat's voice cracked through the haze of rage clouding DJ's head. "That's enough!" The sound of Kat's voice echoed through the ringing in her ears, and DJ backed away. She'd lost it.

She heard someone shout, "Call an ambulance." Two of the ranch hands pushed by DJ into the stall, one running to Kat and the other to Victoria.

DJ turned to Kat, who lay curled into the corner of the stall. DJ couldn't tell if Victoria or her own rage had forced her there. The frightened look in her eyes sliced through DJ's heart. The pulsing pressure in her veins made her head throb. She took in a breath to calm herself before she turned and gathered Kat into her arms, carrying her out of the barn to the porch for Rebecca to tend to her.

"Don't let your mother take you away from this place. No matter what she tells you," DJ said, staring into Kat's confused eyes. She left her with Rebecca, walked across the yard to the water spigot, and washed the blood from her bruised knuckles. When she heard the sound of sirens increasing in the distance, she dropped to the ground and propped herself up against the fence post, watching the police car and ambulance travel up the gravel road. Her mind was cluttered with emotions and guilt. She wouldn't use Kat's feelings for her to take her to Austin as Elizabeth wanted. The deal she'd struck with Elizabeth to pay off her family's farm would be breached. They would lose the farm unless she found another way to raise the money and save it from foreclosure.

Victoria had already been loaded into the ambulance when Kat spotted Mike, the emergency tech, as he stopped to check on DJ. She saw her shake her head when Mike tried to treat her lip and her hands. DJ pointed to the porch. Mike flipped his case closed before he came across to see Kat, where she was rejecting Rebecca's attempts to clean the blood from her face.

"How is she?" Kat asked as Mike approached.

"She has a few broken ribs, but she'll live." He knelt down in front of her and opened his kit.

"Not the one in the ambulance." She looked around him to catch another glimpse of DJ. If she hadn't shown up when she did, Kat might very well have been dead right now.

Mike gave her a curious look as she stared over his shoulder. "She's got a fat lip and her hands are bruised pretty badly, but nothing's broken." He opened a sealed package containing gauze and doused it with something. "Other than the nose, are you hurt anywhere?" He gently wiped the blood from the gaping cut running down the bridge of her nose.

"No. Nowhere else," she said, looking at him directly.

"Does it hurt?" Rebecca asked, watching Mike put a butterfly bandage across the wound.

"Like a mother…" Kat winced when he pressed the bandage down lightly.

"The medication will kick in soon, and she won't feel much of anything." Mike handed her a pill and a small bottle of water. "She's going to have a pretty pair of black eyes, though," he added, closing his case and standing up. "I don't think her nose is broken, but you need to take her to the doctor as soon as possible and have the rest of her checked out."

"Shouldn't you take her now?" Rebecca asked.

"I don't want to go now," Kat said firmly. "We'll go in the morning." She softened her tone. Her sister was only trying to help.

Rebecca lifted her shoulders and smiled at Mike before he went down the steps to his rig.

"Are you sure?" Rebecca turned to Kat, lightly touching the purple area spreading on each side of Kat's nose.

"I'm sure," Kat said, pushing her hand away. "She was going to kill me."

Rebecca's face was blank, and then she took Kat into her arms. "Thank God Dani was here."

Kat stared across the yard at DJ talking to the police and took in a deep, ragged breath. The sudden emptiness in her chest shocked her, and she felt queasy. "I need to go inside and lie down." She clamped her eyes closed to hold back the tears stinging them.

"That's probably a good idea." Rebecca helped her up from the rocker and inside the door.

Kat stopped in the doorway and turned to look at DJ once more. "Would you check on her?"

"Sure." Rebecca peeked over her shoulder. "I'll be right back."

DJ had just finished giving her statement to the police when she glanced over to the house and saw Rebecca helping Kat inside. She swung around, grabbed the fence, and let her head drop between her outstretched arms. She wanted to go to her, but she couldn't stomach the shock she'd seen in her eyes earlier.

"Hey," Rebecca said as she rubbed her hand across the middle of DJ's back.

DJ raised her head. "Hey."

She took DJ's hands from the fence and assessed the broken skin on her knuckles. "Are you all right?"

"I'm fine." DJ turned and took off to her car.

Rebecca kept stride next to her before she took hold of her arm. "Why are you leaving?" Her face wrinkled with confusion.

"She doesn't want me here." DJ looked up at the house. Kat was standing just inside the screen door with her arms wrapped across her chest.

"I don't think you can assume that. You just prevented her from being killed, didn't you?"

A jolt of pure terror shot through her. "Is she all right?"

"She might have a broken nose, but other than that, she's okay. You can't just run away from this like every other relationship you've had. She's my sister, Dani. You owe me more than that." Her tone was low and demanding.

DJ stopped suddenly, and anger bubbled in her chest. "I'm going to ignore that remark."

Rebecca blew out a short breath. "I'm sorry. I'm upset."

"Join the club."

Rebecca followed DJ to her car. "I'll stay here with Kat tonight."

DJ focused on the house. Kat stood at the window now. "Good. She needs someone with her."

"Why are you so sure that someone isn't you?"

DJ shook her head. "I made a deal with your mother, Rebecca. One that Kat will hate me for."

Rebecca narrowed her eyes. "What kind of a deal?"

"Don't worry. It's a deal I can't go through with now." *Now that I love her.* DJ shook her head and continued to the car. "It doesn't change the fact that I made it, just the same."

"She'll get over it, Dani, but you need to work out your own issues."

DJ stopped short. "Let it alone, Rebecca."

Rebecca put herself between the car and DJ. "Your dad's dead, Dani. You can't keep punishing yourself for something you had no control over."

She stared into DJ's eyes as though she could see right into her soul. DJ put her hands to her face, trying to conceal the tears she couldn't hold back any longer. "I didn't think the day I left would be the last time I saw him." She shook her head. "I didn't know what I was doing. I was too young and stupid to realize he was trying to do what he thought was best for me." The regret was suffocating her. If she could rewind time, DJ would change every minute she'd lost with her father.

Rebecca took DJ's hands in hers. "Why haven't you been to see your mother?"

DJ closed her eyes and choked out a cough, clearing the emotion knotted in her throat. "It's hard, Rebecca. You have no idea."

"Strength doesn't come from what you *can* do. It comes from doing the things you thought you couldn't. You really don't want to lose any more time with your mom." Rebecca wrapped her arms around DJ. "Or Kat." She forced DJ to look at her. "No regrets, remember?"

"I already have plenty of those." DJ shrugged and dropped into her car. "Tell her I'm sorry." She looked straight ahead, threw the car into gear, and fishtailed in the gravel as she drove off.

CHAPTER TWENTY-SEVEN

Kat entered the lobby of the Montgomery Building. She was ridiculously nervous about what was to come in Austin today: the board meeting, going up against her mother, and most of all, the possibility of seeing DJ again.

She'd kept in contact with both Rebecca and her mother throughout the past month but hadn't tried to contact DJ. Nor had DJ tried to contact her. After Virgil was released from the hospital, it didn't take long for Kat to make her peace with him, but she was still trying to work out her issues with her mother.

As she passed the security desk, Kat gave the guard a wave, then entered the elevator. She pressed the button for the twenty-fifth floor and hoped to avoid running into DJ on her way to Rebecca's office.

After exiting the elevator and heading down the hallway, she heard DJ's voice and quickly ducked just inside the door to Rebecca's office. She shivered. The butterflies fluttering in her stomach had suddenly turning into seagulls avoiding a storm at sea.

Through the small crack she'd left in the doorway, Kat could see DJ at the end of the hallway talking to a small red-haired woman. DJ's presence was all business, and it seemed to fit her well. Just one more affirmation that she'd done the right thing. Kat was acutely aware of the muscular body beneath the midnight-blue Theory pants and jacket. Kat didn't need to see DJ's legs to know they were gorgeous. She closed her eyes, trying to purge the image from her mind.

"Hey, sis. Who we spying on?" Rebecca whispered behind her, and Kat slammed the door shut.

"DJ's down the hall," she said as she crossed the room and slung her suit bag over the chair. She'd planned to change into her jeans after the board meeting.

Rebecca pressed her lips together. "You can't avoid her forever."

"I know. It's just safer to see her when other people are present." Kat noticed the stack of folders on the edge of Rebecca's desk.

"Safer for whom, Dani or you?"

"Both." Kat had had a lot of time to think in the past month, but her feelings hadn't changed. She'd only become more in love with DJ. "Are these for the board meeting?" She took a folder off the top of the stack and thumbed through it.

"Don't change the subject." Rebecca sat in her chair and crossed her legs.

Kat dropped the folder onto the stack, then turned and walked across the room to the coffeepot on the table. After pouring herself the usual mixture of half cream and half coffee, she slid down onto the couch and sat quietly sipping the mocha-colored mixture.

"How can you drink that? It can't taste like coffee." Rebecca followed her over and poured herself a cup.

"I don't like coffee. I only drink it for the caffeine." She took another sip and scrunched her nose in response to the bitter taste.

Rebecca chuckled, sitting down on the couch next to her. "Why don't you just have a soda instead?"

"Too much sugar makes me jumpy, and I don't like diet."

"Same here." Rebecca smiled, bringing her cup to her lips before setting it on the table in front of her. "Why won't you talk to her?"

Kat twisted a strand of hair between her fingers as the complicated thoughts clouded her mind. "Have you ever thought you had everything you could ever want in life and suddenly had it ripped away?" Her voice quivered unexpectedly.

"No. I can't say that I have."

"Well, I've had it happen twice now." Kat's voice cracked with a painful sound of acceptance.

"It doesn't have to be that way, Kat," Rebecca said softly.

Kat squared her shoulders and pressed her lips together. She was not going to cry. "Her life is in Austin and mine is in Kerrville."

"Nobody says that has to change." Rebecca's voice rose sharply. "I'm sure the two of you can work something out, if you'd just compromise a little."

"She'd be working here most of the time, and I'd be at the ranch."
Kat's stomach quivered, and she took in a deep breath. "I don't think I
can settle for just having her part-time."

"So it's all or nothing? That's crazy." Rebecca's cup rattled against
the saucer as she dropped it onto the table. "People need lawyers in
Kerrville too, you know."

Kat popped forward, trying to keep her composure. "I can't ask DJ
to change her entire life for me."

"Honestly, I think that's *all* you'd have to do." Rebecca took Kat's
hand to regain her attention. "You know she'd be there in a heartbeat."

"I don't know that," Kat said firmly, still feeling as though she
were just an assignment, a job that produced a wonderful, momentary
distraction in DJ's life.

"She loves you."

"Stop." Kat shook her head. She'd been over it a thousand times
these past few weeks, trying time after time to find a way to make it
work. "This is hard enough already. Please just leave it alone." She
threw herself into the couch, kneading her forehead with her fingers.
"I'm sorry, Bec."

Rebecca frowned and raised her cup to her lips. Kat knew this
discussion was far from over, but she was thankful Rebecca was letting
it lie for now.

"You look very nice today. Red certainly seems to be your color."
Rebecca reached over and touched the silk lapel of Kat's Chanel suit.
"It brings out the blue in your eyes."

Kat blinked rapidly, halting the tears threatening to spill out.
"Thanks." She let the corner of her lip curve up slightly as she tugged
on the bottom of her skirt to flatten the creases. The suit wasn't at all
in Kat's budget. It had cost much more than she'd anticipated, but she
wanted to make an impression at the board meeting today.

"So how's everything at the ranch?"

"Good. We finally finished building the new stable."

"That didn't take long, did it?"

"It would've been done a lot sooner if we'd had better weather.
Nothing like a few tornadoes to slow down construction." Kat touched
the tip of her nose lightly, a habit she'd acquired after the injury to
remind herself how miserable her life had become.

"Does it still hurt?" Rebecca asked.

"It's tender." It'd been almost a month to the day since Victoria attacked her at the ranch. Kat's nose had healed well. Luckily it hadn't been broken. Her self-confidence, on the other hand, had been irreversibly damaged.

"At least you won't have to worry about Victoria anymore."

"That's true." Kat crossed her arms to avoid the shiver threatening to quake through her. "Funny how her men were so willing to turn on her to save their own hides." Knowing she wouldn't have to see Victoria ever again had put Kat's mind at ease for the time being. She'd been indicted for murder, along with fraud and embezzlement, and the district attorney had assured Kat they wouldn't need to add assault charges to convict her.

"How's Virgil? I'm sure taking care of him has been a full-time job."

"Let's just say it's been a challenge." Kat smiled and let out a sigh. "If Arizona were here, she'd already have him up and riding again."

"Tell me about Arizona," Rebecca said, shifting in her seat. "I've always wondered what kind of love could be so strong it would possess you to give up the finer things in life."

A feeling of contentment washed over Kat, and she let her gaze wander the room. "It's hard to describe, Bec. She was the love of my life."

"I always knew you had a crush on her when we were kids, but I thought that was because you wanted to be like her. Did you ever have an interest in boys?" Rebecca cocked her head slightly.

"No, never boys. There were a few other girls." Kat smiled shyly. "But that's exactly what they were, *girls*."

"I can't believe I never saw that." Rebecca scooted closer. "So when did things change between you and Arizona?"

"The summer after I graduated from college."

"What? How?"

"Something was just different. She didn't seem to be as comfortable around me as she was in the past. Our usual banter just wasn't there." Kat's smile widened. "After all, she'd politely rejected me hundreds of times before." She laughed. "I thought that maybe she was mad at me or something. Then as we got further into the summer, things seemed to return to normal. So I just shrugged it off as my own insecurity."

"And?"

Kat sipped her coffee and laughed. "And you sure are nosy."

"Your life was always more interesting than mine."

"Not always." Kat slid the cup onto the table in front of her.

Rebecca smiled widely. "You might as well tell me. I'm going to pry it out of you sooner or later."

Kat shook her head and rolled her eyes. "We were out riding one afternoon. She'd managed to avoid my advances once again." Her face warmed and she shifted, throwing her arm across the top of the couch. "I was totally flirting with her, glancing over my shoulder, giving her my sexiest look, when a snake slithered across the trail. Before I could get a handle on the horse, it bucked me."

"My God. Were you all right?"

Kat nodded. "The fall dazed me. When my head cleared, Arizona was hovering over me with this frantic look on her face. Then she kissed me and…" She gave a soft smile. "That's when it all started." She bit her bottom lip. "We made love for the first time that day."

"Really?" Rebecca's eyes widened. "Right there?"

"Well, not right there on the trail." Kat stilled for a moment as the memory washed through her as though it had only just happened. She took a deep breath and smiled. "Needless to say, she was pretty ecstatic I wasn't hurt, and I was enormously grateful there were snakes in the world after that." She stroked the inside of her wedding band with her thumb and re-filed the memory into the archives of her heart.

"I'm so sorry you lost her, Kat." Rebecca stared at the thin gold band on Kat's finger. "You know you're going to have to take that off someday."

"I know." *But not today.* Kat looked at the band as she twisted it on her finger. It had been her safety net for far too long. She abruptly flipped her hair out of her face and let her hand fall to her lap before shifting into the corner of the couch. "Enough about me. How have things been for you?"

"Some of the board members have been a little testy with me lately. Too bad we didn't have any of those tornadoes here." Rebecca gave a wild-eyed gesture, prompting an abrupt laugh from Kat. Rebecca leaned forward, clutched her stomach, and laughed along with Kat. "Sometimes, I think I might be better off if one of those twisters sucked me up into it."

"You and me both." Kat nodded. "So what happened with Mark?"

"In exchange for his testimony, he received a suspended sentence." She tried to disguise her regret. "He can't practice law in Texas anymore."

"I'm sorry, Bec."

Rebecca shook her head. "Dani was right about him all along. I guess I deluded myself into thinking he wanted me more than my money."

"He probably did at first, but Daddy was pretty persuasive when he wanted to be. Money does funny things to people."

"It sure does."

Rebecca seemed sad, and Kat didn't have the slightest idea how to fix it, so she just nodded and pressed her lips together into a thin smile. "What time does the board meeting start?"

"Ten sharp." Rebecca reached for the coffeepot and refilled both of their cups. "I'm looking forward to a weekend away. Do you want to go straight to the ranch after the meeting or have lunch here in town?"

"We can have lunch at the ranch. Virgil's a pretty good cook."

"Virgil. Hmm." Rebecca twisted her face into a grimace. "I still can't believe he's our father."

"Come on, Bec. You promised." Kat had answered all the questions about Virgil that Rebecca had thrown at her over the past few weeks, and now it was time the two of them came together to finish the evaluation.

Her hands flew up. "I know. I said I'd try, and I will."

"He's really not such a bad guy, once you get to know him."

"I'll be the judge of that." Rebecca lifted her cup and drank one last sip of coffee. "Finish up. We need to drive out to the estate and pick up Mother before the meeting."

Kat rolled her eyes and groaned. "If you insist." She didn't know if she was up to dealing with her mother today, but there really wasn't any day she was up for that.

❖

Maggie met Kat and Rebecca with hugs at the door as they came in. "It's so wonderful to see you girls together again."

"Is the old matriarch up yet?" Rebecca asked with a grin.

"Oh, yes. She's been up for hours waiting for the two of you. I was hoping you'd come for breakfast."

"You know I could never resist your cooking, Maggie." Kat smiled. "If I had stayed in Austin, I'm sure I'd be at least twenty pounds heavier."

Maggie took Kat's hand and assessed her. "If you ask me, you could use a few more pounds on that skinny little body of yours."

"Maybe one or two." Kat smiled.

"I made French toast with butter and powdered sugar, just the way you like it." Maggie's voice rose sweetly.

Kat gave Maggie's hand a light squeeze. "You're going to spoil me, Maggie."

Elizabeth appeared at the top of the stairs and began to descend them slowly. "Good morning, girls."

"Good morning, Mother." Rebecca started up the steps to her. "Why aren't you using the elevator?"

"The doctor says I need to use my legs."

Rebecca held out her hand. "Do you need some help?"

Elizabeth waved her off and grasped the banister firmly. "No, thank you, dear. I can make it."

Elizabeth had slowly but surely improved the use of her legs over the past few weeks. It was apparent to Kat she had no intention of slowing down anytime soon.

"It's nice to see you, Kathryn." Elizabeth stepped off the last step onto the marble floor. "I'm so glad you could make it for breakfast this morning."

Kat kissed her lightly on the cheek. "It looks like you're doing well."

"I am. Please come in and sit down." Elizabeth took Kat's arm and led her into the dining room. "Now tell me how everything is at the ranch."

"It's certainly been a challenge lately. But now that Virgil's feeling better, life should be back to normal soon." Kat helped Elizabeth into the chair at the head of the table before settling into the one just to the right of her, where a full plate of French toast was already waiting. "This looks delicious, Maggie."

"I put the shaker of powdered sugar right there in front of you,

Miss Kathryn, just in case you need a little more." Maggie gave her a wink, then waited for her to take a bite.

"Is there any maple syrup?" Rebecca asked.

Maggie frowned. "French toast is meant to be light and delicate."

"I know, but I like it sweet, like me." She grinned.

"If you must have it, Miss Rebecca, it's right here." Maggie leaned forward and moved the crystal boat closer to her plate.

Kat smiled as she remembered how Rebecca and Maggie had gone round and round about the syrup when she was a child. Apparently, Rebecca still loved to torment Maggie.

"And I was thinking you didn't love me. Thank you, Maggie." Rebecca's voice was as thick and sweet as the syrup itself.

Kat chuckled as she picked up her knife and fork, cut a small piece off the corner of her French toast, and put it into her mouth. "Um..." She closed her eyes in delight. "This is perfection, just the way it is."

Maggie turned, donning a smile of satisfaction. "I'll be in the kitchen if you need anything else."

"You always were a suck-up." Rebecca raised her eyebrows and twisted her lips into a grin. "It's nice having my big sister back."

"Virgil told me you've been working very hard lately," Elizabeth said, ignoring their banter.

"You've been in contact with Virgil?" Rebecca blurted, failing miserably to conceal the surprise in her voice.

"We used to be quite close, you know, and I was hoping we might possibly recapture the friendship we once had."

Rebecca's mouth dropped open. "You mean you want to—"

"Yes, Rebecca, that's what I mean. He is your father, after all."

"I think that's a fine idea," Kat said, fighting to hold back a chuckle.

Elizabeth glanced over at Rebecca and frowned. "Don't look so surprised, dear. I may be old, but I'm not frigid."

Rebecca gave her a wide-eyed look. "I'm sorry, Mother. I just never thought about you and Virgil that way. Or even...Oh God!" Her face contorted and she dropped her fork. "You and any man, for that matter."

Elizabeth narrowed her eyes. "Rebecca, I don't find this at all amusing."

"Nor do I, Mother." Rebecca's voice rose. "I just found out that I have a stable hand for a father."

Elizabeth took in a deep breath, and Kat knew she was summoning her patience. "At one time, Virgil and I loved each other very much. But he knows how much you girls mean to me."

"It's hard to believe you gave him up for us. Not for the money." Rebecca picked up her knife and fork to cut her toast.

"Rebecca." Kat leaned forward. "Do we have to do this now?" She knew Rebecca was upset, but this kind of jousting wouldn't do anyone any good.

Elizabeth raised a hand. "It's fine, Kathryn. Let's bring it all out in the open." She looked down into her bowl of oatmeal. "Maggie, do we have any fruit?" She looked up at Maggie's scowling face, who took her half-eaten bowl of food and then slid a plate of fruit in front of her. "Thank you, dear. Try the strawberries, girls. They've been delicious lately." Always the consummate hostess, she smiled and looked down at her plate. "You may not believe it, but I love both you girls, and I've always wanted what's best for you."

Kat stabbed at a blueberry, bouncing it across her plate. "So why didn't you tell us any of this before now?"

"What was the point? There was no chance for us then." Elizabeth took the knife from the table and sliced a strawberry into fourths before placing one in her mouth.

"You make it sound so easy," Kat said softly, her mind still cluttered with the persistent emotions created by DJ. The feelings hadn't diminished, even with the distance she'd deliberately put between them.

Elizabeth clanged the knife down onto her plate. "On the contrary, Kathryn. I think you're well aware that giving up someone you love is far from easy. Virgil and I both knew that someday we'd be together again. We just had to let each other go until then." She stared at Kat as she moved the fruit around on her plate with her fork. "My reasons were quite valid. Are yours?"

Blindsided by the question, Kat snapped her head up and stared at Elizabeth. "My reasons, whatever they may be, are *my* reasons, and they're personal." She blotted her lips with her napkin and tossed it onto the table. The chair scraped against the floor as she pushed away, bolted up, and charged to the French doors that led to the garden.

"Damn it, Mother." Rebecca threw herself back into her chair.

"Well, someone had to say something. You and Danica may be willing to let her go, but I'm not."

Rebecca sprang up and followed Kat. "This isn't about letting her go. It's about letting her be happy."

"Do you really think she can be happy without Danica?"

"No. I don't." She stopped in the doorway. "But she's the one who has to recognize that."

Kat took in their conversation as she left the house. She was halfway across the garden before she felt the moisture streaming down her face. She dropped down on one of the many concrete benches placed strategically throughout the garden and admired the beauty of the flowers. A few of them were still at their peak, but with the ensuing summer heat, the majority had already begun to die.

She felt like one of them. Just a few short weeks before, she'd been gloriously happy, reveling in the new love life had given her. Now she felt as though she were withering inside, dying just like the flowers.

Kat cradled her head in her hands. She'd made her decision about DJ without taking time to deal with her feelings. Her mother never sugar-coated her methods. Maybe a reality jolt was exactly what Kat needed. She was finally realizing just what she was giving up.

Rebecca touched her shoulder. "Are you all right?"

"I will be." Kat wiped away her tears before taking Rebecca's hand. "I guess with everything that's been going on lately, I haven't dealt with my feelings for DJ."

Rebecca slid onto the bench next to her and lifted Kat's chin with her hand. "Just promise me you'll be open-minded about her, okay?"

Kat nodded, agreeing even though she wasn't sure she could.

Rebecca stood and offered Kat her hand. "We should really go if we want to make a proper entrance at the board meeting."

Kat took her hand and walked along the garden pathway with her. "I should check my makeup before we go. I must look a mess."

"You're beautiful, Kat." Rebecca smiled, wiping the remaining moisture from Kat's face. "And you're going to be all right." She pulled her into a hug.

Kat had regained her composure and was once again in control of her feelings as they drove downtown to the Montgomery Building.

"It looks like we're going to have a lovely day," Elizabeth said, looking out the window.

"Hopefully it won't be above eighty degrees before noon." Rebecca reached for the air-conditioning knob. She turned it up a notch and peeked into the rearview mirror at herself. "I'm already beginning to glow."

"Are you going to be available for all the board meetings, Kathryn?" Elizabeth asked.

Kat kept her gaze constant on the endless string of oak trees mesmerizing her through the smoked-glass window. "No. I won't be here for them. I'm giving my proxy to Rebecca."

Elizabeth's soft disposition changed quickly. "But I gave you that stock so you would remain active in the company."

"And I told you, I'm not interested in the company." Kat's voice was firm.

"You know the rules, Kathryn. Rebecca doesn't have enough stock to carry your proxy."

She shifted sideways to look over the seat at Elizabeth. "She does now. I gave her half of what you gave me."

Elizabeth sprang forward. Clutching the headrest, she dug her fingernails into the soft leather. "You can't do that."

"Oh yes, I can." Kat smiled broadly. "I had the papers drawn up last week, and there's not a single thing you can do about it."

Elizabeth sank against the seat. "You're going to leave your poor mother out in the cold?"

Rebecca chuckled, glancing into the rearview mirror. "You'll be far from out in the cold, but things are definitely going to change around here."

"You ungrateful—"

"Be careful, Mother," Kat said. "Do you really want to alienate your last link in the company?"

Elizabeth crossed her arms. "Drop me off at the rear entrance. I'll go up alone." Her lips puckered as the words flew out impatiently.

"No, you won't." Kat gave her a don't-cross-me look. "We're going to walk into that boardroom with esprit de corps." She reached for Rebecca's hand. "Everyone is going to know that Rebecca is in control and we're behind her one hundred percent."

Rebecca glanced at her in the mirror again. "Contrary to what you may think, Mother, this isn't about you. The board needs to know, along with every other predator out there, that this company is *not* vulnerable."

"What are you talking about?"

"Since Daddy died, at least two other companies have been waiting to swoop in and take control," Rebecca said as she parked the car in the space reserved for her in front of the Montgomery Building.

"I didn't know anything about that." Elizabeth's voice had quieted.

"Exactly," Kat said. "If Rebecca wasn't here, your precious little company would already be in someone else's hands." She slid out of the front seat and then opened the door for Elizabeth. "Now come on." She took her mother's hand and helped her out. "If we're going to make the meeting on time, we need to head out now."

Elizabeth shot out in front of them, plunking her cane to the ground. "You girls have certainly become more commanding as you've matured."

"Like mother, like daughters." Kat winked, putting her hand out. Rebecca took it and clasped it in hers.

CHAPTER TWENTY-EIGHT

Kat paced the hallway just outside the conference room. "I hate having to stand up in front of these people and talk."

"Tell me about it." Rebecca let out a chuckle. "The first time I made a presentation, I was so nervous, I whipped the pointer around like it was a lightsaber. Halfway through the meeting, Daddy took it away from me."

"I wish I'd been here to see that," Kat said, giving her a wide smile.

Rebecca bumped Kat with her shoulder. "You would have enjoyed it. I almost poked his eye out."

Kat raised an eyebrow. "Oh, yes. That I definitely would have enjoyed."

Rebecca's attention veered to the elevator, prompting Kat to peek over her shoulder. *Zing!* There DJ stood, hair spiked and looking awesomely dapper, dressed in the midnight-blue suit that emphasized her athletic build and accented her already impressive physique. Kat swallowed hard as DJ approached, trying to fight the persistent yearning running through her veins.

"Ladies." One by one, DJ took each of their hands and raised them slowly to her lips.

DJ let Kat's hand linger beneath her lips just a bit longer, and Kat felt the familiar jolt she'd tried so desperately to ignore. DJ's gaze moved slowly up, and Kat was caught by her intense sea-green eyes. She couldn't suppress the sensations that rushed her as the woman she loved stood before her.

The door opened, and Rebecca's assistant poked her head out into the hallway. "They're just about ready to start."

"Come on, Kat." Rebecca moved to the door. "Kat, it's time," she repeated, breaking the trance in which DJ seemed to have her captured. "You'll have to excuse us, Dani." Rebecca looped her arm in Kat's and led her to the door.

Elizabeth, Rebecca, and Kat made their entrance and sat at the rear of the room until the chairman called the meeting to order. After welcoming everyone, the chairman asked if any of them would like to address the board, and Kat politely accepted.

"Go get 'em," Rebecca whispered, slipping a silver telescoping pointer into Kat's hand. Kat smiled. The gesture actually helped calm her nerves.

Kat made her way to the front of the boardroom, lightly touching a few shoulders along the way. She'd been gone a long time, but some of the faces, though somewhat older, were still familiar.

"Hello, everyone. My name is Kathryn Jackson. A few of you may remember me." She let her gaze dart back and forth among those she recognized, who smiled and gave her a nod of acknowledgment. "But I'm sure the majority of you haven't the slightest idea who I am." She rolled the pointer between her thumb and fingertips. "I'm the other daughter, the one who doesn't want anything to do with this company." She tossed the pointer onto the table, and it clanged and rolled until someone reached out and stopped it. "However, if anyone in this room has any ideas about taking control away from my sister Rebecca, you'll be seeing a lot more of me than you'd ever dreamed."

She picked up a pile of folders and passed them around the table. "As you can see from these figures, your stock has continued to grow without deviation over the past few months." She paused a moment, giving everyone a chance to look at the reports. "You all know from experience what Rebecca can do, and with your support, she'll continue to be instrumental in the growth of this company."

Kat became momentarily distracted when she saw her mother whisper something in DJ's ear. When DJ crossed her legs and shifted to face Elizabeth, she couldn't help but wonder what her mother was saying. When DJ changed her focus to the front of the room and smiled at Kat, she lost her train of thought.

To cover her momentary lapse, Kat cleared her throat and said,

"Is there something you'd like to add, Ms. Callahan?" The question came out louder than Kat had intended, and the sound of her voice reverberated throughout the small boardroom as she stared into DJ's shimmering green eyes.

DJ uncrossed her legs and sat up squarely. "Just that I'm behind you and Rebecca one hundred percent." She lowered her chin and gave her a supportive smile.

Kat was fully aware of the warmth lingering behind DJ's smile, and the response her body gave was more intense than she'd expected.

She poured a small amount of water into the glass on the table in front of her and took a drink. "Now, unless anyone has any questions for me, I'll turn the meeting over to Rebecca." She waited momentarily, fully prepared to field any questions, but none came. Apparently, the board members were satisfied with Rebecca's performance for the time being.

"Looks like you're in charge." Kat swiped the pointer from the table and handed it to Rebecca before slipping to the rear of the room, then out into the hallway, where she flattened herself against the wall and closed her eyes. After she'd locked eyes with DJ, the whole experience had been a blur.

"I think you made your point."

DJ's voice startled her, and Kat opened her eyes. "I hope so." She let out a sigh of relief. "We appreciate your help. Hopefully Rebecca won't have to worry about battling anyone for control ever again."

DJ searched Kat's face. "Each and every moment I know you, I'm more impressed." Her eyes seemed to reflect genuine admiration, and Kat gave her smile in return. "I miss that." DJ reached to touch her, and Kat retreated. "I miss *you*, Kat." She closed the distance between them, cupped her cheek in her hand, and let her thumb drag across Kat's lips.

"DJ, please don't do this." Kat closed her eyes and begged for the blaze DJ ignited in her to diffuse.

"What about us, Kat? I can't just let you go."

Kat opened her eyes and studied DJ's face. She knew every line, every crease by heart. She'd seen it every night in her dreams for the past few weeks. She didn't want to look, but knowing she might never be this close again, her mind demanded it. She brushed her fingers through the sprigs of blond coloring her temples. They looked remarkably white now against the dark color of her suit.

"DJ, like it or not, you *are* a city girl, and I'll forever be a country girl." DJ had her wondering for a while, but after seeing her today, in this drastically different element, Kat knew where DJ belonged, and Kat just didn't fit here. Kat draped her hand across DJ's and removed it from her face. "Your life is here, and mine is at the ranch. You know if I stayed, I would never be happy." She turned to the window and stared out over the city.

"Kat, please, can't we make this work, somehow?" DJ snaked her arms around Kat's waist and immersed her face in Kat's hair.

"I've distanced myself from this place for several reasons. You were sitting right next to one of them in that boardroom. She tried to manipulate you as well." Kat understood DJ's reasons for wanting her in Austin, but she couldn't come back to this life or to her mother's control. "I'd end up hating you for it." Kat didn't want that. She wanted the passion igniting within her right now—DJ's body close with her arms around her, the very things Kat knew she couldn't have. "It would be a weekend romance at best." The emotion choked inside her, almost suffocating her words. "I need more than that. We both do."

Rebecca poked her head out of the conference room. "I'm sorry, Dani. We need you in here." DJ hesitated. "Now, Dani," Rebecca snapped, apparently seeing the tension between them.

"All right," DJ said, her frustration coming through loud and clear. "I'll be back in a minute." She gently pressed her lips to Kat's ear. "Please don't leave before we have a chance to talk more." She gave Kat one last squeeze and left her feeling cold and alone.

Rebecca started toward Kat as she shot to the elevator. "It looked like things were a bit tense between you two."

Kat jabbed the elevator button with her finger. "Nothing more than usual. Thanks for the interruption."

Rebecca followed her into the elevator. "Are you all right?"

"I'm fine." Kat forced herself to hold the tears until she reached Rebecca's office. She pushed through the door, picked up her bag, and went into the bathroom. She stared into the mirror at her red eyes, begging for the incessant pain in her heart to stop. The only thing keeping her going was telling herself everything would be fine as soon as she got to the ranch.

After wiping the streams of moisture from her face, she took her clothes from her bag and removed her suit. She put on a pair of blue jeans and a pale-blue T-shirt. Then she checked her reflection in the mirror one more time before going into the office.

Rebecca was waiting just outside the door. "What are you doing, Kat?"

Kat kept herself remarkably composed as she walked across the office to the couch. "Changing my clothes."

"Stop. You know what I mean." Rebecca's voice was firm yet gentle.

"This isn't me, Bec." She shrugged and held her palms upward as she looked around the room. "This is DJ's world. My life is at the ranch."

"Damn it, Kat. Haven't you ever heard of compromise?"

"Any compromise would only end up being a sacrifice on my part." She laid her suit bag across the top of the couch. "I'm too old for that."

"Too old or too stubborn?" Rebecca shot back.

She tossed Rebecca's bag at her. "I'm leaving in about fifteen minutes. You'd better change if you're still going with me."

"Bullheaded…" Rebecca mumbled as she went into the bathroom.

Kat was well inside her head when she heard DJ's voice in the distance, coming down the hallway. She moved from the window to the bookshelf in the corner of Rebecca's office, where she found Rebecca had placed several pictures of the two of them as children.

The door flew open and DJ rushed through it. "Rebecca."

"She's in the bathroom," Kat said softly, without turning. She plucked a picture from the shelf in front of her and stared at it. No, she stared through it, trying to rebuild her faltering resistance.

DJ's demeanor seemed to change instantly. "I thought maybe you'd already left."

Kat set the picture in its place on the shelf. "We had to change before heading to the ranch. Somebody's draggin' her tail." She tipped her head toward the bathroom.

"Don't go," DJ said as she came closer.

Kat took in a slow, even breath, swung around to face her, and was startled to find herself in DJ's arms. Her eyes were soft and gentle, nothing at all like the angry, dark hollows she'd seen when DJ was beating the life out of Victoria Maxwell. Kat had never seen such rage in anyone, a frightening rage prompted by DJ's need to protect her. She remembered how they immediately softened when she'd picked her up and carried her from the barn.

"Have dinner with me tonight?" DJ stroked Kat's cheek, and she inched up against the bookshelf.

"I can't," Kat said, trying desperately to contain her jumbled feelings. "We're finished here. I have to get to the ranch."

DJ's lips closed in on hers, and Kat felt the heat in light-seconds. The soft, gentle kiss morphed into the erotic dance of tongues Kat had been aching to replay since the last time DJ kissed her. The familiar combustion was too much for Kat to ignore. DJ's hands slowly roamed the curves of Kat's waist, and as the kiss deepened, every one of her nerve endings fired. Kat responded out of utter need for this woman who fit her in every way. She slid her arms up around DJ's neck and pressed her body hard against her. All seemed right in her world again. How could she let her go?

"I'm all set," Rebecca said as she came out of the bathroom. "Whoops...Sorry." She whirled around and headed back in.

Kat ripped her lips away. "It's okay, Bec." Debating whether to stay or go, she leaned against the shelves to steady herself. She was grasping at something she knew would end if she stayed here. She slid along the wall, avoiding DJ's gaze, afraid she might fling herself into her arms.

"I was just trying to convince your sister to have dinner with me tonight."

"Oh." Rebecca looked at Kat and nodded. "If you want, we can wait until morning."

"No. I don't want to stay." The words flew out abruptly, and Kat could see the sadness in DJ's eyes. "I really have to go," she said, softening her tone as she picked up her suit bag from the couch and slung it over her shoulder. "I've already been away too much this summer. I really don't like leaving Virgil alone."

"Some other time, then." DJ's voice rolled with disappointment.

Or you could come to the ranch. She thought it but couldn't say it. She wouldn't beg. Kat headed to the door. "You ready?"

"You go ahead. I'll be just a minute," Rebecca said.

"Meet you at the truck. I'm parked right out front." Kat felt DJ watching her as she left the office. Her heart tightened as she turned and gave her one last look before the elevator doors closed.

Kat slid into the driver's seat, took the wedding ring off her finger, and tossed it into the console. She pressed her forehead to the steering wheel as she waited for Rebecca. Her resolve had weakened, and she was on the verge of crumbling. She wanted to run back upstairs to DJ, if only to spend one more night with her. But making love to DJ now would only be an impossible reminder of what she was giving up. She needed DJ to love her enough to come with her to the ranch.

Chapter Twenty-Nine

The doors to DJ's future had just snapped shut right in front of her. She'd known when this whole thing started that it would end this way. But knowing it didn't make it any easier. DJ would never take Kat away from the life she'd built at the ranch, a life that she, herself, had cherished at one time. Giving it up had been the hardest thing DJ had ever done, until now.

When DJ had sat next to Elizabeth at the rear of the boardroom, she hadn't expected Elizabeth to tell her she'd paid off the mortgage to her family farm. Nor had she expected to hear that Kat had signed over half her stock to Rebecca, as well as giving Rebecca her proxy. Kat had outsmarted Elizabeth after all. The board would have someone to guide them, and Kat would return to the ranch. Kat's performance impressed her. She'd learned more about this company in the past month than most of the board members had in years. She and Rebecca could run the company together with ease.

Rebecca's voice jarred DJ out of her thoughts. "My mother's still upstairs." She touched DJ's shoulder lightly. "Will you see that she makes it home?"

DJ punched the elevator button with the side of her fist. "I'll take her."

"You don't mind?"

"What else do I have to do?"

"I tried." Rebecca shrugged as she stepped into the elevator. "I'll talk to Kat again this weekend."

"Thanks," DJ said as she sank into the corner of the elevator, knowing full well Kat wouldn't change her mind.

Rebecca grabbed the elevator door, and it shot open as she stepped inside. "What the hell's the matter with you, Dani?"

DJ snapped her head up. "What do you expect me to do? I can't force her to love me."

"She *already* loves you." Rebecca's eyes were wide. "I've never known you to walk away from anything you really wanted."

"This is different." She plowed her fingers through her hair. "I can't buy her. This has to be her choice."

"Do you love her, Dani?"

"I love her too much to make this any harder for her than it already is."

"Then you should know there's no choice for her. Don't *make* her choose. Follow her, damn it!" Rebecca narrowed her eyes. "Your father's dead. You can't do anything about that." She let out a heavy breath, and her voice softened. "It wasn't your fault. Stop punishing yourself for something you had no control over. You've more than fulfilled your promise to him. Now follow the woman you love and live the life you deserve." The elevator doors opened, and Rebecca started out, but she turned and made the doors bolt open again. "If you don't, maybe you deserve to be alone."

DJ pushed the elevator button, prompting the doors to close. "Maybe I do."

DJ sat behind her cherrywood desk staring blankly at the laptop monitor. She couldn't think today. Hell, she hadn't been able to think since Kat went back to the ranch. For the first time ever, DJ was uncertain about her future. She'd thought she had the life she needed. She was financially secure and successful. She could pretty much have any woman she wanted. But all that seemed unimportant now. She'd buried the only real part of her life long ago, and now she'd let any hope for it walk out the door. She slapped her laptop closed. DJ didn't want just any woman. She wanted Kat.

Marcia poked her head just inside the doorway. "What's wrong?"

"Can't concentrate."

Marcia crossed her arms and leaned against the doorway. "Then go after her."

"Can't do that. I have my own issues to resolve."

Marcia frowned and disappeared from the doorway for a minute, then returned with a small yellow sticky note. "Here's the number. Why don't you do us both a favor and call her?" She stuck the note to the closed laptop in front of DJ.

"Why don't you get to your desk and mind your business." Marcia was only trying to help, but she had no idea what she was asking.

Marcia put her hands on her hips. "Maybe I should take the rest of the afternoon off."

"I think that's a fine idea."

"Alrighty." Marcia headed out of the office. "Anything else you need before I go?"

"Just shut the door, please." DJ looked at the number on the note and picked up the phone. She looked again, crumpled the paper in her hand, and dropped the receiver into the cradle. She had no idea what to say. Had it been too long? There was only one way to find out. She took a breath, picked up the phone again, and punched in the number.

When DJ heard the voice on the other end, she struggled to speak. "Mom. It's Dani."

"It's so good to hear your voice, honey." The sweetness in her mother's voice rang through, and DJ's anxiety vanished.

"It's good to hear yours too," DJ choked out.

"How are you, baby?" The love in her mother's voice overwhelmed her, stirring emotions in her she thought were long gone.

"I'm all right. How are you?" DJ asked, but she was far from all right.

"A little tired right now." Her mother let out a sigh. "I just finished tendin' the garden."

"You shouldn't be outside in this heat." The humidity was high this time of year, and it would be hard on her mother. She was probably in her mid-sixties now. She didn't know exactly. She'd lost track.

"I have to take care of my tomatoes." She sounded weary.

"The best tomatoes in Texas," DJ said, remembering the way her mom used to slice a plateful for every meal.

"You're sweet, honey."

"I was wondering…" She cleared the lump in her throat. "Would it be all right if I came out to visit for a day or two?"

"I'd love that, sweetheart."

"You sure you have room?" DJ asked, half-hoping her mother would say no.

"I always have room for you, baby girl."

"I should be there by sundown."

"I'll put a roast in the oven."

"I'd like that. Would you make some of your biscuits too?" DJ quickly wiped away the warm moisture running down her cheeks. All the feelings she'd kept locked inside engulfed her.

"I'll make two pans, so you and your brother won't have to wrangle over them."

DJ cleared her throat, trying to hide the emotion spilling out. "I love you, Mom."

"I love you too, darlin'."

"See you this afternoon." DJ dropped the receiver into the cradle and hopped up from her desk. "Marcia," she said as she opened the door.

Marcia looked up from her desk and seemed to notice DJ's emotional state. "I'll cancel them. Just give me a call when you're ready to come back, and I'll reschedule."

"Thanks, Marcia." The woman was irreplaceable.

"Not a problem."

That afternoon, DJ made it to Johnson City in close to forty-five minutes, though it was a little over an hour's drive. She slowed as she turned onto the dirt road leading to her childhood home. Her stomach knotted. The last time she was here they'd just buried her father. DJ hadn't stayed long then and had only spoken to her mother a few times since. As she passed the hundred-acre wheat field, she thought of the day the fire had claimed it years ago. She could still hear the disappointment in her father's voice. She'd shirked her responsibility to her family, and because of her that year's crop had been lost. After DJ left, it didn't take long for her to realize that her father was right about the fire, but she intended to prove to him she wasn't useless. She'd worked hard, graduated in the top of her class, and taken a job at a prominent law firm in Austin. She'd done it, she proved her father wrong, but it was a hollow victory, and she still couldn't bring herself to face him again.

As she neared the house she could see them all out on the porch waiting—her mother, Marilyn, Junior, and his wife Judy. She'd had second thoughts after she'd gone home to change her clothes and pack a bag, but she couldn't turn around now.

When she cut the engine and stepped out of the car, her family members came down off the concrete porch. Her mother was the first to grab her and give her a big hug. The rest followed, all except Junior. He circled around the BMW.

"You're just in time. Dinner's about ready." Her mother put her arm around DJ's waist and gave her another squeeze. "Come on, girls. Let's go set out the food while Dani and Junior visit a minute."

"Thanks, Mom. I'll be right in."

DJ watched her mother go inside, leaving her and Junior alone to talk. She had a way of making people work out their problems whether they wanted to or not. When they were kids she used to lock them in the storm cellar until they reached some sort of truce. Their reunion wouldn't be easy. She didn't expect everyone to welcome her. Life on the farm had been tough after she'd left, and her brother had shouldered all the work.

"That's quite a fancy machine you have there," Junior said, swiping his hand across the flop-top. "Not much good for farmin'."

"You could drive her into town later if you want," DJ said, trying to make peace.

Junior leaned down and peeked inside. "What for? Can't fit no supplies in it."

"Well, then maybe you could just take her out on the highway. See how she handles." DJ knew Junior wouldn't make it easy.

Junior took one more look at the car. "Maybe."

"How was the crop this year?"

"Purdy good. Soil's good. Should be good next year too." Junior looked out at the newly planted field. "Thanks for sendin' the money and all. It really helped out." He didn't look at her. "I had to buy a new tractor. The old one just up and quit on me."

"The old tractor finally gave out, huh." DJ smiled. She remembered it well. "I learned to drive on that tractor."

"Me too." Junior almost smiled. "I remember. You drove it right through the side of the barn."

"That I did." Back then the tractor was shiny and new, but DJ's father had put her up in the seat, fired it up, and said, "Go to it, girl." She wished she could hear his voice just one more time.

"The new one's got air-conditioning. That sure helps on these hot summer days." Junior offered his hand to shake.

"I wish I could do more." DJ took Junior's hand and pulled him into an embrace. "You be sure and let me know if I can do anything else."

"Come on, you two. Supper's waitin'," her mother said through the screen door. She must have been watching them through the window.

"You could do one thing for me," Junior said, looking out at the yard.

"Name it."

"Come around a little more." Junior looked toward the door. "Mom's not gettin' any younger, you know."

"I'll do my best, Junior." DJ couldn't tell her brother just how hard it had been for her to make it there today. She hoped it would be easier the next time.

Junior raised his eyebrows. "Joey Meteer just got divorced. You could come home and settle down with him…or maybe his ex." He winked. "They only have four kids."

"Don't even think about it." She shot Junior a playful look of warning. "I have enough trouble in that department as it is. I don't need him tracking me down again." Joey had chased DJ all through high school and had everyone in town convinced they were getting married. When DJ left for college, Joey had followed her and acted like she'd broken his heart. He'd finally left her alone when she introduced him to her girlfriend.

"It ain't easy living in a town where everybody knows you."

"You ain't kiddin', brother."

Junior threw his arm around DJ's shoulder. "Let's go eat some of Mom's home cookin'."

They headed up the steps into the kitchen, where DJ spotted her mother at the stove dipping out bowls of pot roast, carrots, and potatoes. "Sure smells good in here." She gave her a hug and kissed the side of her head.

Her mother handed her a bowl of biscuits. "Put these on the table between you and your brother, honey."

DJ slid them onto the table and sat down. "Where are the kids tonight?"

"Hank's workin' down at the grocery store, and Janie's at a

sleepover." Junior reached into the refrigerator, took out a pitcher of iced tea, and set it on the table.

"That's too bad. I was hoping to see them." DJ guessed she had no right to think they'd want to hang around to see her. They didn't really know her. "How about Dwayne?"

"Bowling night." Marilyn said.

"They'll be around for breakfast in the morning," Judy said as she slid a bowl of pot roast in front of her.

DJ had missed her mother's cooking. Rosa did pretty well for her in Austin, but there was nothing like down-home country cooking. They waited until everyone was seated, and Junior said a prayer.

DJ dug a fork into the roast and took a bite. The flavors brought her childhood flooding back. "Just as good as I remember, Mom."

Junior took a biscuit from the bowl and then passed the bowl to DJ. "I bet you can't get cookin' like this in the city."

"Nope. Sure can't."

The meal was topped off with her mother's famous cherry pie. DJ hadn't eaten that much in years. She'd had seconds of pot roast and two slices of pie. She was definitely going to have to do double time on the treadmill when she went home.

Junior cleared his plate and handed an envelope to his mother. "I'll be in the other room if you need me."

"We'll be fine, Junior."

"What's that?"

"Something your daddy left for me." She took the letter out of the envelope and handed it to DJ. "Both your brother and sister have seen it. Now I want you to read it."

DJ unfolded the paper, and her neck bristled as she immediately recognized her father's handwriting. It never did have much style. Just plain writing with a mixture of upper- and lower-case letters.

My Dearest Virginia,

If you're reading this, darlin', then I guess I'm already gone. I know you'll never forgive me for pushing Dani away. It wasn't easy doin' it. She was your baby girl, and I know how much you love her. Believe it or not, I love her too. Maybe I didn't go about it the right way, and we lost a lot of years with her because of it, but I thought sending her away was the best thing to do at the time. We couldn't afford to do it for Junior, but he's put a lot of sweat into this farm, and now that I've passed, he'll take it on. It's his birthright. I couldn't do much for Marilyn either, but she has Dwayne, and he'll take good care of her. Dani was my last hope for this family to have a better life. The time will come one day when she'll have to decide about who she really is and what kind of a woman she's become. She may never come back to our way of life, but at least she'll have a choice. That's all I wanted for her. I hope you can forgive me for not being a perfect husband and father. I tried my hardest and did what I thought best. Ginny, believe me when I say you were the love of my life.

Henry

DJ swiped the tears from her eyes before she folded the letter and slid it across the table. "Why couldn't he just say that to me?"

"Your daddy was a very prideful man, Dani. Besides, would it have made any difference?"

"You're damn right it would have." She popped up from the chair. If her mother knew the turmoil she'd dealt with because of the words she and her father had exchanged, she'd understand.

"Dani. I won't have that kind of language here." Her mother's voice shook.

She paced the room a few times before she picked up their empty dessert plates and carried them to the sink. "I'm sorry, Mom."

"Just leave those, honey. I'll put them in the dishwasher later."

DJ reached down, pinched the handle, and opened the dishwasher door. "When did you buy this?" she asked, placing the dishes in the rack.

"A few years ago, with one of those checks you sent."

DJ smiled. "Good. I'm glad you've put them to good use." When she'd first started sending the checks, she wasn't sure if her father would accept them. The first few went uncashed. After that, they cleared the bank each month, like clockwork, on the first. DJ guessed her mom had something to do with that. She was a practical woman. She wouldn't let one man's pride stand in the way of taking care of her family.

DJ turned to the sink and gripped the edge of the counter as she looked out the three-by-three wood-paned window. "Did you ever forgive him?"

"Your daddy? Course I did. I loved him too much not to." Her mother joined DJ at the sink with the coffee cups. "What's brought you here after all this time, honey? Don't read me wrong. I'm glad you're here, but this isn't just about your daddy."

"You're right, Mom." It was about Kat, this farm, that city, and her ranch.

"What's her name?"

DJ grinned. She never could keep anything from her mother. "Kathryn."

"That's a beautiful name."

"I'm in love with her, but I'm afraid she can't forgive me for what I've done." She had no right to ask her to either.

Her mother took DJ's chin in her hand and made her look at her. "Sweetheart, if she loves you as much as you love her, she can't do anything but forgive you." She hauled her into a warm embrace. "She won't have anything else in her."

DJ smiled at her mother. It was funny how she had the power to put everything into perspective. "I'll be leavin' out after breakfast in the morning."

"When will you be back?"

"Soon." DJ would make sure not to stay away too long. Once she'd seen her family again, she'd realized how much she missed them. She wanted to be part of them again.

"Will you bring Kathryn with you?"

She nodded. "If she'll have me." Kat and her mother would get along well.

"She will, darlin'," her mother said as she took DJ's face in her hands and kissed her forehead.

CHAPTER THIRTY

Kat rolled over and slid her hand across the cool, empty sheet. Another morning waking up alone. She'd never really liked the feeling but was learning to live with it.

Things might not have worked out the way she wanted with DJ, but it was a journey she'd cherish forever. The voyage back, however, would take some time. It had been close to two weeks since she'd left DJ in Austin, and she hadn't stopped thinking about her since.

Rebecca bounded onto the bed. "Wake up, sleepyhead."

Kat pried her head from the pillow and looked at the clock. "You're up bright and early this morning." Not primed with her morning coffee yet, Kat's voice croaked out in a low, gravelly whisper.

"Yep. I'm ready to watch my big sister break that filly today."

Kat let out a grunt and dropped her head onto the pillow. "Has the rain stopped?"

"Not a cloud in the sky," Rebecca said cheerfully.

It had only been a few days since Rebecca drove in from Austin for the week, and it hadn't stopped raining since she'd arrived. She'd developed a critical case of cabin fever and was driving Kat absolutely crazy.

Kat wadded the pillow up under her head and turned onto her side. "What about that cowboy you were snuggling up to last night in the bar?"

Rebecca's smile widened. "He's on horse detail today too."

Kat chuckled. "Imagine that." She found that Rebecca enjoyed playing with the weekend cowboys who frequented the ranch much more than she enjoyed riding the horses. They were all friendly and eager to teach a city girl the ins and outs of ranching.

Rebecca tugged at her arm and bounced off the bed to her feet. "Come on. Let's go. We're burnin' daylight."

Kat blinked. *Who the hell is this woman?* "Coffee," she grumbled, rubbing her face. "I need coffee."

"I'm way ahead of you." She took a mug off the top of the dresser and held it up. "Half and half, just the way you like it."

"You'd better put on some old jeans. It's going to be messy out there today." Kat rolled out of bed, swiped the mug from her hand, and took a big gulp.

"But I don't have any old jeans."

"Then wear the pair you like the least." Kat headed into the bathroom.

"I like them all," Rebecca said, her voice rising. "Maybe I'll just watch today."

"No way, little sister. Find a pair in my dresser. It's time you got your feet wet."

Rebecca searched a few of Kat's drawers until she found a pair of jeans. She held them up to check the size, then flipped them over her shoulder and headed to her room. "Oh, I almost forgot. Mother's coming out today."

"What?" Kat took the towel from the rod on the wall and threw it over the top of the sliding shower door.

"I told her how nice it is here, and she couldn't wait to see for herself."

Kat flipped the knob in the shower and the water spurted out. "Great. I get to break the filly *and* my mother."

"Come on. She's not that bad."

"Speak for yourself." Kat inched the door closer to the jamb and then swung it open again. "You'd better be ready, little sister. Just for that, you're going to help me out in the corral today." She had to make Rebecca pay for bringing the warden out. "Wait till your cowboy sees you all muddied up."

"Hey. That's not fair."

Kat lifted her eyebrows. "I wasn't aware we were fighting fair." She clicked the bathroom door shut.

❖

Virgil was sitting in his usual chair at the end of the table reading the morning paper when Kat drifted into the kitchen.

"Anything good in the news today?"

"Nope." He turned the page. "Ain't been nothin' good since they threw Victoria in jail."

Kat poured herself another cup of coffee and doused it with the usual amount of cream. "You comin' out today?"

Virgil continued to skim the paper. "Whatcha got goin'?"

"I have to break that new filly."

"The one DJ did so well with?" Virgil threw DJ at her again in the same obvious manner he'd been using for the past few weeks.

Kat glared at him over her cup as she brought it to her lips. "Apparently she's partial to city girls."

"Or maybe just one in particular." Virgil continued to push. "Doncha think it's about time you gave that girl a call?"

"Virgil." Her voice was firm, letting him know, once again, he was entering territory she didn't care to discuss. "Don't you think it's about time you got off your butt and did some work around here?"

Still on the mend, Virgil wasn't moving around much yet. Since his room had burned along with the stable, he'd moved into one at Kat's and spent most of his time yammering at her about DJ. The only other two things that occupied him were keeping up on the investigation into Victoria's case and sitting on the porch watching whatever was happening in the corral.

Virgil folded the paper neatly and slapped it to the table. "Now don't get your dander up, missy. I just want you to be happy."

Kat clanged her mug against the bottom of the old porcelain sink. "I'm perfectly happy with the way things are." She took her baseball cap from its usual hook on the back of the door, shot him the smooth, impassive smile she'd cultivated over the years, and headed out onto the porch.

"In a pig's eye," Virgil mumbled, pouring himself another cup of coffee before moving out into the rocking chair on the porch.

Kat glared at Virgil but knew he was right. DJ had made her happier than she'd been in a long time. God only knows she'd thought about her more than once during the past few weeks. She'd even started out for Austin once to ask DJ to come back. She'd made it halfway there before realizing it would be just as hard for DJ to live at the ranch as it would be for her to live in the city. She adjusted her cap low on her forehead and headed down the steps. She couldn't help but think that if DJ was serious about wanting a relationship with her, she'd already be here. She sucked in a breath of fresh air to clear her mind. Today was a beautiful day, and she refused to waste it thinking about what could've been. No clouds, no wind, just pure blue sky. After being cooped up inside for the past few days with Rebecca, she intended to make the best of it.

❖

When Rebecca strolled out onto the porch, her mother had already arrived and was seated in the rocker next to Virgil. He'd even taken the old rickety chair and let Elizabeth have his good one in the corner.

"Would you like a cup of coffee, Mother?"

"I'd love one, dear, but I can get it myself." She leaned forward in an attempt to stand.

What was that all about? As long as Rebecca could remember, her mother had never volunteered to do anything for herself.

Virgil hopped up out of his chair. "Stay put, Lizzie. I'll getcha one."

Lizzie? What the hell kind of alternate universe am I in? She shook her head. "I have one right here she can have." Rebecca attempted to hand the piping-hot cup of coffee she'd brought out for herself to Elizabeth, but Virgil plucked it out of her hand and passed it to her.

"There you are," Virgil said to Elizabeth before turning to Rebecca. "Mornin'."

"Good morning." She gave him a polite smile. Rebecca hadn't seen Virgil much since she'd found out he was her father and still wasn't comfortable with the newfound knowledge. When her mother slid him a smile, her insides twitched. She turned and went inside to pour herself another cup of coffee. Watching the two of them interact wasn't on her list for entertainment today, far from it, but she'd promised Kat she'd try.

"Where's Kat?" she asked, returning through the doorway.

"In the stable gettin' the filly ready."

There was an uneasy silence.

"I think I'll head over and see if she needs any help."

"You ride horses?" Virgil asked.

"Not since I was a teenager."

"She's just looking for a way to avoid us," Elizabeth said in her all-knowing tone.

"This little threesome wasn't quite the picnic I'd planned on today," Rebecca shot back.

Virgil rolled his lips against each other and blew out a short breath. "I know findin' out I'm your father hasn't been easy for you."

"You're right about that." Rebecca sipped her coffee, scowling when it scalded her tongue.

His lip hitched up at the quick answer. "I'm not askin' for any more courtesy than you'd be givin' a stranger."

Rebecca turned and gave him the once-over. "You *are* a stranger to me."

The deep creases in his weathered forehead rose. "Then it shouldn't be too hard, should it?"

The old guy had a point, and she really wasn't up for taking this particular type of mud bath today in the corral. She smiled reluctantly, then walked over to him and extended her hand. "Rebecca Belmont."

A smile poked out from beneath his thick handlebar mustache, and he took her hand. "Virgil Jackson."

"Nice to meet you, Virgil." She settled down into the bench swing.

"Likewise," he said, giving her a wink. "You ever seen Kat break a horse?"

"No. I've never spent that much time around horses. They're not my kind of fun."

"You didn't like the Belmont Ranch when you were younger?" Virgil asked.

Elizabeth shrugged. "Horses were always Kat's passion. Rebecca never had much use for them."

"She doesn't know what she's missin', does she?" Virgil smiled at Elizabeth, and her eyes sparkled.

Oh, God. Not again. Rebecca didn't know how much more of this she could take. She pushed her foot against the railing, and the bench swung back and forth. "I guess I'm about to find out."

Virgil chuckled. "I don't know how two sisters can be so alike and so different at the same time." His eyes focused back on the corral. "Well, anyway, I think you're in for a treat this mornin'." He watched Kat back the filly against the railing and grinned as she slid the saddle across its back and cinched it tight.

"You taught her how to do this?" Rebecca asked.

"Gave her a little guidance, maybe." Virgil shrugged. "Didn't really have to teach her. Most of it just came natural." He touched Elizabeth on the knee. "Must've got that from her mother."

Kat stroked the horse's face and then its neck to calm it before putting her foot in the stirrup. The filly inched away from her. She let her foot fall to the ground and pressed her face against the animal's neck. The filly seemed to settle as she spoke to it. She put her foot into the stirrup again but didn't let it drop this time when the horse inched around. She held on until the horse slowed up, then swung her leg up across the saddle. The filly spun and threw her off.

Virgil sprang forward in the rocker. "You all right?" Rebecca could see the excitement and then the concern fill his eyes.

Kat looked over and gave him a nod, then danced around the filly with one foot in the stirrup, trying to mount it again.

"It usually doesn't take her long, but with the amount of rain we've had these past few days, it's gonna be messy."

"Oh, my!" Elizabeth slapped her hand to her mouth when Kat went flying again.

"She's all right," Virgil said, patting her on the knee. "You almost broke her that time," he shouted, watching Kat drag herself out of the mud.

Rebecca shook her head as Elizabeth's watchful gaze transformed into a horrified stare. "This doesn't look like any fun at all to me."

Virgil smiled widely. "But aren't *you* having fun watchin' her?"

"Yes, I am," Rebecca said with a grin. "But look at her." Kat gained a new layer of mud with each attempt.

"Believe me, she's lovin' every minute of it. Besides, maybe gettin' thrown off the horse a few times will knock some sense into her." Virgil gave Rebecca a wink, and she knew exactly what he was talking about.

"It couldn't hurt." She laughed. The old guy was sweet and funny. Maybe having Virgil for a father wasn't so bad after all.

"She hasn't called Danica yet?" Elizabeth asked.

"Nope. Dadburn stubborn girl. Says she's not gonna." Virgil slapped his hand to the arm of the chair.

Elizabeth pushed forward in her chair and looked over at Rebecca. "Have you talked to her?"

"Till I'm blue." And then some, but Kat was going to have to reach that decision on her own.

"Well, she certainly won't listen to me." Elizabeth relaxed into the rocker and looked toward the corral. "Without Danica, Kat's going to be miserable for the rest of her life."

Her mother seemed lost in thought, and Rebecca could tell she was remembering her own unhappy life with Charles Belmont.

Rebecca let her gaze veer to the corral. "Is she going to stop now?" Covered in mud, Kat leaned against the fence to catch her breath for a few minutes.

"Not yet. She'll try a few more times 'fore she quits," Virgil said as he unscrewed the top from the small round tin he'd taken out of his shirt pocket. He dabbed a bit of wax onto his fingers and twisted one end of his mustache up before swiping his finger through the wax again and twisting up the other.

Kat walked cautiously to the filly and looped the reins in her hand.

"See? There she goes." Virgil popped the tin into his pocket and motioned to Kat in the corral, sliding her foot into the stirrup.

Rebecca winced, watching the filly whirl around and throw Kat off again. "Damn, that has to hurt." She jumped to her feet and shouted, "Are you sure you're okay?"

Kat waved her off and went back to the horse.

"I can't believe she doesn't give up."

Virgil let out a chuckle. "Sit down and enjoy the show. It's gonna get better."

Chapter Thirty-One

Kat gave Rebecca a wave without turning her attention from the horse as she made another attempt to tame the filly. Rebecca, Elizabeth, and Virgil had been on the porch all morning, completely engrossed by the show Kat was giving them. She threw her leg over the filly, and it managed to throw her for the fifth time, knocking the wind out of her. *Show over.* Kat struggled to her feet in the slippery mud and calmly stroked the horse before leading it into the stable.

"You could be a little more agreeable, you know," she said as she slid her saddle from the filly's back and led it into the stall. She secured the latch across the front and rested against it. "You're really trying my patience today, and I don't have a lot of that left right now." She stared into the big brown eyes looking back at her. "I have the whole family out there trying to fix my problems for me." She glanced down at her jeans. "And you've got me covered in mud from head to toe." She reached in and stroked the horse's face. "Yeah, I know. You have your own problems." She tossed in a few handfuls of hay before she strolled out and headed for the house.

Kat heard Virgil chuckle and shook her head. "Gotcha again, huh?"

She tugged her boots off at the bottom of the steps. "I don't know what I'm gonna do about her."

"Why don't you call DJ." Rebecca lifted her eyebrows. "I bet she could do it."

Virgil nodded in agreement. "That's a darn good idea, young lady."

Kat looked over at her mother. "You have anything to add?"

Elizabeth shook her head. "I've already spoken my piece."

"I could think of a few more things to add," Virgil spouted.

"Me too," Rebecca said.

Kat flattened her lips and flashed Virgil a glassy stare before swerving it to Rebecca. "Let it go, you two." She swiped a gooey glob of mud from her arm and threw it at them. The mud sailed past Rebecca's head and stuck to the house behind her.

"Hey!" she said as she wiped a few stray splatters from her face.

Kat gathered another handful and threatened to throw it Rebecca's way. "Say another word…" She was tired of having this conversation over and over again.

Rebecca clamped her lips together into a scowl.

"Okay, then." Kat tossed the mud into the dirt and swiped her hands across her shirt, which didn't help much. "I need to shower." She looked down at herself and decided it would be better to take her clothes off on the porch rather than drag the mess inside. Quickly surveying the grounds, she climbed up the front steps and began to unbutton her shirt.

Virgil's eyebrows rose slightly. "You gonna undress right out here in front of all the guests?"

She frowned. "I don't see any guests, do you?"

"Looks clear to me," Rebecca said.

He skimmed the grounds from the corral to the barn.

"Everyone has already left out for their morning details." Kat continued with the buttons.

He turned his head and scanned the grounds. "All right then. Go ahead. I'll keep an eye out."

"Thanks." She let her shirt fall to the porch, then slid her mud-covered jeans halfway down before sitting on the bench, peeling them off, and tossing them on the pile.

Rebecca raised an eyebrow. "That's a nice look."

"Shut up." Kat clamped her lips into a tight smile and hurried inside.

She flipped the knob on the shower and looked at herself in the mirror. It wasn't one of her best days. She had mud streaks across her face, and the dark circles under her eyes had become more prominent than ever over the past few days. As she went into her bedroom, she took the hat from her head and dropped it on the dresser. She picked up the picture of her and Arizona and ran her fingers across the glass. *Maybe I can't do this alone.* She hated the thought of needing anyone again as much as she'd needed her. *Maybe I just don't want to.* She set the picture in its place on the dresser and then grabbed a towel from the hall closet. *What's so wrong about that?* She stepped into the shower. *DJ doesn't want to do it with you. That's what's wrong.* She ducked her head under the stream of steaming water.

Kat had just stepped out of the bathroom when she heard Virgil and Rebecca's voices trail down the hallway. They were still laughing at her. Her cheeks heated. *They think I put on a good show for them, huh? Well, I'll show them funny.* She rushed into the bedroom and put on a clean pair of jeans and a red T-shirt before wrapping a towel around her hair and going into the kitchen.

Kat narrowed her eyes and stood with both hands planted firmly on her hips. "I'd like to see either one of you try to break that filly next."

"Settle down, Kat. We were just havin' a little fun."

"At your expense, of course." Rebecca jerked the metal handle on the old refrigerator door and reached inside. The old metal shelf rattled as she searched through it. "Don't you have any bottled water?"

Virgil chuckled. "The only water we have in this kitchen comes from right here." He flipped the faucet handle up, letting water stream out.

Rebecca scrunched her nose, then reached into the refrigerator and took out a soda. "I'll just have this."

"One of the boys came in from the trails while you were in the shower and said there's someone up on the north-forty messin' around with your new fence."

Kat unwound the towel from her head, tossed it across the chair, and let her wet hair drop to her shoulders. "What do you mean, messin' around with the fence?"

"Looks like they're taking it down."

"What? Who the hell told anyone they could do that?" Kat let her stare bounce from Virgil to Rebecca.

Rebecca threw up her hands. "Don't look at me. I didn't give anyone permission. The sale hasn't finished escrow yet."

"Damn. This would've never happened if you'd sold the land to me." The screen door slapped against the house as Kat threw it open and headed for the stable. It had to be the new owner. Who else could it be? Victoria was long gone.

Rebecca followed her out the door. "Hey, I tried to give it to you, remember?"

"I wanted you to keep it. I didn't think you were gonna sell it."

"You know I don't have any use for it."

"Now I have to deal with a new frickin' neighbor." Kat shoved her foot into the stirrup, threw her leg over Minow, and took off up the trail. She couldn't believe she was going to have to deal with this situation all over again.

Kat leaned down and patted Minow on the neck. "I'm sorry, baby, but we need to move fast," she said as she bounced her heels against the horse. Except for a few spots where Kat had slowed to cross gulches, she'd had Minow in a gallop most of the way, and the horse was breathing hard. As Kat neared the fence line, the memory of the day she'd spent up there with DJ popped into her head. She tried to shake it, but it was clear that all of her memories of DJ would be with her forever.

"There they are." She saw a truck in the distance on the far side of the fence. "Come on. Just a little farther." When Minow galloped closer, Kat found two men working on the fence, one removing fence staples and the other rolling the wire.

"Hey, stop that. What do you think you're doing to my fence?" she shouted.

One of the men's heads popped up. It was George, her bartender at the ranch.

"Hi, Mrs. Jackson. I thought you knew about this."

"No, I didn't. Who told you to take the fence down?"

"Your new neighbor," George said as he popped a staple from the fence post. "This here's my buddy, James."

"Glad to make your acquaintance, ma'am."

"James." She dipped her chin. "Don't you still work for me, George?"

"Yep, but your neighbor's paying me pretty good for this." George went to the bed of the truck, picked up a plastic cup, and put it under the tap of the water cooler strapped to the side. "Seems to be pretty well-off."

"Where'd you meet this new neighbor of mine?" Kat was curious. It seemed everyone had met this presumptuous ass but her.

"Came into the bar last night lookin' for you." He took a big swallow, then splashed what was left in the cup to the ground and tossed it into the truck.

"I was at the bar. I didn't see anyone looking for me."

"It was pretty late. Close to midnight, I think. You'd probably already turned in."

"Yeah. I was gone by that time." She'd worked hard moving hay in the barn yesterday and had turned in about ten.

She mounted Minow. "Don't take any more of that fence down until you hear from me, George."

"The boss isn't gonna be happy about this."

"You know something, George? I don't really care if your boss is happy or not." Kat tugged at the reins, and Minow turned around. "And, George. You need to decide which job you wanna keep," she said, looking over her shoulder.

George tossed his pliers into the truck bed. "Pack it up, James."

Kat nudged Minow with her heels and headed down the hill. This guy had balls. She had to give him that. He was overstepping her boundaries. It had taken her weeks to put that fence up, and she wasn't about to take it down again. When she got to the house, she was going to have a nose-to-nose conversation with her sister. She wanted to know who this guy was, and she wanted to know now.

"Where is she?" Kat yanked the screen door open and let it slap against the house.

"Inside washing her hands. We just came back from visitin' with your new neighbor," Virgil said.

"My new neighbor?" Kat's stomach knotted. "Where?" Finally, she was going to meet this pompous ass. She picked up the towel from the chair she'd left it on and peered out the window.

"I think you might like this one a little better than the last." Virgil smiled. "Had some remarks about the show you put on out there on the porch earlier." Virgil held the screen door open, letting Rebecca lead the way out onto the porch.

Rebecca stifled a giggle. "Very complimentary."

"What?" Kat followed them out the door, rubbing the moisture from her palms with the towel. All she needed was for her new neighbor to have seen her in the altogether before they'd even met. What an impression to live down.

She stared across the grounds, where she spotted a shiny, new black truck parked next to hers. "Where'd he go?"

Rebecca pointed to the stable. "Checking out the new filly."

"Virgil, you know I don't like strangers left alone in there anymore." She threw her towel over the railing and marched down the porch steps.

Virgil raised his eyebrows. "Everyone who comes here's a stranger. Seemed nice enough."

Kat turned and shouted to him, "What's his name?"

Virgil shrugged. "I didn't catch it."

As Kat approached the stable, she caught a glimpse of the muscular figure, dressed in khaki shorts and a polo shirt, standing just inside the door. Her heart thumped.

"DJ?" she said softly, but as her eyes adjusted to the lowered light, she could see right away it wasn't her.

"No, ma'am. I'm Matt Wilson." He turned around to face her.

"You're my new neighbor?" Kat's voice rose as she gave him the once-over. This guy was no rancher.

"No. I'm just here for a little rest and relaxation."

A loud burst of laughter came from the other end of the stable. "I'll tell you right now, buddy. You're in the wrong place for that."

Kat's breath caught, and the voice sent all kinds of crazy sensations through her. She knew in an instant who it was. She swung around quickly, and there was DJ, just standing there, grinning. Kat's stomach made the familiar bounce. Dressed in jeans, boots, and a teal V-neck shirt, she looked as good as ever. Her mind raced. Why was she here? Had she changed her mind? Had she given up her life in the city and come to be with Kat at the ranch? She paced herself, trying to slow her thundering heart as she walked slowly toward her.

"Back for another stay, Ms. Callahan?" She cocked her head and somehow managed to keep her self-control as a jumble of uncertainty and pure happiness deluged her.

"Would that be so bad?" DJ said, giving her a smile that blew right through her cool composure and melted all her defenses.

"That depends." Kat moved closer, and a familiar jolt zapped through her.

"On what?" DJ reached behind her for the bridle hanging on the gate.

"On how long you plan on staying." Kat waited for the answer she needed.

"I just came by to see how this little filly's doing." DJ slid the bit into her mouth and tied the reins to the railing.

"Oh." Kat's voice deflated, and she let out a sigh. She knew better than to think DJ'd left her life in the city just to be with her.

"You didn't seem to be having much luck with her earlier."

She dropped her shoulders. "You were watching?" She didn't understand. "How long have you been here?"

"All morning." DJ stroked the horse's neck.

All morning? What the hell? Why hadn't she shown herself earlier?

"You mind if I give it a try?"

"You can if you like, but those hundred-dollar jeans of yours are gonna get mighty dirty."

"I went with a different brand this time." She twisted around, showing her the letter stitched on the back pocket.

Kat took a look and realized DJ had slipped her perfect ass into Wranglers this time. "Well, it won't be any different with those." Kat turned to walk away.

DJ took her arm and swung Kat hard against her. "One more thing."

Kat eagerly threatened to subdue the heat of DJ's breath as it rolled across her lips.

"While I'm here, we need to get the boundaries straight."

"Boundaries?" Kat's thoughts clouded as she watched DJ's shifting green eyes flicker with impatience.

"That is, unless you're open to a merger." DJ pressed her mouth to Kat's.

At that moment, everything went hazy for Kat. *Merger? What the hell is she talking about?*

DJ broke away momentarily and smiled. "I'm your new neighbor."

EPILOGUE

DJ shoveled the last pile of manure from the horse stalls into the cart and drove it around behind the barn to the compost pile to be picked up by a nearby nursery. Her life had changed dramatically over the past few years. She hadn't expected to ever live in the country again.

Rebecca had given DJ a great deal on the land neighboring Kat's, and she'd sold her penthouse apartment in the city to afford the down payment. She'd decided to change her life to be with Kat. If she hadn't been in Kat's future plans, she'd prepared to build a small one-bedroom cabin on the land and do her best to make amends. She'd hoped Kat would find a place in her heart to forgive her, and when DJ had returned to the ranch close to two years ago, she had. Kat's voice had been decisive when she'd told DJ she wanted to live life with her together on the ranch. She'd moved in that week and hadn't had a second thought since.

They'd rebuilt the stable and added a nice apartment on the side for Virgil. Having him living in the house made the honeymoon phase of their relationship an adventure. They'd managed to find special places around the ranch to spend intimate time together and camped out frequently near the river. The countryside was a beautiful backdrop for the intimacy involved in cementing a relationship. Skinny-dipping and making love in the moonlight was the most breathtakingly magnificent honeymoon they could've ever imagined.

DJ had just brought her horse out of the stable and was getting ready to check the trails when she heard the screen door slap shut.

"Breakfast is ready, darlin'," Kat shouted.

DJ looked up at the house and smiled as Kat waved her in. She tied the horse to the railing, rushed up the steps, and took Kat into her arms and kissed her. "Good morning, Mrs. Callahan."

"Good morning, Mrs. Callahan," Kat said softly and kissed her again.

DJ slid her hand across Kat's growing belly and let the happiness wash through her. Kat had become more beautiful with each week during her pregnancy, and today, at twenty-six weeks, she was more stunning than she'd ever been. Future dreams in the country were something DJ hadn't let herself entertain before she'd met Kat, and she'd certainly never planned on having a family. But with Kat by her side, it felt right.

About the Author

Dena Blake grew up in a small town just north of San Francisco where she learned to play softball, ride motorcycles, and grow vegetables. She eventually moved with her family to the Southwest, where she began creating vivid characters in her mind and bringing them to life on paper.

Dena currently lives in the Southwest with her partner and is constantly amazed at what she learns from her two children. She's a would-be chef, tech nerd, and occasional auto mechanic who has a weakness for dark chocolate and a good cup of coffee.

Books Available From Bold Strokes Books

A Country Girl's Heart by Dena Blake. When Kat Jackson gets a second chance at love, following her heart will prove the hardest decision of all. (978-1-63555-134-1)

Dangerous Waters by Radclyffe. Life, death, and war on the home front. Two women join forces against a powerful opponent, nature itself. (978-1-63555-233-1)

Fury's Death by Brey Willows. When all we hold sacred fails, who will be there to save us? (978-1-63555-063-4)

It's Not a Date by Heather Blackmore. Kade's desire to keep things with Jen on a professional level is in Jen's best interest. Yet what's in Kade's best interest...is Jen. (978-1-63555-149-5)

Killer Winter by Kay Bigelow. Just when she thought things could get no worse, homicide Lieutenant Leah Samuels learns the woman she loves has betrayed her in devastating ways. (978-1-63555-177-8)

Score by MJ Williamz. Will an addiction to pain pills destroy Ronda's chance with the woman she loves, or will she come out on top and score a happily ever after? (978-1-62639-807-8)

Spring's Wake by Aurora Rey. When wanderer Willa Lange falls for Provincetown B&B owner Nora Calhoun, will past hurts and a fifteen-year age gap keep them from finding love? (978-1-63555-035-1)

The Northwoods by Jane Hoppen. When Evelyn Bauer, disguised as her dead husband, George, travels to a Northwoods logging camp to work, she and the camp cook Sarah Bell forge a friendship fraught with both tenderness and turmoil. (978-1-63555-143-3)

Truth or Dare by C. Spencer. For a group of six lesbian friends, life changes course after one long snow-filled weekend. (978-1-63555-148-8)

A Heart to Call Home by Jeannie Levig. When Jessie Weldon returns to her hometown after thirty years, can she and her childhood crush Dakota Scott heal the tragic past that links them? (978-1-63555-059-7)

Children of the Healer by Barbara Ann Wright. Life becomes desperate for ex-soldier Cordelia Ross when the indigenous aliens of her planet are drawn into a civil war and old enemies linger in the shadows. Book Three of the Godfall Series. (978-1-63555-031-3)

Hearts Like Hers by Melissa Brayden. Coffee shop owner Autumn Primm is ready to cut loose and live a little, but is the baggage that comes with out-of-towner Kate Carpenter too heavy for anything long term? (978-1-63555-014-6)

Love at Cooper's Creek by Missouri Vaun. Shaw Daily flees corporate life to find solace in the rural Blue Ridge Mountains, but escapism eludes her when her attentions are captured by small town beauty Kate Elkins. (978-1-62639-960-0)

Twice in a Lifetime by PJ Trebelhorn. Detective Callie Burke can't deny the growing attraction to her late friend's widow, Taylor Fletcher, who also happens to own the bar where Callie's sister works. (978-1-63555-033-7)

Undiscovered Affinity by Jane Hardee. Will a no-strings-attached affair be enough to break Olivia's control and convince Cardic that love does exist? (978-1-63555-061-0)

Between Sand and Stardust by Tina Michele. Are the lifelong bonds of love strong enough to conquer time, distance, and heartache when Haven Thorne and Willa Bennette are given another chance at forever? (978-1-62639-940-2)

Charming the Vicar by Jenny Frame. When magician and atheist Finn Kane seeks refuge in an English village after a spiritual crisis, can local vicar Bridget Claremont restore her faith in life and love? (978-1-63555-029-0)

Data Capture by Jesse J. Thoma. Lola Walker is undercover on the hunt for cybercriminals while trying not to notice the woman who might be perfectly wrong for her for all the right reasons. (978-1-62639-985-3)

Epicurean Delights by Renee Roman. Ariana Marks had no idea a leisure swim would lead to being rescued, in more ways than one, by the charismatic Hudson Frost. (978-1-63555-100-6)

Heart of the Devil by Ali Vali. We know most of Cain and Emma Casey's story, but Heart of the Devil will take you back to where it began one fateful night with a tray loaded with beer. (978-1-63555-045-0)

Known Threat by Kara A. McLeod. When Special Agent Ryan O'Connor reluctantly questions who protects the Secret Service, she learns courage truly is found in unlikely places. Agent O'Connor Series #3 (978-1-63555-132-7)

Seer and the Shield by D. Jackson Leigh. Time is running out for the Dragon Horse Army while two unlikely heroines struggle to put aside their attraction and find a way to stop a deadly cult. Dragon Horse War, Book 3 (978-1-63555-170-9)

The Universe Between Us by Jane C. Esther. Ana Mitchell must make the hardest choice of her life: the promise of new love Jolie Dann on Earth, or a humanity-saving mission to colonize Mars. (978-1-63555-106-8)

Touch by Kris Bryant. Can one touch heal a heart? (978-1-63555-084-9)

A More Perfect Union by Carsen Taite. Major Zoey Granger and DC fixer Rook Daniels risk their reputations for a chance at true love while dealing with a scandal that threatens to rock the military. (978-1-62639-754-5)

Arrival by Gun Brooke. The spaceship *Pathfinder* reaches its passengers' new homeworld where danger lurks in the shadows while Pamas Seclan disembarks and finds unexpected love in young science genius Darmiya Do Voy. (978-1-62639-859-7)

Captain's Choice by VK Powell. Architect Kerstin Anthony's life is going to plan until Bennett Carlyle, the first girl she ever kissed, is assigned to her latest and most important project, a police district substation. (978-1-62639-997-6)

Falling Into Her by Erin Zak. Pam Phillips, widow at the age of forty, meets Kathryn Hawthorne, local Chicago celebrity, and it changes her life forever—in ways she hadn't even considered possible. (978-1-63555-092-4)

Hookin' Up by MJ Williamz. Will Leah get what she needs from casual hookups or will she see the love she desires right in front of her? (978-1-63555-051-1)

King of Thieves by Shea Godfrey. When art thief Casey Marinos meets bounty hunter Finnegan Starkweather, the crimes of the past just might set the stage for a payoff worth more than she ever dreamed possible. (978-1-63555-007-8)

Lucy's Chance by Jackie D. As a serial killer haunts the streets, Lucy tries to stitch up old wounds with her first love in the wake of a small town's rapid descent into chaos. (978-1-63555-027-6)

Right Here, Right Now by Georgia Beers. When Alicia Wright moves into the office next door to Lacey Chamberlain's accounting firm, Lacey is about to find out that sometimes the last person you want is exactly the person you need. (978-1-63555-154-9)

Strictly Need to Know by MB Austin. Covert operator Maji Rios will do whatever she must to complete her mission, but saving a gorgeous stranger from Russian mobsters was not in her plans. (978-1-63555-114-3)

Tailor-Made by Yolanda Wallace. Tailor Grace Henderson doesn't date clients, but when she meets gender-bending model Dakota Lane, she's tempted to throw all the rules out the window. (978-1-63555-081-8)

Time Will Tell by M. Ullrich. With the ability to time travel, Eva Caldwell will have to decide between having it all and erasing it all. (978-1-63555-088-7)

Change in Time by Robyn Nyx. Working in the past is hell on your future. The Extractor series: Book Two. (978-1-62639-880-1)

Love After Hours by Radclyffe. When Gina Antonelli agrees to renovate Carrie Longmire's new house, she doesn't welcome Carrie's overtures at friendship or her own unexpected attraction. A Rivers Community Novel. (978-1-63555-090-0)

Nantucket Rose by CF Frizzell. Maggie Jordan can't wait to convert a historic Nantucket home into a B&B, but doesn't expect to fall for mariner Ellis Chilton, who has more claim to the house than Maggie realizes. (978-1-63555-056-6)

Picture Perfect by Lisa Moreau. Falling in love wasn't supposed to be part of the stakes for Olive and Gabby, rival photographers in the competition of a lifetime. (978-1-62639-975-4)

Set the Stage by Karis Walsh. Actress Emilie Danvers takes the stage again in Ashland, Oregon, little realizing that landscaper Arden Philips is about to offer her a very personal romantic lead role. (978-1-63555-087-0)

Strike a Match by Fiona Riley. When their attempts at matchmaking fizzle out, firefighter Sasha and reluctant millionairess Abby find themselves turning to each other to strike a perfect match. (978-1-62639-999-0)

The Price of Cash by Ashley Bartlett. Cash Braddock is doing her best to keep her business afloat, stay out of jail, and avoid Detective Kallen. It's not working. (978-1-62639-708-8)

Captured Soul by Laydin Michaels. Can Kadence Munroe save the woman she loves from a twisted killer, or will she lose her to a collector of souls? (978-1-62639-915-0)

Under Her Wing by Ronica Black. At Angel's Wings Rescue, dogs are usually the ones saved, but when quiet Kassandra Haden meets outspoken owner Jayden Beaumont, the two stubborn women just might end up saving each other. (978-1-63555-077-1)